James
Phelan

Patriot
Act

CONSTABLE

CONSTABLE

First published in Australia and New Zealand in 2007 by Hachette Australia,
an imprint of Hachette Livre Australia Pty Limited.

First published in ebook in Great Britain in 2018 by Constable

This paperback edition published in Great Britain in 2019 by Constable

1 3 5 7 9 10 8 6 4 2

Copyright © James Phelan, 2007

The moral right of the author has been asserted.

A CIP catalogue record for this book
is available from the British Library.

ISBN: 978-1-47212-928-4

Typeset in Simoncini Garamond by Bookhouse, Sydney
Printed and bound in Great Britain by CPI Group (UK), Croydon CR0 4YY

Papers used by Constable are from well-managed forests
and other responsible sources.

MIX
Paper from
responsible sources
FSC® C104740

Constable
An imprint of
Little, Brown Book Group
Carmelite House
50 Victoria Embankment
London EC4Y 0DZ

An Hachette UK Company
www.hachette.co.uk

www.littlebrown.co.uk

In memory of Shirley Phelan

AUTHOR'S NOTE

Since the forming of the UKUSA (pronounced U-KU-ZA) Treaty in 1948, the parties involved have developed ever-capable electronic Communications Intelligence services. Put simply, the intelligence agencies of the five member countries (USA, UK, Canada, Australia and New Zealand) currently have the capability to intercept every spoken or written word that travels via telephone, fax, email, radio, microwave, satellite, fibre-optic transmission, etc., *in the world.*

Since day one, France has been opposed – they want in. While military and terrorist communications are targeted, Echelon (the main UKUSA program) spends most of its time and resources targeting political and economic assets around the globe. This information is disseminated to US companies via the Advocacy Center, set up by the Clinton Administration in 1993 and that year alone added $35 billion to the US economy through export gains.

Being responsible for the security of Echelon's information is an enormous burden. If it were to fall into the wrong hands – those outside the UKUSA Treaty – the consequences would be tantamount to national disaster. That is the subject of this novel.

James Phelan
Melbourne, 2007

PROLOGUE

PARIS, APRIL

Joseph Cassel knelt in a pool of blood, the hot metal of the silencer pressed against his forehead.

The assassin was losing his patience.

While skilled in torture and interrogation, he didn't have the time to get the information he needed. Given that luxury, he was confident he could crack any man – soldier, spy, terrorist, whatever. And the naked man on his knees before him was a politician.

Well, he *was* a paratrooper once, the assassin conceded. Not that the fat-framed Cassel showed any signs of being agile or fit. But there was a steely composure and hardness in Cassel's eyes that came from witnessing death and destruction first-hand.

The assassin pressed the silenced IMI Jericho pistol to the politician's lips.

'Don't want to talk? You can see what will happen to you if you don't,' the assassin said.

The message was clear to Cassel – the corpse of his mistress was spread-eagled on the floor, her head a ragged mess of gore. He had tried to protect her, reaching out to grab her in an embrace as she darted out of bed, but now he knelt in a pool of her sticky warm blood on the polished floorboards of his weekend retreat's master bedroom.

It never ceased to amaze the assassin how much blood a shot to the head generated. It reminded him of his first kill over a decade ago, when he had been a member of Israel's Sayeret Matkal special operations force.

'You'll never stop it,' Cassel said. 'It's far too late for that.'

'Perhaps,' the assassin said in French. 'Then again, perhaps your daughter will be more helpful?'

The assassin could see Cassel's neck flush red with anger, his muscles flexing at his urge to fight, to strike. He was getting through to him. Excellent.

'Shall I pay her a visit?'

'Fuck you, ghetto dog.' Cassel faced upwards, leaned forward and spat at the assassin.

The assassin sighed while he checked his watch. He casually wiped his face, pressed the pistol to Cassel's temple. Time to go.

'*Au revoir*,' and with a squeeze of the trigger, the wall behind Cassel was painted red.

The assassin moved quickly downstairs, stepping over the two dead bodyguards on the way out the back door. He closed the gate behind him, kick-started his motorbike and took off down the lane, just as Cassel's next appointment arrived out front.

•

'To my sole heir, my daughter Sianne Cassel, I bequeath the Pres—'

A gasp from the assembly broke the solicitor's speech. Sianne Cassel's mouth moved into a thin smile, shielded by the black veil over her face.

'I bequeath the Presidency of the National Front Party of France, effective immediately. All powers of that office are to be transferred to her, and in accordance to the party's charter, Sianne may appoint her own caucus . . .'

The solicitor looked up from his notes at the man who was now coughing with emphysema.

Sianne Cassel turned around, annoyed at the interruption. Why was decrepit old Lopin here anyway? Sure, he'd helped to found the party, but her father had distanced him years ago. He had no influence any more, no allies in this room.

The aide standing by Lopin's side – built more like a soldier than a physician – started up an oxygen bottle and held a mask to his charge's mouth.

Cassel turned her attention back to the solicitor and waved at him to go on.

With a raised eyebrow, the solicitor resumed the reading.

An hour later, Sianne Cassel was riding in the back seat of a black Peugeot 607, talking on a cell phone. The dark-tinted windows shielded her from public view, as the ex-military driver navigated the Arc de Triomphe with a couple of toots of the horn. In the passenger seat sat a bodyguard with the proportions of a champion weightlifter.

'Madam President,' the voice said over the phone.

It was the first articulation of her salutation, and she liked it.

'Mon General Danton – you are well-informed indeed!' Cassel said, smiling.

'Like any good chief of intelligence . . .' Danton's tone turned more serious. 'I take it we are still moving forward?'

Cassel stared out of the window as the car pulled up to a traffic jam. Light drizzle had fallen all morning, and she focused on the windowpane. Several drops of water streaked together, forming a larger mass that settled for a while, before sliding away with the car's motion.

'Everything has come together, General. My father's death shall be his greatest triumph. I hope to see things move more quickly now.' Cassel idly watched as the car detoured around the roadworks and took a side street.

'*Oui* – we will await your arrival tonight.'

'Excellent,' Cassel said as she tapped her fingers on the armrest. 'And your team are already in the field?'

'Yes. They will avenge your loss.'

'*Merci, mon General. Au revoir.*' Cassel ended the call by closing her Motorola, and looked in annoyance through the windscreen as the car came to a sudden stop on the cobbled laneway.

A garbage truck was backed into a loading bay, blocking off the way ahead. A man in overalls and a woollen hat turned after throwing a bag in the back of the truck, signalling to the Peugeot to wait a moment.

Cassel's driver gave a gesture of annoyance and put the car into reverse, then turned in his seat to look out the back window. In an instant the driver's eyes squinted into sharper focus.

Cassel turned to stare in the same direction he was looking, to see a black BMW 5 Series speeding up the lane behind them, closing fast.

The two occupants of the BMW wore ski masks.

Cassel's driver shared the briefest of glances with the man next to him, who was in the process of pulling a submachine gun out from under his seat.

'Hold on!' the driver said as he planted the accelerator. The V6 turbo diesel roared as the tyres fought for traction on the wet cobbled road.

Cassel prepared herself for the impending collision by putting her hands on the back of her driver's headrest, her head braced on her hands as she'd been taught.

The impact crumpled the rear end of the Peugeot, and the manoeuvre bought some time as the BMW's airbags disoriented its occupants.

The driver slid the gear into drive, the Peugeot surged forward.

A rocket-propelled grenade streaked towards them from the garbage truck, and as the driver kept his foot hard on the accelerator, the grenade scraped over the roof of the Peugeot and exploded into the ground under the front of the BMW – sending the car flipping end-over-end down the lane in a ball of flames.

Leaning out the passenger window, Cassel's bodyguard had his FN P90 submachine gun firing hard towards the garbage truck ahead, where the man in overalls now had a black ski mask pulled down over his head. While reloading his RPG launcher, his body was ripped to shreds as at least twenty 5.7 mm rounds found their mark.

The Peugeot braked hard, the ABS still gripping the road when Cassel saw her bodyguard tumble out of the door, ejecting his spent magazine and inserting a fresh one as he rolled to his feet. He never stopped moving as he stepped over the corpse and disappeared around the back of the truck.

A quick burst from the FN P90 rang out, followed by the sharper report of a pistol. The passenger-side window of the truck splattered with thick crimson.

'Get me out of here,' Cassel said, her voice steady and calm. The driver nodded to her, pulled an automatic pistol from under the steering column and left the car.

She watched him approach the truck, pistol trained ahead as he moved. He glanced around the corner of the truck's cab, gun still in his outstretched arm, then disappeared from view in the direction her bodyguard had gone.

Two quick sets of gunshots rang out, followed by silence. Cassel waited, looked for a sign from her driver or an attacker, but nothing came. Moments later she steeled herself, took a small pistol from her purse and left the car. The laneway behind was blocked with the flaming wreckage of the BMW, so the way ahead – past the truck – was her only choice.

From around the cab of the truck she saw the back of a masked assassin move with military precision towards her prone driver. He never moved the bead of his aim, ready to administer the kill shot.

A tiny pop of a gunshot rang through the air, in contrast to the louder sound of approaching sirens. The assassin turned around to face Cassel. She still had the pistol pointed at him, and smoke trailed from the short barrel. She could see his surprise as he looked about himself, checking for the wound that only she could see. She kept her gun trained on him as he turned his own from the driver to her.

But he couldn't finish the movement. As he raised his arm he tore the coronary artery in his neck, blood spraying violently with the pump of his heart through the small entrance wound. He fell to the ground. Another shot to the head left him motionless.

Cassel helped her driver to his feet.

'Let's go.'

PART ONE

1

NEW YORK CITY, JULY

Lachlan Fox felt as though he were looking into a mirror. The man opposite looked tired and undernourished, the dark rings under bloodshot eyes masking what was usually a guy in good physical shape. Both men looked older than the early thirties they were.

•

Fox had been back in New York for just five minutes when he'd got the call over the PA system at JFK International Airport. At the United Airlines service counter, a typed note was waiting for him.

'*Go to the third payphone near the first set of toilets ahead of you. It will ring at 9.45 pm. Answer it.*' Fox looked at his watch – 9.42. This person was punctual.

'*I need to meet you, tonight, regarding an article you wrote,*' the voice said. It was metallic, spoken through one of those scramblers you could get from prank stores.

'Which article?' Fox said, wiping the sleep out of his eyes. In the past year of being an investigative reporter, he'd written dozens of in-depth articles.

'*No Such Agency*,' the voice said. It was the insiders' nickname for the National Security Agency. The NSA. The largest and most advanced intelligence agency in the world. The scrawled nickname had adorned an envelope of information that had landed on Fox's desk a month ago; an envelope that kicked off his initial interest in the story and proved to be the centre-piece of the biggest investigation Fox had worked on. Illegal phone intercepts of UN delegates in New York. Transcripts of ambassadors' emails. Embarrassing material emerged for many countries and the repercussions of international relations were still being felt, even among the closest of allies.

'*Take a cab to the East Village, I'll call your cell in fifteen minutes with a meeting place.*'

Fifteen minutes later Fox relayed directions to the cab driver. The streets were packed with the usual late-evening rush and Fox got out two blocks before his destination and walked the remainder of the way.

•

'How do I contact you?' Fox said, drinking the last of his pint of beer. He could sense the meeting was over, as his NSA informant had stopped talking and become fixated on checking his watch and the hundreds of faces around them. It was a Thursday night and the Irish pub on East 24th was crowded well over fire regulations.

'You don't,' he said, finishing off his scotch. The ex-NSA agent was struggling, and judging from his pupils and tapping hands, Fox suspected he was high – undoubtedly some kind of amphetamine to keep him awake. Having the world's most advanced intelligence agency harbour a grudge against you tended to do that.

He rose from the booth to leave. 'I met you in person this time so you'd take me seriously.' He looked startled as someone bumped into him, a seemingly harmless brush past by a guy carrying three beers.

'I took your last message seriously,' Fox said. 'It kicked off stories in papers all around the world.'

'That's why I know I can trust you with this. We won't need to meet again. Make sure it gets out, fast.'

'What's the rush?' Fox asked, but the guy had already turned away. 'Cheers,' Fox called to his back, watching as the man melted into the crowd. He'd left a copy of the *New York Times* on the table, folded in half, which Fox took as he departed. An unseen envelope added weight to the paper.

•

'Subject is walking eastbound on East 24th, approaching First Avenue,' the agent said into his sleeve mike as he followed Fox's brisk walk through the busy night-time crowd.

'Copy that,' the agent in the command centre said. 'You got a good description?'

'White, about thirty years old. Make him six two, 198 pounds, short dark hair,' the agent said, panting as he talked and moved after Fox. 'Wearing black jeans, green t-shirt and a large black backpack.'

'Keep tight on him, two vehicle units are on their way,' the other agent said.

'ETA on that backup?'

'They're on Broadway and Fifth, ten minutes out.'

'Copy that.'

•

Fox thought about the meeting while he weaved his way through the crowded intersection at First Avenue.

One drink. Under five minutes. Busy place. Nothing revealed in their discussion for fear of being overheard. As one past intelligence officer weighing up another, Fox respected the man's caution. And this guy deserved respect, going to the trouble of looking Fox in the eye this time around, rather than simply posting him the information as he'd done previously. Fox knew too well what it was like to work in an area where trust meant saving lives. It was something drummed into intelligence operatives, enough to stick with them even when on the outer. *Particularly* when on the outer.

And Lachlan Fox knew what that felt like.

The walk signal changed and Fox jogged to get ahead of the pack.

•

'Subject is moving double-time, in pursuit.' The agent bumped his way through the milieu of pedestrians, and settled into a half run like his quarry.

'Has he made you?'

'No, he just seems to be in a hurry,' the agent replied.

•

Fox kept up his pace until he reached the Manhattan Marina. He couldn't yet be sure but he suspected he was being tailed. He put his ticket through a turnstile and joined the throng boarding the ten-thirty ferry. As he walked across the gangplank he took the opportunity to check behind him in the reflection of the pilothouse window.

This was the third time he'd seen this face in half a mile. Young guy in a suit, always looking intently at Fox's back, never too far behind.

Moving as fast as him.

Following him.

His meeting hadn't been a secret at all.

•

'Copy that, backup is headed for the Williamsburg Bridge, keep me posted on the drop-off point in Brooklyn and they'll take over from exit on your visual handover.'

'Got it,' the agent said, catching his breath as the ferry cast off.

•

Fox stayed on the ferry past the stop closest to his house and waited for the next stop to get off. On the way to the gangplank he released a latch on a life boat and let the winch play out a little.

As he walked across the gangplank, he saw in the reflection of the ticket booth the man following him, four people behind. This time Fox caught a glimpse of him talking into his sleeve, in what would be notification to another party of his location. Another party he may not be able to detect until too late.

Fox walked deliberately slowly to the newspaper vendor, buying the day's *International Herald Tribune*. After another glance to be sure his follower was still acting alone, Fox walked into the men's room.

Looking around, he figured he had two options.

Escape via a small window with the hope of losing his pursuer, or waiting long enough for the man to come in and check. He knew he only had a few minutes, as the ferry crew would check all lifeboats and moorings before casting off. The loose raft might buy him an extra two minutes, tops.

•

Fox's decision was soon made for him.

The man entered while Fox washed his hands at the basin. Fox watched his back as he moved to the urinal.

Leaving the faucet running, Fox took three quick steps and was behind the man, pressing his keyring into the back of his head.

'Turn around and you'll have a new hole in your head,' Fox bluffed, hoping the bulbous keyring felt metallic enough to pass as a pistol.

The man didn't move but for the instinctive raising of hands to show compliance.

'Who are you?' Fox said, pushing the keyring harder.

No answer.

'Who do you work for?'

Still no answer.

A whistle blew and Fox knew it to be the ferry's last-minute warning.

With a sharp blow to the side of the neck, the man went limp and hit the wall in front of him. Fox hefted him backwards, sitting him on the toilet in a cubicle. Using a handful of tissues, he brushed aside the man's jacket.

A pistol in a hip holster. Glock 19.

A badge on his belt. FBI.

'Shit.'

A minute later Fox was back on the ferry. The warm summer-evening breeze blew down the East River as he stood at a side rail looking at Manhattan.

A million little pieces ran through his mind.

Within fifteen minutes Fox stepped on the deck of his houseboat and punched the code into the security pad by the door.

The lights flashed in sequence: it signalled secure, with no internal motion detected in the past 24 hours.

Dumping his bags in the entry, he walked into the kitchen and put some coffee on. On the bench was a pile of mail collected over the past three weeks by his friend, Alister Gammaldi. The phone that hung on the wall was flashing with messages, and he picked up the receiver with a grimace.

'*You have . . .*' the metallic voice said, taking time to compute the number, '. . . twenty-seven messages.' They could wait until morning.

He dropped the thick brown envelope that had been in the *New York Times* onto the sofa on the way through to his bedroom, allowing himself a moment to lie down. His own bed, the smallest and nicest of missed luxuries.

Despite himself, Fox felt his eyes growing heavy and he slept. The adrenalin that had fuelled his weary body over the past hour had subsided, leaving him exhausted.

And he dreamed. Always the same. He always dreamed of dead people, two in particular. He saw the face of Birmingham, a soldier under his command on a UN peacekeeping mission in Timor. Fox watches on helpless as Birmingham is killed. In the dream Fox isn't there but he's omniscient, he's looking from above, he's looking into the man's face. Into his eyes. Fox hears all and sees all, and there's a moment in that final look of Birmingham that asks Fox 'Why?'.

The dream shifts to Venice, he sees a boat. Fox's view zooms in from the heavens, the picturesque location turning to shit as his mind's eye enters a cabin to close in on a woman's face. Alissa Truscott. She is young, beautiful, broken. Fox wants to empathise with how she feels but he can't. He tries to tell her it will be okay, as if he is in a position to provide deliverance, but nothing comes out. The scene switches to a bird's-eye view, so that Fox this time sees himself there too. He knows this is not how it happened exactly. He's sure the figure of him standing there in complete stillness had some emotions at the time, some movement. He sees a tear run down her face, he tracks it in slow motion as it leaves her eye. Those eyes. They say, 'save me'. Fox watches in slow motion as the silhouette of a man fires a gun and Alissa's head buckles from the shot. He sees the life leave her eyes as . . .

Fox jolted up, rolled from the bed and pulled his .45 calibre SOCOM pistol from a holster under the bedside table. Purpose-built for the US Special Operations Command, the Heckler & Koch slide was silent as he chambered a round, his back against the wardrobe as he closed his eyes and waited for the sound again. It was the first time that he had held the pistol, like this, since Venice. He blinked hard to get the dream world out of his mind.

Sweat ran down his face. His heart topped out steady at one-eighty. He again saw the faces of Birmingham and Truscott. Their expectant but lifeless gazes straight at him. He shook them away.

There!

The sound of footfalls on the upper deck, constant and heavy this time. Walking towards the unlocked front door.

He waited out of sight behind his bedroom wall as he heard the glass door slide open. The safety off on his pistol, he closed his eyes and concentrated on the sounds. Having lived on the boat for almost a year, he knew every creaking board of flooring: someone had just stopped at the kitchen bench.

Thump.

A heavy sound reverberated through the boat and Fox took his chance. Rolling out of the bedroom he came up on one knee behind a sofa, pistol raised in a steady two-handed aim.

'Don't move!' Fox shouted, the figure silhouetted in the dark kitchen.

The sound of breaking glass rang out as a bottle hit the ground. Fox squeezed more pressure onto the trigger.

'Jesus Christ, Lachlan! You've been in the African sun too long!' The voice was instantly recognisable – Alister Gammaldi, Fox's best friend since high school.

Fox laughed and put the pistol on the coffee table before squeezing his friend in a bear hug.

'Shit, sorry, Al – thanks,' Lachlan said as he took an offered beer from the case Gammaldi had brought in.

'You going to shoot me?' Gammaldi asked as he eyed the pistol.

'Why would I shoot you?' Fox said. 'Especially when you bring imported beer around.'

'How was Zimbabwe?' Gammaldi asked as he cleaned up the dropped bottle.

'Hot, miserable, and full of trouble,' Fox said. He sat on a stool at the kitchen bench, picking at his beer label. 'I've collated enough dirt on Mugabe and his government over the past three weeks to have the UN sit an emergency meeting to see about forcing an election and taking the bastard to the International Court. Well, that's if they bother to read what I filed.' Fox shook his head to clear some of the horrific images he'd seen, still blending with the dream world he had just been in.

'And, by the looks of things, you haven't eaten for a while,' Gammaldi said. 'You've lost about ten kilos, I reckon.'

'Mostly in my writer's paunch,' Fox said and rubbed his stomach. 'Seriously, though, humping it around the country-side in forty-plus degree heat with nothing but MREs to eat – yeah, you lose weight pretty quick. That, and what witnessing several mass graves dug up by UN investigators does to your appetite.' Fox shook his head again, thinking about all the interviews he had done with widows and orphans of political dissidents, many guilty of nothing more than speaking out.

'Well, mate, I've got just the thing,' Gammaldi said. He threw the dishcloth in the sink, went outside and returned with two pizzas. 'I had to put them down to get in the door.'

'Good man!' Fox said, as they moved over to the sofas. 'Ooh, it's from Grimaldi's Pizzeria no less. A Gammaldi with a Grimaldi.'

'Spare no expense,' Gammaldi said with a mock Italian accent. 'Why do you think I followed you over the river to live in Brooklyn? This pizza is as close to my mama's as we are ever gonna find.'

When he sat down, Fox felt the newspaper push into his back. He pulled out the plain envelope and considered it – he was too tired right now for another burden.

'What's that?' Gammaldi asked, almost a full slice of Capriciosa stuffed in his mouth.

'This . . .' Fox looked at the envelope, then the pizza, then to the muted sports channel Gammaldi had put on the television. He looked out the windows across the East River to the twinkling Manhattan skyline. Coming from strife-torn Africa had awakened him to the liberties that, like so many westerners, Fox took for granted. And those liberties came at prices that were unavoidable.

He pulled the sheets of folded paper out and flipped through them, scanning each page.

'Oh shit . . .'

2

MONT BLANC, FRANCE

Mont Blanc is the highest peak in Western Europe. From atop its 4807 metres the snow stretches as far as the eye can see, westwards over the Rhone Alps and into the interior of France, and to the east into Italy and Switzerland. At its base sits the picturesque town of Chamonix, home of the first ever Winter Olympics and one of the most popular ski fields in the world.

Twelve kilometres north of Chamonix, sunk deep into an inhospitable mountain, is France's most secure and secretive military base, Fort Gaucher. Nestled into a sheer rock basin, the bare, craggy cliffs surround a permanently frozen lake, the snow-capped rims measuring five hundred to a thousand metres on every side. Tens of thousands of years ago it was the site of one of the most violent volcanic eruptions the world has ever seen, millions of tons of rock being blown skyward, leaving a deep, desolate sinkhole.

The site, a region cordoned off for training by the military, was found to be the perfect hiding place by France's first military imaging satellites in the late sixties. Originally set up in 1974 as a secondary command post for the French forces in the event of an all-out war in Europe, by 1983 it was being run by the French external intelligence service, the DGSE (Direction Générale de la Sécurité Extérieure). Now, there are two twenty-metre satellite dishes housed in fibreglass radomes that resemble giant golf balls situated there. The radomes, used the world over by communications intelligence agencies to hide the direction their satellite dishes are pointed, in this case also keep the snow off and the equipment inside from freezing.

To further protect from observation from above, twenty-six turbo-fans surrounding the basin provide cloud-cover for the entire area, the mist settling just below the ridge line. A mixture of water vapour and chemicals brought to the right temperature and dissipated into the atmosphere, the cloud is thick enough to shield all outside installations and activity from the likes of imaging satellites and reconnaissance aircraft.

To keep away the occasional adventure-seeking skier or snowboarder who may manage to hike the five kilometres from the nearest public road, the company of white-clad commandos stationed at the base can have a squad anywhere on the outer-rim within three minutes of a sensor or alarm being triggered.

Put simply, Fort Gaucher is as secret and secure as an intelligence base can be.

Major Christian Secher blocked the first two blows with ease, taking the hits to his forearms while he made a move of his own: a feigned upward thrust of his left knee, followed by an extended right arm. His palm to the instructor's throat sent the man spattering to the ground, where he then kicked him over onto his back.

'You're dead,' Secher said, stomping on the gym mat next to the fallen man's head, then walking off towards the shower.

The sound of clapping rang through the open space of the gymnasium. It was the first time in the week he'd been on the mountain that someone had watched his 5 am judo class.

Secher turned to see General Danton leaning against a doorway.

'As impressive as ever,' General Danton said, stubbing out his cigarette against the steel doorjamb. 'Be in my office in five minutes.'

•

Secher, dressed in gym clothes with a towel around his sweating neck, entered the general's office ten minutes later. Big for a Frenchman, he stood at six-three and around 210 pounds, and spent every possible spare moment doing judo and gymnastics wherever in the world he was stationed.

'Well, Major?' General Danton leaned forward in his chair, looking over his reading glasses at the agent he had hand-selected for the mission. He was as impressed as ever by Secher's physique, and remembered back to when he had recruited him as a pugnacious teenager. Back then, the lean and lanky Secher had been a reserve member in the French Olympic gymnastic team. That all changed when the intelligence agency got its claws into him.

'My current assignment is on track, if that is what you are concerned about.' Whenever Secher spoke it was in a lyrical way, his tone at once comforting and persuading, measured and exact. He was used to getting his way, Danton knew, but it would be different today. He needed straight answers from this young man, and hoped the sweat coming off his temples did not appear as conspicuous as it felt. This was quite literally the operation of a lifetime.

Secher helped himself to a bottle of water from his boss's bar fridge.

'We have less than a week,' Danton said. 'Just over five days to make the on-location connection. You've had months of planning, an unlimited budget and manpower . . .'

'You're questioning me?' Secher said.

'Still you do not have the key,' Danton replied, drying off the palms of his hands on his pants. 'You planned to have it by now.'

'My plans are fluid, organic, ever-changing,' Secher said. 'It's what has made me succeed.'

'This is for the future of France.'

This made Secher smile. He knew well what this was for. Danton included him on all the intricacies of the plan. He knew that France would soon be radically and forever changed politically.

'The connection will be made – you will get your Sixth Republic,' Secher said, taking a long pull of the water and staring at Danton. 'By the time your computers are ready, you will have the key in your hand. Get the key earlier than you are able to use it, and the risks escalate. Much like your cleaning operation is doing.'

'Excuse me?' Danton felt his reply did not match the expression on his face. He knew what Secher was alluding to.

'You have to stop killing these men. It makes my job much harder.'

'It's not me.' Another lie. Danton knew this man could see through it but he had to play this out for his audience.

'Of course it's not.' Secher leaned on the back of the chair facing Danton. 'You don't know what it's like being a field officer. If you think a few dead Europeans won't make the Americans suspicious, you are wrong. If they change their security patterns now, when we are so close, the failure will be yours.'

Secher went to the door and dismissed himself, turning at the last moment, smiling.

'France is close to being great again, Monsieur Danton,' he said. 'We both know it.'

Danton sat pensively behind his desk, staring at the back of the door after Secher's departure.

'An interesting choice, mon General.' The voice came from the videophone on his desk, which had been on through the meeting for the benefit of his boss.

From the LCD screen, a pair of light-green eyes pierced out from a round face. Her wispy blonde hair was tied back, her lips thin slits of pale pink. Sianne Cassel.

'He's the best agent in France,' Danton said, knowing there was some degree of uncertainty in his voice. Cassel had been around the political scene long enough to pick up on it.

'But you have doubts?'

'He's a bit . . . reckless, a bit ruthless,' Danton said. 'The price of brilliance.'

'We are so close, mon General. The success of our plans is on your shoulders,' Cassel said. 'Can you stop your other agents?'

'It was an order-and-forget mission,' Danton said. 'The assassins will work until their job is done.'

Danton shifted in his chair. He'd gone too far over the past few years, failure now was treason. His palms still sweated, and a bead ran down his temple. He hoped it didn't show up over the video feed. The silence meant he had to answer her question.

'It's too late.'

3

NEW YORK CITY

The headquarters of the Global Syndicate of Reporters (GSR) occupied the top five floors of the Seagram Building. Between exposed bronze columns that soared up to the sky, the dark amber glass façade reflected the morning sun onto the neighbouring towers of Manhattan.

Fox rode his bicycle across the stark expanse of the grey granite plaza, dismounting without stopping and hoisting the bike across his shoulder, moving through the revolving doors and past the security desk. A nod to the guards behind the desk – who replied with a casual salute out of respect to the ex-navy officer – and they allowed the secondary set of glass doors to slide open, which Fox continued through to the fire door.

He took the stairs, running the flights to his thirty-seventh-floor office, the bike over his shoulder. His iPod pumped Jay-Z and Linkin Park through headphones, drowning out the background clutter of his mind as his thoughts and heart raced.

Three months ago the Frenchman Joseph Cassel was killed. Decorated war hero during World War II and Algeria. Leader of the extremist National Front Party. A founding member of the right-wing Euro power group LeCercle.

Since then, six Bilderberg Group members have been killed. Bilderberg could be seen as a rival group, on political and economic grounds.

All six of those men had attended the last LeCercle meeting.

So someone's cleaning out the group. But which group is doing what? And who could do it? Someone connected, either with intelligence ties or within one of the groups. Given the membership list, it could be any high-placed official who owed his or her position thanks to either exclusive club's significant global influence.

It's like warring mob clans. But why? What's to gain?

Fox scanned his eye on the optical identification pad by the door and jogged the hall to his office, hanging his bike on the wall and plugging in his notebook computer.

It was 6 am and the office floor was deserted. He took his change of clothes from his pack and made for the bathroom.

•

At 9 am every Monday morning, Managing Director Tasman Wallace held a meeting in the briefing room with his senior investigative journalist team. They first went through the top news items from around the globe, each member collating stories in their respective fields of expertise for their teams to chase up.

Fox noted down the latest reports coming out of Iraq and replayed what his guy on the ground in Baghdad had sent through to him overnight.

'CNN's crew is stuck out of the city for forty-eight hours, think you can get them some coverage of the next parliamentary press conference?' Wallace asked.

'Yep, Ray Cassin is on station in the Green Zone, he's done plenty of TV work, I'll have him get a crew ready,' Fox replied.

'Good,' Wallace said, sitting back down after refilling his tea from the side table.

For the next fifteen minutes, Fox listened as the other eight bureau heads went through their latest work. Every day was school for Fox, as he watched and listened as eight of the smartest reporters in the world, each hand-picked by Wallace for their tenacity to bring their chosen field to the light of day, went through some of the most up-to-date investigative reporting to be found anywhere.

The last few minutes were taken by the Chief of Staff, Faith Williams.

'I need everyone's quarterly budgets and team expenses in by the end of the week,' Faith said, to predictable groans all around.

'Come on now,' she jibed, to precede her oft-heard spiel. 'GSR is renowned for spending more time and money on investigative stories than any other news source on the planet – and your diligence in managing your financial affairs is what keeps us afloat.'

'And I thought it was our brilliant reporting skills that kept the electricity on,' Fox said with a smile.

Faith stared back, her green eyes turning mischievous.

'Well, Mr Fox, I'm happy to share with the others in the room that your department is breaking records when it comes to expense accounts,' Faith said as she looked down to check her figures. 'Your costs are up around forty per cent on your predecessor for this time last year.'

'War is an expensive undertaking,' Fox retorted good-naturedly. 'You've got to spend money to make money.'

The room laughed as one, as they all knew too well that the world was increasingly a hostile place. They also knew that the stories Fox was filing and coordinating were the most lucrative in the building. Media outlets, and ultimately the viewing, reading and listening public the world over, had an insatiable appetite for news from the frontline.

'Okay, people,' Wallace said. 'Go find the truth.'

After his usual sign-off, the reporters filed out. Fox waited to be the last to leave with Wallace and Faith.

'Lachlan, how was Africa?' Wallace asked as they walked to his office. On the other side of his fifties, Wallace looked paternally at Fox from under bushy white eyebrows – he was always relieved to see staff return safely from an assignment, particularly from a trouble spot.

'Miserable,' Fox replied, making way for Faith to precede him into Wallace's office.

'You look like you've fallen asleep on a sun-bed,' Faith said.

Fox checked his reflection in Wallace's mirror-backed bar. He was deeply tanned to the point of having skin peeling from his nose and cheeks.

'I've got a good few weeks' worth of leads to chase up, on top of this month's Middle East load. Gammaldi is briefing a research team for me right now,' Fox said, taking a seat across the desk from his boss. 'In a nutshell, our reports will be enough to put Mugabe and his cohorts on trial in The Hague, and that's just a start.'

'About bloody time that bastard was out. The sooner that continent gets rid of the old guard, things will be that much easier to fix,' Wallace said.

Fox nodded absently, thinking over the events that were coming together, slowly connecting the dots that were the European killings.

'You look like you had a tough time over there,' Wallace said. 'Make sure you see the med team and have them check you over and design a program for you – I can't be having you go soft on me.' Wallace's concern was more that of a friend than employer.

'Yeah, too much sun and not enough food,' Fox said. 'Amazing what most of Africa does for the appetite – if they ever went into the business of tourists coming for health retreats, they could make a killing.'

'Rather than just killing their own,' Wallace said.

'Ain't that the truth,' Fox replied.

'The UN is making some progress?'

'The UN is about as useful in Africa as the rest of the world,' Fox said, putting his folders on Wallace's desk. 'I guess that's unfair, the UN ground-staff are trying their best to make a difference. But the problems in Africa, while so simple, are on such a massive scale . . .'

The three sat in the office for a moment in silence.

'While over there I got wind of a couple of CIA camps in the Sudan,' Fox said. 'Until six months ago they were used as terrorist training camps, set in forts originally built by the British in the nineteenth century.'

'What's the CIA doing with them?' Wallace asked, sipping tea as he paced his wood-panelled office. The streetscape of Manhattan was alive below as the morning sun streamed in through the tinted glass.

'My guy says they have some interrogation centres set up there, transit points for Extraordinary Rendition,' Fox said, referring to the politically spun euphemism for Americans moving people around the globe into countries with far less human rights concerns. 'Basically they're black-op camps away from any press, so naturally I'm interested. I'm planning to go in and check it out in a couple of weeks.'

'I thought you were going back to Africa in a few days?'

Fox leaned forward and opened the top folder, passing over the material he had been given at the bar the night before.

'I have to look into something else,' Fox said as Wallace scanned the folder, marked simply: 'The groups that control the world'.

'What, is this your novel outline about the Knights Templar or something?' Wallace asked with a crooked smile until he registered the seriousness on Fox's face.

'Tas – this is regarding something I've been working on for a couple of months. It started with my article in the *New York Times* that linked deaths of dead European leaders. It's part of something that's going to blow up in some important faces real soon.'

'What is this list – looks like a Washington powerbroker's phone book.' Wallace flipped through the first few pages, taking his time as he went. He stopped about midway.

'What's up with these people? Some of these names are untouchable – I mean if you've got anything incriminating them it's gotta be solid, you'll have to run it past me and legal . . .' Wallace trailed off, his eyes went wider and wider as he continued through the list.

'They're not party specific . . .' Faith said, getting up to read over Wallace's shoulder. 'Lachlan – what does this mean?'

Fox looked at Wallace, not sure where to even begin.

'In a nutshell, it's . . .' Fox began. 'No, wait. I'll go back a step.'

Fox dragged his chair closer to Wallace's desk, as if fearing being overheard in the office.

'Last night I was given a lead that ties in on this story,' Fox said. 'Transcripts of chatter among right-wing groups in Europe. Nothing specifically targeted by the NSA, but picked up by them through their following of economic angles. Many of these guys head up the biggest continental businesses.'

'I'm not sure I'm following . . .' Wallace said.

'Last night I received that from my NSA source.' Fox pointed at the stack of paper in Wallace's hands. 'A complete list of every attendee of the groups I've been writing about.'

Fox passed over another stack of printed paper.

'And these are the transcripts,' he said. 'They're of phone and email conversations that I have had in this investigation.'

'Why would he give you these?'

'Proof of authenticity,' Fox said. 'They're legit. I made those calls, I typed those emails.'

'So we assume the rest is legit too,' Faith said. 'So what's going on?'

'I'm working on an answer to that,' Fox said. 'But what I finally have now is a list of surviving attendees of the Bilderberg Group.' Fox again pointed to the papers in Wallace's hands.

Wallace flicked to the last page and scanned upwards:

Wallace, Tasman, Director GSR.

'I attended a meeting in '94,' Wallace said.

'I know, but look at this.' Fox leaned over and flipped through the pages Wallace was looking at.

'This,' Fox said, tapping the page, 'is the list of the last annual meeting of LeCercle, held in Nice two months ago.'

'They're basically the right-wing equivalent of the Bilderberg Group?' Wallace said.

'Yes, it's as right-wing as they come, and like Bilderberg they are made up of the world's powerful elite. Leaders of business, government, the military.' Fox paused. 'Big difference is, LeCercle is totally Eurocentric, rather than having the Bilderberg's purpose of bringing the US and Europe together. That article I filed a couple of weeks ago opened the floodgates; I had to sort through a million and one conspiracy emails in my inbox this morning.'

'And I thought you were clutching at straws on this group connection,' Wallace said. 'Your source is trustworthy?'

'Tight as. Ex-NSA, now on the outer for calling attention to domestic spying, similar to the much-publicised case in Britain's GCHQ when they blew the lid on spying on the UN delegates.'

'What if he's got a grudge against his former employer?' Wallace said. 'It may compromise what he's feeding you.'

Fox spread out the pages of the transcripts on Wallace's desk.

'He may well have a grudge, but he's got the goods. These are the raw transcripts of NSA phone and email intercepts,' Fox said. 'The first couple are from inside the UN headquarters, between Security Council members and their governments during the lead-up to the Iraq war.'

'What's the significance of that, the story broke years ago,' Wallace said, reading over the calls that the delegates thought were secure conversations at the time.

'Further proof of authenticity, like evidence of a proof of life. It was a big story at the time, and this shows that my source is genuine. Next up, these,' Fox said, handing over several pages.

'They're eavesdropping on your whole team?' Faith asked, reading the transcripts of Fox's investigation phone calls on the dead Euro leaders. Calls to their businesses, the police agencies involved in the investigations, and journalists who covered the events in their own backyards.

'Yep. My communications, the research department's, my people in the field,' Fox said.

'So we've now got the NSA spying within the US,' Faith said. 'Not that we didn't suspect it was going on, but this is proof.'

'They could deny these are genuine,' Wallace said. 'Or say that it came up as the communications were between US parties and overseas persons of interest. The Patriot Act covers them for that.'

'Going public with this will force their hand,' Fox said. 'Make them comment, make others look closer at what they're doing.'

'But you're not planning on doing that . . .' Faith said, watching Fox closely.

'Not yet,' Fox replied as he met her gaze. She knew how to read him almost too well. 'First I want to know the *why*. I think that this spying on me is proof that these hits in Europe are part of something bigger. You don't take out such high-profile targets, particularly in such quick succession, without something big going down.'

'Hmm . . .' Wallace stacked all the papers in front of him into a neat pile. 'You do realise that you're the only one to be linking these deaths. Interpol, Europol, Scotland Yard, none of the Euro agencies are banging this drum.'

'That's why I'm on *your* staff,' Fox said, getting a grin from the old man. Fox tapped the list of the group's attendees. 'Look, Tas, I can taste it now. This is the tip of the iceberg. And it's enough to have this NSA guy put his neck out and start running for his life.'

'Who are these names you've got highlighted?' Faith picked up on the six names, the six *same* names, who were highlighted on each list.

'Those were six members who have also attended a Bilderberg conference in the past.' Fox cleared his throat. 'The five I wrote about in that *Times* article, and a sixth who was killed last weekend. All up, there were seven attendees out of the 126 who attended the last LeCercle meeting who had also attended a Bilderberg conference in the past.'

'And this one you've circled – John Cooper, Senior Partner at Cooper and Patterson in Washington?' Faith asked.

'He's the seventh.'

Wallace looked at Fox, getting the point.

'He is the only surviving Bilderberg member who attended that conference in Nice.' Fox looked from Faith to Wallace. 'Cooper's time is ticking.'

•

Half an hour later, Fox and Gammaldi were riding in the back of a GSR car, heading to JFK airport.

Fox tapped his fingers on the windowsill, not in tune to the top forty song blaring loudly over the radio at Gammaldi's request, but for the adrenalin running through him.

'This John Cooper guy's in Russia?' Gammaldi said, rifling through the contents of his carry-on bag.

'Just got there, a trade conference in St Petersburg tomorrow,' Fox said. 'He's giving us some time for a chat tonight.'

'What if he's targeted over there?' Gammaldi asked, pulling a packet of M&Ms from his bag.

'We've got the warning through,' Fox said, taking a few of the offered chocolates. 'He's got extra protection. Hopefully, it's enough.'

4

RUSSIA

The black Citroën C5 waited at the border while the two French DGSE agents handed over their passports.

'Returning from Poland?' the border guard said, inspecting their visas. Another guard walked an Alsatian around the car, the big dog pulling on his chain, sniffing, checking, eager to find something.

'Would have been a good trip, if we didn't have to come back through Belarus,' the agent behind the wheel replied in Moscow-accented Russian. 'Full of pigs.'

'And ugly women,' the other agent said from the passenger seat.

The guard grunted and handed back the passports. He took a close look at their registration, not picking up on the French forgery of Russian officialdom.

'We have nothing to declare, but for some American porn,' the other agent said loudly, passing over a DVD. 'For you, comrade.'

The guard laughed and took the DVD, waving them through.

The agent looked into his rear-view mirror as he got up to speed, pocketing his fake passport.

'Fucking Russians,' he said, in his native French. 'Maybe we can take a few days rest on the Black Sea after this final hit. Our Euros go far over here.'

'Hmph,' the other agent grunted, opening his briefcase and removing a thin file.

A series of photos were in there, and he looked at them for the tenth time. John Cooper's image and biography were seared in his memory.

'Russians,' he said. 'Almost as bad as Americans.'

5

NATIONAL SECURITY AGENCY HEADQUARTERS, FORT MEADE, MARYLAND

Ira Dunn wore his marine dress uniform with his test pattern of service ribbons pushing out from his barrel chest. He strode in his mirror-finish patent leathers through the halls of Foggy Bottom like he owned them. Hell, the guy practically did, certainly more so than anyone else on the planet.

'Why do they call it Foggy Bottom?' the computer contractor asked his military minder.

Dunn considered the pair of them standing behind him in the elevator. He'd been young and full of questions once too.

'Foggy Bottom is the affectionate, yet deservedly unfortunate, name we gave this HQ,' the young officer replied. 'As you'll find out if you start work early enough, this here basin in Virginia is often fog-filled. Officially we're designated as Fort Meade.'

'What's with the black glass façade of this building, is it just to look ominous?'

'It has the reflective qualities of mirrored sunglasses. It's part of a security system known as Tempest. The windowpanes are triple-glazed, each space between the panes has a pocket of air in-between and a current buzzing through the specially made glass. Different levels and combinations of steel in the glass further add density. Put simply, this building is a vault. No sound waves get in. More importantly, nothing gets out. It's kind of a motto around here. That, and the other expanded meaning of NSA being "Never Say Anything".'

The elevator chimed and the pair got out, Dunn waiting alone in the lift as it went up another level to the executive floor.

The scale of the operation he was a part of no longer impressed him like it did that starry-eyed visitor. While people the world over had heard of the CIA, until recently few were aware of the United States' largest intelligence agency. Unlike its more famous cousin, which was primarily charged with operating human intelligence, or HUMINT, NSA was in the communications intelligence, or COMINT, business. Employing more mathematicians than any other organisation in the world, and housing the most supercomputers on the planet, it was an expensive ship to run. Dunn's section of the NSA was charged with two primary missions: to intercept foreign communications, and to secure US communications. Code-breaking and code-making. Unveiling and veiling.

Ira Dunn walked into his office on the seventh floor, the executive level largely deserted. Dunn was a military man born and bred, and some things, such as an early roll call, were hard to dispel.

Certainly not as hard as following the directive of a government, a battle of temptations that his patriotism fought with daily. Nationhood versus political whim. Posterity versus a term in office. Historical identity versus modern spin.

'Fuck'n 'crats,' Dunn said, tossing his copy of the *Washington Post* on his desk. He moved to the coffee percolator in the corner, filled the pot with hot water, added his daily measure of fresh ground beans, and flicked the well-worn switch. The pot percolating, he walked back over to his desk and switched on his computer.

Again, the *Post*'s headline story caught his attention, a piece about Secretary of State Adam Baker, and the deal he had made with the Israelis on the Lebanon issue. Capitulation again for the Americans. Might as well have walked into the negotiation room, put a tub of lube down on the table and bent over.

After reading the article, Dunn smashed his fist down on the newspaper in disgust.

The nation as it was now – as it had been for the past thirteen years – wasn't what he'd worked hard at building. It sure as hell wasn't one he was content with.

Dunn logged into his computer and opened the browser, SIPRNet coming to life immediately with a stream of messages for him to follow up. The Secret Internet Protocol Router Network looked much like its successor, the civilian version of the World Wide Web. Outside the US Department of Defense, there were few people in the world cleared for access to this secret network. His homepage started up with a CIA briefing of up-to-the-minute news. Sourced from legitimate news services and supplemented with further intelligence information from various hot-spots around the globe.

An article halfway down the page caught his interest.

'*Russian trade conference tomorrow, free trade on the agenda.*' He clicked the link and read the CIA brief. Over a dozen news pages were linked, and he clicked on the *New York Times*.

'Hmm . . .' The piece pretty much told him the same as the CIA brief notes.

On his keychain was a 512-bit encryption coder that loaded via a firewire plug on his NSA-designed keyboard. A twelve-digit alpha-numeric code changed every ten seconds. Inserting the firewire plug, Dunn read the current code and typed the digits into the computer.

While SIPRNet was the most secure version of the internet, Dunn was one of just three people in the world to have access to the SIPRNet gateway to Echelon. In a nutshell, this was the only way you could access the information remote from the few key supercomputing terminals at NSA bases around the globe.

He clicked through to the Dictionary commands area and scanned through the Russian list to make sure they were targeting the appropriate keywords. The file was extensive, by far still the biggest of any targeted country thanks to a largely bygone threat, and he tapped in a translation priority request.

Within seconds the commands fed into the biggest collection of supercomputers in the world, disseminated within nanoseconds to the appropriate information bank.

Until otherwise directed, the Russian economic COMINT in and out of St Petersburg would be higher on the priority list for the NSA. Anything written or spoken in the world that travelled over a communication device that contained relevant words, in any language, would be recorded, and an analyst would manually go through each entry.

'Targeted data mining, my Russian friends,' Dunn said to himself, closing the Dictionary control panel. Hunting, rather than simply gathering. Measuring voice patterns. Tracking locations of targets. Dunn was wielding the latest tool in the world's fight on terror. The most important tool in the US economic arsenal. An integral component to the superpower status of his nation.

Dunn logged out of the command screen and clicked through SIPRNet to the page of one of his divisions, the Advocacy Center.

'. . . $4B contract won through Boeing and Raytheon for new missile defence system for Japan . . .'

'. . . $720M of new wheat sales Iraq . . .'

'. . . Lockheed wins $4.9B contract in Canada, in purchasing the new C130J over the Airbus A400M . . .'

Dunn leaned back and cracked his knuckles.

On the wall of his office was a tattered US flag, a big ship's ensign. A glass case kept its burned and bullet-ridden fabric from falling apart. Every morning Ira Dunn looked at this flag and said the same thing.

'It's all for you, boys.'

6

WASHINGTON

Fox and Gammaldi arrived at Dulles International Airport and looked up their next connecting flight. With some time to kill, they went to a café adjoining the terminal's main bookstore.

'Two double espressos please,' Fox ordered, surprised to see Gammaldi lean forward to pay. He put his change into a stuffed wallet.

'Al, not that I'm complaining about you paying, but why are you carrying so much cash around?'

'We're going away, you never know what I might need to buy in Russia,' Gammaldi said.

'You've got enough in there to buy a nuke,' Fox replied. 'At least a tank.'

'Maybe I will,' Gammaldi said. 'Tom Clancy has a tank.'

'Good for him. Seriously, you didn't get money out before we left, which means you already had it on you,' Fox said, watching as Gammaldi struggled to fold his wallet so he could squeeze it into his back pocket. 'I know you are normally pretty liquid, I put it down to your grandparents going through the war. But dude, you've got like a couple of grand in there?'

'A few,' Gammaldi said, taking his coffee and following Fox into the bookshop.

'Where'd you get a few thousand dollars?' Fox asked, watching his friend's face through the steam from his cup as he sipped his drink. 'I know we get paid pretty well and I've been watching you spend your easy – ah, hard-earned – cash on decking out your snazzy Brooklyn brownstone. Next you'll be buying a DB9 or a stretch Hummer.' Gammaldi was silent through Fox's jibes. 'Seriously, are you the local Park Slope stand-over man or something?'

'If you must know, nosy one, I sold my place back home,' Gammaldi said.

'What's that?' Fox replied, eyebrows raised.

'I sold my homestead back in Oz a few months ago,' Gammaldi said. 'I like it over here. The food, the people, the work. Even getting used to the sport.'

'In that order too, I bet,' Fox said, putting his bag down inside the bookshop. 'Seriously, you're gonna stay here for a while? That's a big decision. And you're just telling me now . . .'

'Did I give you grief when you sold your place on Christmas Island?' Gammaldi asked while he dropped his carry-on bags onto Fox's. 'You did that and decided to stay here within the first month. At least it took me closer to a year.'

'Yeah, but I had nothing left at Christmas Island. You're close to your family, I mean your house was even physically close to them. And you still had the navy job to go back to next year.'

'Told them I'm out,' he revealed. 'Sick of flying the shit helos we have in the navy anyway. Every time I'd go up I'd be wondering how I'd get back down – the easy way, or the flaming-wreck way.'

Fox finished off his coffee and tossed the cup, shaking his head at the revelations of his mate.

'And here I was thinking you were just hanging around to make sure I settled in,' Fox said with a grin.

'You settle anywhere. You're like a nomad, or a member of the Rebel Alliance –'

'Okay, I'll stop you there before you go on another two-hour rant about *Star Wars*,' Fox said. He turned away to look over the contents of the new releases, amazed by the sea of covers that seemed to change every week or so.

'A lot of crap gets written . . .' Fox said to no one other than himself. Gammaldi was already lost in a *Sports Illustrated*.

'People love it,' a man's voice behind them said.

Fox turned around and recognised him. Bill McCorkell, National Security Advisor to the President of the United States. He bore an uncanny resemblance to Napoleon Bonaparte, and always seemed to wear the same cut of pinstripe suit. A close inspection of the stripes bore the name WILLIAMMICHAEL-MCCORKELL in a superfine constant font. Bill Clinton got him onto the master tailor in Hong Kong.

'Bill, good to see you,' Fox said with a smile, shaking the man's hand. They had met on only a couple of occasions, but McCorkell's close ties to Wallace at GSR meant he was an invaluable resource. As the military and intelligence brain for the President, McCorkell knew it all when it came to global security. And he understood the power that the media could wield for him when he needed it.

'This mug here is Al Gammaldi, GSR's handyman and occasional pilot,' Fox introduced.

'I've heard only good things,' McCorkell said. Gammaldi gave an inquisitorial eyebrow dance at Fox. 'Sorry I'm a bit late,' McCorkell said. He passed Fox a manila folder.

'I thought we were early. Thanks,' Fox said. He flicked through the printed pages in the folder, scanning the information that he'd read with greater detail on the flight.

'Bit of background on John Cooper,' McCorkell said. 'As he heads the Advocacy Center, it's a glowing report. Also in there is what we have on LeCercle that isn't readily available in the public domain – sadly, not that much. They've never made any threat lists. Same goes for Bilderberg, and while there are administration officials and business leaders from here that attend that annual gathering, there's virtually nothing I can tell you that isn't in the press.'

'And they've been good at flying below the press radar,' Fox said as he tucked the folder into his leather satchel and they left the bookshop, joining the throng in the main international terminal.

'Well, like all those power groups, they're a secretive lot,' McCorkell said. 'First rule for attendees is that they don't talk about what goes on.'

'Kinda like the first rule of *Fight Club*, I guess,' Fox said with a grin. 'I'm surprised you haven't attended any meetings by the likes of Bilderberg.' From what he knew of McCorkell, he had a good idea in which direction his answer would be.

'Not for me, I'm afraid,' McCorkell said. 'Always made it a point to keep a clean nose from affiliating myself with any of these types of special-interest groups – not an easy thing to do in my line of work.'

'Kissinger has done all right by it,' Fox said, baiting him good-naturedly.

'Yeah, don't get me started on that man,' McCorkell replied.

'They're calling our next flight,' Gammaldi said.

'Listen, on the off-chance something happens while you are in Russia, you may need this.' McCorkell passed over a business card. 'A friend at the US Embassy in Moscow, should you need one. Just mention my name and he'll get me on the blower, and I'll vouch for you bums.'

'Thanks, Bill, I'm sure we won't need it but I never pass up a "get out of gaol free" card,' Fox said. 'I'll be in touch when we're back.'

'Sure.' McCorkell checked his watch, and nodded to his Secret Service agent fifteen paces away that it was time to go. 'I kinda wish I could join you on this little adventure, sure sounds more interesting than the state dinner I've got to get ready for.' McCorkell walked off, his Service agent leading the way to the car park.

'He seems like a good guy,' Gammaldi said with a mouthful of chocolate bar as they walked to their departure gate.

'One of the best,' Fox replied. 'Been a friend of Wallace's from way back, and now has the ear of the President. Thank God this country has guys like him.'

'Always good to have friends in high places.'

7

FRANCE

'Arsehole,' the pilot muttered under his breath, levelling the aircraft out.

'Faster!' echoed up into his cabin again.

The pilot tapped the throttle in a futile gesture as the small twin-engine jet was flying at its maximum cruising speed. He was used to being chartered by the French government for VIP shuttle service, but this Secher character had some kind of death wish to get to Russia.

At least he was being paid well, the pilot reconciled. Ten thousand Euros cash for a round trip. Not bad for a day's work. He could put up with the irritating passenger for that.

•

Secher leaned back in the leather seat and opened a bottle of sparkling water. In an attempt not to think about the pressing situation at hand, his mind raced as he went through what he had to do over the coming days.

Having called in a favour from the director of his agency's Eastern Field Operations, he knew the location of the final assassination. He'd also learned that it was an order-and-forget mission from the outset, some three months ago, and this last target could not be worse for Secher's end of the mission. Everything was coming to a head; everything was close to making or breaking point.

It was down to the wire, as always. His adrenalin was pumping, nervous sweat breaking out across the back of his neck.

Part of him liked it. The challenge. The game. Yet part of him hated the frustration of it.

Secher threw his water bottle across the empty cabin.

'Faster!'

8

ST CATHERINE'S PALACE, ST PETERSBURG

Fox and Gammaldi walked into the opulent foyer of St Catherine's Palace.

'I'm impressed, you're even wearing a cummerbund,' Fox said out of the corner of his mouth.

'I'm surprised you're not wearing your medal,' Gammaldi retorted.

The interior of the palace was a sea of colour and all that glittered in modern Russia. Fox recognised a few faces, a mix of business and political leaders in a showing of East/West economic and military cooperation.

'Not quite my scene, old boy,' Gammaldi said to Fox in a mock toffy accent.

'Who you calling "old boy", fatso?' Fox replied. They had to wait in line to get through a security checkpoint. 'Officially this function is a preamble to free-trade talks with key economic partners, for the opening up and management of the resource-rich and still largely untapped south-western Russian states, and a crackdown on terrorism in the region.'

'Okay, you've sold me, this is just my kinda party.'

'Unofficially,' Fox continued, looking with raised eyebrows at his sarcastic mate, 'this is an opportunity for the legitimate businesspeople to mingle with underworld figures. Hardly a rarity in Russia. In fact, often these people are one and the same.'

It was their turn to go through some airport-like metal detectors, complete with armed guards carrying trays for the guests to place their metallic objects in prior to being scanned. A security guard waved them forward and Fox and Gammaldi placed their watches and belts in the offered tray and passed through.

Fox set off the alarm, and he shrugged at the guard on the other side, a man a head taller than Fox's six foot two and almost twice the weight.

'Boots,' Fox said in Russian as explanation, as Gammaldi walked through and got the all-clear.

Another guard patted Fox down, not caring about ruffling the guest's tux. He nodded and the big security guy let the pair through.

'I'll look for Cooper,' Fox said as they climbed the ornate main staircase. 'You check the place out.'

'Onto it,' Gammaldi replied, taking a handful of canapés from a passing waiter and a champagne from another.

'And stay sharp,' Fox added before Gammaldi peeled off. 'The night is still young.'

'What, you're worried about Cooper even with all this

security around?' Gammaldi said. 'There are more guns here tonight than in Baghdad.'

'Only one of them has to be in the wrong hand,' Fox answered, checking his watch. 'If I don't bump into you before, we'll meet back here in an hour.'

They went their separate ways at the top of the stairs and Fox walked along the Vaulted Passageway. He strolled up to a long bar and waved over a barman.

'Vodka, crushed ice, lime and sugar,' Fox ordered, the drink being shaken before his eyes within seconds. 'In a short glass, thanks.'

While the bar tab was on the house, Fox passed a twenty-dollar Euro over in an exchange that would mean the barman would remember his drink of choice for the night.

Fox turned around and leaned on the bar. He took his time to survey the scene before him, and sipped his drink as he watched the passing crowd. He only noted a couple of body-guards, unusual given the stature of the guest list but not surprising given the overt security in and out of the palace's entry points.

Plenty of new money here. Dirty money, those who had cashed in on the rapid shift to capitalism at the right time. Also, plenty of English, French and Italian accents. By their look and dress, this was an opportunity for older money to forge ties with the shifting tide of wealth on the continent. Old-money families, representing finance and industrial sectors, making bonds with the emerging resource, manufacturing and information technologies rooting themselves in the developing East. Survival of the richest. He recognised some European Union parliamentarians, the Chancellor of the Exchequer, football players, military leaders, royalty. All in black tie but for a few dress uniforms.

As he approached the Great Hall, the sound of a modern take on a classical Russian composition spilled from the room. A table by the large gilded entry doors was piled with sequined masks, with a sign that read in Russian and English: *'For the after-dinner dance'*.

In the Great Hall, the official ballroom of the palace, Fox casually looked about, searching the faces for Cooper's, which he had memorised on the plane flight from the States. The black and white tuxedos in here were accentuated by splashes of classic and fashionable colours, as the women made their presence felt. Most were very young, tall, exquisitely curvy, dark-haired Eastern-European beauties. Below their flawless exterior and designer clothing was a hard and sad look in their eyes.

It took Fox under five minutes to find his target.

John Cooper was talking to the former head of NATO. The woman standing by Cooper was different to the others Fox had seen so far. While equally as elegant and beautiful as any other, she carried herself with a confidence and grace that was her own.

Five strides away from an introduction to Cooper, a man blocked Fox's path. His jarhead haircut belied his occupation, despite the rent-a-tux.

'Marine?' Fox asked, passing him his GSR business card.

'Delta,' the soldier said, reading over the card. 'Lachlan Fox. I was told you'd be coming. Cooper will meet you in the Marble Study after the first dance.'

Fox watched as the woman standing by Cooper came over. She wore her auburn hair up in a loose bun, and her face and neck were accentuated by a jewelled lattice of a choker necklace that spilled across her shoulders and décolletage. Her black dress was a shimmering slip that clung to her as she walked.

'I'll take care of him,' she said.

'Yes ma'am,' the soldier responded. He peeled off into the crowd, his stance wary and alert.

'Kate Matthews,' she said to Fox, her hand dwarfed by his as they came together in greeting.

'Lachlan Fox. Shall we get a drink?' Fox asked, with a hand gesture towards a waiter on the other side of the room.

'Sure,' she said and they walked off.

'You work with John Cooper back in DC?' Fox asked.

'Executive assistant,' Kate replied, in the accent of a true New Yorker. 'Sounds better than "right-hand woman". Been to Russia before, Lachlan?'

'Once, as a tourist,' he said.

'Not exactly a tourist hot spot,' she replied. 'You're an Aussie?'

'Yep, although I live in the States now,' he told her, taking two glasses of champagne from the waiter. 'And to explain my backpacking to far reaches of the globe, it was just after high school so I wasn't exactly cashed up. Eastern Europe was a damn sight cheaper back then, particularly the booze.'

'To cheap booze,' she said, taking a glass of champagne from him and raising it to accentuate the point. 'And the beautiful St Petersburg.'

Fox raised his champagne glass to her. 'Here's to beauty.'

'A beautiful city?' she said. She held her glass just short of cheers.

'From what I've seen so far, a city full of beauty,' Fox replied, and they clinked glasses and sipped while looking into each other's eyes.

'The Venice of the north. Incredible palaces, canals,' Kate said, still holding Fox's gaze with hers. 'In that respect, it sure beats New York.'

'I like New York, although it's taken me the good part of a year to find my own space there,' Fox said. Stood to reason she'd look up on him prior to this meeting, he'd have done the same. 'You spent much time there?'

'Grew up there, parents still live near the boat basin on West 79th,' she said. 'How about you, a West Side boy too?'

'No, but it's a nice area where your folks are,' Fox said, studying her dark eyes. She would be about his age, maybe a year or two younger, late twenties somewhere. 'It's been bugging me but I just figured it out. You look a lot like Eva Green.'

'The Bond Girl? I can live with that,' Kate said. She smiled over her glass, her eyes looking Fox up and down. 'Let's see . . . Jake Gyllenhaal, perhaps?'

'Yeah, I get that,' he said. 'Look a bit like him yet sound like Heath Ledger. I've got the whole *Brokeback* thing going on.'

'Oh, great film!'

'Best on-screen love story since *Casablanca*,' Fox agreed. 'But to answer your question, no, I don't live in Manhattan. I'm over in the DUMBO area of Brooklyn.'

'Oh, it's fantastic over there,' she said, putting her hand on his arm. 'You're in a loft space?'

'Houseboat at the moment, one of those little old converted ferries from the Naval Yard,' Fox said, trying to figure her out.

'The dream is to find a nice roomy warehouse space and do it up myself.'

'Ah, well, living on a boat is my dream,' Kate said. 'Sailing around the world, going from port to port, following the sun.'

Fox noticed her eyes change as she said this, her expression lost in the dream. *What are you hiding?*

'You have to live in Washington for work?' Fox asked.

'Yeah,' she said, as Fox took a couple of masquerade masks from a waiter and passed one to her.

'Don't tell me you dance,' Kate said. 'Tall, dark and handsome Fred Astaire, where were you when I needed you for my prom?'

'Ha! I move, that's about it,' Fox said. He glanced over at Cooper who was still wrapped up in conversation. The Delta guy was scanning the crowd, the bulge in his open tux jacket suggesting a submachine gun. Probably the compact MP-7, smaller than its older MP-5 cousin but still gets the nickname 'room broom' for its high rate of fire.

Kate put the mask on and followed Fox out onto the parquetry dance floor. The music changed to a waltz and soon the floor was filled with masked couples slowly moving to the string orchestra. She put a hand on his shoulder and reached the other out to hold his. Fox's left hand rested above her hip, noticing in their movements that she wasn't wearing any underwear. He looked into her eyes, and started leading slowly to the music. She smiled, her orange mask setting off her big dark eyes and red lipstick.

'So, what do you do in your role?' Fox asked. Kate held tightly to him, the crowd on the dance floor brushed by.

'Well, it's not all Bond Girl stuff, let me assure you!' she said. 'I'm a lawyer at Cooper Patterson, handling corporate affairs for the firm. Basically, I field most of the groundwork tasks for John Cooper with relation to government and corporate relations.'

'Sounds intriguing . . .' Fox said, the pair sharing a laugh.

Kate ran her hand down Fox's arm as the music sped up a little.

'Okay, since you're picking on me,' she said and squeezed his arm. 'You're tall, tanned, and clearly you work out. Most reporters I've met are fat and pasty.'

'Well, most lawyers I've met are – well, let's just say, you stand out in a crowd in a good way,' Fox told her. 'To explain away your suspicions that I am not a journo for lack of fat and pastiness, my tan is from a job I just did down in Africa. I guess I'm fit because I've been in the job only about a year, having spent a fair bit of time in the navy before that. When in New York I ride to work and swim every other day.'

'I assume this was in the Australian Navy?' Kate asked.

'Yep, officer for about five years, then bugged out and had a nice tropical-island life,' Fox said. 'A quiet life that a big part of me wishes I still had . . .'

'A tropical-island life does sound ideal,' Kate said, holding on tighter as the floor became more crowded. 'Why on earth did you leave that behind?'

The music changed and Fox noticed that Cooper had moved on.

'Kate, can we continue this chat another time?' he asked. He scanned the crowd and saw the Delta guy leading the way for Cooper at the far side of the room.

'Sure.'

•

'How is old Tas Wallace and GSR?' Cooper said. He looked for all the world like Truman Capote, dressed in a classic one-button tux, it was hard to imagine him not wearing the formal gear. He had the air of one that could go anywhere in life he wanted. If he'd had strong enough ties to a political party someone would have made him run for President by now.

'He's fine, and we're busier than ever. I see you got our warning,' Fox said as the Delta guy closed the study door and stood outside it. 'Looks like he could stop a few bullets, and make them pay for their trouble.'

'Hopefully he'd send off some bullets of his own before any come my way,' Cooper said, passing over a Cuban cigar to Fox. 'An academic pondering, though, don't you think?'

'Better safe –'

'This study was built for Alexander the First, you know,' Cooper said, cutting Fox off. He took a seat on a small settee, pouring two glasses of red from a bottle.

Fox sat down opposite, registering that Cooper was not the slightest bit concerned to have a DoD escort from the Moscow embassy shadowing him. Clearly a man used to armed protection, used to being known as someone who had something worth killing for.

'Mr Cooper, I've linked the recent deaths of six Bilderberg members to a conference in Nice early this year,' Fox said. He clipped the cigar and lit it up, passing the cutter/lighter combo back to Cooper. The smoke definitely had the big heavy rolls of flavour that only a Havana number could produce, hardly the type of import you'd expect from a man who was a gatekeeper for a major part of exporting for the US economy. *Little wonder the budget deficit was so high. Not that this Cuban would show up on any official lists . . .*

'I read your *Times* piece. I went to that conference of LeCercle, and I've been to a few Bilderbergs in my time,' Cooper said, staring levelly at Fox over the rim of his wine glass. 'But I'm sure you know all that already. So what, you think I'm next to be pushing up daisies, do you?'

Fox had a mouthful of cigar smoke, and he let it swill around with the taste of the 1970 Château Montrose.

'You don't seem concerned at that prospect,' Fox said.

'I've been a corporate lawyer my whole life,' Cooper said, blowing a puff of smoke up to the ceiling. 'A master of the universe in a litigious society, if you like. I've made more money and more enemies than most.'

Fox found himself on the receiving end of a smug, question-if-you-dare gaze.

'What happened in Nice?'

'A lot happens in Nice,' Cooper said. 'Big place.'

Fox watched as Cooper continued to sip his wine and smoke his cigar.

'This is all off the record,' Fox offered.

'Off the fucking record?' Cooper spat the words out. 'Who do you think you are talking to? I'm giving you five minutes because of who your boss is. You think I'm chatting with you about a fucking story you wanna write? My backyard ain't the place to go diggin' for your first Pulitzer.'

Fox leaned forward, and waited a couple of seconds for Cooper to look him square in the eye.

'McCorkell thinks this is serious enough to have you protected outside the US.' As Fox spoke he hammered his points home with a pointed index finger hard onto the tabletop. 'These six guys that were *killed* were better protected than you.'

Silence for a beat. Fox set his glass on the table, tapping his cigar in a crystal ashtray.

'What do you think is going on?' Cooper said, watching his wine as he swilled it about, the sticky red legs slowly running down the sides of the glass.

'Someone is cleaning out Bilderbergers who attended Nice –'

'You've said that. But it doesn't scan. Why now? Why that conference? It's not like members have not gone from one club to another before.' Cooper spoke rapid fire. 'It's illogical. These clubs are legitimate, made up of some of the most powerful people in the world. Something illegal on the scale you are suggesting is far too big a risk for any of them to get involved with. Try another angle.'

'That's why I need to know what happened there,' Fox said. 'For now, all I've got is a list of dead attendees. I need to know why.'

'You're tenacious, I'll give you that,' Cooper said, taking another sip of wine and putting the glass down on the table. 'Look, you'll never find out what went down at Nice, and I don't mean to say I won't tell you what I know. First rule of a meeting like that, no one talks about what went on afterwards – so don't go expecting anyone to be as forthcoming as me. No minutes are taken, no press are allowed inside for interviews or to cover the goings-on.'

'Were you there for the whole duration?' Fox asked, pouring more wine for them both.

'I was there for the first day only, and that was in the official talks. The real stuff happens outside the structure of the scheduled talks, during the quiet meetings afterwards, over dinner, while they smoke cigars and fuck Eastern-European prostitutes.' Cooper let a swirl of smoke lift into the air. 'Well, not *while* they fuck, but you get my drift. Not unlike what is going on with this trade conference here in St Petersburg. Everyone pushing their own agenda, always the same routine.'

'And money continues to make the world go round,' Fox said. He could see his cynicism was not lost on Cooper. 'Anything you saw or heard that rattled any cages?'

'Certainly no disagreements that were worth killing allies over, which is why, Mr Fox, I think you are way off the mark,' Cooper said. 'Look at these two groups you are talking about. LeCercle is similar in organisation to Bilderberg but very different in ideas and objectives. Bilderberg is about breaking down political barriers, opening up economies, promoting trade, commerce and friendship between the US and Europe. LeCercle is all that but from a totally Euro angle, bent on minimising the influence of the US.'

'Who was there, anyone unusual?' Fox sat forward again and had a sip of wine.

'That's one thing about that group, they're all unusual.' Cooper tapped the ash from his cigar while he thought. 'Very right wing, which is their thing, but there were some nutters there. From those exiled for war crimes, banned from politics, to the more "acceptable", for want of a better word.'

'And that's different to the usual mix?'

'Hard to say, it was my first time to one of their meetings. I was the only American there that I noticed – you getting the very Eurocentric point? I think they have the odd Yank and Jap there only when they recognise that what we have to offer may be of some use to them and their objectives, hence we usually make brief appearances. But, yeah, it was an unusual mix for any gathering, like a who's who of the extremist Euro hawks. Hell, if Hitler and Mussolini were still around they would have fitted right in, pardon the pun.'

'How about the mix of politicians and business leaders?'

'Mainly politicians, military and intelligence types at this one. Not sure if that's the norm for them or not, but I know with Bilderberg we normally go for a fifty–fifty government to business split. Nice was more ninety–ten.'

'What did you talk about?'

'A few things, but basically what my office does. Of course, I gave them the Disneyland tour of what goes on, with an intro of what you'd learn from the Advocacy Center's website. Presented it from the point of view of having business to government relationships that work, while being transparent and accountable. The importance of being current in a rapid marketplace. Reinventing your business model before it's outdated. Learning from the recent mistakes of ours, Enron, WorldCom, etc.'

'How were you received?'

'Look, Lachlan, I think your twenty questions are warming me up for something.' Cooper took a big toke on his cigar, savouring the smoke.

Fox stared at him for a beat.

'Okay,' Fox had a sip of wine, working the angle. *Fuck the angle.*

'Your firm handles the Advocacy Center,' Fox began.

'I'm director of the Center, you know that.' Cooper smiled, parrying the question. 'Nearing the end of my five-year tenure actually, so I'll be back to earning some real cash soon.'

'Care to give me a version of what your Center does?'

'You know what we *do*, Lachlan.' He took a sip of wine, waiting.

'Okay,' Fox said. 'The Advocacy Center legitimises industrial espionage.'

'Ha!' Cooper slapped his thigh. 'That's it exactly. How?'

'The US and allied intelligence agencies, led by the NSA, feed you with economic communications intelligence.' Fox talked quickly, leaning forward in his chair and putting the cigar in the ashtray. 'The Center makes sure that where that information helps US companies win contracts over foreign rivals, the information gets its way to that US company at a useful time. Boeing winning contracts over Airbus, that sort of stuff.'

Cooper had another sip of red. He too leaned forward, eyes narrowing on Fox's in a level stare.

'That's a step or so past my Disneyland version but I'll pay it.' Cooper looked about the room, and cringed slightly. 'Probably not the best place to talk about this,' he said. He drained his glass and put it on the table. 'You think somehow my role is tied to the Bilderberg Group? That my role is significant in this investigation of yours, if I'm the last surviving member . . .'

'Perhaps,' Fox said. 'I think it's significant that you represent the economic arm of the US intelligence community and some serious shit is going down with these two groups that are economically and politically focused. I don't like coincidences.'

'What else do you want to hear from me?' Cooper asked, arms outstretched and palms facing up as if surrendering.

'Anything you might know about the possible linked motives for the killings of those men.' Fox delivered his punchline, knowing it would not be answered today.

Cooper took another puff, and scratched his head.

'Honestly, I hadn't even remotely thought about it until I read your connections piece in the *Times*,' Cooper said. 'But I'm still having trouble coming to terms with these groups at war. This ain't the Bloodz versus the Cripps, Lachlan. These are guys with a hell of a lot to lose by going out on murder campaigns. I think you're barking up the wrong tree.'

'You don't think it's bizarre to have these six murders within three months? That doesn't set off any alarms bells for you?'

'There are plenty of people who die in Europe. These guys were old, and if the papers and police in their countries say they had heart attacks, what's not to believe. Hell, I'm probably one shrimp cocktail away from a bypass myself.'

'It's not that hard for an intelligence agency to stage a murder to look like a heart attack,' Fox said. He could see some of what he was saying was finally being absorbed by Cooper. 'Perhaps I can talk to you some more back home, when I've chased up a few more threads.'

'Sure, come to me with something that does scan,' he said, smoke following the words out of his mouth. 'But let's be clear on something. You ever print anything I say –'

'We won't –'

'You fuck'n' say I met with you, that I spoke to you –'

'I've got it,' Fox said. 'Loud and clear.'

Cooper settled back into his chair.

'Okay, I think we've said enough in a Russian palace. And you're a journalist; they're an endangered species in this country. Work out with Kate a time for a meeting in DC when we're back. You show me some evidence of this hypothesis, whatever these strings are you're grasping at, and I'll see what I can do about steering you in the right direction.'

'The right direction?' Fox asked.

'The right person, someone who may be able to give you some answers. Ira Dunn, for a start,' Cooper said. 'He's more the guy you should talk to, but he'll want damn more than a few loose ends.' Cooper stood up and offered his hand. *Meeting's over.*

'Ira Dunn,' Fox repeated, shaking his hand. 'At?'

'You'll find him. That's your job, isn't it, investigating things?'

'Okay,' Fox said. 'But what if time's ticking?'

'What, my time?' Cooper saw the look in his eyes. 'That army guy can babysit me. Back at DC both my office and home are guarded round the clock, I have a government driver service. Besides, considering the amount of money my office brings in, the shit-storm that would descend if I were killed . . .' Cooper looked into his empty glass. Fox could see his comment from before was ringing in Cooper's ears: *The other targets were better protected than you.*

'Thanks for your time,' Fox said. 'I'll get in touch via Kate.'

'You do that,' Cooper said. 'Send her in on your way out, will you?'

9

ST PETERSBURG

Secher's aircraft touched down at St Petersburg's airport and taxied down the tarmac to a row of private hangars. A dim light illuminated from within the giant rusty mouth of a curved corrugated-iron hangar that the aircraft disappeared into, coming to an abrupt stop inside.

'Refuel and be ready to take off as soon as possible,' Secher ordered the pilot before walking down the fold-down stairs. He was greeted by a strong sea breeze blowing the summer winds down from the Arctic.

'Welcome to Russia, Major Secher,' the local DGSE agent said, handing over two sets of keys. 'Your car and hotel.'

'*Merci*,' Secher said, walking to his BMW sedan.

He tossed his rucksack onto the passenger seat and took off in a squeal of rubber. He tossed the hotel key in the centre console, the rule of never staying in prearranged accommodation as fresh in his mind as it was when he learned the craft of being a field operative. Regardless, he wasn't going to be here long enough to stay overnight.

Driving out of the airport, he got onto the highway heading south, and set the car on cruise control at 120 km per hour. He'd have gone faster if the condition of the road permitted it, but he didn't need to attract unnecessary attention. He knew the quickest way to St Catherine's Palace, and the time it would take to get there.

He pulled his SIG Pro 9 mm pistol from his bag and loaded a full mag of hollow point rounds. His hand gripped the pistol tight, the uncertainty running through his mind that he may already be too late.

10

ST CATHERINE'S PALACE, ST PETERSBURG

'Good meeting?' Kate asked.

'It's a start,' Fox said as Gammaldi came up, the expression on his face unusually serious.

'This is my colleague, Al Gammaldi,' Fox said. He noticed the look on his friend's face but couldn't read it. 'Al, this is Kate Matthews, and this guy here is a Bragg boy.'

'Hi Kate, BB.' Gammaldi shook hands with them both. 'Lach, you gotta sec?'

With the vocal tone to back it up, now Fox knew the look in his friend's eyes. *News. Haste. Desperation.*

'Kate, I'll call your hotel tomorrow morning to organise a follow-up meeting with Cooper back home,' Fox said. 'Oh, and he wants a word with you in the study.'

'No problem, lovely meeting you, Lachlan – you too, Al,' Kate said, turning towards the study.

'What's up?' Fox asked as he and Gammaldi walked along the corridor and down a small service staircase.

'Something's not right,' Gammaldi said. 'I was looking for the kitchen – did you try those caviar boats, amazing, has to be Caspian – and I heard something coming from behind there.' He pointed to a side door that Fox had to duck to get through.

'You went through here?' Fox asked. The walkway was a damp stone hallway that curved around into darkness, a few greasy bulbs lighting the way. It was lucky if it were six feet tall and three feet wide. It looked and smelled ancient.

'I though it might be a cellar,' Gammaldi said. 'But it's a tunnel out of the palace.'

'So what's the problem?' Fox said as he went to turn. Gammaldi caught his arm, his grip like a vice.

'I heard a scuffle, and a muffled scream, so I ran back out and waited behind some crates. A few minutes later two security guards came out.'

'Yeah, and?'

'Their uniforms didn't fit right. They didn't seem right.'

Fox looked from Gammaldi to where the passageway disappeared. Without word he walked forward, Gammaldi close behind. Fifty metres along, a dark off-shoot led away into nothingness. Fox paused there, squinting into the pitch black to wait for his eyes to adjust.

'See anything?' Gammaldi asked.

Fox took a few steps and looked down – feet, two pairs. Two corpses.

'Shit!'

Two men lay there, naked but for their underwear. Both tall, one a huge mountain of a man. It was the two guards from the entrance security. Both had been strangled, their bodies still warm.

11

ST PETERSBURG

Secher banged the steering wheel in frustration, nipping the car into the other lane to glance ahead of the truck convoy. He ducked the car back behind the truck as an oncoming van flashed past on the single-lane highway. He went out wide again and dropped the BMW down a gear, overtaking the first two ancient Russian-made trucks before having to slam on the brakes and drift into the small space between the enormous eighteen-wheelers as another with dim headlights came lumbering from the other direction and nearly wiped him off the road. He ducked back into the oncoming lane, setting the three-litre BMW into third and surged past the next truck, working up through the gears as he clicked over a hundred and sixty to make up time.

12

ST CATHERINE'S PALACE, ST PETERSBURG

Fox bounded up the stairs three at a time, Gammaldi behind, his shorter legs moving fast to keep up. They took a left down the hall, turned again and ran towards the study.

'Delta boy's gone, they must have moved on,' Gammaldi called out to Fox as they reached the door.

It was locked.

Fox put his ear against it. THUMP.

'Break it down!' Fox called as he and Gammaldi shouldered the big door at the same time, the wood splintering in.

The Delta soldier was on the floor, dead. The garrotte burn around his neck matched those on the two corpses in the tunnel.

Two men dressed as palace security were in the room. Assassins. Wearing dead-men's clothing in the ultimate false-flag tactic.

One had his back to the open doorway, lying over Kate, one hand over her mouth and the other lifting her dress. Her bare legs writhed into the air.

The other assassin had a plastic cord wrapped around Cooper's neck, intently watching his face redden and his eyes bulge.

Cooper's hands gave up the futile effort of trying to loosen the constricting force around his neck.

The brutish figure of Gammaldi rushed headfirst into the room, doing a quick scan before charging the colossus lying on top of Kate.

Fox was a step behind coming through the door, his tall athletic frame straightening and charging shoulder first into Cooper's attacker, crash-tackling him in a manoeuvre that would make the coach of any football code proud. The mayhem that followed in no way resembled a fight aired on the sports channel. In the savage rampage for life and death, there were no Queensbury Rules.

Gammaldi hit the hulk of a man off Kate with an elbow to the head. He went off to the side and Gammaldi followed through with a kick to the ribs, pulling Kate to her feet like a rag doll and pushing her clear of the brute.

On the other side of the room, Fox saw the motionless form of Cooper lying face down on the carpet but didn't have the time to check for a pulse. His attacker kicked out at Fox, sending him smashing into Alexander's desk. Fox grabbed a silver candelabrum in his fist and swung around, connecting with the assassin's face, sending teeth and blood spraying through the air. Still he fought back, setting on Fox before he could swing the stick again, wrapping his hands around Fox's throat.

The hulk got off the ground and Gammaldi stood in front of Kate, shielding her.

'Lachlan, little help over here!' he said as the man leapt at him, an up-swinging fist collecting Gammaldi on the chin. The pair swung limbs in a furious exchange of blows, Gammaldi the quick-hitting in-fighter versus the powerhouse out-fighter.

Having dropped the candelabrum to try and prise his attacker's hands from his throat, Fox leaned into him, twisting himself as he did so in a move that dislodged the man's hands and turned him around. Using that vital second of disorientation, Fox grabbed onto the assassin's head and twisted it as quickly as he could, the life ending in an audible death knell of broken vertebra.

The body slipped to the floor, and Fox turned to help Gammaldi. As he walked over he picked up a heavy antique stool, and with an arcing swing through the air he smashed it against the back of the assassin's meaty neck. The colossal man slumped to the ground with a grunt, Gammaldi just managing to avoid being crushed by the human avalanche.

Fox moved to Cooper, rolled him over and felt for a pulse. None. His neck was crushed to pulp and turning deep purple.

He turned and moved to Kate, an arm outstretched to deflect her gaze away from the lifeless form of Cooper.

'Let's get you out of here.'

•

Secher pulled into the gated entrance of St Catherine's Palace and roared up the drive, the big diesel engine and low-profile tyres throwing up the gravel as it fishtailed with the speed.

At the front of the palace he jumped out of the car and passed the keys to an attendant wrapped with a fifty Euro note.

'Keep it right here,' he said in perfect Russian.

'Yes, sir.'

•

Fox led Kate out of the east wing and around the rose fountain to the car park. Gammaldi, a few paces ahead, called up a taxi from the rank.

Fox opened the door and put Kate in the back seat. He turned to Gammaldi, and saw that he was still jacked full of adrenalin. When Fox spoke he was quiet, calm, clear, in charge.

'Al, I need you to head to the US Embassy in Moscow, go and see this guy,' Fox said, handing Gammaldi the business card McCorkell had given him in Dulles.

'Who is he?'

'He'll be CIA,' Fox said. 'Tell him he can verify us via McCorkell at the White House. Kate and I will need visas and help getting across the borders of Latvia and Lithuania, and a plane back into the US from Vilnius.'

Gammaldi nodded, staring wide-eyed at the blank look on Kate's face as she peered up from the back seat of the cab.

'Al, you got that?' Fox said, shaking his mate's shoulder.

'Yeah, sorry. See the CIA guy, get you two visas and a plane Stateside from Lithuania, got it.' Gammaldi looked again at Kate.

'You'll be fine to leave via Moscow on a regular flight,' Fox said. 'I want to get Kate out fast, below the radar.'

'I understand. How are you getting out?'

'We'll get a train to the east, head for an airbase the CIA leases outside Vilnius,' Fox said to Gammaldi, his stocky friend standing diligently by his side, alert now and scanning for threats.

Fox climbed into the cab.

'You'll be okay?' Gammaldi asked Fox quietly, standing by the open back door of the cab.

Fox looked at Kate. She was staring out the other door's window in a daze, not moving at all.

'We'll be fine, just get to Moscow as fast as you can.'

•

Secher walked up the grand staircase and towards the ballroom, scanning the faces as he went.

'Fucking Russians,' he muttered, straightening the cheap polyester tie the security guard had insisted he had to wear.

He smoothed his blond hair and took a breath to gain composure, as he received a drink from a waiter. Then he surveyed the scene around him. Hundreds of faces, some covered with masquerade masks. He moved slowly about the room, fitting in yet scanning each person top to bottom.

A woman's scream echoed from upstairs, and he turned and bolted toward the sound.

A young woman was being comforted by a portly man as Secher arrived outside the study. His stomach turned as he went into the room. It looked like a bomb had gone off, bodies and furniture askew.

John Cooper was dead. His eyes were bulging, his face purple from the burst capillaries. Another dead American was splayed out on the floor, with an MP-7 submachine gun holstered under his jacket. The guy hadn't even had the time to pull it out.

Two palace security guards lay motionless – and then one moved.

Secher leaned down next to him, rolled him over.

The man's eyes went wide in recognition and he began to speak in French before Secher put a finger to his lips.

There was a commotion behind Secher as three uniformed palace guards arrived at the door, pistols drawn.

'Don't move!' was yelled.

'Call an ambulance!' Secher ordered.

'Hands in the air!' shouted one of the guards, pointing his pistol at Secher.

The Frenchman stood and walked up to the guard.

'FSB!' Secher yelled at him, producing a false identity card. The Federalnaya Sluzhba Bezopasnosti, or Federal Security Service, was enough to strike compliance in any Russian. The ruse worked, the guard lowering the pistol and taking a step back out of the doorway.

'Call an ambulance, and keep this door shut,' Secher ordered. 'No one in or out of the building!'

The guard nodded and his companions ushered people out of the hallway.

The door was hefted to as shut as it could be in its damaged state, and Secher was alone with the surviving assassin.

He knelt down next to him, and the man's eyes widened on recognition.

'What happened here, soldier?' Secher said quietly.

'Monsieur –' Blood trickled from the corner of his mouth as he spoke.

'In Russian,' Secher said, looking about the room for a

moment, sure there'd be bugs. 'Whisper,' he said, putting his face close to the other man's.

'Major Secher,' he said in Russian, accented with a gurgling dialect due to blood filling his lungs. 'This was our last hit, and we . . . we were interrupted, I think they were American, or English, two of them . . .'

Secher looked at the other DGSE operative, his lifeless neck twisted awkwardly.

'These two, they beat you unarmed?' Secher was a little surprised. He'd helped design the latest unarmed-combat training doctrine in the French intelligence service. It was the best such program outside an Asian country.

'Yes – they were . . . fast.'

'Where's the girl?' Secher asked.

The agent was fading, not registering what Secher had said.

'The American woman.' Secher slapped his face to stop him from disappearing into unconsciousness. 'Where is she?'

The agent was drifting; Secher shook him hard.

'What happened to the American woman?' Secher was angry this time. He watched as the expression on the man's face changed.

'They – they must have taken her. Women . . .' he grinned through bloody teeth, 'my weakness . . . I was going to have some fun with her, I – my – I had my back to the door . . .'

Before he could finish, Secher leaned on his windpipe in a swift, crushing blow.

13

WASHINGTON

'Mr McCorkell, you have a call from the Moscow Station Chief,' the White House operator said over his cell phone.

McCorkell looked across at his alarm clock, rubbing the sleep from his face.

'Put it through on my home line.' McCorkell hung up his cell and waited for his landline to ring. A call from the CIA Moscow Station Chief at this hour was something you wanted to keep secret. To that end, his apartment was swept for bugs each week, and his windows had been fitted with a version of the Tempest security system. An outer layer of reflective polycarbonate, a pane of heavy lead-content glass with a vibrating current running through it, and an inner pane of regular laminated glass. Supposedly impenetrable to all foreign-signal intelligence tools. Even his encrypted cell phone had to have a long-range booster built into the apartment to get the minimal reception it received.

His bedside phone rang.

'Hey, Mark.'

'Bill, I've got a quick one,' Mark Rubbo, the MSC, said.

'Go ahead.'

'Just got word that Cooper and our Delta section head were killed in St Petersburg. I'm waiting for definite verification.'

'Shit!' McCorkell pounded his side table. 'How solid's your source?'

'I was hoping you could tell me. I have an Alister Gammaldi, US permanent resident with Australian citizenship, in one of my interview rooms here at the embassy. He says he urgently needs visas for a Lachlan F –'

'Mark, whatever the man wants, you organise it for him ASAP, got me?' McCorkell said. 'Whatever, wherever, just do it.'

There was a pause on the other end, and McCorkell could sense where this was going.

'You wanna give the CIA a heads-up –'

'Mark, it's nothing you need to know,' McCorkell said, about to play his infrequently used trump card. 'Want me to have the President send you a letter to make you sleep easy about it?'

'No need, Bill, but so you know I'm not gonna wear this in my local budget. We can't afford to crap around here any more.'

'Well I'll see what we can do about restarting the Cold War for you kids in Moscow,' McCorkell said, hearing the humour had worked at the other end. 'Seriously, send my office the expense details and we'll work that out, and I'll inform your Director of this first thing in the morning. In the meantime, keep me posted on what happened to Cooper.'

McCorkell hung up his connection and stared out the window
at the glow of the Washington night.

14

RUSSIA

Fox returned to the sleeper cabin with a bottle of Smirnoff and two glasses.

Kate sat facing the window, watching as the clear moonless night sped past. The occasional streetlamp and house lights flashed by, strobing into the cabin. Fox could see her face in the reflection of the windowpane, her cheeks glistening with tears. She had put his suit jacket on over her dress, its sleeves coming down over her hands.

'Please, leave the light off,' she said as Fox latched the door and reached for the switch.

'Okay,' Fox replied. He put two shot glasses on the small side table, and poured out two vodkas. 'I needed a drink,' he said. He held a glass out for her. The liquid spilled slightly over the edges of the glass as the carriage rocked rhythmically over the tracks. 'Here, it'll help.'

She got up and wiped her eyes on the jacket sleeve, taking a shot of vodka and downing it in one gulp. She winced, put the glass down and took off the jacket, laying it on the fold-down bed.

'Don't leave me alone again,' she said, moving into Fox, wrapping her arms around him. She put her head hard against his chest and held him tight, as if he might otherwise disappear.

'I won't,' Fox assured her. Throwing back his drink, he pursed his lips and blew out a deep breath as the liquid coated his throat with fire. 'I'll be right next to you all the way home. I just rang Al in Moscow. We'll be met at the border with passports and visas in about an hour. Once we're in Lithuania, we've got a direct flight to New York.'

Kate turned to the fold-down table and poured two more vodkas. She sipped at hers this time.

Fox could see the fright in her eyes, the look that he'd seen on so many young soldiers' faces in Afghanistan and Iraq. The expression on the faces of civilians, all those orphaned kids and widows who'd seen what no one ever should. A look that accompanied seeing first-hand the messiness and brutality of killing for the first time. Nothing a movie or video game could prepare you for. The gore, the smells, the sounds. A part of you never recovered from that.

'Kate, I don't know what to say . . .' he said, watching as she poured herself another. 'I'm so sorry you had to see that, to experience that.'

'It's –' Kate took a sharp breath, swallowing her tears for a moment. 'It's nothing to do with you.' She took a sip and then stared into her drink. The train rocked rhythmically and the clear liquid swilled around in the small confines of glass.

It appeared pure, alluring, toxic.

Fox put a hand on her shoulder, ran it up her neck and steered her face up to meet his.

'I know it's hard, it's fucking awful . . . No one should ever have to see what just happened. No one should know what that's like.' Fox had a distant look of his own, and Kate put her glass down on the table and wrapped her arms around him again.

'Somehow, sometime, part of it gets easier . . .' he said, stroking her head, burying his nose in her hair.

They stood there like that, the train rocking, the sad countryside passing by in darkness and silence.

Kate looked up into his eyes. He could see her gaze had softened; there was some comfort there now, a sense of being secure with him so close.

'And part of it gets harder?'

Fox didn't have to answer her. She could now empathise with him in that regard, could already sense what thinking about it could do to you. It was a new collection of emotions that knew no reasoning, deservedly had no grounding in modern life's experience.

'Thank you.' She buried herself into his embrace and he rested his chin on her head. 'For everything.'

'Thank me when we're in New York.' Fox smelled the coconut of her hair conditioner, losing himself in the sensory distraction. A few minutes passed and Fox felt they had both relaxed into each other.

Nestling into his chest, a series of tears dropped from Kate's eyes down his open shirt collar.

Fox loosened his arms and moved them down to her waist. Her black satin dress clung to her figure, and he ran his hands down her waist to where it moved out at her hips. He let go and moved to step back, ashamed to be having such thoughts . . .

She pulled into him, her nipples hard and brushing against him through their clothes. Her open lips brushed his neck, and followed with soft kisses that slowly marched up and along his jaw line.

'What –'

'Kiss me,' she whispered into his mouth.

Fox took her face in his hands and kissed her slowly. Soon they were moving fast, kissing long and passionately, sucking and biting each other's lips.

They eased back onto the fold-down bed, Fox first. Kate slipped the straps off her shoulders and the dress shimmered to the floor.

She climbed onto him, unbuttoning his shirt and pants.

'Are you sure?'

'Shh . . .' Kate said, eyes welling with tears that threatened to overflow. She pulled down his underwear and tossed them away. 'I need you,' she whispered as she pushed her hips down onto his.

Fox felt her smooth skin goose-bump against his. She moved slowly, leaving her hands on his chest. He felt her tears falling down onto his face, the little warm drops sparkling in the occasional light flashing by the window, a few of them landing in his own eyes.

PART TWO

15

THE WHITE HOUSE

'Good morning, Mr President,' Bill McCorkell said as he entered the Oval Office. As National Security Advisor to the President, McCorkell's daily 8 am meeting was the first official appointment of the President. He carried a folder marked PDB – President's Daily Brief.

'Morning, Bill,' the President said, without looking up from his newspaper, skimming the articles in the sports section. 'You do a good job of keeping me informed, Bill, but your brief doesn't cover any sports worth a damn,' he said as he turned the pages. 'Well, that depends on what one classifies as sport, I guess, but let's not get into that this morning.'

McCorkell poured himself a coffee from a trolley by the Resolute Desk, and sat opposite the President. During the wait, McCorkell looked at the man in his third year of power and gave an imperceptible nod.

McCorkell had held his position at the White House before the current Commander in Chief had come to office, and it was a testament to the latter man's judgement that he remained. McCorkell was recognised by both sides of politics as the best in his field, and working for a new administration, under a new leader of the opposite political persuasion, proved this. Simply, McCorkell was an expert on world affairs: from military and intelligence to politics and economics, there was not a person in Washington who could match his foresight on world vision. While many were surprised that he had not been appointed Secretary of State, insiders acknowledged that it was further credence to the man's solidity in that he did not want to be seen as a mouthpiece for an administration abroad, but as a shaper of policy and direction from within. Indeed, no less than three consecutive Presidents had offered him his choice of job.

The current President surprised McCorkell in how to be adaptive. That, and having the ability to continually exceed all expectations of durability and performance. No matter what crisis or hurdle, this man in the Oval Office gritted his teeth and ploughed through it, each time proving his worth to those around him, and the world. Well, he was a fellow Notre Dame *summa cum laude*.

'Looks like New England is set for a good year,' said the President. He took off his glasses, set aside the *Post* and had a sip of coffee. 'NFL will be the better for it.'

'The Jets will make a comeback,' McCorkell said. 'I feel it in my bones.'

'Just don't use those same bones to predict any global crises,' the President said in a good-natured jibe. 'Seriously, Bill, you've been telling me that same Jets cockamamie since I met you, and I've yet to see them come close.'

'Thankfully I'm not a betting man, Mr President,' McCorkell said. 'That said, I'm still spending the proceeds of that lazy Benjamin I won from you on the '04 Super Tuesday results.'

'Yeah, yeah, well the joke's on us both for having public-servant salaries in the first place,' the President said over the steam of his coffee. 'So, what's new in the world outside sport?'

'First up, a car bomb in Basra killed two US security contractors. Literally happened an hour ago, and the Iraqi police have found possible remains of the bomber,' McCorkell said, handing over the PDB folder. Its classification was stamped *'POTUS Eyes Only'*, POTUS being the common-usage acronym for President of the United States.

'Again, with the IEDs,' the President said, putting his glasses back on and skimming the first report. 'You'd think they would have gotten the picture when the Brits swept the city last week – have a statement worked into this afternoon's press con.'

'Yes, Mr President.' McCorkell continued, 'We also had a close call with Task Force 145 in Kirkuk, involved in a six-hour fire fight with an al Qaeda safe house in the northern suburbs. The Shadow Wolves outfit tracked down the targets, their first big success since they arrived in the country six months ago.' McCorkell flicked to this second report in his own folder. A condensed version of the major intelligence stories, each IntRep blurb was a pointer to a fuller document available on Intellipedia, the nation's latest intelligence-community version of the internet.

'Four friendlies wounded, all rangers who routed the enemy in a fire-support role. Eleven enemy combatants taken captive,'

McCorkell said. 'Big weapons cache was recovered, about a thousand small arms and a hundred RPGs. Tracked as being some of that looted from the Baghdad armoury after the initial invasion.'

'This out with the sharks?' the President asked.

'Yes, sir. It has been leaked to the wire services as those Task Force boys can do with some positive press, so it will come up today in the press-con questions,' McCorkell replied.

'Okay, thanks,' the President said, reading over the brief. 'A couple of commendations coming through on it?'

'I'd say so, they've been light in this campaign and it's an issue that's still getting coverage,' McCorkell said with a sigh, flipping through his notes. 'Next item is that the French have almost their entire surface fleet on station in the South Pacific to conduct live-fire exercises,' McCorkell said. 'The Aussies and Kiwis are keeping their eyes and ears on it for us.'

'How long they staying down there?'

'Couple of weeks, no firm date has been communicated.'

'Nice if they could have spared a few more resources in the Middle East, rather than pussyfooting around their Pacific playground.'

'Yeah, well, they're doing their own thing, as usual. That said, they've got quite a few boots on the ground in Africa at the moment.' McCorkell closed his folder. 'I'm still prepping for Iraq and Africa for the Security Council agenda later this morning.'

'Quiet day then,' the President said, putting his PDB folder down. 'Thanks, Bill.'

McCorkell got up to leave.

'I, ah, had a call early this morning from Moscow Station,' McCorkell said. 'John Cooper was murdered over there last night.'

The President looked puzzled for a few seconds and then McCorkell could sense that the image of Cooper came clearly to him.

'Cooper? Advocacy Center Cooper?' he asked.

'Yep. Murdered in St Petersburg while attending the Russian trade conference.'

'What do our guys in Moscow say?'

'Nothing yet, should have some answers in a few hours,' McCorkell replied. 'This stuff is fresh, yet to hit the press, as their intel agency, the FSB, are running a tight ship around this trade conference.'

'At times I envy Russia's power over their press.' The President squinted hard, which was what he did when he was listening hard, taking it all in, kicking the information around. 'NSA got anything to say on it yet?'

'Meeting with them right after this, and you can bet they'll be going ape over translating all traffic in and out of St Petersburg on this one,' McCorkell said. 'I was scheduled for a tour of their new cryptography lab.'

The President tapped his pen on the credenza, which displayed a map of the Presidents Cup course. 'Shouldn't affect their schedule?' he queried, getting a cigarette from his top drawer and standing up.

'The quantum cryptography switchover?' McCorkell asked.

The President nodded.

'It can't, they're locked in, and Cooper's murder doesn't mean there's a threat to anything NSA are doing.'

'Well, I guess the MO on this is about as broad as it could get,' the President said, fishing around in his pockets for a lighter. 'Any obvious threats?'

'In Russia? Anyone with enough cash can do anything. At this stage we've got nothing but bodies. The two assassins were also killed in the incident; FSB have communicated that they've come up clean, no records at all. Cooper's DoD bodyguard was killed in the attack as well.' McCorkell checked his watch. 'I have a sit-rep with the CIA and FBI this afternoon, linked through to the embassy in Moscow. Should have some news by the end of the day.'

'Okay, we'll chat about it after today's Security Council, get my body man to make some time,' the President said, looking through the bullet-resistant glass door at the ever-green White House lawn.

'Will do.'

'And Bill, if you can get me the details on this DoD guy, I'll write his family a letter.'

'Yes, Mr President, I'm waiting on the Pentagon's personnel file,' McCorkell said. 'Of course, Mr President, for SOCOM operational reasons it cannot list where this Delta soldier was, or what he was doing.'

'I know, no details, hero and all that,' the President replied. 'You ever meet Cooper's family?'

'Yes, Mr President.' McCorkell crossed his arms against his chest, holding his files in close. 'Met his wife at Clinton's inauguration and one other time, I think it was a Gore fundraiser. Last I heard they divorced about five years ago, never had any kids, she lives down in Florida now.'

'Okay, thanks, Bill,' the President said, nodding to the agent outside the door who opened it for him. He turned before walking out. 'Oh, Bill, what's your read of France – think the NFP will make much of a show in the run-off?'

McCorkell thought about it. The French political system was two-staged, where the run-off meant the final going to the polls of the two most popular candidates.

'Will they take many seats? I think they will, yeah,' McCorkell replied. 'Cassel has the sympathy of many moderates with the assassination of her father, and they are already coming off a high platform from the 2002 election, where they were the first extreme-right party in French history to make it to the second round of a presidential election. Back then it was an accident they made it to the second round. This time, the public have made a statement.'

'But they don't have a chance of taking power?'

'A chance so slim as to be almost nonexistent. Europe, particularly France, has more trouble than we do with illegal immigrants, and a tough stance on that is the NFP's and every other right-wing Euro party's war cry. But it's not enough to win over Paris, no matter how many students may riot for a decent pay rate – something that could happen if the flood of illegals was slowed to a trickle. If they get more than twenty-five per cent of the vote, I might just put some hard-earned down on the Jets making the Super Bowl after all.'

'Okay, I'll take your money. Anyhow, come into senior staff tomorrow morning. State is presenting an Old Europe run-down,' the President said, lighting up his cigarette as he walked outside. His chocolate-coloured Labrador, Tenzin, appeared from behind the Resolute Desk and followed him outside.

'Will do. Have a good day, Mr President.'

•

McCorkell walked down the corridor of the West Wing to his office, a mid-sized room overlooking the Rose Garden. He moved his gym bag off the spare seat and sat down, pouring a tea. Irish Breakfast. He'd gotten the taste from his days in England, first the four postgrad years he'd spent at Oxford, and then a five-year stint a decade later working in the embassy. It was his small gesture of going against the establishment over there.

He put his feet up on the coffee table and sat back in the cushioned armchair, a little fifteen-minute ritual he allowed himself each morning to go over the contents of the main dailies.

His eyes skimmed the news but his brain was working overtime. He checked his watch, waiting for the next call from Fox when he landed in New York. Should have been by now . . .

16

NEW YORK CITY

The summer sun was beating down mid-morning, setting the day up to be a scorcher, the humidity hitting Fox and Kate as they walked out of the air-conditioned sanctuary of JFK Airport. Outside the terminal they were met by Richard Sefreid, the head of security for GSR. The big no-nonsense former army ranger walked ahead of them to the waiting car, scanning for threats as he went.

'Head for West 76 and Riverside please, Richard,' Fox said, sitting with Kate in the back seat.

'Got it,' Sefreid said, pulling away from the kerb with a squeal of tyre rubber, checking his mirrors every few seconds. There was a chase car behind them, an identical black Mercedes ML320D, with two armed GSR security operatives inside. The small outfit of ex-military and law enforcement personnel were used to their role of protecting company journalists who stuck their necks out too far.

'You okay?' Fox quietly asked Kate, putting a hand on her leg.

'Yeah,' she replied, looking out the window at the city she'd grown up in.

At least she got some rest on the flight, Fox thought, catching a glimpse of himself in the rear-view mirror. He certainly hadn't received any such respite. He'd stayed awake the entire time while with her, ever watching, ever there, always on his game. Her sleep on the flight had been fairly sound, he was glad to see. She didn't need to know what the nightmares were like.

She was silent, and Fox wondered what that silence meant to her. They'd stayed in their dark sleeper cabin the entire train ride to Lithuania, hours of hot, sweaty entanglement and quiet embrace. Was that something she'd already forgotten?

In the capital city of Vilnius they'd met a local mob boss on the CIA's payroll. His private airfield, guarded by the country's military, was frequently used by the CIA and DoD to move prisoners around Europe and the Middle East. From there a jet leased through a Canadian-based business, untraceable back to the CIA, took the pair straight to New York.

Fox took Kate's hand in his for the drive to her parents' residence in Manhattan. He noticed she no longer squeezed his hand as if from fear of him leaving. Now it was as if she was ready to move on and rely on her parents for support.

•

At the Matthews' apartment building on West 79th, Kate's parents met her at the door.

'Mum,' she said, falling into her mother's arms as she entered. They went off to Kate's bedroom, and he could hear her crying the tears she'd been holding on to since Russia.

'Thank you for bringing my daughter back,' Mr Matthews said, offering his hand. 'Frank Matthews.'

'Lachlan Fox,' he said, shaking hands with the guy who measured a good six-four, looking all the world like a smiling Clint Eastwood.

'I just made a pot of coffee,' Frank said, leading the way out of the entry hall. 'Real, too, no decaf in this house.'

'Sounds good,' Fox replied, figuring the coffee comment was a parental way of trying to bring some normality to the bizarre events they'd heard about over the phone from the plane. He followed Frank Matthews through to the sitting room. Persian rugs covered walnut timber floorboards, the dadoes and walls were a calming shade of pale green and the timber blinds let light through.

'Take a seat,' Frank said, gesturing to an overstuffed armchair. The coffee was set up on the low table between them, the dark brew in the French press promising a good wake-up call.

'Black is fine, thanks,' Fox said, settling into the chair and taking the steaming mug.

'So, is there any more information on what happened to my daughter?' Frank asked, leaning back in his chair.

'Other than what Kate told you from the plane, that's all there is for now,' Fox said.

'Who would do this?' Frank asked.

'I'm afraid I don't really have the answer to that,' Fox told him. 'The who, the why, I have no idea.'

'Who will be investigating this? Americans, I hope.'

'The FBI will be investigating, I'm sure, with the cooperation of the Moscow CIA office and federal Russian authorities,' Fox said, and he could see the man was not impressed by this latter piece of information. 'You'd be surprised, their security services are actually pretty capable, particularly when the case involves a high-value foreigner like John Cooper.'

'Okay,' Frank said, leaning forward with his gangly elbows resting on his knees. He stared at the coffee table for a while, his expression a mixture of frustration and anger. 'What can we do? I mean, what happens from here for Kate?'

'My colleague has given details of what happened at the palace to the US embassy in Moscow along with government offices here,' Fox replied, sipping his coffee and putting it down on the table. 'The State Department will be sending someone here at noon today. They will need her account of what happened, and they'll supply a psychologist to help her work through the trauma.'

'You've been through this before?' Frank gave Fox a look that further reminded him of Eastwood – more Eastwood the fatherly director than Dirty Harry.

'Unfortunately, I've seen my fair share of death,' Fox admitted. He looked into his coffee, then up at Frank. He didn't know what else he could say to this man, other than he'd do his best to find out the truth.

'How long have you been a journalist for?'

'Spent some time doing my own little rag back in Australia. A few investigative pieces got me noticed, and I've been with the Global Syndicate of Reporters for just over a year now,' Fox said. 'We're a team of investigative journalists, and I always seem to get the gigs where I'm in the worst places in the world, where morality – or rather humanity – has left in favour of desperation through necessity – or just plain evil.'

'There's certainly no shortage of that, and it's something I'm sure we could discuss at great length another time,' Frank said. Fox could see the man was genuinely interested in what he would have to say. 'And you spent some time in the military, as an officer?'

'Yeah,' Fox said, giving him an inquisitorial look. 'What gives it away?'

'How you carry yourself. My brother, father, grandfather, all went through West Point,' Frank said. 'Although they'd all say that your hair is a little over regulation.'

'Yeah, well, I spent some time in the military, back in Australia,' Fox said. 'Working for GSR I'm now based here in New York, and I travel the world looking after the military portfolio. I became an expert by default, in a field that's in high demand these days, what with Iraq and all.'

'Been over there?'

'Yeah, served there for a bit,' Fox said. 'Not in a hurry to get back, though. It gets a huge amount of coverage anyway, more than ten times what a crisis place like Darfur gets, which, when you consider the body-count comparison, is a criminally disproportionate press skew.'

The pair sat in silence for a moment. Fox looked at his watch; he should have checked in with McCorkell by now.

'Do you think this attack on Cooper and my daughter was random?'

'Unlikely,' Fox replied.

'And no leads whatsoever?' Frank asked.

'I'm sorry, Frank, I know it's frustrating as hell,' Fox said. 'I'm determined to find out, though.'

The phone rang and Frank picked it up. Fox took the opportunity and stood to leave.

'I'll just be a sec, Lachlan,' Frank said, covering the mouthpiece. 'It's Kate's boyfriend, I'm sure it would do her good to talk to him.'

Fox watched as Frank walked out of the room with the portable handset. He was disappointed, but it now started to make sense. That look in her eyes when they'd met, there was something she was hiding, something she was not letting out. At least she had a lot of support right now.

•

Across the street from the Matthews' building, behind the blacked-out windows of a contractors' van, a DGSE agent aimed at Fox as he walked out onto the sidewalk. He had watched as the pair entered twenty minutes earlier, Fox's back to the agent as he led Kate into the building.

Now the agent had a good, clear shot, and as Fox walked to the waiting SUV the agent's finger squeezed, the button held down as the digital camera clicked away.

17

FRANCE

'Keep a tail on him,' Secher said to his lead DGSE agent in New York.

'Yes, Major.'

Secher's mind raced. The verbal description matched those from the scene at the palace – this was the man who had intervened on the attack on Cooper. Yet again, Danton's near-sighted actions were making his job that much more difficult. While Secher thought Danton a fool for thickening the plot with the last assassination attempt, part of him relished the uncertainty of it. The fear of walking into the unknown. The challenge ahead. The game.

'Visual observation, plant some bugs, whatever it takes. I want to know who he is, where he works, sleeps, eats.' Secher paused while a navy pilot in a Libelle G flight suit similar to his own entered the terminal. He made eye contact, tapping his watch to Secher, who nodded in reply.

'In twenty-four hours I want to know who this man is,' Secher said into the phone. 'Send me a message via the consulate in Sydney.'

'Sydney, Australia?'

'Yes,' Secher said. 'And keep on him. By the time I get to New York, I want to know more about this man than he knows about himself.'

'Yes, Major.'

Secher hung up and followed the pilot out onto the windy tarmac of the Istres Air Base in the South of France. A row of delta-winged Dassault Rafale multi-role fighter aircraft lined the main taxiway, and Secher walked past the gleaming jets to his waiting ride.

Closing up his state-of-the-art flight suit, he walked up the ladder and climbed into the aft seat of the production-line-fresh French Navy Dassault Rafale N. The pilot closed the canopy, getting the thumbs-up from the ground crew after they removed the wheel chocks. The plane taxied the short ride to the end of the runway, turning sharply and coming to a complete stop.

'Hold on, Major,' the pilot said as he brought the engines to full burn, the airframe trembling under the pressure as the pilot released the brakes. The two-seater fighter jet, specially designed for aircraft-carrier use, shot forward and left the runway in three seconds, the afterburners blasting a sonic boom through the sound barrier.

18

NSA HQ
FORT MEADE, MARYLAND

McCorkell followed Dunn into the supercomputing wing of the NSA headquarters. The noise inside the double-walled concrete building was an electrical buzz that sounded like a billion bees, and the air carried the electrical smell that came from having the world's biggest and most powerful computers in a controlled air-space.

'The basement here has its own power plant working parallel to the Maryland supply to maintain the cooling power needed by the machines,' Dunn said. He stopped at a viewing platform on the metal-meshed walkway.

'This is it,' Dunn said, waving a hand around the open expanse of the floor. From this mezzanine level, they looked down at the computers, arrayed around what resembled a foil golf ball the size of a small house.

'So in that structure is the code-maker that's going to make us unbreakable?' McCorkell said.

'Yep,' Dunn replied. 'Quantum cryptography. Amazing to think it, but the small array of lasers in there provide an endless stream of photons that produce encryption for all our stored information. Other crypto systems are being implemented over the next six months to replace all security measures for our outside customers. That little room will do what ten thousand cryptographers and the biggest supercomputers on the planet cannot do.'

'Photons, hey,' McCorkell said.

'Yeah,' Dunn smiled. 'Quantum does the crypto work, the latest Cray HPCS supercomputers system handles the grunt work. But I'm just an analyst by trade these days. You'll need to speak to one of the tech boys if you want a deeper quantum physics explanation.'

'Think I'll pass, all the same,' McCorkell said.

'Well, the beauty in her is this: as we are working with light, any disturbance, such as an attempted eavesdropping, is detected as it disturbs the carrier.'

'So we'd know as soon as someone tried to hack in,' McCorkell said, starting to cotton on to one of the new system's strengths.

'Straightaway. And even if someone did tap into it, they'd never get any usable data. It's faultless, bullet-proof.'

'Not something I often hear from intel chiefs,' McCorkell mused.

'You wouldn't believe the amount of hacks we get on sensitive government networks each day. And it's not just geeks doing it for kicks, now the terrorists have gone high-tech on us. Cell in Bahrain nearly shut down Pensacola air-traffic control last week.'

'Why Pensacola?' McCorkell asked.

'Why Bahrain?' Dunn walked McCorkell to a better vantage point. 'And what's more, beyond the security implications, switching to quantum cryptography is going to free up around half of our technical division who normally spend their days working on ways to build better encryption technology for securing our own communication traffic.'

'An increased workforce overnight,' McCorkell said. 'Just don't let Congress cotton on to that one, they'll think there's room for some fat to be trimmed.'

'Don't you worry about that. Shit, you know what kinda workload we got ahead of us.' Dunn motioned for them to walk back towards the doors leading into the operations building. 'NSA grew up for the first forty years to spy on the Ruskies. Follow their fleet traffic, intercept their military communications and signals intel. Now we're tracking millions of cell phones across the world, mining billions of emails . . .'

'Sounds like you need a bigger vacuum,' McCorkell said. He followed Dunn into the lift, watching as the NSA Deputy Director pressed his thumb on the pad to access the executive floor.

'Our vacuum's plenty big enough. You say it, we record it.' Dunn shot McCorkell a sideways look. 'Well, of course, not if *you* say it, nor any upstanding US citizen for that matter.'

'Of course,' McCorkell said, certainly not needing to remind Dunn of the bad press the NSA got when listening in on UN Security Council members during the lead-up to Iraq. Like all intel news to hit the press, it's only when they did something wrong that it was brandished around for the world to see. He knew Dunn was still paying for that one.

'Imagine what Hoover's boys would have made of this,' Dunn said. 'FBI would love the keys to this place if they had the chance. And in a way I don't blame them. Their problem's almost getting too big too. Shut the borders, look within. We got enough problems in our backyard, let alone everyone else's.'

'So you've joined the isolationist camp?' McCorkell said, following Dunn out of the lift and down the white marble corridor.

'No, not on your life, but I can see their point,' Dunn replied.

'Hell, I wouldn't mind if we adopted some of the foreign policies we had prior to the Second World War,' McCorkell said. 'If we just concentrated on our own nation-building again. Hell, being more of a closed society would give you guys less foreign data to mine.'

'Well, the data-mining capability is not so much the issue. We've got the computing power and storage space of God. As September 11 proved, what we don't have are the fifty thousand linguists we need to properly translate all those communications in time. We have had to switch from simply gathering to *hunting.*'

McCorkell cringed. The September 11 intelligence blunder was the worst press the NSA had ever received. Its network of intercept systems picked up communications between the terrorists before the attacks, but the translation of those COMINT files occurred after the event. Hence the change in doctrine to go looking for the threat, rather than waiting for it to be fulfilled.

'You have your Senate hearing in a couple of days?' McCorkell asked.

'Yeah, I put it off as much as I could,' Dunn said. 'The last change in the Senate means they're dragging us over those same 9/11 coals again. The Democrats have been waiting for their chance to question me, and to do what they can to pull the Patriot Act apart. A waste of bloody time, of course, there's nothing new the SSCI are gonna learn from me.'

'Well, the Senate Select Committee on Intelligence was set up for just that purpose, wasn't it?' McCorkell said. 'Being so good at wasting time puts a new meaning to oversight. The price we pay for living in a democratic republic.'

Dunn grunted.

'How about computer programs, they still can't make up the shortfall with translating the collected comms?' McCorkell asked.

'To some degree,' Dunn said, showing McCorkell into his office. 'We're constantly upgrading them, working on hundreds of joint programs with DARPA and some of the off-the-shelf tech companies, and some good-looking stuff is coming out of it.'

'Maybe I should buy some tech stocks again,' McCorkell commented.

'There's money to be made. But our problem here is that you can't beat a pair of human eyes and ears to detect meaning in a person's communication. Not yet, anyway.'

'Makes the concept of Total Information Awareness not as impressive as it sounds,' McCorkell said.

'We'll get there.' Dunn sat down behind his desk, an old relic of a thing from the seventies. The chairs were new, though, upgraded every twelve months as part of an occupational health and safety measure in all government agencies and departments.

'Thing is,' Dunn said, 'as we get better, and as we get more results in the field, more military strikes and grabs of key assets, the sons of bitches are getting smarter. Used to be the terrorists would use disposable mobiles, use them once and chuck them out. Didn't worry us too much, as we'd then go hunt their voice pattern. We've taken out half the al Qaeda leadership through that. The smart ones that are left know this, and they don't use phones at all any more. We joke about bombing places like 'stan and Iraq "back into the Stone Age". But that's the hardest place for us to find anyone. Put them in a first-world city, with modern communications, and we have control. We hear and see everything they do. Give them carrier pigeons and human messengers, and we're lost.'

The pair sat silent for a moment, thinking about the gravity of it all.

'Cooper was a great loss,' Dunn said. 'Who's handling the investigation?'

'Moscow CIA Station Chief and the local FBI attaché,' McCorkell said. 'And the FSB are pulling St Petersburg apart for leads.'

'Forgive me if I don't have much faith in the FSB,' Dunn said. 'When they were the KGB, they had reach. Damn, they were fuck'n good, and they worked in numbers. Something to be said for having no gloves to take off. Now, as none of the poor sons of bitches are getting regular paycheques from their half-assed government, they stick their hands out to the local business oligarchs. But of course, you know that as well as I do.'

'That I do. Just don't piss the FSB off – a sprinkling of polonium or dioxin in your dinner is not a nice way to go,' McCorkell said.

'Litvinenko and Yushchenko certainly proved the FSB still has some reach, and a long memory – if it was our Russian friends, of course,' Dunn commented with a wry smile.

'Of course . . .' McCorkell said. 'Ira, there's an investigative journalist on this Cooper thing, Lachlan Fox. Good guy, ex Aussie Navy. He might pop by soon.'

'He's not a spook?' Dunn said, jotting down the name.

'No, Wallace's GSR. He was in St Petersburg when this went down, almost in time to save Cooper, he took out the assassins in the process.'

'Okay, I'm impressed,' Dunn said. 'How is Tas? Haven't heard much about him for some time.'

'Great,' McCorkell replied, happy to be thinking about his old friend. 'Still taking on the world, going where news corporations with shareholders and commercial interests dare not tread. Just has his own little army of reporters to do the dirty work now.'

'Fuck'n' admirable, some of the stuff he's championed,' Dunn said. 'You two old boys still go rowing?'

'When we can.' McCorkell checked his watch. 'And while I like to pretend I didn't hear you mentioning "old boy", I'm afraid my knees are finally putting an end to running.'

'Know how that feels,' Dunn sympathised.

'Ira, we'll need to put our heads together for a replacement for Cooper,' McCorkell said as he stood to leave. 'I've asked Treasury to compile a short list by tomorrow, and I want your approval before I take it to the President and Cabinet.'

'Let's do it after we switch over to this next-gen encryption,' Dunn said, coming from around his desk to walk his guest out. 'The economy can handle the Advocacy Center being run by the deputy for a couple of weeks.'

'Fair enough,' McCorkell replied. 'So, when does your Quantum baby come online?'

'Friday. A week from now there's not a person on earth who will be able to hack our secure information. We even quietly put a challenge out there to some allied agencies, the Brits, the French, the Ruskies: go try and hack into our government computers a week from now. Can't wait to hear back from them! In a few days time, we flick the switch and nobody, ever, will be peeking in our window. The walls are going up.'

19

NEW YORK CITY

Fox and Gammaldi had just finished their debrief to Wallace in his office. Faith Williams sat to the side of Wallace's big oak desk, intently listening in on this pair of investigators who for the past year had made a game of making her life harder.

'I spoke to Bill McCorkell about an hour ago,' Fox said. 'I've got a meeting time set up to speak to Ira Dunn tomorrow evening.'

'Sounds good,' Wallace said, noting down the meeting. 'Nice to hear we still have some people putting in the hours down in Washington.'

'Who's Ira Dunn?' Faith asked.

'The last thing Cooper said to me was to speak to an Ira Dunn,' Fox told her. 'He's a deputy director at NSA, in charge of their Communications Intelligence Directorate.'

'Well, I want you to talk to the shrink before you go,' Faith said. Having personnel authority over all GSR employees, most had learned early on that it was wiser to follow her directive to the letter than be on the receiving end of her usually well-hidden wrath. 'If for nothing else, to make sure you're on the ball enough to keep putting in the hours.'

'Okay, you don't need to justify it to me,' Fox said. 'I'm understanding this American preoccupation with psychiatrists more and more each day.' He gave her his most charming smile and she looked back down at her notes.

'Do I have to see the shrink too?' Gammaldi asked.

'I don't know, Alister, do you?' Faith retorted.

'I think I'm okay,' Gammaldi said. 'Bit homesick, though, missing Vegemite, that's for sure.'

'Well why don't you tell Dr Bender all about it then,' Faith said. 'I'm sure you don't have to hold Fox's hand on his trip to Washington.'

Gammaldi made a mock gesture of stretching out his arm and offering his hand to Fox, sitting in the chair beside him.

'Lachlan, I take it you're not planning on getting involved in any assassinations on this trip?' Faith asked, her thinly sculpted eyebrows raised. 'No showdowns with madmen who have their fingers on WMD launch buttons?'

'Nah, WMD-wielding madmen were so last year,' Fox said. He was fast adding to his unenviable record in the building for being caught in hot spots, not exactly being a magnet for trouble but often putting his nose a little too deep into a story.

'You'll have to take a commercial bird,' Wallace said, bringing the meeting back on track. 'Both Gulfstreams are out at the moment.'

'Okay,' Fox said, standing up. 'If that's it, I'm going down to have a chat to Ben Beasley.'

•

'Hey, Lachlan, check this out,' Ben Beasley said, looking up from his MacBook. The comms expert in the small GSR security team, Beasley had spent the first ten years of his career working for the FBI in their Baltimore office, specialising in communications interception. More listening in on small- to large-scale crime than what the NSA was tasked with, but for Fox it was a level of expertise into a world he felt he knew too little about, considering he was about to head down to NSA headquarters itself.

Fox looked over Beasley's shoulder, at what was an image of a city, zooming in.

'Google Earth, seen it some time back,' Fox said.

'Not quite, my learned Aussie friend,' Beasley said, zooming in even further.

'Good res– holy shit!' Fox said, reading a newspaper, watching as the person sitting in the open café turned the pages.

'DoD Earth,' Beasley said. 'Not much of it is real-time footage like this, but in a nutshell it's as sexy as the world mapping images of the Department of Defense get.'

'Nice,' Fox said. 'Don't suppose I should ask how you've got access to it?'

'I access it through a NIPRNet emergency CAVNET gateway in their SIPRNet Intellipedia network . . .' Beasley slid his glasses higher onto his nose. 'Lost you, haven't I?'

'Lost me at NIP-something,' Fox said.

'Well I'll explain it in layman's detail sometime, if I ever see you logging in to play Warcraft online.'

'Dude, I so don't have time for computer games,' Fox said. 'Anyway, I'm here because of your time with the feds.'

'Oh?'

'You were in their communication division, right?' Fox asked. 'So you know a fair bit about phone and email intercepting?'

'I'm your man,' Beasley said, clearing some of the clutter off his desk. It wasn't that the room was small, it was simply full of tech gear. Radios, LCD screens and computer terminals were stacked everywhere. 'What's it to ya? Want me to bug someone? An ex-girlfriend perhaps? Ex-boyfriend even, I've often wondered about you and that Gammaldi character . . .'

Fox humoured him with a laugh, before slapping a strong hand on Beasley's shoulder.

'What do you know about the NSA?' Fox asked.

'Ah, the holy grail of the intelligence community,' Beasley said, then turned more serious. 'How long you got?'

Fox gave him a look that said as long as it takes, minus the wisecracks. He took a seat on the swivel chair next to Beasley.

'Well,' Beasley began, 'they're our biggest intelligence agency by far. Comes under the umbrella of the sixteen-member National Intelligence Community, and it's a part of the DoD. Tasked with protecting US communications and intercepting those of others.'

'What do you know about their intercept programs?' Fox asked, taking an Oreo from the open pack on Beasley's desk.

'Well, they've got the best gear out there by far – help yourself by the way,' Beasley said, stuffing a cookie in his mouth before continuing. 'They've got hardware and software that other intelligence agencies won't get access to for years and the public sector will probably never see. Supercomputing power that NASA would cream their pants over. In terms of intercept programs, they're part of the biggest global network of spying the world has ever seen, thanks to the UKUSA Treaty.'

'The Anglo alliance?' Fox asked.

'Yeah, the US and UK are the main players, along with Australia, Canada and New Zealand. A few other allies have stations on their soil too, although they don't get to play the game like the UKUSA countries. It all came together after the Second World War as a way to keep tabs on the Ruskies and the new international body, the UN. In a nutshell, by having such a spread-out range of sensors and satellite dishes across the globe, they can get it all. Anything said or written that travels via satellite, radio, microwave, cable, fibre-optic – you name it, they can intercept it.'

'And Echelon?' Fox asked, circling 'UKUSA' in his Moleskin notebook.

'Don't know if Echelon is still a code name they'd use, as it's pretty commonplace in the thriller genre now,' Beasley said, taking a sip on his 7-Eleven Big Gulp. 'You know, shows like *Alias*, *24*, *NCIS*, you hear Echelon mentioned there and in espionage novels and stuff all the time. Of course, most of the references to it could not be more wrong.'

'What's its purpose?' Fox asked.

'I'm not sure of its official mandate, but basically it's a program used by the UKUSA countries, mainly driven by the NSA, that hunts for data.'

'Their spying capabilities,' Fox said.

'Yeah. Punch into a specially programmed supercomputer – they call them Dictionaries – some keyword or phrase, like "nuclear bomb" or "hijack", and it will record every conversation, fax, email, whatever containing that word. Eventually, an analyst or linguist at NSA or another UKUSA country will go through the communication and see if it's a threat. I'm sure it's more refined than that but that's the gist of it.'

'How many keywords can the system track?'

'Theoretically, these days it's limitless,' Beasley said. 'Any word, phrase, whatever, the computers can handle it. The weak link in the chain is the human time it takes to establish if it's a credible threat. This leads to failures such as with 9/11, where the terrorists' calls were intercepted prior to the attacks but not translated and analysed until after the event.'

'That would come down to a shortage of manpower?'

'Fuck'n' A. The intelligence community have got themselves plenty on the payroll who can convert Russian. But all the Middle Eastern languages? Those linguists are not exactly the nationality of civil servant the intelligence agencies jump over themselves to recruit, if you know what I mean.'

Fox nodded and made more notes, crossing off his list of questions. 'How about the Advocacy Center?'

'Never heard of it,' Beasley replied, shaking his head.

'It's a DC-based outfit that disseminates NSA-collected industrial espionage of foreign companies and governments,' Fox explained, 'and passes it on to US businesses, to help them abroad.'

'Gotcha, I know they've been doing that sort of thing for a while, particularly since the end of the Cold War when globalisation filled the vacuum. Spending time chasing economic shit like that is why they were caught with their pants down on 9/11.'

'But to be fair, the whole world has gone that way with their communications intelligence?' Fox said. 'Everyone's now after the economic advantage.'

'True, but we were the ones that paid the ultimate price, and, given the capabilities we have, there's no excuse it panned out like it did.'

Fox felt for the former lawman. He could sense the raft of emotions headed by anger and frustration shared by so many of his countrymen, particularly those in his adopted city of New York where 2001 was still so raw.

Fox raised his fist and had it punched in a friendly little salute.

'Thanks for that, Benno,' Fox said.

'Go get 'em, Lach.'

20

FRANCE

Sianne Cassel looked out the floor-to-ceiling tinted windows of her coastal villa. The headland of Mogiou was buffeted by a white foam of crashing surf as the sun shone upon the south-eastern cliff face. The brilliant summer rays of light twinkled across the choppy Mediterranean and gleamed in Cassel's eyes. Hearing the last person entering and taking a seat, she turned around to face the board table.

'Thank you for being here,' Cassel said to the assembled foreign guests and handful of French military leaders. Their cover for the meeting was a regular briefing for the Identity, Tradition and Sovereignty political group of the European Parliament. Not that word would get out. These were allies. Leaders and potential leaders who she could depend on for immediate support. 'We are now taking the final steps in the operation.'

She smiled, and nodded to Danton.

He flicked the digital projector on, showing a map of the world.

'Within the next twenty-four hours we have teams infiltrating two American spy bases, in New Zealand and Greenland,' she said, the spots lighting up on the map. 'Both teams will be delivered by the French Navy –' a nod from the chief of the navy '– and executed by special-operations forces.'

'Why wait until now to place these hacking devices?' This came from an airforce general.

'To best avoid detection,' Cassel said. 'The longer our intercept devices are there, the more chance we run of being discovered. This way, they will be in place for less than forty-eight hours by the time they are activated.'

'Why this local connection?' the chief of the French Navy asked.

'We need these planted so that we can piggyback onto the American satellite feed,' Danton fielded the question. 'As these will be locally attached to the computers at the two stations, they run the risk of discovery, as Mademoiselle Cassel has explained. That is why the final steps are happening so close together.'

'And once you're connected, how long do you need the window to be open?'

'An hour at the most.' The chief of the navy looked impressed at this.

'That's enough time to get all the information you need? All the inside information on competing American businesses? The dirt on our political opponents?' the ex Prime Minister of Italy said. He was clearly desperate to resume power and avoid his pending legal wrangle.

'We now have a gathering of linked supercomputers set up to rival the Americans' NSA headquarters,' Danton said. 'We are well up to the task. Inside of an hour we can download all the stored information in NSA's databanks.'

'And if they detect these devices, before or after the data download?' the foreign minister of Sweden said, ready to assume power once he had the dirt he needed to overthrow the incumbent Prime Minister.

'We are targeting the two locations to safeguard against that – we only need the one uplink to succeed,' Danton said. 'And I'm sure they will discover the devices afterwards, but they will be untraceable and meaningless by then.'

'And, needless to say, it will be too late by then,' Cassel added. She smiled, pleased to see the assembly were now at ease.

'Where is our computer facility, at Domme?'

'No, we could not have increased our facilities there as it is watched by foreign satellites,' Cassel said. 'We have been procuring supercomputers through back channels for the past twelve months. The networked system has been set up at Fort Gaucher.'

There was surprise on the faces of the military men present.

'You should step up heavier security there,' the French chief of the navy said. 'Air cover at least.'

'No, we cannot arouse suspicion by overt actions,' Danton said. 'The fort cannot be observed from satellites or spy planes. It is well guarded by a company of commandos, and it's practically impenetrable because of its location.'

'If I had known you were running this from Gaucher, I would have allocated some resources there,' a French Army general said.

'We have kept it to ourselves until now for fear of your generosity, mon General,' Cassel said with a smile.

'You don't trust us?' the Italian asked.

'We trust you all, without question,' Cassel said. 'But as the generals have mentioned, should they feel compelled to provide more security it may compromise the mission by attracting suspicion. Secrecy is our best security.'

'But there is so much invested in this, our careers, our lives if it fails –'

'Failure, *mon ami*, is not an option,' Cassel said. 'My father worked his entire life towards setting up a Sixth Republic for France, for a unification of Europe into a single economic state. It was he who included you in on this plan, all those years ago. Indeed, it was he who steered many of you into the high-ranking positions you enjoy today. His untimely death will not be in vain.

'While we all share in the dream of a greater European state, and indeed a Sixth Republic for France,' Cassel said, motioning to her French military chiefs, 'so you too want similar goals for your own countries. We have all invested our lives towards this – it is the only dream I have ever known. And as we shall go into the annals of history as the parents of the greatest republic France has ever seen, we will all share in the glory when a unified Europe will be the leading superpower of the twenty-first century.'

'We are behind you with our lives, Madame President.' Nods all around.

'I know, as my life is in your hands.' Cassel flicked the projector to show a map of continental Europe. Another click and a line went around the shoreline, the only land borders are Russia and Turkey. 'With the rest of our allies, we have representatives in every nation either already in power or ready to assume power once we give them the information they can use to oust the current governments.'

'How immediate will the information be handed to us?' This came from the only German present, an ex-officer in the Stasi who now had his own political party – and a side job of selling NATO supplies to terrorists.

'Within days,' Danton said. 'Our own DGSE interceptions have quite a few dirt files that you will find useful too.'

'The line you see, gentlemen,' Cassel said, 'is what will occur over the next twelve to eighteen months. Russia is still to be left out, initially, until they prove their worth in terms of securing their borders and managing their own population. But their resource wealth will prove to be a necessity for us.'

'So we will need to militarise the eastern-border states?' the opposition leader from Poland asked.

'I can't see why,' Cassel said. 'Our power will be economic, and countries like Russia and Turkey will want to comply to join the fold. We will spend a great proportion of the new EU's budget on border security, though, to stem the flow of illegal immigrants from Africa and the Middle East.'

'I don't want Turkey in the EU,' the German said.

'It won't be, at least in our lifetime. They would be far too much of a drain on us.' Cassel clicked the monitor again and the projector showed the world map. She used a laser pointer as she spoke. 'Without these actions we are undertaking, the

USA will continue to be the dominant world power, with China and India emerging as rivals for that power around the middle of this century. Without our actions, terrorists and refugees will continue to flood Europe's shores, our shores, and slow us down. This has gone on for far too long already.'

'And what of China and India?' the Austrian Prime Minister asked. 'They are still emerging superpowers, China particularly.'

'Their rate of economic growth is slowing, and they will soon face their own political dangers,' Cassel said. 'Their power is reliant on a populace that functions as a cheap labour force. While the rich get richer in that nation, and the middle class expand, a billion people remain in or near poverty. That is a time-bomb that will occupy itself for the immediate term.'

'Regardless, I for one have no qualms about another fifty-year cold war, and I'm sure we will have many more meetings such as this to plan what to do,' Danton said, adding his voice to what he planned would be a commanding role in Europe's future military and intelligence leadership. 'But my gut says let China and India have Asia. A united Europe, a closed Europe, has almost everything she needs.'

There were smiles all around the table.

'But please, Madame Cassel, tell us, how will the data be accessed?' the current French defence minister said. 'How on earth are you hacking into the Americans' most secure intelligence apparatus? Surely we are close enough now for you to tell us?'

Cassel looked about the room.

'Indeed we are close enough,' Cassel said. She took her time, choosing her words carefully and speaking them deliberately. 'We learned of a vulnerability in the American security system some time ago, a vulnerability that will only be apparent for a short while longer. To access the Americans' information two things must occur: the planting of the hardwired key at a relay station, in order to pick up their coding information and to piggyback on their data transfer frequency.'

Cassel paused for effect, and the Italian could not contain himself:

'And the second part of the operation?'

'We must log into the mainframe at NSA using a specific one-time remote-access key,' she said. 'Because of the timeframe, this will be activated via a burst transmission from a submarine in the North Atlantic.'

'Why the Atlantic?' the navy admiral asked.

'Due to the timing constraints,' Danton said. 'We will pick up the DGSE agent with the access key from the United States' east coast, drop him via helicopter into the Atlantic – in international waters – and transmit the NSA key data from the submarine's burst transmitter. Relayed to our military satellite in Fort Gaucher, we then have access to download whatever we want.'

'Then,' Cassel smiled with all her teeth bared, 'we shall see the rightful place of Europe in the world order.'

21

NEW YORK CITY

'I really don't have time for this,' Fox said, lying back on the couch.

'And yet here you are,' Dr Bender said, writing down some notes. 'It's GSR policy, and while I don't care what you all may say about me when I'm not in the building, I'm here to make the workforce as stable and efficient as possible.'

'Stable, efficient,' Fox said, closing his eyes. 'I just need a holiday.'

'Your humour is your holiday, Lachlan. You use it to avoid thinking deeper about the problem at hand.' The psychiatrist made more notes. 'And we've discussed your running-away issues. It's a temporary fix, until something happens where the issues rise again. Like at Christmas Island last year.'

'I need a holiday from my mind,' Fox said, as if he hadn't heard what she had just said, 'from those "deepest, darkest terrors that linger in there".' Fox was quoting her, something from their last session about obtaining wisdom and knowledge from ordeals, but she didn't take the bait.

From the corner of his eye Fox caught her looking him over.

'You look like you've lost weight,' Dr Bender said, taking him in lying there in his rolled-up shirtsleeves and slim-fitting trousers. 'Have you been sick?'

'I'm trying out to be a model for Paul Smith,' Fox said, smiling at her. She didn't look impressed.

'I've been away, in Africa,' he relented. 'Didn't do much for the appetite. Not that the past twenty-four hours helped.'

'What did you see there?' she asked, scribbling away on her pad.

'In Africa?' Fox looked at her with raised eyebrows. 'Death.' He turned to look at the ceiling and closed his eyes.

'Still having the dreams?'

'Still having the dreams,' he replied.

'Have they changed at all?'

Fox thought about it for a while. 'They're worse since coming back.' He opened his eyes, looking up at the white ceiling. 'I only dream of dead people. And the dreams are always worse after I've seen people die.'

'Did you see people die in Africa?'

'I saw too many people dying, too many dead people,' he said. He closed his eyes again, thinking. 'I was somewhere else yesterday, another country, another continent.' He couldn't say anything that would require her to make a police report. 'More death. I saw someone die, killed quite brutally actually.'

The psychologist waited for Fox to go on, but he was finished. She'd learned that she could not push him further for details.

'Let's talk some more about the choices you have made,' Dr Bender said.

'I decided to eat fruit for –'

'Lachlan.'

He turned to look at her. 'The choices? I assume you mean the choices I've made over the past two years that resulted in me watching two people being killed in front of me.'

She nodded.

'We've talked about that,' he said, attempting to close the issue.

'That was months ago. Refresh my memory.'

Fox sighed. 'I was given the choice to save the soldier under my command, John Birmingham, or some hostages. That is, to walk away with him, alive, and leave behind a village full of captured East Timorese. Instead, I tried to save him with force, with the thought to saving the others after that, and I . . . I lost them.'

'Your decision wasn't the problem there, Lachlan, it was the outcome. At least in your mind, at the present.'

'I went against the odds. I took them on. I gambled with his life. I lost . . .'

'Generally one loses when one gambles,' she said. 'But again, Lachlan, surely you can see that the decision you made, the choice under extreme pressure, was worthy of that risk.'

'At the time, yeah, I thought that. He was a soldier under my command. I did what I was trained to do. The only saving grace, I later learned, is that some of the East Timorese escaped in the pandemonium.'

'You decided to be a frontline soldier, you could have stayed behind a desk,' she said. 'Surely you would have known the decisions you'd make out there, at the "pointy end" as you have called it before, would result in some choices that led directly to loss of life. Results that are not without heavy consequences, James Bond-like actions, are firmly placed in the realm of fiction.'

'Tell me about it . . .' Fox said. 'It's not like I trained to be an assassin. We were water-born recon troops, marine and shore-assault specialists, waterway clearers. Until I went under fire I thought it was a thousand times better than an office job. God, there was no way I could have gone back into military intelligence,' he said. 'I wasn't the right thinker.'

Dr Bender made more notes, tapping her pen on the pad when she finished.

'And the second incident?' she asked. 'I'm not letting you off. Tell me about this other scene that haunts you.'

Fox closed his eyes again. He could see her face, her eyes full of tears, pleading. The face of Ivanovich, the Chechen leader, his hand pushing a pistol hard against Alissa Truscott's head.

'Again, I was given a choice. I had the option to leave a scene, with the life of this young woman being threatened before me, in place of averting a catastrophic terrorist attack,' Fox said. 'Wallace's only daughter, no less. Not that that really makes it any different. But you know . . .'

Dr Bender waited a moment before prompting him further. Her voice was soft, caring.

'And the decision you made?'

'It came almost too quickly,' Fox said. 'I chose to let her die. Didn't even hesitate that time around.'

'And the result? Thousands lived in her place?'

'In her place?' Fox looked to her, anger there. He turned back to the ceiling, closing his eyes, pinching the bridge of his nose. 'The result, for me, was just as bad that time around. Seeing an innocent killed. Explaining that loss of life to a parent.'

'It was another example of your character coming out through choice in dilemma, Lachlan,' she said. 'The true Lachlan Fox shining through.'

'I guess there's a brighter side to anything if you're prepared to look hard enough,' Fox said, with a degree of cynicism that he immediately regretted. 'I'm sorry, I don't think I want to talk about this more today.'

'Okay, let's finish off with a different topic,' Dr Bender said, pausing as if thinking what to ask, but Fox knew she always had her questions well and truly planned. 'What do you think makes you happy?'

'Part of me wants to reply that I can't remember being happy,' Fox said. 'Seriously. But that's another issue you'll want to delve into for months on end.'

It took him a minute or two to think about it in the silence that the psychologist provided. 'I think I'm happy when I'm busy, like, really busy,' Fox offered into the silence.

'Or rather, your mind is more at ease when you are busy because your mind is busy,' she said. 'Busyness that is double-edged, as is evident when you have these dreams. And now, while you are very busy here at GSR, and you immerse yourself in your work, you have your downtime. Those times when you are alone, when it's just you and your actions that you are reflecting upon.'

'What, you're thinking I need a wife or something?' Fox said, trying to avoid the situation with humour. 'Think I'll start with a puppy.'

'A partner would probably help, or even a pet, but at the end of the day it's still you and your mind, alone, that you have to deal with.'

'I like my alone time,' Fox said, looking at her. 'Sometimes I really need to just be alone, surrounded by silence. Some space around me. Actually, that's something I really miss since leaving Christmas Island, those silent horizons that disappeared into the sky. Here all you see are buildings.'

She made more notes, tapping her pen at the end of the thought.

'What's happening with your drinking?' she asked. 'How many a day?'

Fox didn't respond.

'Lachlan?'

'I don't know, a few. Hardly drank a thing in Africa, though,' he said. 'I'm telling you, that place would make a fortune on health tourism.'

'Lachlan, you need to confront your demons. Own up to them, explore them. It's natural to have regrets, but you can't have them rule your life, pushing your thoughts and future choices into negative space. You can't keep avoiding the seriousness in what's driving you right now.'

'Sounds very Zen-like.'

'I'm not saying that you should be happy every second. Hell, if I knew how to condition my patients with that kind of therapy . . .' Dr Bender said. 'We just need to find some methods that work for you to deal with these thoughts. Not to distract you so much as to lead your mind in another direction at times. Have you been keeping the dream journal?'

'For a couple of weeks,' Fox said. 'It was always the same. Well, not exactly the same, but the same result. I was useless, couldn't move. I was watching myself making all the wrong choices, all the wrong moves, again and again.'

'We've been over this, Lachlan. There were no right choices. There were snap decisions that were made that saved lives. No one said it was easy being a hero. You choosing to go through that door is something you can't take back.'

'If only,' Lachlan Fox said.

22

NEW YORK CITY

The DGSE agent dressed as an electrical worker knocked on Fox's houseboat door. He knew Fox was at GSR but he had to be sure it was deserted. He picked the lock, sliding the glass door open.

'Hello?' he called out, walking through, holding a small pistol in the pocket of his overalls. 'Electricity man . . .'

He smiled to himself, dropped his toolbox on the table, and turned his attention to the alarm pad by the front door. He punched in the override code to the alarm system. Off-the-shelf devices were far too easy to disable, particularly American brands.

Opening his toolbox, he removed a plastic packet of listening devices, each smaller than a dime. He placed one in each room, the adhesive backing sticking under furniture. A few went hidden behind the lapels and collars of Fox's work-wear.

His job almost done, he reset the alarm, and went up to the top deck. He taped a signal-booster device to the far side of the rooftop exhaust stack, out of view except if you were looking from the direction of the water on the East River.

23

SOUTH PACIFIC OCEAN

Secher looked out of the canopy of the fighter jet as it banked sharply to an approach run.

De Gaulle, France's only aircraft carrier, and the only nuclear-powered surface vessel outside the US's arsenal, sat in the middle of the carrier battle group doing exercises. Four *Cassard*-type air-defence frigates rimmed the perimeter, while two *Rubis* attack subs trawled somewhere in the waters. Inside the protective ring, two landing ships and three replenishment ships steamed behind the carrier's wake. She was big, but from where Secher was seated she looked like a postage stamp.

He closed his eyes as they touched down on *De Gaulle* in the Dassault Rafale N fighter jet, the arresting hook pulling them to a violent halt on the short runway deck.

Secher climbed down from the cockpit and landed on the flight deck with wobbly legs. The ship captain greeted him.

'Major Secher, your team is in the ready room, this way,' the captain said. Secher trailed behind, amazed that even a ship of this bulk was moving so much with the sea.

'We are nine hundred nautical kilometres north of New Zealand,' the captain said as they walked. 'This is the biggest display of French naval power in the Pacific since Chirac's resumption of nuclear testing at Mururoa Atoll back in 1995.'

A sleek black Eurocopter Panther was being readied on the aft section of the deck. A dozen mechanics worked with tools, removing any unnecessary weight to get maximum fuel range in the flight. Long-range fuel tanks hung from stubby wings.

'Our ride?' Secher said, unzipping his flight suit as he walked.

'That's her,' the captain affirmed. 'She'll go up in about thirty minutes, as soon as it's dark. Not that you can see them, but we have a New Zealand frigate and an Australian sub to our south.'

'Will they be a problem?'

'*Non*, the frigate is not Aegis equipped,' the captain said with a smile.

'Aegis?' Secher asked.

'An American radar tracking system – it's good, believe me,' the captain said. 'I'm going to put everything we have into the air and conduct live-fire exercises to cover your flight path. They will have so many targets to track, your flight will go undetected.'

'Excellent.'

•

Three hours later the Panther slowed its full-speed wave-skimming flight and hovered. Secher and his two-man DGSE operations team were dropped into the ocean, wetsuits and flippers keeping them buoyant. Each man was tethered to their own assault bags with their own flotation devices.

Secher pushed the button on his backlit GPS locator strapped to his arm. They were on time, on location. He motioned with hand gestures to his team to hang tight, and the three of them came together and linked arms in the calm swell. The moonless night was green from within their night-vision world as they trod water for five minutes.

At a squeeze on his arm from a team-mate, Secher turned his head to see the submarine break the surface a hundred metres away. It was massive, the black prow foaming the sea as it levelled out before them.

The team swam the distance, and by the time they reached it they were greeted on the anechoic-tiled deck by a wetsuited sailor.

'Welcome aboard, my wet spy friends,' he shouted over the sound of the sub exchanging air. He pulled the three of them up with knotted rope. 'Next stop, sunny New Zealand.'

24

NEW YORK CITY

Fox sat at his office desk after the morning meeting, typing an email to the research department two floors below. His MacBook computer took up the only space on the desk that was not covered with files and articles on the groups and the slain men.

Gammaldi sat at the coffee table with his own laptop computer. Two trolleys of files delivered from the research department were parked next to him.

'How you getting on over there?' Fox asked after sending the email. 'Making a dint in it?'

'You serious?' Gammaldi said, not looking up from his computer. 'There's no way that we are going to be able to get through all these papers.'

'We've got to,' Fox replied, opening a fresh stack of folders in front of him. 'Welcome to the true world of investigative journalism. About as exciting as being an analyst at an intelligence agency. Or a detective. Or a PhD candidate.'

'Or a proctologist,' Gammaldi added.

Fox smiled at him.

'Somewhere buried in the papers in this office will be a piece of information that matters,' Fox said. 'Something that will make a connection. A break in the investigation.'

'Well, Sherlock, when I'm done compiling all attendees of the Bilderberg and LeCercle meetings of the past fifty-something years, I'll get right into this first trolley,' Gammaldi said, shaking the trolley with a bit of anger. 'By then I'll be ready to break into a case of bourbon.'

'Good man, Watson, that's the spirit,' Fox said, chewing on his pen.

'Hey, the attendee list of Bilderberg really is a who's who,' Gammaldi said. 'Thatcher, Blair, Kissinger, Rumsfeld, Wolfowitz, Rockefeller, Clinton . . .'

'That's great, Al. Just keep searching.'

'Says here that Clinton's real dad is Winthrop Rockefeller,' Gammaldi said.

'What crazy website are you on?'

Emily McDonald, Wallace's executive secretary, came into the room with a tray of coffee and breakfast. Her appearance, with bobbed hair and checked one-button suit with matching skirt, gave her a Jackie O look.

'You boys look like you could do with a feed,' she said, winking at Gammaldi. Easily passing for mid-thirties, Emily was closer to fifty and had been with GSR since its inception as a small club of investigative journalists.

'Thanks, Em, don't know if fatso here quite needs it,' Fox said, taking a croissant.

'Wha –?' Gammaldi said, already half through a bacon and egg roll. His short but stocky Italian frame had softened around the edges in the year they'd spent in New York.

'Just give me a call if you need anything else,' Emily said, closing the door behind her, leaving Fox and Gammaldi alone with their veritable mountain of paperwork.

'Dude, how about you start reading through those LeCercle files, huh?' Fox said, pointing to Gammaldi's trolley.

Gammaldi closed his computer with a bang and pulled a handful of files from the trolley, opening them onto the coffee table.

'Sianne Cassel, Deputy Leader – now Leader – of France's National Front Party and the Identity, Tradition and Sovereignty group in the EU, born . . .'

'Al, read them in your head, okay?' Fox interrupted, flipping through pages of his own.

'What is it we're looking for exactly?'

'You'll know when you see it. A pattern, some coincidence, something that doesn't add up. Something in someone's past or something they've done. There's gotta be a connection between members of the group that will point to a motive to kill these guys,' Fox said, holding up the seven files of the murdered attendees. 'These are the files on the attendees of the last LeCercle conference, who were also Bilderberg members.'

'Whaddya doin' with 'em?'

'Ha, listen to you, gone all New Yorker on me,' Fox said. 'What would your mama say?'

Gammaldi turned his attention back to his open file in protest of his much-missed mother being brought up in conversation.

'These folders are everything research could dig up on the group,' Fox said. 'Currently I've got them contacting the families, friends, colleagues, everyone possible, to see what the seven dead guys were about. Full profile, top to bottom.'

'I don't care much for her bottom,' Gammaldi said, holding up a picture of Cassel for Fox to see. She was dressed in bike shorts and singlet, riding along with the masses following the Tour de France.

'Please don't show me that kind of shit, I sleep badly enough as it is,' Fox said, and the pair of them went about laughing their way through hundreds of thick folders.

25

COOK STRAIT

The wetsuited Secher climbed into the airlock and his two-man team followed. They each wore thick rubber wetsuits, flippers, and re-breathers for the short journey to the surface, where they would inflate their zodiac deployed from one of the submarine's vertical launch tubes. Secher tightened the front straps on his waterproof backpack filled with various field gear.

'First time in New Zealand?' the junior member asked, the small talk to settle his own nerves on being on an assignment with two of the most decorated agents of DGSE. Both Secher and his long-time lieutenant on such missions laughed.

'Not quite. We were here in 1985, when we were about your age.' The young agent's eyes went wide in recognition of that earlier mission. It was infamous in DGSE after all, and put the French intelligence agency in the unwanted position of being in the eye of the world's media.

'Fuck'n' Greenpeace sons of bitches,' Secher said. He faced his lieutenant. 'You should have used twice the explosives.'

The hatch beneath them hissed closed, and the flooding light blinked.

'Let's go.' The three masked up as the water foamed in around their ankles.

26

NEW YORK CITY

'Now this is interesting,' Fox said, standing by the window in his office with an open file in his hand.

'Ex Italian Prime Minister desperately wants to resume power. He's under covert surveillance as the state brings corruption cases against him. They have him photographed meeting with Cassel senior three times in the past year. Since the latter's assassination, he's met with your girlfriend in the spandex, Sianne Cassel, twice – the last meeting in southern France, left for there as early as . . . yesterday.'

'Girlfriend, thanks, that's a nice touch,' Gammaldi said. He rummaged through the stack of files he'd already read. 'I've got three more people who have had recent known meetings with Joseph Cassel.'

Fox gazed at the file in his hand, not focusing on the information in front of him but the words of Gammaldi ringing in his ears. *Meetings with Joseph Cassel.*

He turned to his desk, flipping through the stack of forty or so targets that he'd read through already.

'Here,' Fox said, separating a file onto his chair. 'Here, here, here,' he went on until he had filtered seventeen files into a pile on the high-backed leather chair.

'All these are members of the LeCercle group – all foreign nationals to France – who have been aided to their positions of power through the financial clout of the National Front Party and the influence of LeCercle. And most are members of the European Parliament's Identity, Tradition and Sovereignty group.'

'NFP is the party Daddy Cassel co-founded,' Gammaldi said. He scanned his own notes. 'Co-founded with Pierre Lopin.'

Fox looked at his list. Some threads were coming together, a pattern emerging, but it still wasn't clear enough.

'Keep piling these separately, and any that have no clear reference we'll take down to the research department to dig a little deeper. I think we've found our connection, I think we've found the current president of LeCercle.'

'The person who may well have answers on the Bilderberg slayings,' Gammaldi added.

'At the very least an insider's insight, Scooby.'

•

Two hours later, Fox dialled McCorkell's number at the White House.

'The National Front Party in France is the biggest member of the EU's Identity, Tradition and Sovereignty political group.

Together they've been channelling funds through to sympathetic European political parties,' Fox said.

'That's old news,' McCorkell replied over the line. 'The whole concept of the EU's ITS group is to support their sympathisers and to have a disproportionate say on the European Parliament floor. Where they are getting their funds from, however, is information that our State Department would thank you for.'

'Who knows. Many of these guys are minted, though, heads of big businesses mixing with politicians, you know how it works,' Fox said, reading through several cross-checked files. 'And it's on a grand scale. Cassel senior had the European Parliament halt a long-running investigation into our UKUSA Treaty and Echelon program three years ago, as it was starting to dig too deeply into the capabilities and activities of France's own intercept program run by the DGSE.'

'France is the only other power with a global network to rival the UKUSA alliance,' McCorkell said. 'With all their foreign territories, it's easy for France to go it alone and still manage to eavesdrop on most of the world. You're sure it was Cassel that halted that investigation?'

'Absolutely. It's the "why" that I need to find out. Sure, he was patriotic as hell, I get that much. I need to know how this French system works,' Fox said. 'If I'm right and they're using their version as a right-wing fundraiser, I need to know what makes it tick, and who's on the inside of the DGSE who might be a sympathiser with these Euro hawks. It's treasonous if the government's offices are kicking back to political parties and foreign nationals, so there's got to be a pretty big motivation for this.'

'Ira Dunn will know their capabilities as well as anyone,' McCorkell said.

'He'll tell me what I want to know?' Fox asked.

'He's been in the game since before you were born, he'll know how their op works,' McCorkell replied. 'At any rate, he'll tell you what you need to know about them. Just don't expect him to be so forthcoming on his own agency's capabilities.'

'Well I leave for DC in an hour, hopefully I'll return with some answers,' Fox told him.

'Lachlan, Dunn can be a bit cagey at times, NSA to the bone, old-school patriot,' McCorkell said. 'I sold your meeting to him purely on the basis that you were there in St Petersburg and that I thought it would be a good idea for you to give him the run-down in person.'

'Perfect,' Fox replied. 'I'll start with that.'

'It's my rep, so don't go getting his nose out of joint with some line of questioning. And don't forget he's a deputy director. The National Security Agency is a tight ship, as secretive as things get around here.'

'Hey, who do you think I am, Diane Sawyer?'

'Ha,' McCorkell said. 'Anyway, Dunn's old-school American, ex-marine, so he'll be keen to hear what you have to say about the French connection.'

27

NEW ZEALAND

Secher sat at the prow of the black zodiac, using his night-vision goggles to guide them through the sandy fjord into the mouth of the Wairau River. Having been deployed into the Cook Strait between New Zealand's North and South Islands, the calm waters of the river were a welcome respite from the surf.

Constantly checking his GPS coordinates, it took them almost thirty minutes to reach the point where they pulled the craft up onto the overgrown eastern riverbank. In silence Secher left the two agents to cover the zodiac with foliage, while he walked up to a low fence. In the dark night's sky, he could make out the long expanse of a vineyard, and just beyond that the tops of the giant white radomes of Waihopai Station. In the wine-making Marlborough Region, they stuck out like dogs' balls.

Secher chuckled to himself at the thought.

His lieutenant came to his side, preceded by the long suppressor on his FAMAS assault rifle, ever scanning for threats. He pointed to the junior agent and motioned him to take point position.

'Stick between the vines,' Secher said, tightening the head strap on his night-vision goggles. 'You take the lead to the perimeter fence. Don't engage any contacts.'

28

NSA HQ
FORT MEADE, MARYLAND

'Well, thanks for taking the time to come here and let me know in person,' Dunn said, pouring another round of bourbon from the bottle he kept in his bottom drawer.

'I'm just sorry I wasn't through that door a minute earlier,' Fox said, taking the glass from the desk. It was surely against the rules, Fort Meade being military property and all, but the hour was well past the yardarm.

'World's full of lost minutes. Had my fair share,' Dunn said, raising his glass in Fox's direction. 'To John Cooper, yet another fallen comrade.'

'Cheers to that,' Fox replied. He leaned over the desk and chinked glasses, then he looked up at the wall behind Dunn.

'You started as a marine,' Fox said, motioning to the glass-encased Mameluke sword. Earned by all US marines on graduating officers' school at MCB Quantico, it complemented their full dress uniform in a tradition dating back to 1825.

'Six years, then naval intel, then got swallowed into NSA. Still rank as a colonel,' Dunn said, leaning back in his chair and sipping his bourbon. 'You were Australian Navy?'

'Yeah,' Fox said, standing up to inspect Dunn's photo wall. 'Started out in intelligence but stayed for only a couple of years before bugging out to a more hands-on role.'

'What put you off intel?' Dunn asked.

Fox thought about it for a moment. He looked over the photos of Dunn as a young officer, standing shoulder-to-shoulder with other fresh-faced servicemen in combat zones, on beaches and at the desks of big ships. Everywhere, their expressions were hopeful, confident, assured.

'I think it was the people more than anything else. No offence, Colonel,' Fox said.

Dunn waved it off.

'I was consistently amazed at the type of people that came through the door,' Fox said. 'They were recruiting the *right* thinkers, rather than free-thinkers. You know the type, they can't see outside the square, give the politicians and brass the answers that they want to hear rather than the answers that they should hear. The convenient truth instead of an inconvenient truth. Back home, it really came to a head in the budget boosts following the start of this War on Terror age. They let anyone in to boost the bums on seats. Not the way an intelligence outfit should be staffed, if anyone asked me.'

Fox had felt Dunn was measuring him, and the mood in the room shifted slightly as if the more experienced officer finally approved.

'Your recent articles on Extraordinary Rendition really rattled some cages around here,' Dunn said. He had a big Cheshire Cat grin that Fox couldn't figure out.

'Oh?' Fox was intrigued. He'd co-authored a few *Washington Post* pieces on the process the CIA used to move terrorist suspects across borders into countries that turned a blind eye to torture. Places where the US administration didn't have to worry about the laws of due process when concerned about the dubious grounds for holding and questioning captives. Transporting for torture. The same network of transport that Fox had used to bring Kate home from Eastern Europe.

'Not here in NSA,' Dunn said. 'Didn't bother us any. But you could smell the shit-storm in Washington, our inherently nervous ugly step-sisters over at Langley were having kittens.'

'Well, that transport network came in handy when I had to bug out of Russia in a hurry,' Fox said. 'Thankfully the CIA guys in the field didn't hold any grudges towards me.'

'Give 'em time,' Dunn replied. 'They're a bit slow in reading the news.'

'Yeah, well, not that their helping hand means I'll pull any punches on them in the future,' Fox said, raising his glass in a mock toast.

'Glad to hear it.'

'From the *Liberty*?' Fox asked, pointing to the framed US ensign hanging on the wall. He got up for a closer inspection.

'Yep,' Dunn said, draining his bourbon. 'Know what happened?'

'Only what's been printed,' Fox said. Two photos on the wall showed the USS *Liberty*, before and after she was put out of service by the Israelis. In the centre of the wall was a framed large US flag, torn and burned in places; a flag that Fox had read was hanging in the National Cryptologic Museum across the road. He'd researched the *Liberty* incident prior to the meeting. Always be prepared when heading into an interview with a subject. Where possible, know that person as well as they know themselves.

'Damn fine men lost that day,' Dunn said. 'You know what that's like.'

'I do.' Fox sat back down. A plaque from GCHQ, Britain's NSA equivalent, was on the wall behind Dunn, celebrating 'sixty years of partnership'. With the world's biggest intelligence agency at his fingertips, it stood to reason that Dunn had read a report on him prior to the meeting. 'Colonel, what motive could you see for Cooper's murder?'

'Plenty of motive. Cooper looked after Advocacy Center stuff, so there are hundreds of big foreign companies that would wish he and his outfit didn't exist.'

'I have spoken to some of the businesses that have profited from Advocacy Center dealings,' Fox said. 'They are unwilling to say what information was provided by that office.'

'Part of the deal, for operational security reasons,' Dunn said, clearly pissed off that Fox had contacted these companies. 'If the foreign companies wised up to what information we're gathering from them, they may try to shut that door. Besides, much of the info we are passing these American companies are details of bribes being offered by their foreign rivals to sweeten the so-called tendering process.'

'Sounds fair enough,' Fox said with double meaning. 'Does that information cost the US companies anything?'

Dunn locked Fox in a hard stare.

'The government gets reparations through the taxes involved,' he replied. 'Raises the GDP, gives US companies a foot in the door into new markets they otherwise might miss out on.'

What else are you lying about? Fox thought, and reminded himself that this man was in a profession of lies and deceit.

'I've put together a list that shows all members of the Bilderberg Group who attended the last LeCercle meeting have been assassinated,' Fox said.

'Yeah, I had a read of your hypothesis piece in the *Times* that this is a warring-groups thing,' Dunn replied. 'Assassinated or murdered? And only them? No other wealthy or high-profile people killed in the same time-period?' He leaned forward on his desk. 'I don't believe in coincidences, and what you're saying seems too blatant. One special-interest group taking out another. These guys are connected, sure, but they're glorified country clubs. What you are saying just doesn't scan.'

'That's what Cooper said,' Fox went on. 'Blatant as it may be, these guys were killed after that last LeCercle meeting.'

'So what's your read on that; they saw or heard something they shouldn't have?' Dunn asked.

'France's National Front Party has been funding key members of the LeCercle group to assume positions of power,' Fox said. 'Joseph Cassel was head of NFP and LeCercle. His murder kicked off this spate of killings across Europe.'

'I didn't mind Cassel, pretty spot-on for a French guy,' Dunn said. 'So you're thinking these other deaths could be reprisal for his assassination? By who?'

'That's one explanation I'm looking at,' Fox replied. 'His daughter, Sianne Cassel, has taken the reins of the party, and she is the current head of LeCercle. She has a motive if she thinks that her father was taken out by Bilderberg. She's rich, powerful, well connected.'

'So it may have nothing to do with the groups, other than her using them to gain her own foothold in Europe?' Dunn asked. 'Like her father, she's been in and out of the European Parliament over the years, a position only obtained through the international connections she would have made from LeCercle.'

'Perhaps. The sticking point that I keep coming back to is that these were all invited guests *to the same conference*,' Fox said. 'With no LeCercle members willing to talk to me about that meeting, I can only assume something was learned by these men that cost them their lives.'

'Lachlan, it's assumptions in this game that kill, take it from a wiser man than you,' Dunn said, leaning back and sipping his drink. 'Whatever the case, this stinks.'

'I for one am not gonna wait around for six months to read an obscure FBI report on Cooper's death.' Fox tried that hot button.

'Fuck'n' feds,' Dunn said, staring into his drink.

'Anything remarkable that Cooper had done lately?' Fox asked. He leaned forward in his chair. 'Advocacy Center made any extraordinary deals, big deals?'

'They consistently play a hand in signing big deals,' Dunn informed him. 'The Advocacy Center adds billions, tens of billions, to the economy every year through what they do. They're the point guys making a path for our exporters to follow. You name a big American company, find their overseas rivals, and bet your ass they have been pipped at the post by what the Center does.'

'Uncovering bribes, giving the good guys the inside info on rival bids . . .'

'Where's this going?' Dunn fixed a stare on Fox.

Fox went for it.

'Ever include me on any target lists?'

'What?' Dunn looked surprised but confidently steadfast. 'I could say that I don't comment on intelligence issues but this is just too much. We don't intercept COMINT of journalists in the US. I mean, if something like that were done, such as if we suspected you were communicating with a foreign person of interest, I'd know about it as it would be me who'd have to okay it before obtaining a FISA court warrant.'

'So neither me nor anyone at GSR has been listened in on?' Fox asked.

Dunn leaned forward, elbows on his desk. 'What have you got? I take it you're not asking me this for nothing.'

Fox took the printed transcripts from his satchel, and passed them over to Dunn.

'Okay, these look like ours,' Dunn said, surprised. 'Where'd you get them?'

'A source.'

'These originals?' He scanned through the pages, turning them with care.

'Yeah, I've got copies back in New York,' Fox said.

'Can you leave these with me? I'll run them through our archives to see if we pulled this down,' Dunn said. 'If these are ours, then I'll find out who authorised them and why; I get his ass and you get your story.'

'*If* they are yours?' Fox said.

'I said they look like ours,' Dunn replied. 'It's our format, our font, our classification codes . . . but I've been in this game long enough to know that you need to chase down every possibility before coming to a conclusion.'

'You think they could be fakes?' Fox asked.

'That never crossed your mind?'

'It did, until you just confirmed that they look exactly like what you produce,' Fox said, cottoning on to what Dunn had said earlier. 'You have those originals, I presume you're going to check them for prints and other evidence of an origin?'

'Right after I check with our intercept team to see if these are legit,' Dunn replied. 'These could be wiretaps set up to look like ours. If they are, they're damn good, which means it's someone who's seen our docs before. Whatever the case, you've got me concerned.'

Fox watched as Dunn slid the papers into an envelope and put them in his out-tray.

'That it?' Dunn asked, eyebrows raised.

'Colonel, I'm not letting this Cooper thing go,' Fox said. 'It's part of something big and I'm going to find out what. Has there been an increase in chatter between right-wing European groups and individuals?'

'As in LeCercle members?' Dunn asked with raised eyebrows, as if he knew the question was coming.

'Them or anyone related,' Fox replied.

'Can't say,' Dunn responded.

'Something's going down with them. Do you at least target them for interception?'

'Lachlan . . . One, I can't tell you what or who we target, and while I'm not surprised you've asked, I'm surprised you are persisting. Two, we're a little busy dealing with real national-security problems at the moment to worry about a European right-wing group bumping off rivals – if indeed that is what they're doing. Seriously, who or what organisation is doing this, right now, in the scheme of things, I couldn't give a fuck about it.'

'It doesn't warrant a closer look?' Fox persisted. 'Even now that they might have targeted one of your own?'

'Lachlan, we're not the world police, we're charged with securing America. That's it, it's that simple.'

Fox shook his head like he wasn't agreeing with what Dunn had said, his own mind driving thoughts that came out of his mouth as he clutched at possibilities.

'Why now?' Fox asked. 'What's significant about the timing?'

'Who knows.' Dunn could see Fox was not satisfied. 'Look, this intercept stuff,' he tapped the envelope, 'if it leads to an NSA mole, then I'll see what we know about these LeCercle guys, okay? As a courtesy to you for bringing this to my attention. Not that I'm offering to show you anything raw, but if something stinks then I'll point you in a direction.'

'Okay,' Fox said, getting up from his chair to leave, picking up his bag. 'What's your read of Europe right now?'

'What, politically? The last French election outcome stirred the pot over there. Cassel has a huge following, and she's well-connected through LeCercle. And France is hosting the next EU summit. Austria, Belgium, Spain and the Netherlands are headed for the polls soon, many more coming up next year. But this is your story, you tell me.'

Fox stared at the big old tattered US ensign on the wall behind Dunn's chair. A few seconds passed in silence.

'What if it's not just about Europe?'

'Well, if LeCercle is your only lead then it has to be Eurocentric. That's their mandate, they're driven to make Continental Europe the leader in every aspect.'

29

MARLBOROUGH, NEW ZEALAND

'No visible targets,' he said.

'Let's move,' Secher commanded, climbing the cyclone-wire fence and vaulting over the barbed wire at the top. The station was surrounded by rolling green lawns, and Secher was surprised to see a handful of sheep wandering around to keep the grass low. High-tech global surveillance installation surrounded by the world's lowest-tech lawnmowers.

The three agents moved silently towards the transmission building, where Secher paused and took the thermal imager from the backpack of the junior agent. Holding it close to the concrete-block building, he lifted his night-vision goggles and peered through the scope.

Two figures sat in the far room of the complex, at the opposite corner of the building. They showed up as flaring white heat among a sea of dark blue inanimate space.

Secher nodded to his lieutenant, who picked the lock on the double doors. Inside, Secher motioned for the junior to wait inside the doors to safeguard their exit.

Walking the dark corridor, Secher pulled one of the two USB transmitters from his breast pocket, as they moved along the tiled floor in their silent-soled combat boots.

Left, Secher motioned with his hand, and they came to another cyclone-wire fence that divided the room. Beyond the locked fence was their objective. This was not on the design specs that they had been provided with back at Fort Gaucher.

The pair traded a look, and Secher pointed to an alarm that linked the steel-framed gate. If it was opened, the lack of connection would set off the alarm. He motioned a cut across his throat and pointed to the wires. The lieutenant nodded, and pulled a small pack of electrical equipment from a thigh pouch and went about diverting the alarm trigger.

Secher took a few moments and looked around the dark room. If the fence was not on the plans, he wanted to know what else wasn't. Again, he lifted his night-vision goggles and looked through the scope of the thermal imager.

One target.

Secher scanned the vicinity where the other had been. Nothing.

He stepped around a wall, scanning further, in the other corner, the image clearer now through less concrete.

Still nothing.

Click. The gate opened behind him, and he backed through with his lieutenant, passing over the imager once inside.

One target, he held up a finger, circled it and pointed to the thermal scope. *Find the other.*

Secher took the six quick steps he knew he had to take, turned right behind the supercomputer, and bent down to the maintenance panel.

He was surprised to find the panel cover off, indeed nowhere to be seen. This would mean their USB stick would be visible if anyone bothered to bend down and look in the space.

He looked at the empty space for a moment, weighing up his options.

The lieutenant came to him and motioned, *Time to go. Fast.*

Secher plugged in the special DGSE-designed USB stick and they left the room and building in double-time.

30

NEW YORK CITY

Fox landed back in La Guardia late, thankfully missing the last true rush of commuter airline traffic for the day. The Delta flight had been a rough one, the weather this week really turning up the winds as the night rolled in.

Travelling only with his leather file satchel, he skipped the luggage carousel and headed for the exit. Almost there, a familiar face caught his eye and he headed for the nearest bathroom.

Standing at the urinal, he heard the door open and from the corner of his eye he could see the man he'd spotted a couple of times before leaving New York that afternoon. About his height, ten years older, a good thirty kilos heavier. And he'd seen a glimpse of a pistol on his hip.

Fox waited until the other man was standing at a urinal too, and then turned to head for the washbasin. He took his time washing his hands, leaving the faucet running as it became clear that the man was not going to turn around until he heard the water stop. Fox called his bluff.

'Long way from Quantico,' Fox said, baiting him. There was no one else in the room, so the man must know he was talking to him. Fox turned off the running water and went to the hand-dryer. The man still did not turn around, remaining silent.

'You always posted to the New York office?' Fox asked, and the man turned around to face him. He gave Fox a blank stare. 'On second thought, you look more than a little too out of shape, even for a fed. Suit's a bit too tatty as well.'

'I think you've got me confused,' he replied.

'That may be the case,' Fox said, finishing up with drying his hands, then taking his satchel from under his arm and holding it in his left hand. 'But you have been following me.'

'Fuck off or I'll make you eat that bag,' the man said. He put his head down and moved for the door.

'Okay, I'll follow you for a while,' Fox replied, stepping in line to follow him out, the man turning in a pace that belied his bulk to hit Fox with a right hook to the jaw.

Fox leaned out of range, swinging with his left hand as he did so, the satchel hitting his target flat on the face. A crunch came with the weight breaking the man's nose, the force making him lose his footing on the tiles, and he went crashing flat onto his back.

Fox knelt down to question him but was confronted with a gun coming up to his face, the man's finger moving inside the trigger guard of the old Colt .38 revolver. As Fox registered the weapon it settled his mind that this guy wasn't law enforcement. He chopped his two hands together in a blow that flicked the Colt from the man's hand and sent it rattling across the floor. Fox kicked the pistol under the washbasin counter and as he turned back the man grunted through his pain and sent a meaty fist up into Fox's stomach, the blow knocking the air out of his lungs.

While Fox was stepping back and heaving in some deep breaths, the man got to his feet, pulling a knife from his ankle as he did so.

Fox surged forward, deflecting the blade away with his forearm and crashing the man into a cubicle. He sent two quick punches into his bloody face as he went down, then dragged him around and put his head into the toilet, standing on his knife-wielding hand until he let go. Kicking the knife into the next cubicle, Fox pushed the man's gorilla-like neck down into the bowl and pressed his knee against it to add force. Holding the flush button down, he kept the man's head in the wet confines until he felt him starting to sputter for breath.

Fox pulled the man's head clear of the toilet bowl, forcing him to face upwards. He looked down into the man's eyes, and noticed his own arm was spewing blood to the floor from the knife encounter.

'Who are you?' Fox said, watching the man gain some composure. Five seconds later and no answer forthcoming, it was drink time again. The floor was slippery underfoot, a mixture of Fox's sticky, thick blood pooling with the blue chemical-laden toilet water.

Fox pulled the man back up, and turned his face away as he coughed sprays of toilet water everywhere.

'Who are you?' Fox asked, holding the man by the hair at the back of his head. 'Who are you working for?'

The door to the restrooms opened and Fox quickly closed the cubicle door behind his back. A hand pressed tight against the man's mouth, thumb and forefinger pinching his broken nose in an action that sent his eyes wide with pain. Fox held the man's head hard, forcing him to look up at Fox's eyes. Fox was giving his best 'dare me to' stare.

A couple of minutes passed until the restroom was theirs again, and Fox released his hand from the man's mouth.

'Crunch time,' Fox said. He shook the man's head by a handful of hair, and waited as he gasped in deep breaths of air. 'Talk, or this gets nasty.'

The man spat out a mouthful of blood and water.

'I'm a private investigator,' he said, face down towards the bloodied toilet bowl. 'In ten years, tailing you's the biggest paycheque I've ever seen.'

'Who's employing you?' Fox demanded. He let go of the PI, unlocked the cubicle door and walked out backwards.

'No name, no contact,' the PI replied, getting groggily to his feet. 'Just a voice over the phone.'

Fox grabbed some paper towels and held them to his arm. The cut looked half the length of his forearm and needed stitching. He started to feel light-headed at the sight of the crimson dripping from his fingers.

'How long?' Fox asked.

'Not yet twenty-four hours,' the man said, holding a handful of toilet paper to his nose.

'What are you meant to do? How do you report in?'

'I'm paid to follow you,' he said, pausing to retch out some blood and toilet water. 'Keep you in sight. I have no way of contacting the guy who contracted me. He said he'd contact me.'

'I'll double whatever he's offering you,' Fox said. 'Come into my office tomorrow, let us talk some more then.'

Fox winced as he fought some bile from rising in his throat from the ordeal. Dark blood was streaming down his arm and running off his elbow despite the pressure and elevation.

There was silence from the PI, as if he were weighing up the pros and cons of this new arrangement.

'Do it, and you can still stay on me, collect your other paycheque,' Fox said, taking a step forward, up close into the other guy's face. There was something to be said for overt force, the shock and awe of Fox's actions sinking in to gain the required outcome. Amazing what people will do to avoid conflict. 'Or walk the fuck away – but by God, if I see you again, I'll tear you apart with my bare hands.'

'Okay,' the man replied, reaching in to his pocket and taking out a business card. 'This is me. Come to my office tomorrow morning.'

After a moment of cleaning the blood off themselves as best they could, Fox and the PI left the restroom, heading their separate ways out into the hot New York night.

31

NEW YORK CITY

'Well, good evening there, sir,' Gammaldi said, opening the door dressed just in his grey cotton boxers, a decidedly out-of-place experience for the Brooklyn neighbourhood of Park Slope. Fox entered without a word, Gammaldi looking out the door into the deserted streetscape as if there was something sinister lurking out there.

'What's up?' Gammaldi said, watching as Fox peered out of a crack in Gammaldi's blinds at the street outside the brownstone building. Dim lights and music emanated from other brownstones in the street, the neighbourhood in their own little world outside the circus of Manhattan.

'There's – you drunk?' Fox asked, looking at his mate in his jocks, empty beer cans and pizza boxes covering the big square coffee table. He walked back over to the front door and flipped the intrusion lock across.

'Been watching the game,' Gammaldi said, offering Fox a beer from the bar fridge next to his armchair. A ninety-inch plasma screen took up most of the lounge-room wall.

'It's actually starting to make sense,' Gammaldi said, sitting back into his leather recliner and popping a fresh Bud.

'NFL making sense? Now I know you're drunk,' Fox responded, looking around the litter on the ground-floor living room. 'And you're drinking Budweiser, sweet Jesus, man. That stuff's filtered through horse kidneys.'

'Drink of kings,' Gammaldi replied, raising the can in high salute without taking his eyes off the screen.

'You got any weapons in this pigsty?' Fox asked. He walked towards the kitchen nursing his forearm.

'Yeah,' Gammaldi said, taking a big gulp of beer, 'I'm packing right here.' He hefted his groin with his free hand, and took another swig of beer, all while still keeping both eyes firmly planted on the TV.

'How about a first-aid kit?' Fox asked.

'There are some Band-Aids and stuff under the sink,' Gammaldi said.

Fox walked into the adjoining kitchen and rummaged through the cupboard. The few loose plasters were not going to help. He wrapped a clean tea towel around his forearm, covering the makeshift pressure bandage he'd made from a sleeve of his shirt.

'My cell phone's flat, I'm just gonna use your phone,' Fox said, taking a seat at the kitchen bench and dialling a number.

'Just not a sex line – I've seen *Punch Drunk Love*!' Gammaldi replied, accentuated with a hiccup. 'Hey, make some nachos while you're in there!'

Fox returned a couple of minutes later.

'Sefreid's coming over,' Fox said, brushing off a chair to sit on. 'I'm gonna crash here tonight to lay low for a bit.'

'Cool, party time,' Gammaldi said, accentuated, this time, with a burp. 'Hey, wanna do a *Scrubs* marathon? *Arrested Development*? Don't tell me you've still got your grudge against television programs since *The West Wing* ended. Kevin Smith movies?' Gammaldi held up the seven-hour *Evening with Kevin Smith* DVD box.

'Tempting, but I'm not really in the mood for dick and fart jokes,' Fox said, nursing his arm.

'Hey, the dude makes a decent living from it,' Gammaldi replied. 'I know you dig Smith, hell you even like Affleck in his films.'

'Smith would cast Affleck as the shark in *Jaws 5* if he could,' Fox said, playing along with the joke. He switched off the lamp near the front windows and peered out into the street again. 'You just go back to your game, mate. I'll hang here by the window.'

'Hey, what happened to your arm?' Gammaldi said, looking at Fox properly for the first time.

'Just a cut, Sefreid's bringing over a med pack,' Fox replied.

'You should have a drink.' Gammaldi pushed an unopened beer across the table with his foot.

'Yeah, thanks,' Fox said, leaving it there and resting in a leather armchair by the window. He settled in and tried not to move too much.

Twenty minutes later came a knock at the door.

Gammaldi had flaked out by the end of the game, snoring louder than the expert commentary over the highlight replays.

Fox looked through the peephole and opened up.

'Lach,' Sefreid said, walking in with a duffle bag.

'Thanks for coming, Rick,' Fox said, taking the bag.

'That's everything you wanted?' Sefreid said, walking over to the snoring Gammaldi.

'Yeah, thanks for popping by my place,' Fox said, rifling through the clothes Sefreid had picked up from his houseboat on the way, making sure his SOCOM pistol was tucked in there too.

'I've got Goldsmith and Pepper waiting in a car out the front, they'll take you two into GSR in the morning,' Sefreid said, poking Gammaldi in the cheek. He didn't even flinch. 'He drunk?'

'Yeah, a rare sight actually,' Fox said.

'I'll say,' Sefreid replied, picking up an empty Bud to inspect the label. 'He's been drinking lights too.'

'Come check this out, will you,' Fox said, taking the med pack from his bag into the kitchen.

'Ooh, I guess I'm gonna be the lucky one who gets to stitch that up,' Sefreid said, looking at Fox's arm oozing blood into the sink from the ten-centimetre-long cut.

'If you would, that'd be great. It's a neat and straight one,' Fox said, while he cleaned up the wound in the sink. Fox knew both of them had been on either end of a decent stitching job in the field before, and they knew the task as well as any general practitioner.

Fox gritted his teeth as Sefreid did the job in under a minute, finishing off with a coating of spray-on bandage that sealed the wound.

'No sign of anything at my place?' Fox asked.

'Nothing. I've actually outsourced the night watch to a couple of ex-secret service guys from a private security firm,' Sefreid said. 'When it's light tomorrow morning, we'll go in and do a full sweep, top to bottom.'

'Thanks,' Fox replied, putting on a clean shirt. 'I came here thinking it was best to get patched up and rested before having to confront someone as I walked in my front door.'

'Fair enough, and don't worry about the security,' Sefreid told him. 'You're not the first reporter at GSR we've had to put round-the-clock protection on and I'm sure you won't be the last.'

'Perhaps that should be our motto: *Pissing people off where no one else dares*,' Fox said.

'Journalists are good at that,' Sefreid replied. 'It's pissing off the *wrong* people that's the kicker. But I guess that's the fun part of the job.'

'Yeah, laugh a minute,' Fox replied, holding up his arm. 'I'm gaining plenty of mementos of those zany times.'

He walked Sefreid back to the front door.

'So this PI guy will come in tomorrow?' Sefreid asked. He walked out the door of the brownstone and waited on the tiled landing.

'How about you go to his office and pick him up,' Fox said, handing over the business card. 'He'll cooperate. Find out everything you can.'

'I'll go and get him first thing, before I sweep through your place,' Sefreid said, walking down the few entry stairs to the pavement, and calling out with a wave over his shoulder, 'Sleep easy!'

32

CLOUDY BAY,
NEW ZEALAND

At the entrance to the fjord, Secher sent his countrymen back to the sub and walked south-west along the beach towards the main road. Dressed in jeans and shirt, he had given all his equipment over to them, pocketing a second USB stick and putting on a small backpack.

Walking along the highway towards the township of Blenheim, he kicked stones as he went. He still fumed at the blunder in the layout of the station. In those extra seconds he could have hidden the device somehow. Danton had guaranteed the information was up-to-date *to the day*. Idiot. No wonder Danton had gone nowhere since his planning of the *Rainbow Warrior* attack. Incompetent fuck.

He picked up a rock and skipped it along the road, and found the way ahead becoming lighter as a truck rounded the corner behind him. He waved his arm in the air and the big eighteen-wheeler came to a slow halt.

'Thank you,' Secher said with an American accent. He climbed into the cab and held his backpack on his lap.

'Backpacking?' the truck driver asked. Secher nodded. 'Where you headed?'

'Christchurch,' Secher said. 'A few hours south, right?'

'Yep, and it's your lucky night,' the driver said, working up through the gears.

Perhaps it was. He watched the lush green farmland whoosh by in the big lights of the truck. With any luck the next part of the plan would go off without a hitch. It was his plan, after all.

Secher unzipped his bag, pulled out a couple of chocolate bars, and the driver took one with thanks. Secher pulled a photo from a side pocket in the bag, looking at it in the dim light of the cabin.

'Your girl?' the driver said with a grin.

'Yeah,' Secher replied, looking down at the smiling face of Kate Matthews. He had taken the picture the day he recruited her, on their second liaison. The sun and fun times of Monaco had worked a treat, as expected. 'She's my girl.'

33

NEW YORK CITY

'If you like her so much you should see her again,' Gammaldi said, breaking the silence. Fox and Gammaldi rode into GSR in the back of a Mercedes ML320D, the morning traffic a sea of fury around them. Pepper was in the passenger seat scanning for threats, with Goldsmith behind the wheel.

'Kate?' Fox queried, getting a nod from his friend. 'I'd like to, but she's already seeing someone.'

'Oh,' Gammaldi replied, turning his attention elsewhere.

'I could get used to this!' Gammaldi said to the guys in front, watching the hubbub of early-morning New York come to life.

'How do you normally get to work?' Goldsmith asked.

'Train,' Gammaldi said, still watching the traffic.

'You mean subway?' Goldsmith asked, stopping at the lights.

'Huh?' Gammaldi replied.

'The train, it's called a subway,' Goldsmith told him, taking off in the traffic again.

'All right,' Gammaldi said, twirling his finger around his temple for Fox's benefit.

Fox cracked a smile.

'Ah, that's what I haven't seen all day,' Gammaldi said to Fox.

'Why are you so chipper?' Fox asked, holding on to the hand grip as Goldsmith took a hard turn down into the undercover car park of the Seagram Building.

'Another day in sunny New York,' Gammaldi said. 'What's not to like? We're raking in the green here at GSR, and you can't say the work isn't interesting.'

'Good for you,' Fox replied, exiting the car. 'Thanks boys.'

The SUV peeled off and Gammaldi followed Fox to the elevator.

'Seriously,' Gammaldi said, 'aside from you fighting off guys in toilets, things are pretty sweet here in the mighty Apple, aren't they?'

'It's the Big Apple, and yeah, they're sweet,' Fox said, getting into the elevator. 'I was being sincere when I said *good for you*.'

'Yeah, well, are you being sincere to yourself?'

'Whaddya mean?' Fox said.

'Nice New York lingo, but it ain't gonna get you outta this.'

'Outta wha'?' Fox asked.

'Kate, Faith, your minimal fucked-up sleep,' Gammaldi said.

Fox looked to the floor. 'What, my shrink talk to you?'

'I know you, buddy,' Gammaldi said, looking Fox square in the eye.

Fox shrugged and presented his eye for the retinal scan. 'Access thirty-seven.' A vivid green light waved over his eye and the elevator rose.

'Okay, I tell you most things . . .' Fox said, 'but how'd you know about Faith?'

'Like all great investigative reporters,' Gammaldi replied in a theatrical voice that sounded like Russell Crowe's character in *Gladiator*, 'my sources will never be disclosed.'

34

MARLBOROUGH, NEW ZEALAND

One of the night-shift workers at Waihopai Station went to the computer room before heading home.

Punching in the alarm code, he opened the steel-framed wire door and walked around to the back of the main super-computer. He reached into his pocket and pulled out the four small screws and screwdriver. He felt around the top of the computer, a good seven feet high, and retrieved the access cover.

Sure, using a government supercomputer that was tasked with spying for his own interests on the side had its risks. But he always double-checked he left nothing behind, and always made sure he left things as they were expected to be.

So what if he used the massive supercomputer to download eighty gig of lesbian porn once a week onto his iPod. In minutes it did the job that would take his home computer, with its so-called 'high speed broadband' connection, a month to do.

And this computer even found the porn for him, or at least the little program he'd inserted did the job for him.

He knelt down, holding the panel up, and rested the screws on the floor, taking one. While lifting the panel into position, he saw it. An ordinary-looking USB thumb drive.

'What the . . . ?'

35

NEW YORK CITY

'Hey, Lach,' Sefreid said, coming into Fox's office, out of breath.

'What is it?' Fox asked, registering the look.

'That PI's dead,' Sefreid said. 'Murdered.'

'Fuck!' Fox exclaimed. He stared at Sefreid for a while then shook the surprise from his head. 'When?'

'Some time last night or early this morning.'

Fox pounded his fist on the table. 'Should have seen that coming.'

'Went to pick him up half an hour ago, the coroner and CSI were already on site,' Sefreid said. 'It might not be a hit connected with you, though. In the guy's line of work, it could have been a pissed-off spouse, some crook or stand-over man . . .'

'The timing is far too coincidental,' Fox said. 'His employer must have found out that I'd approached him, and is trying to clean things up. Reckon you can find out what the police know?'

'Yeah, I'll get Beasley to call some of his old bureau colleagues,' Sefreid said. 'As I bugged out a couple of feds showed up, so I thought it best to hightail it before they started asking me questions.'

Fox leaned forward in his chair, his elbow on the desk, resting his forehead on his hand, his jaw clenched tight.

'All right, thanks, mate,' Fox said.

Sefreid left the office and Fox yelled into emptiness, 'Fuck!'

36

NORTH CAROLINA

Located outside the sleepy town of Hertford is a slice of DoD property officially known as Harvey Point Defense Testing Activity. In the CIA they aptly called it 'The Point'. Its purpose: to train the National Clandestine Service personnel in paramilitary skills. It's where they teach the pointy end of spy-craft, as opposed to the more cerebral activities undertaken in the classes at 'The Farm' in Virginia.

CIA Director Robert Boxcell had dual purposes to his visit, and he'd just completed his officially scheduled tour of a new kill town. The live-fire range was set up to resemble an exterior and interior of real-world buildings, complete with doors and windows that could be blown in and out, to be replaced by the base carpenters within an hour of the exercise ending. Several agents and agents-in-training had demonstrated their small-arms skills before the director, in a rescue scenario of hostages and clearing rooms of life-sized cut-out terrorists.

Boxcell was met as he exited the operations observation room, where instructors could watch every inch of the training facilities to judge their charges. Members of the clandestine action group Task Force 121 had just finished up, and his contact, once a high-ranking member of the team, had been required to attend.

'You look like shit,' Boxcell said, shaking the man's hand. About thirty years old and six foot two in height, the agent was underweight and looked harrowed from lack of sleep and rest.

'Thank you, Director,' he said, taking a walk out towards the deserted rifle long-range. 'I had to get in character for a meeting in New York, a couple of nights ago. Keeping it up just in case I need to make another appearance.'

'How's it tracking?'

'Good. Lachlan Fox is onto it,' the agent said. 'Bought that I was ex-NSA, he just went down to Fort Meade to follow up on the intercepts I fed him. We planted some listening devices in his home, and have been scanning his computer in his office. He's investigating it, just like you want.'

'It's no good to me if he doesn't get the story out,' Boxcell said. 'What's your read? Should we create and leak some more transcripts to journos in DC?'

'Not yet,' the agent said, stopping at the sandbags facing the far-off targets. 'Let Fox run with it for a couple of days. We scouted for a long while to set this up with the right guy, he'll see it through.'

'I want it out before Friday,' Boxcell said. 'NSA are going to have a good news day on Friday, better to have the garbage out in the open before then.'

'Fridays are good garbage days for the press,' the agent said, referring to the Washington practice of letting the bad news out on Friday to be swallowed up in the weekend news cycle.

'That's right, so let's get it out before then, got it?' Boxcell replied, looking into the man's bloodshot eyes.

'All right, I'll give him a nudge.' The agent bit his lip, plans going on behind his tired demeanour.

'Okay, we done here?' Boxcell said, hands in pockets.

'Yeah, leave it with me,' the agent replied, resting his foot on a sandbag and squinting off at the furthest target almost a kilometre away. 'What about the bullshit that's been fed to the French outfit?'

'You just worry about your end of the op,' Boxcell said, turning back to face his bodyguard, spinning his finger in the air to announce his intention to head back to his helicopter. 'Then you've got your pick of postings, no more Stateside babysitting assignments.'

'I've been stuck here on this plan for so long, I was beginning to think you'd never offer me a passport,' the agent said with a smile.

37

NEW YORK CITY

Fox tapped his fingers on the desk. His head felt like it was going to explode. His arm throbbed. And he missed his morning exercise. He was on his fifth coffee and it wasn't even noon. His cell phone chimed and roused him from his thoughts.

'Yeah?'

'Lachlan, it's Julian,' the voice said. The background noise sounded like a million seagulls.

'Oh – hey, Julian, what's up?' Fox replied. He sat up straighter in his chair; there was only one reason why this guy would call him.

'You upstairs? You've got a visitor down here.'

'Oh thanks, be there in a sec,' Fox said.

He closed up his cell and walked out of his office and to the lift, pressed the button and waited, tapping his steel-capped RM Williams boots on the floor. His thin cotton trousers and polo shirt were not quite up to the dress code of where he was headed, but hey.

The lift pinged and the doors opened, Gammaldi emerging with two big brown paper bags. 'Where ya headed?' he asked while he stood in the open doors of the elevator.

'Just outside for a breather, back in five,' Fox replied, stepping around his mate.

'Ah, a little nip at your local, hey. Well, at any rate, hurry back. I got us a couple of pastrami Rubens from Katz's,' Gammaldi said, holding up the two paper bags. The weight and grease of big sandwiches within threatened to burst them.

•

Fox walked across the plaza that opened out onto Park Avenue. The day was another summer blast-furnace with high humidity, the westerly wind offering little respite as it blew through the built environment of Manhattan. By the time he had walked around the corner of the Seagram Building onto 52nd Street, he was beaded with sweat from the humidity, all the moisture that the heat sucked from the harbour being dissipated upon the city's inhabitants. He entered the Four Seasons Restaurant and took a seat at the front bar.

'Hey, Lachlan,' the barman said, passing over a short glass of Bombay Sapphire and tonic.

'Thanks, Julian,' Fox said, looking around at the few scattered faces in the big square bar. Certainly no one familiar in the mix.

'Dining Room Three,' Julian said, motioning with his head to the opposite corner of the restaurant. 'Two guys, came in about ten minutes ago. Asked me to contact you for a chat like they know you regularly meet people here.'

'But you've never seen them before?' Fox asked, leaning forward on the timber bar so they could converse quietly.

'Nope.'

Fox took his drink and left the bar, walking through the grill room and up the short staircase to the private dining rooms.

Two men were in the hardwood-panelled room, behind the table facing the door to the grill room. The one seated he knew from the photo in the LeCercle file: Pierre Lopin, a founding member of the group and long-time stalwart of the French political scene. He was old, well on the other side of eighty, and sat low in his wheelchair with an oxygen bottle on the floor beside him.

The other man was around forty, and stood close by Lopin's side. Upon Fox entering, he walked over and handed him a note and a Barneys shopping bag. Fox couldn't help but notice the massive automatic pistol under the guy's open suit jacket as he leaned towards him. The way he passed the note, Fox knew he was expected to read it straightaway.

There is a listening device on you. Go to the restroom, change all your clothes over, leave your old clothes in the wastepaper bin.

'Are you serious?' Fox asked, cocking his head to the side at the absurdity.

The man nodded, and Fox looked at the pair of them closely for a while. The old guy looked as though he was fading before Fox's eyes, so he left the room and did as instructed.

He was back in the room in two minutes, dressed in a new shirt and pants.

'Okay, what is going on?' he asked.

'Take a seat, Mr Fox,' the younger man said.

'I'll stand, thanks,' Fox responded. 'Who are you?'

'Akiva is my man,' Lopin said, his voice coming in raspy tones.

'And you're Pierre Lopin,' Fox said.

'Yes,' Lopin replied, adjusting his nasal tube which pushed air into his lungs.

'We are here to help you,' Akiva said. 'You had a listening device on your shirt.'

'From?'

'They are watching and listening to you,' Lopin said, leaning forward in his wheelchair. 'Hence the unusual circumstances of this meeting.'

The bodyguard leaned against the far wall of the room, giving Fox space with Lopin.

'Who are "they"? LeCercle?' Fox asked.

'No,' Lopin said. 'DGSE.'

Fox couldn't help but look startled.

'French intelligence? What would they want with me?' he asked, drinking the last of his gin.

'Akiva here made sure that the agent is tied up with the consular general until our meeting is over,' Lopin said. 'Nice to see an old man still has some friends.'

'How do you know that they are following me?'

'Akiva hears things,' Lopin said, waving to his bodyguard. 'They know you have been investigating the murders in Europe, that much is in the public domain. And as a result of your continued interest, and the actions that they are undertaking, we know they are following you.'

'Old news, Mr Lopin. In the past couple of days I've been followed, beaten, cut,' Fox said, holding up his bandaged arm for evidence. 'I feel I'm getting close but still can't see where this is headed.'

194 • JAMES PHELAN

'It's because you're getting close,' Lopin told him, taking his time to get more oxygen, 'that I think you may be able to stop them.'

'Stop them?' Fox asked. He decided to take a seat close to the old man so that he was not straining so much to speak. 'I'm writing up some newspaper pieces that can bring to light the truth behind the killings, but *stop* them?'

'That may be enough,' Lopin said. 'But you have to hurry.'

'What can you give me?' Fox said. 'Do you have proof that members of LeCercle sanctioned these murders?'

'Forget LeCercle. And forget these murders,' Lopin said. 'Sianne Cassel is the danger. And she has grand plans.'

'You're no longer part of the group?'

'LeCercle was designed to keep European identity after the Second World War. A national flavour, unique,' he said, taking some deep breaths. 'We were always conservative. But what they are now . . .' He nodded to Akiva, who came over behind Lopin to wheel him out.

'What are they now?'

'Still much the same, in that they are a collective of like-minded peoples. The Identity, Tradition and Sovereignty group is just an extension of that,' Lopin said. 'It's Cassel who's the issue. She's planning attacks. Get that message to someone you trust in the US administration – today.'

Lopin said that like he knew Fox had the ear of McCorkell.

'What's the rush? What are her plans?'

'A chain of events through Europe that will be kicked off with a Sixth Republic for France,' Lopin said. 'It's happening as we speak.'

'A Sixth Republic?' Fox asked. He looked at the faces of these two Frenchmen. They were cold, hard, honest. 'How?'

'A coup d'état,' Lopin said. 'And sooner than you may think possible.'

Fox's eyes went wide.

'It was brought up at that conference in Nice?' he asked. 'That's why the Bilderbergers have been killed? Because of a planned coup in France?'

The old man smiled at his bodyguard, looking back to Fox.

'No. I know these plans because I was the first person Sianne's father told them to, years ago.' Lopin adjusted his air supply. 'What was discussed in Nice, however, was her plans, building on her father's plans, first for France and then for the continent. For a new-look European Union.'

'What's so sinister about that? It's something discussed in many editorials, a new constitution and all that. Hell, the EU as it stands is practically a superpower to rival the US right now. Its GDP is already higher . . .'

'Mr Fox, listen to me carefully. I don't know every detail, as I dismissed Joseph every time he got drunk enough to bring this up with me in his fool-hearted attempt to get me to join the fold. But Sianne Cassel has let it be known that she will disseminate valuable information to all group members to use in their own countries. Information on their political rivals, information on their commercial competitors outside of Europe. She's strengthening the continent, putting the far right into power, and then shutting the gates.'

'Shutting the gates?'

'Putting walls up, however you want to look at it. Limited immigration. Isolationist economic terms. No more American dominance or European reliance on outside resources and services.' The old man shifted in his chair. 'I'm telling you this because you're already in this. You can do something with this information I've just told you. I've seen walls go up before. I've seen the looks in the eyes of madmen being led by a dictator before. I won't allow it again.' The old man lifted up his arm and rolled up his sleeve, showing a line of numbers tattooed into his forearm. 'This is forever my reminder.'

Fox looked into the old man's eyes. This man had seen it all, and once more was once too often.

'Never again will there be fascists ruling my country,' Lopin said, his determined eyes wet with tears. 'I love my country, and I love being free.'

'Why can't you move things through your own channels at home?' Fox asked. 'Alert French and European authorities to what's happening in their own backyard.'

'This has been a plan in the making for all of Joseph Cassel's life. The network is so entrenched throughout Europe, there are few left to trust,' Lopin said. 'Even the centrists and lefts are swayed when such discussion of European grandeur comes up. The recent Iraq and Afghanistan invasions have cemented these sentiments in Europe. The populace are ready to be led by what they see as a way to share their own destinies in the world as Europeans. I fear this is coming to a close so soon that there may be nothing to stop it.'

'But what? What's Cassel planning to use to do all this?' Fox waited for an answer as the old man wheeled closer to him.

'That most powerful of weapons, Mr Fox. Something that everyone wants to have control of. The true weapon of the twenty-first century,' Lopin said. '*Information.*'

38

FORT GAUCHER

The two technicians tapped commands into their chunky military his-and-her laptops. They shared a knowing look; there was nothing wrong with the connection at their end. They worked in a pair to be sure of such things. What had been a strong signal relayed by satellites from New Zealand for the past few hours had vanished.

'Mon general!' the first technician through the door said.

'Yes, what is it?' Danton asked, noticing the pair of them now in his office. 'One of you should be at your station at all times, this mission is —'

'The New Zealand connection has just gone offline,' the other technician said. 'It must have been discovered.'

Once they left the room, Danton stared at his reflection in the blank screen of his video-conference monitor.

Everything now rode on the second connection being made. The stakes had just been raised another notch.

A heat rushed up his neck as he stared at his desk, fists clenched, face flushed.

He picked up his military phone, hardwired into the fibre-optic military communications network that snaked throughout mainland France.

'Put me through to the COFUSCO,' Danton said, pronouncing it *Co-fu-sco*.

The Commandement des Fusiliers Marins et Commandos came onto the secure line.

'Commander,' Danton said, keeping with Bonaparte's tradition since the Battle of Trafalgar of not applying the salutation of '*mon*' before the navy officer's title. 'Your force accompanying our agents into Greenland. I want them to wait there on the station until the mission is complete. At all costs.'

'Up to forty-eight hours? That runs an enormous risk of being found out.'

'If they are found, it will be too late,' Danton said. 'They must ensure that the connection is made, and that it stays secure until activation. The entire mission rides on their shoulders. I will notify you as soon as the mission is completed from our end.'

There was a long pause at the other end of the line, as the commander of France's naval commando force considered this new dimension to the mission.

'All right, it must be done. Contact me the minute that they can evacuate from the site.'

'*Merci*, Commander,' Danton replied. He hung up the dedicated military-link phone and picked up his internal digital handset.

'Find me Christian Secher.'

39

NEW YORK CITY

'French intelligence agents – here in New York?' Faith asked.

'Yep,' Fox said. 'Working out of the French consulate on Fifth Avenue. Every nation in the world has its intelligence staff working in their consulates and embassies, and just because they're an ally doesn't mean they don't want to know what goes on inside our borders. At any rate, you can bet your arse they're who hired that PI.'

'And who got rid of the PI once they found out you made him,' Gammaldi said.

'This is where I'm at,' Fox answered, working with his laptop on a digital projector. 'Sianne Cassel is the current head of France's NFP, which in turn hands her the leadership of the European parliament's Identity, Tradition and Sovereignty group,' Fox said, the image showing shots of Sianne Cassel with the party signage behind her. 'Lopin confirmed her as the head of the last LeCercle meeting.'

'Seems her father was grooming her for leadership,' Wallace said. 'Bet that nepotism put some noses out of joint in both camps.'

'Absolutely. The NFP has a tumultuous history under the leadership of Cassel senior, especially since his co-founder Lopin was forced out in the eighties. Cassel was seen by many party faithful as being too far to the right to ever gain a significant position of power, such as the presidency of France. That outlook proved fairly true, until the 2002 presidential elections, where their strong standpoint on immigration, the death penalty and economic protectionism brought Joseph Cassel forward to be the contender to Chirac.'

Fox flicked to the next image, which showed a map of Europe. Headshots of known LeCercle members came up, lines formed like a spider's web that linked them to their respective countries. 'So far we have uncovered sixty-two members of LeCercle who have direct ties to either the NFP or ITS, either through funding their own political ambitions or using contacts within France's DGSE spy network to eavesdrop on opponents.'

'A bunch of rotten apples,' Wallace said at the named faces that appeared on the screen.

'Rotten as they come. Some are wanted for war crimes,' Gammaldi added.

'So what's the connection with the murders?' Faith asked.

'Lopin told me the motive for the murders was twofold,' Fox said. 'Cleaning out the attendees of the conference who ideologically could not be relied on, and as a reprisal for the murder of her father.'

'Do you think Cassel knows who ordered the murder?' Wallace asked.

'I don't think so,' Fox replied. 'Lopin said Joseph Cassel was killed to stop him from executing his plan. He told me that Sianne survived a hit on the day of her father's funeral, and that she's been out of Paris in hiding and under protection ever since.'

'Do they suspect you are onto them?' Wallace asked.

'Apparently,' Fox said. 'They may have identified me as being present at Cooper's death, linked it with what I've written about. Shows we've been investigating the right path, though.'

'You've sold me there,' Wallace said. 'This Pierre Lopin, what's the information he was talking about?'

'He didn't elaborate,' Fox said. 'The full scale of the plans was not detailed at that meeting in Nice, that was more a final feeler to see who was coming for the ride. Seems this information angle is something that Sianne Cassel brought to the table to enact her father's far-flung ambitions. They use information like that from their DGSE to finance their sympathisers, only on a grander scale.'

'Could be they have set up their own communications eavesdropping capabilities,' Gammaldi said.

'Easier just to tap into existing ones, pay off the right people,' Fox suggested. 'Anyway, the ITS must have been a catalyst in this too, galvanising the far right in a more legitimate political arena. Lopin suspects there are some that know what is planned who can be questioned, people who have been in recent communication with Sianne Cassel.'

'How does he propose those people are questioned?' Faith asked. 'You go over to Europe and grill them?'

'No, this gathering are far too cagey to let a journalist near them,' Fox said. 'Lopin suggested we get word to someone we trust in the administration here. Someone, he stressed, outside of the CIA.'

'Why's that, he thinks they are aiding elements of the group?' Wallace asked.

'Not the groups specifically but some of the nationals involved in this,' Fox admitted. 'The CIA started up and have continued to aid and finance right-wing groups and parties in Europe since the fifties.'

'Operation Gladio being a case in point,' Wallace said. 'I investigated some of their activities when I was working for the *Times.*'

'Absolutely. Operations like Gladio were set in motion to thwart the spread of communism after the Second World War. Now these networks are proving their value in the War on Terror, as they have in their employ members of the intelligence and security apparatus of most European countries,' Fox said. 'They're political and they're of a military and intelligence angle. Rendering foreign nationals across borders in their War on Terror, making strikes in sovereign territories. The scale of these quasi-security outfits is quite staggering, and the fact that they are working outside their home government's sight and control makes them indispensable assets.'

'A network that would be well-placed to make some moves in the EU when the time comes,' Wallace said. The room sat on that bit of info for a while.

'Okay, so we can get the word to McCorkell,' Wallace said. 'Then what?'

'Well, whoever they use to pick up one of these guys for questioning, I can safely say they won't be letting me sit in on the interview,' Fox said. 'So the story, from our point of view, goes cold.'

'McCorkell will keep us in the loop,' Faith said.

'Not if it's known in the administration that he was running the op and something got printed,' Wallace said. 'He'd be made as the leak, and after the Valerie Plame scandal the White House is a tight, unforgiving ship.'

'Which is fair enough,' Fox said. 'I don't think we have a choice. This goes to McCorkell ASAP, while we work other angles.'

Wallace nodded. 'I'm headed to DC tomorrow, I'll tell him in person,' he said.

'We couldn't go in with the GSR security team and pick up one of these guys?' Gammaldi asked. 'They've got the skills to do it.'

'There's only so far I'm prepared to go,' Wallace said. 'Kidnapping and interrogation for a story is far too far.'

The room was silent for a few seconds, and then Fox stood and collected his papers.

'I'll get back to it,' he said, Gammaldi following suit and packing up his briefing notes.

'As soon as Beasley is back I'll get him to sweep all the offices here for bugs, but I'd say the place is clean,' Fox said.

'There's been no unauthorised access into the GSR levels, I can vouch for that,' Faith responded.

'I'd hope not, this place is like a fortress,' Gammaldi put in.

'Your houseboat will be a different story, I'm sure, as that's where they would have planted them on your clothes and wherever else,' Faith said. 'I'd hate to think what they have already overheard.'

'Sefreid and Beasley are pulling my place apart right now,' Fox said, standing by the door to leave.

'You should stay in the sleeping quarters here until this blows over,' Wallace said. The lowest level that GSR leased, on level thirty-five, contained five rooms each set up like hotel suites.

'Thanks, I'll think about it. I'll wait to hear what the boys pick up,' Fox said. 'And it would be a good idea to have Beasley set up electronic interferers to all our computers so they can't read our screens.'

'Read our screens?' Wallace asked. 'You mean over the net?'

'No. You can read the data off someone's computer screen by the electronic resonance put out up to five hundred metres away,' Fox said. 'So anyone in the surrounding buildings here could be picking up what you are seeing, typing, whatever.'

'Geez, this electronic eavesdropping investigation is opening up a whole new world to me,' Wallace said.

'It's a big scary world out there,' Fox replied, leaving the room with Gammaldi in tow.

40

SYDNEY, AUSTRALIA

Secher had a three-hour wait for the connecting flight to Los Angeles. He sat in the QANTAS lounge and enjoyed lunch and a beer, reading the paper. He was in fresh clothes, having bought a few things at the New Zealand airport and changing before his last departure.

A man sat down next to him, the act out of place as the café was largely deserted. Out of the corner of his eye he could see the man had an untouched coffee in front of him, and was looking about himself a little too quickly.

'Mr Secher?'

Cold gaze in reply.

'I'm sorry, I think you have the wrong person,' Secher said.

'My mistake,' the agent said, biting his lip. He looked out the window to the busy tarmac. 'Sir, there was a problem in New Zealand. It's gone offline. And this.'

Secher said nothing, as the agent left a piece of paper on the table and walked away.

Secher read the note and finished his lunch, turning the page of the newspaper every now and then but his eyes registering nothing. His mind was racing.

Contact Apple, the note read. *Telephone the consulate in New York,* is how Secher transcribed that.

He picked up his new duffel bag, left the café and walked to a bank of payphones the furthest away from the food and beverage areas. A quiet, out-of-the-way area of the terminal.

He picked up a receiver, dialled a pager number in New York and hung up after the tone. A moment later the payphone rang.

'What is it?' Secher said.

'The man you have had me following,' the New York agent replied. 'Lachlan Fox. Investigative reporter with GSR, looking into Sianne Cassel. He made the private investigator I hired to watch him, tried to turn him.'

'Don't let anything get traced back to you,' Secher said.

'It's okay, it's all taken care of. But this Fox, he is a capable man,' the agent said. 'And there is something else . . .'

'Yes?'

'He and Kate Matthews . . . we have surveillance of them, together. It appears they are having a liaison.'

Secher's knuckles turned white on the handset.

'Major?'

'Keep on him,' Secher said through his clenched teeth. 'I'll take care of him myself when I get to New York.' He hung up, then dialled a number in France.

'Call me back on this line.'

Exactly a minute passed then the phone rang.

'Get me Danton,' he said as he picked up.

A moment's pause.

'Secher?'

'I got your message,' Secher said.

'Where are you?' Danton asked. 'I was told you were not in New Zealand to wait for confirmation of the connection.'

'Never mind where I am,' Secher said. 'That New Zealand connection was doomed to fail. And now you are hanging this whole operation on the second connection going ahead this afternoon?'

'Not ideal, I know, but –'

'First,' Secher cut in, 'you nearly fuck everything up with your goons cleaning out members of your precious club in a reprisal for Joseph Cassel's assassination. Now this failure. I told you the hardwired link was the weakness in the operation. In a way, I was wrong. You are the weakness.'

'Listen here –'

'No, you fucking listen to me!' Secher said in a staccato voice full of rage. 'I will make another connection, alone –'

'Where?'

'Never mind!' Secher snapped. 'I will make another connection, and if you want the key to it all it's going to cost you.'

'What?'

'Twenty million Euros, into my account, and I hand you the remote access key on time and as planned. If not, no Sixth Republic for France, no fucking super EU . . .'

'We will still have the second connection in Greenland,' Danton said.

'That's nothing without the key.' Secher was calmer now.

'And I wouldn't gamble everything on that connection going as planned.'

'What do you mean?'

'Greenland is a hostile environment,' Secher said. 'Twenty million Euros. I'll check my account when I'm in New York tomorrow. When the money is there, I'll tell you where to pick the new connection from and then deliver the key as planned.'

'The connection has to be in range of one of our satellites, we don't have time to re-task one.'

'I know, and there are nine possible locations where this can occur,' Secher said, his hand ready to hang up the phone. 'Unlike some, I know what I'm doing.'

Secher hung up. Two more calls. A surge of adrenalin. He was liking this, finally he was in complete control. Kate had long been in the palm of his hand. Now Fox had to go.

•

'Global Syndicate of Reporters, how may I direct your call?'

Secher put on an American accent: 'Tell Lachlan Fox that the answer to his investigation will be at the NSA station in Greenland, in approximately . . .' Secher checked his watch '. . . fourteen hours.'

'I'm sorry? Sir? Sir? Hello?'

He hung up.

•

Secher again picked up the handset, and made another call. The US Embassy in Australia, via the operator.

Again with a perfect accent: 'Tell your resident spook to warn the NSA that their Greenland station will be attacked by an armed force in fourteen hours.'

He hung up, and wiped down the phone with a handkerchief.

He walked to the nearby bathroom, headed straight into a cubicle and locked the door behind him, then placed a small toiletry bag on the seat, and set a mirror on the cistern. Within two minutes he had sprayed his hair black, combing it through. Undressed, he wiped instant fake tan over his face, neck, chest, arms and hands. He got changed and put on a pair of rimmed spectacles. Another application of tan, starting to deepen to a dark bronze. He could pass for Middle Eastern or Hispanic. He pulled out a new ID sewn into the lining of his jacket, a passport and a licence, both Brazilian. Then he put all the old stuff and toiletry bag in a plastic bag, and turned his carry-on bag inside out, changing it from blue to red. He left the bathroom, and dropped the plastic bag in the bin in the food court.

He walked up to the QANTAS ticketing counter.

'I'd like to purchase a flight to Puerto Rico,' Secher said.

'We don't fly direct but let me see what I can arrange,' the stewardess said, typing commands into the computer. 'It will be direct to LA, then an American Airlines flight to Puerto Rico. Will you need a return flight, sir?'

'One way.'

41

NEW YORK CITY

Fox was hit in the face as soon as he opened his office door. The culprit was a stench the like of which he had never encountered in his Japanese-inspired minimalist work space, and he squinted his way through it to find the offending package on his desk. The paper bag with the big soggy Ruben sandwich had melted its half-kilo of pastrami, Swiss cheese and sauerkraut onto his desk. The real kicker was the Thousand Island dressing, which had congealed among the papers and files left on the desktop.

'Gee, thanks Al,' Fox said. He walked around and scraped the offending thing into his trash basket.

His desk phone rang.

'Lachlan Fox,' he said, shutting the bin away in a cupboard.

'Lachlan, it's Emily. We had a caller leave a message for you with switch. I just emailed through a digital recording, it may make more sense to you.'

'Okay, thanks Em.' He hung up the phone and clicked his computer from its sleep.

Fox opened the mpeg file of the recorded message. He played it through, stunned the first time, and then played it back at the full volume of his speakers. He picked up the phone.

'Emily – I need you to page Wallace, Sefreid and Gammaldi and have them meet me in the briefing room straight away.'

•

'But you stay here,' Wallace said, bushy grey eyebrows raised in Fox's direction. 'The security team can be in a Gulfstream over Greenland within hours.'

Fox looked to Sefreid and Gammaldi. They both nodded.

'Three days ago the FBI were following you, then the PI, who turns up dead, then you're picked up by Lopin . . . it's very likely that it could be a trap,' Sefreid said. 'Here in New York, you can be protected.'

'Why so elaborate if it's a trap?' Fox asked. 'If someone wanted me dead, they'd do it here. Clearly they've had the opportunity, they've been in my house, for Christ's sake.' Beasley had shown him the packet full of listening devices he'd uncovered doing his electronic sweep. A real medley too, from home-grown spook stuff to the latest European equipment.

'Maybe they want you somewhere quiet where they can question you,' Wallace said. 'Whatever the case, this is too high a risk on something that can be avoided. Stay here and keep on the investigation from this end.'

'They may even want to frame you for something at the station. It's a top-secret military installation, you'd be breaking several Federal laws setting foot there,' Sefreid said. 'I'll take some of the team as a safeguard, and Gammaldi.'

'Me?'

'You're across what Fox is working on,' Sefreid said. 'And clearly you're not a target. I'll leave Pepper and Goldsmith behind on Fox's protective detail.'

'Great,' Fox said, pissed off at having to be babysat.

'If there's something there to find, we'll find it,' Sefreid said. 'If there's hostility, we'll be prepared.'

Fox looked at Gammaldi, feeling as though he'd neglected his best pal for a while now. He could see the stocky little guy had something to say.

'You right with this, Al?' Fox asked.

'I don't really like the cold.'

42

NSA HQ
FORT MEADE, MARYLAND

Dunn walked the executive corridor to the director's office, returning a salute from a visiting junior officer as he went. Base staff knew better. This entire base was a no-salute, no-cover area.

'He in?' Dunn asked, walking past the secretary to the closed door.

'He's expecting you, Colonel.'

Dunn knocked on the door and opened it.

'Ira, take a seat,' the director said.

'Thanks, but this is a quick one,' Dunn said, standing just inside the open door.

The director waved him on.

'I need two op teams for forty-eight hours to respond to a threat,' Dunn said.

'From base detachment?'

'SF unit out of Bragg,' Dunn replied, referring to the heavy-firepower taskforce they could call on, a joint resource between the intelligence agencies and DoD.

'All right. Anything I need to know?' the director asked.

'No.'

'Other resources?'

'Air Force transport, nothing major,' Dunn said, moving back through the door.

'Go.'

43

FORT BRAGG, NORTH CAROLINA

The two sixteen-man Delta teams were in the air within fifteen minutes of Dunn's order coming through. A pair of black Sikorsky H-92 Superhawks transported them to the nearby Pope Air Force Base, clicking over three hundred kilometres per hour on the short journey.

These guys were The Business. Modelled on the venerable British SAS, Delta was comprised of specialist men in what composed the best trained and equipped force in the US Army. They were protected by the latest bullet-proof material in the world, in what was the technology's first real deployment. Covered head to toe in Pinnacle Armour's SOV-5000 Dragon Skin bodysuits, the small linked scales resembling the skin of the mythical beast. Pitted against small arms, they were all but invincible – even the Secret Service was yet to receive this gear.

The soldiers would put on their snowcams on the next flight, where they would ready themselves to deploy via high-altitude jump to their objective. Many punched each other's fists and hooted in eagerness to be going out on what had been described to them as a live run, weapons hot.

44

PUERTO RICO

Secher easily passed for Hispanic in his disguise. With his deep tan, the lean Frenchman wore loose cotton clothing with a worn straw hat pulled down over his head, and old leather sandals completed the picture.

On the outskirts of San Juan, away from the beaches with their five-star hotels and casinos, amid the run-down neighbourhood and dirty streets, he stood with the throng of people waiting for lifts out of the city. Most opted for the overcrowded buses but he wanted something with the least human contact as possible.

He rode in the back of a truck filled with pigs, up through the hills, the forests either side of him. He held a small GPS monitor, checking the coordinates every few minutes. After two hours of bumping along the road in the beat-up truck, he tapped on the window of the cab and the driver stopped.

Secher passed him another ten-dollar note and stood on the side of the road as the driver disappeared around the next bend. Instead of the hunched-over figure that the driver had seen, the man by the road was now upright, purposeful.

Checking off the coordinates again, Secher put the GPS unit in his backpack and switched over his sandals for hiking boots. He took off, running into the jungle up the thickly overgrown mountain.

45

SOMEWHERE OVER THE NORTH ATLANTIC

The Gulfstream X flew at maximum speed, the sleek intercontinental corporate jet making the trip direct. In the cabin, Sefreid's GSR security team opened packs of snow camouflage and unlocked cases of weapons and ammunition. Gammaldi got to choose an outfit from a pile of colourful civilian snow gear.

'You think I'll stand out much in this?' Gammaldi said, trying on a Ferrari-red snowsuit.

'At least I won't mistake you for a target,' Emma Gibbs said, laying out her snowcams to put over her full-body thermal undersuit. Her shoulder length chestnut hair poked through the hole at the back of her ever-present Yankees cap. The only female member of the GSR security detail easily earned the most respect, simply because she could shoot a target through the eye at five hundred metres.

'Used one of these?' Sefreid asked, holding a Falcon parachute up to Gammaldi.

'No, but if Lachlan can do it, it must be pretty foolproof,' Gammaldi said, taking the heavy pack. More than a parachute, the Falcon had its own GPS-guided electric motor that would drop the passenger within a metre of the pre-programmed target area.

'Once on the deck, we'll cover you as you approach,' Sefreid said.

'Or . . .' Gammaldi nodded. 'I can help provide cover, and a big ex-Green Beret like yourself can go knock on the door.'

The team laughed at his antics.

'Seriously,' Gammaldi said. 'How about we all hang tight for a while and watch what's going on?'

'Yeah, we'll do that too,' Sefreid said. 'But the caller into GSR said the answer to Fox's investigation lay at the station, so at some stage we are going to have to go in there and see what's up. And you know what Fox is working on better than anyone else.'

'That's what I'm afraid of,' Gammaldi said. 'Lachlan has probably been strangled to death back in NYC and now I – the last bastion of hope on this investigation for GSR – for the world! – am going into the lion's den.'

'Look, it's a remote listening post in Greenland,' Beasley said. 'Probably totally automated.'

'Hey, you know a bit about communications stuff, how about you come trick or treatin' with me?' Gammaldi was in Beasley's face as he said this, still with humour but his eyes were almost begging the man in front of him.

'Ben, that might be a good idea,' Sefreid said.

'No problemo,' Beasley replied, dumping his pack of snow-cams and picking up a bright yellow parka. He gave a longing look at the .50 calibre rifle he wouldn't get to use. 'Didn't bring my PSP to play with on this mission anyway.'

'Boys, rest easy. I'll be covering your back,' Gibbs said, assembling her Accuracy International AW sniper rifle with its custom-extended ten-round mags. 'I've yet to use Johnny in action. Ten per cent more accurate than my old boy.'

'You named your rifle Johnny?' Geiger asked, the ex-recon marine in the security team genuinely impressed. They all remembered John Ridge well, a soldier who had died fighting shoulder-to-shoulder with them in northern Iran last year. While the team were much like any other private security contractor force, in the seven years they had been recruited to protect GSR personnel, Ridge was the only member to have been killed.

'Yeah.'

'Cool.' Nods all round. That was respect, the pride weapon among the team, the protector in many ways, named for a fallen comrade.

46

THE WHITE HOUSE

Wallace sat in McCorkell's office in the White House, a modestly sized wood-panelled room in the north-west corner of the first floor of the West Wing. Timber Venetian blinds let the bright mid-morning light slice through the room, adding to the relaxing mood that a scented bowl of maple-wood chips created.

'Hi, Tas, sorry to keep you waiting,' McCorkell said, closing the door behind his guest as he entered.

'You know, in all your time here I think this is the first time I've been in your office,' Wallace said, looking around the sparsely furnished wood-panelled walls. 'A cosy little sanctuary in the eye of the storm.'

'My office isn't much to look at, I'm afraid,' McCorkell replied. 'The West Wing is fairly run-of-the-mill compared to the rest of the House. Hell, I'm lucky my cubby hole has windows. The fact it has three makes it prime real estate on this floor – the VP's office next door only has two!'

'Fighting over window numbers, now I know you've been in Washington for too long. Ah, nice mug,' Wallace said, referring to McCorkell's chipped and tea-stained Oxford University mug. They'd met there in the seventies as MA students.

'Yeah, it's my lucky one,' McCorkell said. 'If the President wasn't tied up in the Cabinet Room all day I'd take you into the Oval to say hello.'

'Another time,' Wallace said. 'You guys still crazy busy?'

'It's busy days, Tas, busiest any of us have ever seen,' McCorkell said. 'There were only a few times in the Cold War when things were this frantic on a national-security front. My staff has doubled since the first time I was in this position ten years ago. And still we're struggling just to keep up.'

'So much for a peaceful outlook for the twenty-first century,' Wallace said, taking a cup of tea from a White House catering staffer. 'Thanks.'

'My money's on the twenty-second,' McCorkell said, taking his mug once it had been poured. The caterer left and closed the door behind her.

'Not that you're a betting man,' Wallace said with a smile.

'No, sir. How's Fox getting on with his investigation of the murders – joined any dots yet?' McCorkell asked.

'It's why I'm here,' Wallace said. 'He's got something that you may have to act on, but keep it close.'

'Oh? About time this friendship was a two-way street of valuable information,' McCorkell said in humour, but Wallace was all business this morning. 'Of course, I know my releases to you are used wisely. What's up?'

Wallace put his tea on the desk and leaned forward, his elbows on his knees.

'The Euro Parliament group, Identity, Tradition and Sovereignty . . .' Wallace began.

'Yeah . . .'

'What do you know about them and Sianne Cassel?'

•

Half an hour later, McCorkell had the Chairman of the Joint Chiefs of Staff in his office.

'Thanks for coming in,' McCorkell said, closing the door and sitting back down behind his desk.

'I was already on the Hill,' Admiral Vanzet said, putting his hat on the spare chair and leaning against a windowframe. 'My back's killing me at the moment, I'll stand if it's all the same.'

'Don, this is about something that could be getting huge,' McCorkell said, leaning over and handing Vanzet the list of names provided by Wallace. He decided to keep the NSA Greenland tip-off to himself until he had more to go on.

'Names of some French military, political and intelligence officials who are part of a planned coup in France,' McCorkell said as Vanzet read. 'I want you to keep this on the quiet for the moment, keep it in the family.'

'I read you. *Uniformed eyes only* should be a new classification code,' Vanzet said. 'Damn, some of these names *are* popular with folk in this town.'

'Precisely,' McCorkell said. 'Listen, you got anybody who can do a pick-up and shake-down of one of these people?'

'When?' Vanzet asked.

'Yesterday.'

'That soon . . .'

'This is going down now.'

'I don't know, Bill . . . a coup in France? Seems pretty outlandish,' Vanzet said. 'Surely the Agency would have had a whiff of this before now?'

'They might have, Don, that's my point,' McCorkell said. He watched as the JCS Chairman weighed up his options.

'Okay,' Vanzet said. 'I can see you're really serious about me keeping this close. It's just with something on this scale, we haven't heard a whiff of this from any source, and the amount of people in on it . . . What's their objective, why the coup?'

'A Sixth Republic in France, followed by a redesigned EU,' McCorkell said. 'Why? For the power it gives the newbies on the block. An opportunity for them to make the history books. Money, greed. Why do these things ever happen?'

'I get it,' Vanzet said. 'How tight is your source?'

'Hasn't led me astray before,' McCorkell said, leaning back in his chair.

'What's the source's role?'

'Investigative reporter,' McCorkell said. 'US based. I trust him enough to see this as a problem worth spending some time on.'

Vanzet didn't reply, he didn't need to. He knew as well as McCorkell that the media often had access where spies couldn't reach. That's why the CIA, like so many intelligence agencies over the world, included journalists and NGO staff on their payroll. For those being paid, it would often mean some information coming their way once in a while; or, better still, access to areas and information otherwise unobtainable.

'We watch this guy in Germany,' Vanzet said, tapping a name on the list. 'Defense Intelligence knows he's acting as a middleman in buying NATO weapons and stocks from our base in Wiesbaden and selling them to the highest Middle East bidders – usually Iran. We can take him at any time and shake him down, but it will blow their sting to track and capture his buyers.'

'Take him. We need to confirm on this before I make this list a priority for the President's attention,' McCorkell said.

'I'll have the SSB unit on him to pick him up ASAP,' Vanzet said, referring to the Strategic Support Branch set up by the previous Defense Secretary, Donald Rumsfeld, as his own little CIA.

'Take him and shake him. If he cooperates, we can always offer him a deal,' McCorkell said. 'He can go back to his normal criminal life if he cooperates with us, picking up his buyers as we see fit.'

'Sounds workable.'

'Good, let me know as soon as you get some answers,' McCorkell said.

'What are you doing with these names?' Vanzet asked. 'Hell, there's a third of France's military leadership on this list. If this pans out, it could get messy.'

'Has there been any out-of-the-ordinary French military activity?' McCorkell asked.

'Aside from their exercises in the South Pacific, nothing,' he said.

'Well, I'll work these names some more from my end,' McCorkell said. 'If you can get things quietly moving downstairs, I'll be down when I can. Step up the surveillance of all French military assets, task with everything you've got spare in the Euro theatre and beyond. If it has armour, or weapons, or flies, whatever. We gotta get a head count of their main inventory.'

47

HIGH ABOVE THE NORTH ATLANTIC

'Okay, team,' Sefreid said as he tapped a map of the area. 'Gammaldi and Beasley hump it to the station. Gibbs and myself take position six hundred metres to the nor-west.'

'Done,' Gibbs said.

'Yep,' Beasley added.

'Can't wait,' Gammaldi put in, pulling on a red woollen hat.

'Geiger, you hang on the plane and touch down at Paamiut West airstrip, located about sixty klicks to the north. Nothing there but a refuelling depot, but we had a snow Hummer dropped there for us yesterday by a tour-hire company. There's only one road into the NSA station, I want you to drive straight in, holding five minutes out ready for evac.'

'Got it,' Geiger said, assembling his M4 with underslung M203 grenade launcher.

'We all clear?' Sefreid asked.

'Crystal,' replied Gibbs on behalf of the team.

'What the hell is that?' Gammaldi asked, taking a step back as Beasley hefted a rifle the size of a cannon from a case that measured twice as long as Gibbs' sniper rifle.

'Call me an anti-material boy,' Beasley said, holding up a .50 calibre depleted-uranium round. 'With my thermal scope, if anyone needs a target taken out from behind a concrete wall at two kilometres away, just shout. Not that I'll get to use it this time around.'

'Holla,' Gammaldi said, impressed by a rifle being assembled that wouldn't look out of place on the deck of a battleship.

'Two k's?' Gibbs asked. She was one of the best snipers in the world, and her deadly range topped out at around eight hundred metres.

'Believe it,' Sefreid said. 'A Canadian sniper I served alongside with in 'Stan used one of these to take out a Taliban sniper at about two and a half klicks out. Target practically disintegrated.' Sefreid did hand motions to accentuate the point of impact and disintegration.

'Remember,' Gammaldi said, a meaty hand slapping down on the shoulder of Gibbs. 'I'm the short guy dressed like Schumacher.'

48

NEW YORK CITY

Fox sat with Doug Pepper at Beasley's workstation in the GSR security office. Sefreid had come on the high-frequency radio network right on time.

'We're deploying in half an hour,' Sefreid said over the radio.

'Roger that, good luck,' Fox replied. 'TW went down to Washington earlier today to give them a heads-up, so don't be surprised if some good guys make an appearance.'

'Copy that, we'll play it cool, out.'

Fox signed off too and switched the radio to standby.

'Doug, I'm just gonna pop down to the Four Seasons for a couple of quick ones,' he said, walking to the door.

'I'm on your six.'

'I'm just going downstairs, I'll be fine,' he insisted, getting in the elevator. 'You go do whatever it is you do when you're not babysitting journos.' The doors closed and Fox was pleased to see the annoyed face of Pepper staying behind.

The Four Seasons restaurant was packed with early-evening livery, people having pre-show dinners and drinks. Fox managed to commandeer the far corner of the bar and ordered a beer.

'Hey there,' a woman next to him said. 'Haven't we met before?'

'Is that line seriously still being used?' Fox asked with a smile.

A tap on his shoulder turned his attention away.

Fox took them in within a second. Two guys, mid-thirties, clean-cut and nondescript suits. Open jackets, a sure sign there was a gun within easy access if necessary. One of them was familiar, and had a small plaster bandage on his forehead. Feds.

'Lachlan Fox,' the first guy said, his accent containing the plummy Boston tones of JFK. 'We'd like a word.'

'Sure. Drink?' Fox asked, leaning his back up against the edge of the timber bar when the guys didn't respond.

'Special Agent Andrew Hutchinson, FBI.' Hutchinson flashed his ID. 'You've met Capel.'

'Yeah, sorry, mate,' Fox said, offering a hand to the other agent, which was refused. Capel had a face that would not have looked out of place in the bar scene in *Star Wars*. A face Fox would not forget from three nights ago on the ferry home. *Was that only three nights ago?*

'I've got a problem, Lachlan,' Hutchinson said. 'Three nights ago you turned up at a meeting with someone we're interested in.'

'That so?' Fox responded. 'What's the problem?'

'Well, the problem is, now we have a dead body,' Hutchinson said. 'A PI turned up dead this morning in Queens. His current surveillance case was you.'

'Okay,' Fox said, leaning back on the handrail to signal he wasn't going anywhere. He wanted to say *'That a fact?'* in an impersonation of Bogey's Rick character from *Casablanca* but thought better of it.

'Look, Lachlan, let's start with your meeting the other night,' Hutchinson said. His eyes were blank, nothing to be read there. It's like they were doing all the reading, taking in every move and mannerism of Fox.

'What meeting?' Fox tried.

'With a CIA agent,' Capel said.

Fox looked at the agents, then over at the woman who had long ago turned her attention back to her single friends.

'You look surprised, Lachlan,' Hutchinson said.

'I'm a journalist,' Fox retorted, having a long sip of his beer, taking a moment to get a grip on the situation. 'I don't talk about my sources.'

'Last I checked y'all don't have permanent residency here,' Capel said, leaning in close. An Italian immigrant raised in Texas. By the look of him probably a hint of Kazakhstani in there somewhere too. 'This isn't fuck'n' Deep Throat we're talk'n' about here. We can do this a number of ways . . .'

Fox fought off a smile and stared at the guy, his eyes willing him to make a move so that he could defend himself. Hutchinson noticed the look, and Fox could sense that both these guys had done many hard yards on the beat.

49

THE WHITE HOUSE

'How about the NSA Greenland station thing – do you think there is any cred in that?' Wallace asked over the phone.

'I spoke to the NSA director, he's had no warning come through,' McCorkell said. 'I've got Vanzet down in the Sit Room scouring the North Atlantic Sea and airspace for a possible threat, and the Danish military base is on ready alert if we need them.'

'What personnel have the NSA got there?'

'Two computer technicians with a shotgun for polar bears, hunkered down in the middle of a four-month tour in a collection of snow-covered satellite radomes,' McCorkell said.

'Is there anything there worth getting?' Wallace asked. 'Sensitive info?'

'Nothing that's accessible,' McCorkell said. 'It's all encrypted data that transfers back through to NSA headquarters.'

McCorkell's internal line rang.

'Hang on a sec, Tas,' McCorkell said as he picked up the headset.

'McCorkell.'

'It's Vanzet. We got ourselves a French frigate in the North Atlantic, steaming at flank speed and headed for the Greenland coast.'

McCorkell's jaw dropped. It took him a few seconds to speak.

'Say again, Admiral?'

50

GREENLAND

'Ready?' Sefreid asked his team. They all nodded, Geiger waiting by the door, ready to open it to the freezing and windy elements.

'Why we have to jump out of a perfectly good aeroplane . . .' Gammaldi said, white in the face.

'Relax, the Falcon 'chute will dump you where you need to go,' Gibbs said, triple-checking her sniper rifle's straps were secured across her chest.

'Dump, yeah, that's great,' Gammaldi said.

Geiger hefted open the door, and Sefreid led the way towards the doorway into nothingness.

'You'll be landing on powder snow!' Sefreid yelled into Gammaldi's ear as he launched through the open hatch.

•

Powder fucking snow, Gammaldi thought as he managed to stop slipping about on the icy surface and find his footing.

The Falcon had certainly done its job. The tri-layered honeycomb canopy was controlled the entire way down to terra firma by the GPS-guided motorised backpack. Thirty-six strands of Neolite cord were adjusted at up to six times per second. The result: a landing unaided by the user that a champion skydiver would have trouble matching.

Sefreid came over on short cross-country skis, passing a set to Gammaldi. Unlike Sefreid's and Gibbs's sets, which clipped into their combat boots for a fast release into action, Gammaldi and Beasley had to don chunky commercial gear to go with their cover.

'We're heading three klicks east, let's go,' Sefreid said. The team put their heads down and moved fast, heading towards the unknown.

51

FORT GAUCHER

'That's the best you can do?' Cassel said, her icy gaze piercing Danton over the video call. He knew she was capable of tearing shreds off the most seasoned of European parliamentarians. And he also knew she was a keen shot with a pistol, so thankfully she was hundreds of kilometres away.

'The commandos are more than capable, they will get the job done,' Danton said. Then he remembered Secher. 'And, as a safety net, I have sent an agent to a backup location. Christian Secher, he will make another connection for us.'

'So long as it is more successful than his last one,' Cassel said. 'It's your operation. I expect no more failures.'

The call ended and Danton was left watching the blank screen, his reflection staring back at him. Now he just had to get Secher's twenty million Euros. From where?

A smile crept over his lips as a plan formed. He could order the French bank to transfer the money back to him once he had the key. That way, he'd have the key *and* the money. But what of Secher? He was going to meet with a submarine . . . perhaps the skipper could be ordered to shoot him for treason . . . Yes, that would do nicely.

52

NEW YORK CITY

'Capel, why don't you wait back in the car for me, huh?' Hutchinson stared his colleague down, the agent shaking his head in annoyed compliance and heading off through the crowd.

'All right, Fox, I'll take you up on that offer of a beer,' Hutchinson said. He reached for his wallet but Fox waved him away.

'I've got it,' Fox told him. He waved to Julian, who delivered a couple of fresh beers.

'Cheers,' Hutchinson said, chinking bottles.

'Cheers,' Fox concurred, weighing him up as he drank. He was clean-cut, a little shorter than himself, perhaps what he would have turned out like had he stayed in the office his entire working life.

'I met that PI that was killed,' Fox said, presenting his

bandaged forearm. 'At La Guardia two nights ago. He gave me this, I gave him a broken nose.'

'Yeah, I know,' Hutchinson said. 'After running his mug in the Homeland Security database, the airport CCTV system picked up you guys leaving the terminal. He'd been tailing you and you made him?'

Fox nodded.

'You're pretty alert for a journalist,' Hutchinson said. 'But then you weren't always filing news stories, were you?'

Fox could see it was a rhetorical question, and that Hutchinson was planning on going on.

'We picked up a couple of partial prints from the PI's killer,' Hutchinson said. 'He didn't go quietly, strangled to death, garrotted from behind.'

Fox took it in. Garrotted.

'That mean something to you?' Hutchinson asked, reading Fox.

'No, unusual method though,' Fox said, thinking back to the dead bodies in St Petersburg.

'We'll get him,' Hutchinson said. 'In fact, we have a print match to a French national, we're working through the diplomatic immunity crap right now, so we can pick him up for questioning.'

Fox fought to not let anything show.

'Look, what interests me more is the guy you met with at the Irish bar,' Hutchinson said. 'Goes by a few known aliases. He give you a name?'

'Nope.'

'Well, at any rate, we can't touch him – yet,' Hutchinson said, drinking his beer, looking around casually at the faces in the bar. 'He started with the Agency doing straight spook work, couple of stints in Europe and drove a desk in Langley for a bit, then went off the radar about ten years ago. We think he's a double agent.'

53

GREENLAND

'I'm taking a leak,' the NSA technician said, walking out of the control room and taking a parka off the rack by the airlock exit. 'You kill me while I'm gone, you're a dead man in real life.'

The other technician gave a grunt as he waited with the game paused on the computer screen.

Through the first door, the technician zipped his parka and opened the next, dancing from foot to foot as he waited for the hydraulic steel door to open –

He came face-to-face with the barrel of an M4 carbine. Designed to be a close-quarter assault rifle, it was much shorter than its M16 brother but lacked none of the lethality when up close.

The technician pissed his pants as the eight soldiers in snow combat fatigues and full-faced helmets led him at gunpoint into the station.

54

NEW YORK CITY

'A double agent for who?' Fox asked, putting his beer on the bar and leaning on a barstool.

'Don't know, it's something that's just come to our attention.' Hutchinson looked at the woman next to Fox and smiled. He leaned a little closer to Fox so as not to be overheard. 'How was the meeting set up?'

'That was our first and only meeting. He contacted me, and I have no way of contacting him,' Fox replied. 'I received some printed material from him a few months ago, about a couple of murders in Europe that linked together. And for what it's worth, I didn't know he was CIA. He told me he was ex-NSA.'

Fox could feel that Hutchinson believed him, could see he was street-smart enough to pick a lie. He gave Fox a satisfied grunt in reply.

'What did you talk about?' Hutchinson asked.

Fox frowned, biting his lip. Exchanging some information worked both ways, and this Hutchinson could be a good friend to have onside.

'A couple of articles I wrote; he had some further background info for me to dig a little deeper,' Fox said, and could see Hutchinson wanted more. 'It was about these murders, it ended up being several prominent Europeans over the past few months. Captains of industry, politicians. I ran a couple of pieces in the *New York Times* about a month back, and in a roundabout way I included some NSA intercept traffic he gave me.'

Hutchinson nodded and wrote the information down on a small notepad.

'That sort of thing happen much?'

'People offering info? Yeah, occasionally. You have to be careful of who to trust, how good their info is,' Fox said. 'Why's the FBI investigating a CIA or NSA problem?'

'Counter-intel is our turf,' Hutchinson said. He looked around the bar and saw a couple of guys on the other side, dressed casually and enjoying themselves. He gave them a wave, and they waved back.

'They're with me, couple of local boys,' Hutchinson said. 'We're gonna get this guy, Lachlan. I've got the will, and now, thanks to this PI turning up dead, the New York office has finally seen to it that I have the manpower. I just need a break.'

'I know how you feel,' Fox said, finishing his second beer and banging the empty down on the bar. 'So you think I'm your break? Gonna be watching every move I make in the hope this guy pops up again?'

'Look, Capel is going to watch out for you, just in case,' Hutchinson said. He took a business card from his shirt pocket and passed it over. 'I work between here and DC. Be sure to let me know if you are contacted again. I'm chasing this case to the bitter end, however long that may take.'

'What do you think this is?' Fox asked, getting out a twenty and leaving it on the bar.

'I've been a cop since I could walk,' Hutchinson said, turning to leave with him. 'My hunch on this is that it started out as a turf war between the CIA and NSA. The CIA's been itching for their technical capabilities since day one. And it's getting out of hand.'

'You seriously think the CIA would jeopardise national security to gain access to a sister agency's assets?'

'Yep,' Hutchinson replied.

•

The DGSE agent stayed well out of sight of Fox as he emerged from the bar, and took his time in buying items he had no use for from a street vendor. He didn't recognise the man with Fox, and with having no listening devices still active on Fox, all he could do was watch.

•

The CIA agent posing as the burned-out NSA operative watched the scene with interest. He felt like a buzzard circling above prey, one that was being eaten by lions and about to be picked apart by hyenas. He didn't have to nudge Fox any further, things were coming to a head, fast.

He left the bar after them, no one noticing his disguise as just another lean guy in a thousand-dollar suit with a beautiful woman hanging off each arm. He had heard much of what Fox had said, reading his lips from where he was in the grill room. A useful skill that had taken him a career to perfect.

On exiting the Four Seasons restaurant, the CIA agent watched Fox head back into the GSR headquarters, Hutchinson talking to another agent before getting into a cab. Then he saw another familiar face, walking away from a street vendor across the road, a figure watching the FBI agent and Fox while not drawing attention to himself.

It was the face of the DGSE agent he had delivered information to almost a year ago. Information outlining the weakness of the NSA system.

He smiled, passed his women a roll of hundreds and they peeled off onto Park Avenue. He fished into his pockets and pulled out his cell phone to place a call – and it rang in his hand. Unlisted number, but it was an unlisted cell phone that only a few senior agency staff had access to.

'Hello?'

'It's me,' Boxcell said.

'You can read minds, Director,' the agent replied. 'I was about to call you.'

'No need,' Boxcell told him, the smile evident in his enunciation. 'I have good news. The mission will be successful, something has come up from the other end.'

'Really?' the agent said, smiling to himself, relieved. 'Talk about timing.'

'You can head back to The Point to wait out the next few days, then we'll debrief and organise your next role.'

'Thanks,' the agent said, heading down Park Avenue. 'But there's one loose thread that I have to tie off.'

55

PUERTO RICO

Secher walked for half an hour through thick jungle, the humidity almost unbearable by the time he came to the top of the hill. The thick canopy gave way to a clearing of wild grass, growing in patches between the dead remnants of what was poisoned jungle. Tall steel poles were concreted into the ground at irregular intervals, a helicopter landing obstacle. In the middle of the clearing, at the very top of the hill, was a fenced-in satellite dish atop a squat concrete-block structure.

Taking in every detail with binoculars, Secher could clearly see the signage on the outer fence. Two warnings: MINEFIELD, and a warning of high-voltage current running through the outer fence. The minefield was a ten-metre moat of sand between the two fences, and contained ceramic anti-personnel mines. One gate led in and out, a caged-in walkway with heavy gauge steel doors. If his objective were to infiltrate at any cost, he'd blast his way through there. As his task was to enter and plant a device undetected, he had to take the discreet approach.

Secher spent the next twenty minutes walking around the satellite relay station, staying within the cover of the jungle. He knew the station to be unmanned, but he had to be sure.

In the six months of researching and reconnaissance trips to UKUSA bases across the world, this one had always ranked as a possible target. He knew that the response time to the station from the island's US army base was over an hour.

He walked up to the outer fence, taking a grappling hook and rope from his bag as he went. With the electric razor-wire topped fences, he'd have one shot at this for risk of the rope getting snared if he tried to pull it back.

Secher faced towards where the dish was angling down, and began swinging the grapple around his head. Once the force was right, he released, the steel weight flying through the air up into the dish – and wrapping around the perforated steel bracing that angled within the dish, the grapple hooking back onto the rope. Secher walked backwards as it connected, pulling the rope taut and clear of the fences.

Walking backwards into the jungle, playing out the taut rope as he went, Secher climbed the nearest tall tree and tied it off, inserting a tensioner to wind the rope to its tightest.

He now had a way in and out.

Using a rope-scaling lock handle, he scaled the gradient of the rope while upside down, his legs crossed over the rope to hold his weight. In the heat the sixty metres he travelled had him dripping with sweat, but at least the slide back down the rope would be easy.

•

Two hours later Secher sat in the rear of an open-top bus, heading back to San Juan.

The locals were heading home, having finished their day at work, and their mood was all smiles. A kid sold bottled beer from an ice cooler and Secher settled into his second, giving his empty back to the kid.

He looked out at the jungle rushing by but his mind was elsewhere. He might be able to get an earlier flight into the US than he'd thought. He wondered what kind of yacht he'd buy, and how much of his twenty million Euros he'd spend on it. Thought about what he'd end up doing, perhaps some exclusive private security consulting if he got bored. Yes, it was going to be good.

56

NEW YORK CITY

The setting sun reflected off the glass buildings of Manhattan and shone down onto DUMBO. The Brooklyn area, Down Under Manhattan Bridge Overpass, was becoming more and more gentrified with each day, the docks and warehouses being developed intro trendy apartments and commercial precincts that spread west into the borough of Brooklyn. There was still very much a grittiness to the look and feel, with new graffiti adorning the walls every day, the locals a mix of artists and up-and-comers, everywhere a splash of colour decidedly more Little Italy and Chinatown rather than the lower East Side.

Fox sat on the roof deck of his houseboat, drinking a beer. He watched the occasional boat and ferry chug past, and considered lighting up the barbeque while the sun was still up, but decided there was still a good hour of light left in the summer night. He felt a bit weird having Goldsmith sitting in a car overlooking his houseboat, but given what Beasley had found in his electronic sweep that morning, it was a necessary nuisance.

Kate arrived, a chilled bottle of wine in hand.

'Hey there, sailor,' she said, walking over. Her summer dress waved in the light breeze running up the East River, her hair held in a low, loose ponytail.

'Hey,' Fox replied, about to get up.

'Stay there,' she said, kissing him on the cheek. 'I figured I'd introduce you to a perfectly chilled Napa Valley pinot,' she added, placing the bottle on the timber table. 'Been busy?'

'Just back from Washington last night. Got this for my trouble,' Fox said, holding up his bandaged forearm.

'Ouch!' she replied, holding his hand and inspecting the tightly wrapped arm. 'Workplace injury?'

'Always a workplace injury,' Fox said with a grin. 'Maybe Mum was right, I should have been a primary-school teacher. Make a difference in kids' lives. Nice, quiet, safe work.'

'Sadly, there's plenty of guns and violence in US schools,' Kate said.

'Yeah, that's something that makes my blood boil. Beer?' Fox asked, passing one out of the cooler as Kate sat down next to him on the bench seat.

'Thanks.' She sipped the Asahi. 'And thanks for inviting me over, I needed a change of scene. This is a great spot.'

'Yeah, it's still pretty quiet, for New York. Not sure if I'm game to move right into the middle of Manhattan just yet.' Fox looked over to her. 'How are you going?'

Kate stared ahead for a while then sipped her drink and turned to Fox.

'I'm okay,' she said. 'I've had two days of meetings with psychiatrists, kinda depressed me more than what happened in Russia.'

'They tend to do that,' Fox said, standing up and moving to the barbeque. 'Especially if you have to fork out a couple of hundred bucks an hour to chat about your childhood abandonment.'

'Sounds like you have some experience in this,' Kate said, putting a hand on his leg as he lit the barbeque.

'A little, but I found it easier to move away from all the crap in my life and start again.' Fox blew out the match and sat back down next to her.

'Ah . . . so you're a runner,' she said in humour.

'Don't know about that . . .' Fox replied, picking at the label on his beer bottle.

'That's okay, I think I am too,' Kate said. 'God, how I'd love to run away from it all.'

'From what?'

'Stuff.'

There was silence between them for a moment. Just the sound of distant traffic humming under the current song playing over Fox's iPod music system in the lounge below.

'How long are you in town for?' Fox asked.

'I'm heading back to DC early in the morning, just for the night. I have a few things to take care of before I take some leave.'

'Gonna get away for a while?' Fox asked.

'That's the plan, not exactly sure where to yet,' Kate replied.

'You're . . . you're seeing someone?' he asked, picking more at his beer label. Fox had been thinking a lot about this and he couldn't help but ask.

Kate looked at him as if unsure how to answer, or at least how the answer would go down. She took her hand off his leg. 'Yeah.'

Silence. Fox wasn't quite sure what to say next.

'Look, I'm sorry if I –' Fox said into the space, quickly. 'About – in the train, I mean –'

'Nothing to be sorry about, I'm a big girl.' Kate sipped her beer, pulling a strained face as she looked across the river, staring into the far-off distance at something that was not physically there. She softened and smiled. 'It helped, and it was nice. More than nice . . .'

They were both silent for a while, watching a ferry motor up the river. Fox let out a sigh, leaned over and got a fresh beer.

'Is it serious?' Fox asked.

'What? My relationship?'

He nodded.

'It's . . . different to anything I've had,' she said. 'It's – he's Swiss for a start.'

'Ooh, impressive . . .' Fox said in good humour, popping his beer.

Kate smiled. 'I've been seeing him for a few months. That said, we've only seen each other in person twice. I met him at a party in DC, the type of legal thing I usually hate. He has a business that's moderately successful, and he plans to sell it soon for a bomb.'

'And what, you two will live in the Swiss Alps, raising little watchmakers and living happily ever after?' Fox said, tossing the beer cap across the deck into a trash can.

'Don't know about that.' Kate looked at Fox, stroked his short brown hair that was blowing in the breeze. 'He's offered to take me sailing for a while, to get away from everything for a bit. Six months, maybe a year . . .'

'Sounds like your dream,' Fox said.

'Mmm.'

Fox turned to look at her. She met his gaze, and she still had that haunted look in her eyes. He felt his guilt multiply but couldn't help himself.

'So, what do we do?' he asked, putting a hand on her leg. She picked up his hand and pressed hers against it. She locked her fingers in his and leaned her head on his shoulder.

'Well, after this award-winning barbequed steak you enticed me over here with, I thought maybe I could stay the night,' she said, watching the sun move and twinkle in the glass monoliths before them.

•

On a warehouse rooftop to the north of Fox's boat, the DGSE agent took photos of Fox and Kate sitting on the deck. He had a sound-finder pointed at them, and listened to their conversation through headphones, a program on his laptop computer recording every word. He waited there, took photos of Fox as he cooked, of the pair of them as they ate, and recorded their affair. When the sun went down the couple went below, and the agent, his equipment now useless, packed up and headed for the consulate.

57

THE WHITE HOUSE

Located in the reinforced-concrete basement level of the West Wing, the Situation Room had military aides hanging over laptop computer screens set up along a shallow wall-mounted bench. The long timber table in the centre of the room was vacant but for the Joint Chiefs of Staff. The far wall was covered with big LCD screens and digital clocks ringed the room.

McCorkell entered the Situation Room for the third time that night, on this occasion with urgency.

'Where's Vanzet?' he asked.

'Here,' the Chairman of the Joint Chiefs of Staff said on entering. 'What's going on?'

'France,' the Navy JCS said, pointing to the wall of LCD screens that the aides had readied. 'We've picked up another of their navy assets where it shouldn't be.'

'Their exercise in the South Pacific?' McCorkell asked, looking at the image of the French armada as photographed when they passed Mururoa Atoll.

'That's them. And that,' the Navy JCS said while highlighting a smudge on another screen with a laser pointer, 'is the signature of one of their nuclear boomers entering New Zealand waters.'

'How old is this image?' McCorkell asked.

'Twelve hours.'

'Why send a nuclear submarine in close like that, to test their detection capabilities?' Vanzet looked at the flagged contact point on the digital image of the map.

'There are not that many reasons, beyond an incursion force or tapping an undersea cable,' the Navy JCS said. 'It went within a klick of the coast and stayed at that location for six hours.'

McCorkell's gut turned. There was an NSA station down there somewhere. Surely they wouldn't . . .

'It could have been tapping fibre-optic cable, like we had the USS *Jimmy Carter* do in the Persian Gulf last month,' Vanzet said, exploring all possible angles. 'That there is a busy section of the New Zealand coast, a linking point between the north and south islands.'

'Or the stopover was long enough for an incursion force,' McCorkell said.

'This here,' the Navy JCS added, pointing to an aerial image of a surface warship, 'is the French frigate *La Fayette*. Taken –'

'Just over five hours ago, sir,' a military aide answered.

'Still headed for the Greenland coast?' McCorkell asked.

Vanzet had a closer look.

'Taken with a Global Hawk returning from England,' the Navy JCS said. 'Still waiting on confirm of the real-time sat coverage time.'

'Don, these two locations have one thing in common,' McCorkell said, turning to face him. 'They each house NSA satellite relay stations.'

Vanzet considered this for a moment.

'If it's French, it's military – I wanna know where it is!' Vanzet ordered the room. 'And I wanna know what we've got on or near Greenland. Land, sea, air, a complete inventory.'

'We'll have real-time sat coverage over Greenland in forty minutes,' another aide called out, hanging up the line to the NRO.

'Where's this Greenland station?' Vanzet asked.

'South-east coast, rugged as hell. Danish military is six hundred klicks north-west,' the Army JCS said.

McCorkell motioned to Vanzet to follow him over to the corner of the room.

'My source mentioned there would be possible activity at the NSA base in Greenland,' he said quietly. 'Nothing military was mentioned, though, and certainly nothing on this scale.'

'Well, if your guy got this right . . .' Vanzet said.

'It gives a hell of a lot of credence to the likelihood of this French coup d'état,' McCorkell said. 'I've gotten nowhere with it on the political front. Nothing has popped up in any Europol or Interpol watch lists.'

'Yeah. That's what I'm worried about,' Vanzet said. 'If they're organised enough to keep something like this secret, then they mean business. And this shows they have some of the French military onside.'

'What was that, Lieutenant?' McCorkell said, a puzzled expression on his face as he overheard the air-force officer talking to her JCS.

'We're tracking a US Air Force C-130 in Greenland airspace,' she repeated to the room. 'Heading back to the US on return route from the NSA station.'

McCorkell looked wide-eyed at Vanzet.

'Designation?' Vanzet asked, not missing a beat.

'Black-logged with the Pope flight tower,' the aide replied, pausing to listen to the phone receiver. 'SF designated flight from 43rd Air Wing. Their code word designation has an NSA classification. Flew out of Pope at ten hundred hours, sir.'

'You think the NSA had an early-warning threat they didn't tell us about?' McCorkell asked Vanzet.

'I'll soon find out,' Vanzet said, his neck flushed red with frustration. He turned to an aide: 'Get Pope command on the phone.'

'NSA denied knowledge of a threat,' the Air Force JCS said after putting down a phone handset. 'Their director said so himself.'

'The DNI is over at Meade now,' McCorkell said, referring to the Director of National Intelligence, who had overall command authority over the intelligence community. 'He'll get to the bottom of this.'

'Get this new info to him,' Vanzet said. 'I want to know who ordered that damn plane and what they know. By Christ, if they got wind of a military threat to an NSA station –'

'Who's entering an NSA station?' the President asked. He stood inside the doors to the Situation Room with the secretaries for Defence and State, and his Chief of Staff behind him.

All stood to attention at his presence and he waved them back to their tasks.

'The French, Mr President,' McCorkell said.

The President looked at the seriousness of the faces before him.

'Well this beats what we were just doing,' he said, taking his seat at the head of the table. 'Bill,' he said, turning to his National Security Advisor. 'Tell me, what the hell is going on?'

58

NEW YORK CITY

They lay in bed naked, the linen sheet half-covering their sweaty bodies. They had talked the past hour about growing up, family memories, past loves. What Fox had planned as an evening to make sure that Kate was coping had turned into a night filled with fits of laughter.

'Bullet,' Fox said. He showed Kate his right forearm, sure he'd win this latest round of friendly competition. A neat circular scar the size of a quarter just below his elbow, an identical exit wound on the other side.

'Bicycle.' Kate pulled her leg out from under the sheet and held it straight up. A long scar ran down her shin.

'First time?' Fox asked.

'What, first sex experience?'

'Yeah,' Fox said. 'With a guy or girl, take your pick.'

Kate poked him in the ribs.

'Twenty one,' she said.

'Really?' Fox laughed.

'I was a good girl,' she demurred, playfully biting him on the arm. 'You?'

'Sixteen,' he said. 'I grew up in a small country town, not much else to do . . .'

'Ah, that explains it.'

'Ha. Biggest regret?' Fox asked.

Kate was silent for a while. After two hours of making love, they'd opened another bottle of wine and started with war stories of past lovers, jobs, housemates.

'Okay, and I haven't told anyone this before,' Kate said, sitting up and looking Fox in the eyes.

'Sounds serious . . .' he said.

Kate took her time.

'I was arrested in college,' she began, taking a deep breath before continuing. 'We sent blackmail emails to a congressman after he had raped a friend of ours. She'd been his intern one summer, and when we came back to campus we found she was really messed up.'

'Why is that a regret?' Fox asked. 'I would have done much worse if it had happened to a friend of mine. Probably would have nearly killed the bastard, or worse.'

'Well, we didn't get anywhere with it, so then a couple of guy friends of ours offered to go around and scare him a bit.'

'Okay, that sounds better,' Fox said with a half-smile. 'And?'

'And they were drunk, things got out of hand, and they beat him pretty bad.' Kate was quiet for a while, as if contemplating whether she should continue. 'They never got ID'd, but the feds traced the blackmail back to me. I stayed zip, but still . . . any kind of criminal record in my line of work means no practising law. And that's not to mention the sentence that could have come my way; obstruction of a criminal investigation, conspiracy to attempted murder.'

'Jesus.' Fox frowned. 'If you were arrested, wouldn't it have meant you couldn't get on the bar?'

'They cut me a deal,' Kate said, resting her head on his chest.

'The feds cut you a deal but you stayed zip.' Fox could sense she wasn't going to go further with this, despite his intrigue. 'What happened to the congressman?'

'Didn't run again, wife divorced him,' Kate said. 'Basically got a slap on the wrist considering what he did to our friend.'

Fox lay there and stroked her hair.

'And you stayed zip . . .' Fox said. 'I wouldn't have picked you for the perverting-the-course-of-justice type, keeping secrets like that.'

'What, you think I'm a nun or something?' Kate had a teasing smile, then rolled on top of him and sat up.

'A nun I know you're not,' Fox said, earning himself a playful hit on the arm. 'Can you stay the night?'

She looked down and kissed his lips.

'Sure,' she said, hands resting on his chest, her breasts squeezed between her arms. 'But you're not going to get much sleep.'

59

GREENLAND

Gammaldi approached the station with Beasley behind him. The wind was blowing at gale force and visibility was lowering as a light snow came whipping horizontally, blasting their faces.

A tall cyclone-wire fence surrounded the buildings, the last big snow dump covering every surface with a fresh coat of white. The building was low and squat, no bigger than an average-sized suburban house. Three massive radomes, looking like huge golf balls, and a forest of antennae were dispersed about the compound.

•

'Sniper West to base, we have two contacts approaching from the west,' a Delta sniper called over the tac-mike.

'Say again, West,' the commander replied, sipping a coffee in the mess room of the NSA station.

'Two lone figures, dressed in civilian survival gear, approaching slowly by foot from the west,' the sniper said.

'Expecting anyone from the west?' the commander said to the two base technicians before him.

'No. There's nothing to the west,' one technician responded.

'All the more suspect,' the commander said. 'Sniper West, let them approach.'

'Copy that.'

The commander made for the exit of the mess, flicking the safety off his customised M4 as he made for the building's airlock.

'Commander?' the other technician said.

The no-nonsense Delta Force leader turned around.

The technician went silent, until nudged by his colleague.

'Do we get to have guns too?'

60

THE WHITE HOUSE

McCorkell sat in the silence of the Situation Room, waiting with the rest of the audience in suspense as the main screen was switching from blank to –

'On screen in two, one . . .'

The screen showed the real-time image of the *La Fayette*, sailing full steam across the ocean. It was a thermal image, the frigate a mix of bright colours ranging from warm to the white-hot rim of the exhaust stacks. The sea around it was an eerie black-blue, as if they were watching the ship flying through space.

'Course?' Vanzet asked.

'Same course, sir, she'll be inside Greenland waters in fifteen minutes.'

'Where are the F-15's?' Secretary of Defense Larter asked.

'Eighty-five minutes west of combat station,' the Air Force JCS said, referring to the point of firing.

'Mr President, the French ambassador is rolling up the driveway now,' McCorkell said, relaying the message from a marine corpsman.

'Good. Adam, Tom, come with me,' the President said, the Secretary of State and Chief of Staff rising with him. 'Bill, I want you down here on this. Anything happens in the next ten minutes, I want to know.'

●

'Mr President, such a pleasure,' the French ambassador said, rising from his seat on a couch in the Oval Office in greeting. He put out a hand but the President ignored it. The two secret-service agents who had escorted the ambassador in left the room.

'What's a French warship doing entering Greenland waters?' the President asked, not bothering to sit down and the others following suit.

'Excuse me, Mr President?'

'Your frigate the *La Fayette*. It has sailed from France on a direct course to Greenland,' Fullop said, his short stocky body puffing up a little in his oversized suit.

'I'm afraid I don't –'

'Laurent, your navy exercise in the South Pacific, is it a cover for something else?' Baker asked. The Secretary of State knew this guy well.

'Adam – Mr President –' The ambassador was blinking hard, looking from face to face. Being in this room, with these men, was having its effect. 'We gave your Department of Defense a full briefing on our exercise two months ago –'

'Well they failed to mention a submarine entering New Zealand waters,' the President said. 'Mr Ambassador, this is a serious situation and I need straightforward answers, right now. What is your navy up to?'

The ambassador paled as the words and mood of the men sank in.

'Laurent, we go way back,' Baker said, playing good cop. 'Tell us what you know, or this will escalate to the next level fast.'

'The next level?' the ambassador replied. 'I'm not sure – I don't –'

'If we don't get an explanation, soon,' the President said, taking a step closer to the ambassador, 'that frigate of yours will be on the bottom of the ocean.'

61

GREENLAND

Gammaldi knocked again, the pounding of his double-gloved fist on the steel door reverberating through the airlock beyond.

'Fuck'n' Greenland,' he said through chattering teeth to Beasley. 'Fuck'n' shit cold arse-end of the –'

The door creaked open to reveal the technician, who eyed them suspiciously.

'G'day!' said Gammaldi, rubbing his hands together for warmth. 'Nice beard. Our ride broke down. Can we come in for some hot cocoa?'

The technician nodded, nervous.

That was easy, thought Gammaldi, as he walked through the door with Beasley close behind.

'Bit smelly in here –' Gammaldi stopped as he saw the heavily armed soldiers appear from around the corner.

The door slammed behind him and he was pushed face first into a wall, a gun to the back of his head as hands patted him down.

'We – just – want – cocoa –'

62

THE WHITE HOUSE

'*La Fayette* class frigates are purpose-built to deploy commandos,' the Navy JCS said.

'NSA confirmed there are two unarmed technicians at the station,' an aide called out. 'Still can't get through to them due to weather at their end.'

'Well keep trying,' Vanzet said. 'The Danes just got their helos in the air.'

'Force strength and ETA?' McCorkell asked.

'Two platoons aboard four Black Hawks, eighty minutes out from the north-east, weather permitting. A mechanised company ready to roll as backup, they'll take a good four hours to get to the station.'

'What's – what is that to the aft of the helo pad?' Larter said.

McCorkell squinted at the screen. It looked like two big boxes.

'Zooming in,' the audiovisual aide said, typing in commands to the laptop, the image on the screen tracking fast to keep up with the target.

'Can anyone make that out?' McCorkell asked, looking at two boxy shapes on the aft deck of the frigate.

'Can we get closer?' Larter asked.

The screen zoomed in, closer, out of focus for a moment and then out of shot, as the aide worked double-time with the mouse to catch up with the feed that was slipping to the left of screen.

'Ski sleds?' an aide said. McCorkell looked at him puzzled.

'Snowmobiles,' Vanzet clarified for the room. 'That's their way in. Helo them and two squads ashore for a fast, below-the-radar incursion.'

The room looked at the two white snowmobiles coming into sharper focus.

'I'll tell the President,' McCorkell said, picking up a phone on the desk.

63

GREENLAND

'Our Hummer stopped about ten minutes to the north-west of here –'

'– frozen gas lines, I bet –' Beasley added, nodding to Gammaldi.

'Yeah, so we thought we'd look for some help,' Gammaldi said. 'What is this place, Area Fifty Two?'

The Delta commander eyed them sceptically. They'd been searched down to their underpants, and were just now getting dressed again.

Gammaldi looked to Beasley. Beasley shrugged and looked to the NSA technician. One technician looked to the other, who was busy staring at the commander's M4 and various weapons strapped to his assault webbing.

'Can we –'

'You're not getting fucking firearms!' the commander said to the bearded NSA techs. He turned to a Delta soldier: 'Take these bananas into the mess – and watch the four of them.'

64

THE WHITE HOUSE

In the Oval Office the President hung up the phone. He looked at the ambassador, shaking his head. He pressed the intercom on his desk.

'Get the President of France on the line,' he ordered. 'Wake the son of a bitch up if you have to.'

The French ambassador shrank a couple of inches before the President's eyes.

'The *La Fayette* has two snowmobiles on its aft deck, hardly the usual complement of arms for a warship I would think,' the President said. He walked around and sat down behind the Resolute Desk.

'Mr President –'

'Perhaps you're thinking that this situation is getting me pretty pissed,' the President said, checking his watch. 'I was meant to be having dinner with my family for the first time in over a week. My wife is the one who's going to be really pissed, and so help you God she doesn't come over from the Residence.'

The phone rang and he picked it up.

'Connected through to his personal secretary at Elysée Palace now,' the secretary said. 'Waiting on pick-up – here we go.'

'Mr President,' the President said.

'Yes, Mr President, to what do I owe the honour?'

'I'm going to cut to the chase, so please listen to me closely,' the President said. 'We are tracking a warship of yours, the frigate *La Fayette*, which is about to make an incursion into Greenland.'

'An incursion?'

'Dropping off a military land force, which will be an unwelcome incursion of a foreign force on Danish soil,' the President said. 'We know this as we have real-time visual coverage. We believe they are set to attack our satellite relay station there, which will be seen as an act of war. If we're wrong about that, and this is a test of our tracking capabilities, then call them off before I put that ship on the bottom of the ocean.'

There was silence on the phone.

'Allow me to confer with my defence minister and be back to you within ten minutes.'

'Ten minutes. Any longer, we're taking defensive action.'

'Understood, Mr President.'

•

'Yes, but it's the *why* that beats the hell outta me.' Vanzet turned to an aide. 'What else is on Greenland's south coast that's accessible by snowmobile?'

278 • JAMES PHELAN

'Aside from a few small towns, there are a couple of oil depots, a couple of remote reserve air strips run by the Danish Air Force for NATO refuelling and geographic research purposes, and the NSA satellite relay station.'

'We have a visual yet on the station?' McCorkell asked.

'No. Our only asset is the Warfighter satellite tracking the *La Fayette*,' the Air Force JCS said.

'Leave the Warfighter on the frigate,' Vanzet ordered.

'It'll take them under an hour to get there, less if the helo drops the snowmobiles in real close,' McCorkell said.

Boxcell entered the Sit Room, taking a spot where he could observe the LCD screens.

'I've got an agent heading to Elysée Palace with a CAVNET laptop,' Boxcell said, referring to the military remote-access computer network that proved so valuable to the soldiers on the ground in Iraq. 'He'll be at the French President's ASAP, showing him this real-time footage that we've got.'

'Let him deny what's going down live on screen,' McCorkell said. 'We've got no navy assets nearby?'

'*Seawolf* is closest,' the Navy JCS said. 'Heading in from the south, she was coming back to Virginia to re-crew.'

'I don't like the prospect of an attack sub against the *La Fayette*'s ASW systems,' McCorkell said. 'Nothing with a bit more grunt from the Second Fleet?'

'They're too far south and east. *Wasp* is returning to Virginia from Portsmouth for a full shake-down, so she's now steaming flank speed to back up *Seawolf*, and I've ordered the commanders of the Med and Atlantic fleets to cover the French coast. All our north-east Atlantic coast assets are closing a net from our side. That's two Los Angeles and an Ohio class, and three Arleigh Burke destroyers.'

'I'm recommending to the President that we blockade the French coast until we know what's going on,' Vanzet said.

'Good idea. Weird thing is, most of their blue-water navy has been exercising in their Pacific playground,' McCorkell said.

'Tell me about it. Our entire Seventh Fleet is off the Korean Peninsular doing standoff duty,' the Navy JCS said. 'We've had to rely on the Aussies and Kiwis to keep us posted on their activities down their way.'

'Then why send an unprotected frigate on this mission?' Vanzet asked.

'*La Fayettes* are the most stealthy surface vessels afloat,' the Navy JCS said. 'If we hadn't been scouring the NRO and high-alt images, we wouldn't have found her.'

'Good point,' McCorkell said, after hanging up the phone to the President. He studied the image of the frigate, like a sliver of ice in the frigid sea.

'Admiral.' An aide held a phone to the JCS Chairman. Vanzet hung up after a few seconds of listening intently.

'NSA flight order was a priority-threat reaction force, one C-130 dropping off two Delta squads from Bragg,' Vanzet told the room.

'Who ordered it?' McCorkell asked.

'Ira Dunn.'

65

GREENLAND

Gibbs and Sefreid crawled slowly to their position six hundred metres north of the station by the road leading in. They flattened out under the shrubs, pushing snow forward of their positions to form a low wall, blocking them from sight.

Gibbs clicked in the scope of her sniper rifle and sighted the weapon, chambering a round as she went about her task in automated fashion. She could make out the desolate NSA station, a small jumble of low concrete buildings surrounded by three big round radomes.

'Geiger,' she said over her throat mike. 'Gibbs and Sefreid in position.'

Silence greeted them for a good ten seconds, and Sefreid repeated the call.

'Geiger, you copy that?' Sefreid said over their throat-mike system.

•

'Copy that, sorry for the delay,' Geiger said, turning down the INXS CD he'd put in the stereo. 'Eyal Geiger is currently barrelling in southbound in the Hummer from hell. This baby is chewin' the snow like nothin' else!'

66

THE WHITE HOUSE

The President returned to the Situation Room with his Secretary of State and Chief of Staff.

'Mr President, report just in of an IED going off in Baghdad, two marines KIA, six wounded,' McCorkell said quietly.

The room took in the news in silence, all used to the world not stopping for anyone. Truth be told, McCorkell thought, they could all station themselves in this room and have enough ongoing work to never get any sleep. Bar the two world wars, since September 11th the world they found themselves in was a more threatening landscape than at any time in America's history. At least the Cuban Missile Crisis was over with relatively quickly.

'Any luck with the French ambassador?' McCorkell asked the Secretary of State.

'He doesn't know anything about it,' Baker said, sitting down. 'I've known him for ten years, he's telling the truth.'

'French President will be calling through in –' the President checked his watch '– three minutes.'

'He'll probably play us on the agriculture tariffs from last month's G8,' Fullop said, the Chief of Staff always considering the political angle.

'Let him see how productive his farms are when we have Abrahams churnin' up his countryside,' Larter said, taking a moment to lighten the mood.

'Don, a massive what-if here,' the President said, 'and I'm not seriously thinking about this option . . .'

'We could take them with conventional forces within seventy-two hours on your order, sir,' Vanzet replied. 'And that's without any direct European support, and you could bet your ass there'd be a conga line of NATO countries willing to take pot shots at their most reserved member. Brits and Germans would probably rather we left it up to them to handle.'

'Call from Elysée Palace, Mr President,' an aide said. 'Line three.'

'Put it on the speaker,' he said; then loudly: 'This is the President.'

'Mr President,' the President of France said through the speakers running down the centre of the table.

'Where are we at?' the President asked, his security advisors silent as they all waited for the update.

'I have the defence minister here, along with the chief of our defence force on another line,' the French President said. 'Of the frigate *La Fayette*, it is indeed in the vicinity of

Greenland. The minister of the navy has explained to us that it is a long-planned exercise.'

'An exercise in another country's sovereign waters?' the President asked.

'I admit that it is unusual, and the minister will contact me momentarily with the exact details.'

Vanzet looked to the President to ask a question, and the President nodded.

'Mr President, this is Admiral Donald Vanzet of the Joint Chiefs of Staff. Can you account for the rest of your navy?'

There was a pause on the other end of the line.

'Yes, Admiral, we can,' the French President said.

McCorkell said, holding down the mute button, 'Vanzet, how far are the F-15E's from the *La Fayette*?'

'Sixty-five minutes to combat radius,' Vanzet replied.

'Give 'em an hour?' McCorkell asked, to nods from the Secretary of Defense and Vanzet.

McCorkell released the mute.

'Mr President,' the President said, 'we will give your navy exactly sixty minutes from now to get itself in order. After that, we will be taking action against the *La Fayette* and any other forces we deem as being hostile.'

'Mr President, with all due respect –'

'With all respect aside, that ship is going to the bottom of the ocean unless you convince me otherwise. No ifs or buts. One hour.'

67

GREENLAND

'Good cocoa,' Gammaldi said, smiling to the tech. 'You know, you two guys are dead ringers for Harold and Kumar having a beard off.'

'Yeah, we've been getting that since the movie came out when we were at college,' the Harold look-alike said.

'Cocoa's a home brew,' Kumar said, zoned out of the conversation. He passed over a Tupperware container. 'Have a cookie.'

'Thanks,' Gammaldi said, taking two big homemade chocolate cookies and demolishing one in an instant.

'How long have you guys been here?' Beasley asked, passing on the cookies.

'Four months,' Harold said, looking to Kumar for confirmation, but the man was watching the Delta soldier at the door while nibbling at a cookie. He seemed mesmerised by the soldier's weaponry hanging off his person.

'What do you guys do here?' Gammaldi asked.

'Play games, mostly. Grow a bit of weed in the north radome,' the technicians laughed.

Gammaldi and Beasley shared a look, and Gammaldi sniffed his cookie, smiled, and ate it in a couple of bites. Certainly not the recipe his mama would follow.

'Good, huh,' Kumar said, having another. Beasley helped himself.

'Freeze-dried,' Harold said, tapping his nose. The pair of technicians were clearly high. 'Our patented method.'

'NSA Gold!' Kumar said, the pair breaking into in-joke laughter. 'We had a big stash going on in the south radome, until we saw the spider.'

'Spider?' Beasley asked.

'Fiercest killers in the insect world,' Harold chimed in, the pair nodding.

'Biggest thing you ever seen,' Kumar said. 'Some kinda yeti spider.'

'Okay, dude, this is some crazy shit . . .' Beasley said out of the corner of his mouth to Gammaldi.

'What kinda work do you guys do?' Gammaldi asked, finishing off his cocoa and smacking his lips together. Kumar got up and went to the fridge, pulling out a four-pack of Heinekens.

'The station's automated,' Kumar said, passing around the beers. 'We just debug stuff every now and then, upgrade and fix things when they go bung.'

'Why are these goons here?'

'Don't know, Fort Meade sent them in, probably some kind of exercise.'

'Anything out of the ordinary happen lately . . .' Gammaldi blinked his eyes, shaking his head.

'Ha!' Kumar said, taking a big swill of beer, the surplus running down his chin. 'NSA Gold, unlike any other!' Again the in-joke laughter.

The soldier at the door held up his hand to his helmet-mounted radio, and a moment later turned to the room.

'No one leaves this room!' he said, closing the door and disappearing down the corridor.

Harold and Kumar shared a brief look of panic.

68

THE WHITE HOUSE

'Still no luck in getting through to the NSA station, sir,' an aide told McCorkell.

'There are a number of options, Mr President,' Larter said. 'From dealing with this frigate to a precision strike on their homeland military bases.'

'I suggest we go forward in blockading their coast lines, concentrating on the key ports,' Vanzet said. 'We can have the Sixth Fleet put up a curtain of iron to stop all major shipping within twelve hours.'

'Bill?' the President asked.

'It sends the right message, Mr President,' McCorkell said. 'Shows we mean business, yet it's not aimed at bloodying their nose.'

'What would it involve?' the President said, looking over at his team of advisors.

'The remainder of the Sixth Fleet steamed out of Gaeta, Italy, last night. They'll join up with the rest of the force any minute,' Vanzet said. 'They own the Med by themselves, and considering most of the French Navy is in the South Pacific, the only threat would be from the French Air Force. The Second Fleet are already off their Atlantic coast, and the Brits are itching to come to the party.'

'What's France's air power?'

'Around three hundred combat aircraft, call it two hundred being operational from the mainland, all pretty damn capable but only a third are the latest gen Rafales,' Vanzet said. 'We've got closer to seven hundred in the immediate European Command theatre and we can double that over a twenty-four-hour period. Hell, the amount of air power we have sitting unused in the Middle East right now . . .'

'Okay,' the President said, taking his time to consider his order. 'Keep the fleets steaming to station, ready to impose a blockade. We get the confirmation of a threat from those subs, you roll. We get a confirmation of a clear and present danger to our nation, our air force bloodies their nose good.'

'Yes, Mr President,' Larter said, pointing to an aide to get things moving via the Pentagon. 'Will we be staying at DEFCON Four?'

'I think we have to,' McCorkell said. A raise in the Defense Condition was something rarely undertaken; the last time it had gone beyond that was 11 September 2001. 'At DEFCON Four we've got our European forces battle-ready to move in twenty-four hours.'

'That's right. I've already got the 173rd Airborne Brigade Combat Team waiting on the tarmac in Italy, and the 1st

Armoured and Infantry Divisions are ready to roll across borders from Germany,' Vanzet said. 'That's a hell of a three-punch combo at your disposal, Mr President.'

'We got movement!' McCorkell said, the rest of the room turning their attention to the big LCD screen. The image of the frigate was shown, moving slowly off the Greenland coast.

'That's an NH90, their standard heavy-lifter for the class,' the Navy JCS said. The helicopter was wheeled out onto the deck of the *La Fayette*, a load crew attaching cables to the snow-mobiles. 'Carries twenty troops and close to a tonne of gear.'

'Where's our deadline?' the President asked.

'Just on thirty-five minutes to go, meaning around thirty until the F-15s are in firing range,' McCorkell said, reading a digital timer on a wall re-tasked from its usual function of showing a world time. 'They've been punching it the whole flight, balls-to-the-wall supersonic.'

'This will be touch and go,' the President said. 'Perhaps we'll get the chance to take them from the air, target the helo instead of the *La Fayette*?'

'We've got six Strike Eagles in that formation, we can take both targets,' Vanzet said.

'Losing real-time coverage in four minutes,' McCorkell said, looking at the fast-moving coordinate numbers on the bottom of the screen.

'Robert,' the President turned to the CIA Director. 'Where the hell is your CIA man in Paris?'

69

NORTH ATLANTIC

The NH90 hovered slowly above the deck, a full complement of twenty heavily armed FORFUSCO commandos onboard. The ground crew steadied the two snowmobiles on the air-crate as the helicopter took the load into the air and dipped its nose, heading towards the white coast of Greenland to the north.

It flew low and fast, the main rotor blades whipping up plumes of ice and snow in its wake. Fifty kilometres south of the NSA station, it came to a hover, the air-crate with the snowmobiles touching the ground, then unhooked by the loadmaster.

The pilots went a further twenty metres forward and hovered the helo just clear of the ground, the side doors sliding open and the commandos dropping out onto the frozen surface and running to the snowmobiles.

As the NH90 lifted into the air and banked back to the

direction of the *La Fayette*, the commandos muscled the snow-mobiles off the air-crate and started the diesel engines.

All but four commandos donned skis that clipped into their arctic combat boots, and picked up the water-ski-like handle of the tow cable. With two commandos riding on each snow-mobile and eight towed behind, they took off slowly and powered up to forty kilometres per hour. Resembling two motorised dog-sled teams, the French commandos raced across the surface of Greenland with deadly intent.

70

GREENLAND

'We've got the comms back online!' a Delta soldier said.

'Sir, incoming from Washington for you.'

'Fort Meade?' the commander asked, walking over to the communications desk.

The soldier shook his head, passing the headset.

The commander took it with an annoyed look.

'This is Major Thornbury,' he said, picking up the line.

'Thornbury, this is Admiral Donald Vanzet,' came the reply. 'You hear me, son?'

The commander swallowed hard. He certainly could hear the Chairman of the Joint Chiefs of Staff. Vanzet was as high as the chain of command went, mere paces below God Himself.

'Crystal, sir,' Thornbury said.

'What are your orders there?'

'To stand fast and defend the base until otherwise instructed, sir,' Thornbury said, a little confused that the Chairman of JCS was not aware of his brief.

'Okay, now listen to me closely,' Vanzet ordered. 'We have real-time sat coverage of a French frigate disembarking SF troops, heading fast from the south of your location. They'll be at your door in minutes.'

Thornbury instinctively squeezed the pistol grip of his M4 tighter.

'Say that again, sir?'

71

THE WHITE HOUSE

'I have your CIA man in here now,' the French President said over the speaker phone.

'His monitor has the same real-time satellite footage that we are viewing,' McCorkell said over the line. 'The footage is only up for another minute or so but you can clearly see your ship is receiving its helicopter back from an incursion run.'

There was a moment of silence, and then, to accentuate the point, a replay of earlier footage showed a stream of fast-moving figures disembarking from the superstructure and loading into the helicopter as the rotors started up.

Before anyone in the Situation Room could speak, talking came over the phone at the French end of the connection. Frantic, loud, then silence.

'Mr President,' the French President said. 'I have just been informed that my Chief of the Navy appears to have committed suicide.'

'He committed treason,' McCorkell said matter-of-factly. 'There may be more members of your military in on this, Mr President.'

There was silence for a while, the gravity of the situation settling on everyone.

72

FORT GAUCHER

'Sir,' the female tracking technician said on entering Danton's office. 'We picked up another connection, from the NSA station at Puerto Rico.'

'Excellent!' Danton said. He slammed the palm of his hand down on the desk. 'Be ready to pick up the NSA key data from the submarine transmission.'

The technician left and Danton thought about Secher. Finally, the young officer had proved as capable as he always knew he could be. Such a pity things would have to end like they would.

He picked up the military phone and called through to the Chief of the Navy. Twice the line rang out, and he hung up the phone and typed into his military email system:

Another connection made. Call off La Fayette.

Danton pressed send and got up from his desk, putting on his jacket and leaving his office. He walked through the power plant on his way to the supercomputing room. The massive gas turbine whirred like the sound of a billion bees, the output enough to power a large town. Past the shielding doors, he entered his thumbprint into the biometric door lock. The room beyond was a cavernous expanse of concrete columns supporting the carved-out granite.

In here it was like a fridge. Fans vented the cold air from the basin in, keeping the temperature low. Cut into the mountain, the football-oval-sized expanse currently housed the most numerous collection of supercomputers in the world. Technicians were milling about, connecting hoses that held liquid nitrogen to cool down the conductors. It didn't look pretty but he had been assured countless times it was up to the task.

'We are ready,' the chief tech said as he joined Danton in taking in the view. 'What you see before you is now the most impressive array of computing power ever assembled in Europe. To have it linked like this . . . I have impressed even myself.'

'Well we have our hardwired connection,' Danton said. 'We're piggybacking on the NSA data feed now. I will notify you the instant we have the activation key.'

'We will be waiting.'

'I want to be here when you do the transfer.' Danton checked his watch, smiling. 'Sometime within the next twenty-four hours.'

73

GREENLAND

'Sir, multiple contacts! Bearing fast from the south, ETA three minutes.'

The commander called in reports from the rest of his spotters, and ordered his fire teams to prepare to hold fast against the invading force.

He looked out the small glass window heading south. The sky was darkening and the snow was settling in hard and heavy, the severe elements eerily quiet in the concrete building.

•

'I'd say they would have switched the comms on by now, my quick sabotage work would have only stalled them a couple of hours.' Harold said, hoisting Beasley up and out the window above the sink. They had been going on in this nervous fashion for ten minutes now. Gammaldi had seriously considered knocking their heads together.

'Think they're here about our stash? I think we better go into the north radome and clean it up, I don't wanna go to gaol,' Kumar said. 'I just paid off my MIT loan, I wanna start enjoying life when we get back to civilisation.'

'All clear!' Beasley said from outside, as Gammaldi climbed onto the sink and the techs helped push him up and out.

•

The French commandos shut down their snowmobiles two kilometres south of the station and skied the remaining distance. They split into two teams, one digging in to provide cover-fire positions while the other advanced towards the station. The lead pair of the group raced fifty metres ahead, bolt-cutters out and working fast on cutting a walk-through hole in the wire fence.

•

'South sniper to command, multiple contacts, make that two squads maybe three, humping it in double-time,' the southern Delta sniper said. 'I have two targets at the perimeter fence now.'

'Got a clear shot, South?' Thornbury asked, making sure all lighting in the base was switched off, night-vision goggles on.

'Roger that. Clear shot at two contacts at the south fence,' the sniper said, his finger resting on the trigger as he kept his breathing regular and steady. He had his zero mark on the left eye of the attacker working the bolt-cutters.

'I've got one target in my sight about eighty metres south,' another soldier called.

'Engage on my command and keep things silent,' Thornbury said, readying himself by the airlock with two soldiers beside him. 'Fire!'

•

The French commando working the bolt-cutters flew away from the fence and slid back on the snow as if yanked from behind by a bungee cord. Registering the growing pool of blood from his comrade's headshot, the other commando whipped back to face the station, raising his FAMAS assault rifle – and he too was blown backwards.

•

'The base is crawling with targets,' Gibbs said, looking through the massive thermal scope attached to her rifle.

'How many?' Sefreid asked, holding his night-vision binoculars up, the late twilight conditions not quite dark enough to use them effectively.

'At least twelve in view,' Gibbs said. 'Wait – we got movement, all targets moving, heading around to the south of the station.'

No sooner had Gibbs announced this than there came the sharp report of 5.56 mm assault rifles filling the air from the south.

•

'Where to?' Gammaldi said. He had Kumar by the arm, separating the pair from their argument over whether they should run or stay.

'This way!' Kumar replied. He led the four of them into the entry of the northern radome, punched in a code on an electronic keypad, and the magnetic locks on the heavy steel door clunked open.

Gammaldi was the last through the door, gunfire tearing through the air.

'That's not the Delta soldiers firing,' Gammaldi said to Beasley. 'Their weapons had suppressors.'

'And it's not GSR,' Beasley said as they watched Harold and Kumar disappear behind the base of the massive satellite dish. 'They're not M4s, sounds like a Steyr or FAMAS.'

'FAMAS?' Gammaldi asked.

'French army assault rifle,' Beasley said. 'I'd wager the French have arrived.'

'Jesus, we're in the middle of World War Three here!'

74

NEW YORK CITY

Fox fell asleep with Kate's head on his shoulder, her arm across his chest, a leg over his.

The warm night breeze cooled from the river as it blew in from the open sliding-glass door of the bedroom, the ceiling fan revolving slowly above them and their sweaty sheets.

'Ahh!' Fox said, startling himself awake and sitting up on his elbows, his face beaded with sweat.

'Hey, what is it, babe?' Kate asked sleepily, sitting up and stroking his head.

'A nightmare,' he said. He blinked the images away, and took his glass of water from the bedside table. 'It's all right. Sorry.'

'Shh, it's okay,' Kate said. She waited as he drank and lay back down, rested a hand on his chest. 'I'm here. I'll save you . . .'

Within seconds he was asleep again, and his nightmares were not far behind.

Fox was watching the scene, something he'd played in his mind a hundred times or more, looking down from above. He watched as he walked into a boat's stateroom where a man held a gun to a woman's head. Somehow he knew this wasn't exactly how it happened, and he knew it changed slightly every time. But the result was always the same.

Until now.

Fox watched as his view shifted from that of a bird's eye to through his own eyes, down there in the thick of the action. He was looking at the woman, who he knew to be Alissa Truscott. Her face was always going through the same kaleidoscope: sad, unflinching, knowing. That much never changed.

The man behind her with the gun was in silhouette, as always. This time he came forward, and the gun in his hand disappeared, to be replaced with a hand on Truscott's shoulder. His face became clear. It was Leading Seaman John Birmingham. Never in Fox's dreams had the two of them come together in the same scene. Their expressions were different too. The look of them. The looks they gave.

The two faces that had haunted Fox's nights over the past year were clear, calm. They didn't speak, didn't offer anything. The setting changed, they were all outside now, and the scenery slowly came into focus. They were on the beach, a long, deserted expanse on Christmas Island, the Indian Ocean pouring out to the horizon. It was a perfect day and Fox could feel the warm sand under his feet. Could smell the salty water as the breeze blew over him.

They came closer to Fox, walked right up to him. The silence was broken not by speech but by the sound of the sea, the surf of the ocean breaking on the headlands to the cove. The sound expanded to include that of a small town rising, that familiar milling of families and activity, which filled the morning sky.

Truscott and Birmingham parted, walked past Fox, one on either side of him. He turned around, watching as they walked off together. They were becoming distant when they turned around to face him, and though Fox couldn't be sure, he thought he saw them smiling.

75

GREENLAND

The Delta commander watched as an RPG slammed into the dugout holding six of his troops and light machine guns and mortar. The men scrambled about, shell-shocked from the noise and debris that was still raining down. Their full-bodysuit armour undoubtedly saved their lives.

'Damn it!' he yelled, switching on his mike. 'Snipers, take out those sons of bitches with the RPG launcher!'

•

Atop the windy peak of the southern radome, two Delta soldiers slid to a stop flat on their stomachs. Held in place on the slippery surface by his spotter, the sniper steadied his rifle, scanning for targets.

He felled two before they got through the hole they had cut in the southern fence, and another as he rose to fire an

RPG, the round flying wildly into the air, a trail of smoke spiralling upwards and flaring everyone's night vision.

While the battlefield waited for the grenade to come back to earth, everything fell silent.

•

'What can you see, Emma?' Sefreid asked, as he lay next to Gibbs.

'Gammaldi and Beasley with two others just left the station via a window to the north-east. I tracked them entering the north radome, pretty sure they're still inside,' Gibbs said. While the GSR security team wore tape around their necks to fasten their throat-mikes, the two in civilian clothing wore the tape across their jackets. Appearing to the naked eye like regular black electrical tape, it fluoresced through the film on the scope and night-vision lenses of the team, meaning they could be identified.

'What are they doing in there?'

•

In the radome, Beasley waited by the door as Gammaldi ran around the base of the satellite dish.

The two NSA techs were pulling apart a primitive hydroponics set-up, arguing all the way. Gammaldi considered interrupting them but chose to run back to the door.

'Let's move,' he said, and they opened the door, ran around the radome and headed north.

•

The RPG crashed back down to earth into the ceiling of the station, turning the south-east corner into a pile of concrete rubble.

The French force were firing to protect their retreat while the Delta snipers continued to pick through the ranks at every opportunity.

●

'Our boys are headed our way, six hundred metres out,' Gibbs said, watching them through her big scope.

'Geiger, change of plans, bring the Hummer in fast for evac,' Sefreid called.

'On the way!' Geiger replied.

'I have two armed targets coming from around the north-east corner,' Gibbs said.

'Stall them,' Sefreid ordered.

Gibbs squeezed off an armour-piercing round into the gas tanks along the northern wall of the station. The explosion sent the trailing Delta soldiers through the air, a small mushroom-cloud of fire and smoke erupting into the dark sky.

76

FORT GAUCHER

Back in his office, Danton sat and waited on his phone for a few minutes, tapping his fingers on the desk.

'Hello?' The voice of the French Prime Minister came on the line.

'Prime Minister, this is General Danton of the DGSE. I am sorry to contact you at home at this hour but I have a priority request.'

'Danton, it's late – and I don't have the time, something urgent has come up,' the Prime Minister said.

Danton sat rigid in his chair, his palms sweating instantly.

'Anything I can help with?'

'No, nothing for you to be concerned about. Can I have someone else contact you?'

'Sir, I have the motherlode of intel available but I will need the necessary funds to acquire it,' Danton interrupted. 'I need to access the emergency-response budget.'

'How much?' the Prime Minister said, clearly annoyed.

'Twenty million Euros,' Danton said.

That got his attention.

'That's a lot of unbudgeted money. It will have to come through via the defence funding committee, not the emergency funds.'

'I need it within the next twelve hours,' Danton said.

'So soon?' the Prime Minister replied, annoyed at his previous comment being ignored but intrigued by the urgency. 'What for?'

Danton expected this question and pulled out his trump card.

'It's to pay a long-trusted source that has the exact Afghan location of the top leadership of al Qaeda. Information is less than fifteen minutes old,' Danton said, running further with his own lie.

'How "top" is this leadership?'

'*The* top. *The* head. The entire command structure in one location,' Danton said, enjoying his creativity. What the hell, this guy was only going to be Prime Minister for a few more days.

'That's, that's . . .'

'With this info we can inform the Americans of the location and they can do the dirty work,' Danton said, knowing it would press the right hot button.

'*Non*. Our own Special Forces team will make the strike. We'll turn it into a proud day for the French military. I'll have the treasury wire the funds to your DGSE operations account straightaway.'

77

NSA HQ
FORT MEADE, MARYLAND

Having taken the edge off with his first bourbon, Dunn sat and stared into space. He considered calling the Senate committee and explaining that a matter of national security had come up. Unfortunately, he'd already used that card, twice, and he was told on no uncertain terms to appear. Tomorrow.

Dunn hadn't even planned for the hearing, and for the first time he read over the letter outlining their requirements.

He sipped at his second drink and looked at the photo of his *Liberty* crew on the wall. *Going another round with the Senate Select Committee on Intelligence over those 9/11 coals again . . . give me strength boys.*

78

NEW YORK CITY

Fox's eyes opened slowly, and he focused on the ceiling of his houseboat's bedroom. The view of the timber panelling was lit by the morning sun coming in from his open blinds. The houseboat creaked and moved ever so slowly in the water where it was docked. He listened to the hum and grind of one of the biggest cities in the world, all that life going about another day. The breakfast smells from the close-by DUMBO cafés tempted him up, and then he smelled something else. Sweet, like honey and citrus, a bit earthy with sweat.

He felt next to him, where Kate had been. Cold. Empty.

A note.

'*Thank you. Again. X*'

79

WASHINGTON

Kate arrived at her apartment wheeling a big empty suitcase. A pile of newspapers and mail greeted her, but she didn't stop to look at them. She put her keys in the bowl on the kitchen bench and pressed the flashing message button on her phone. She spent five minutes speed-deleting her way through the condolences of friends and colleagues regarding John Cooper's death. She just didn't have the wherewithal to listen to them properly and respond. She got to the most recent message and paused, her finger over the delete button:

'Hi babe, it's Lachlan. Just calling to say thanks for last night, I had a great time. Sorry I missed you this morning, I actually ended up having a pretty good sleep. I guess I have you to thank for that too. Anyway, good luck in cleaning out your office in DC. Let me know if you need a hand from the airport when you come back here. Call me whenever you need to. Bye.'

She smiled and pressed delete, standing up from the kitchen stool and wheeling her suitcase into her bedroom. She walked over and opened the window overlooking the cobbled paving of Georgetown's P Street. She flicked on her CD player on the dresser, filling the apartment with the sounds of Jewel.

It wasn't until she put her suitcase on the bed and opened her wardrobe that she got the familiar feeling associated with meeting Secher. At once thrilling and dangerous. At least, that's what it felt like on the few occasions she'd been with him. She sat on the edge of her bed and looked in her wardrobe, the half-open, mirrored sliding door reflecting half her image back. She yawned and was reminded of the previous night she had spent with Fox, then stood and pushed the wardrobe all the way open.

She frisked through the contents of her wardrobe, looking for the right dress to wear. She held up a couple in front of her, looking in the full-length mirror at how they clung to her figure. Secher had seen her in her two favourites, so she settled on a jade-green Elie Saab number she hadn't worn this season.

She held it to herself and smiled, heart racing at the thought of what she was about to do over the next twenty-four hours. *Twenty-four hours!* She'd not thought about the details until now. What would she take? She looked over some of her favourite pieces, mostly black, conservative business attire. And then there was her shoe collection . . .

'Don't worry, we'll buy you new things,' Secher had said the last time they were together. They had been laying in bed in his ancient stone townhouse in Bern, almost a month ago now. Had it really been a month? *'We'll shop in Milan, Rome, Florence, then sail the Mediterranean, explore the Adriatic coast . . .'*

Kate shifted from her thoughts to the present, seeing herself there in the mirror, holding the dress. In the reflection she saw the photos on the drawers behind her, felt her hands let go of the dress and it shimmered to the floor. She picked up a framed shot taken of her and her parents, a happy summer from freshman year. Before life became complicated.

She sat on the edge of the bed, holding the framed photograph to her chest, and then lay back, shaking, crying. It was so close as to be real now. Was this really what she wanted? Maybe she hadn't really thought it through. Christian had shared his dream of retiring young and sailing carefree around the world, calling the occasional seaside town home for a while before moving on when they wished, no constraints or burdens. Nothing but the drive to enjoy life. But to leave everything, to not even tell her parents . . .

She would have to talk to him tonight, tell him she needed more time to think about it. Christian Secher would understand, surely, he was sensitive; especially so since what had happened to John Cooper. She sat up, took a deep breath and wiped the tears from her face.

80

NEW YORK CITY

Fox had been back in his office for an hour, sipping at a third cup of coffee to keep alert to the expected news from the GSR team. His desire to be there with them itched at him more than his bandaged arm.

He closed the open file on Kate and put it back on the pile of Advocacy Center personnel.

He sat behind his desk in his thirty-seventh-floor office in the Seagram Building. The blinds were drawn on the floor-to-ceiling windows that looked down onto the plaza. The desk had long disappeared under papers and folders, the lamp providing the only light in his dark office. He leaned back in his Hepplewhite chair, undid his shirt another button and rolled his sleeves up.

He picked up a file from his 'to read' pile.

'The National Security Agency: Quantum Cryptography and the twenty-first century . . .' he said aloud. 'This will be interesting . . .'

81

WASHINGTON

'Welcome back to America, Mr Smith,' the customs woman said, stamping the visa in the English passport of Winston Smith and passing it back.

'Thank you,' Secher said, putting it in his jacket pocket and walking into the main terminal at Dulles. He removed his black-rimmed spectacles as he walked, duffle bag in his other hand. He fished in his pocket for some quarters and placed a call at a payphone.

'You have the helicopter booked?' Secher asked his DGSE agent in New York.

'Yes, I have leased it without pilots, as you instructed,' the agent said. 'I will fly you out to sea tomorrow night myself.'

'Excellent,' Secher said, sensing in the tone that there was something the agent was not telling him.

'What else is there?' Secher asked.

'Major, Lachlan Fox is still here.'

'What?' Secher leaned on the payphone. *This could make things difficult.*

'He did not leave for Greenland, but some others did in his place.'

'Then get rid of him,' Secher said through closed teeth.

'Major?'

'People get shot in America all the time,' Secher said. 'Or make it look like an accident. I don't care.'

'When?'

'As soon as possible. I wanted him out of the picture before and that much has not changed. I do not want him alive by the time I am in New York,' Secher said. A smile crept over his face and he held the handset up to hide it. 'If you can, make it painful.'

82

THE WHITE HOUSE

'There's a procedure in place for this type of threat to intelligence installations and you know it,' McCorkell said over the phone. 'Look, we've still got some issues to work through here this morning, but a friendly heads-up: Vanzet and Larter want blood. Your blood. And on top of your Senate hearing tomorrow, you'll be an easy target to scapegoat all sorts of shit.'

'I appreciate the call, Bill,' Dunn said. 'I had no idea the threat could be something so big. The fucking French of all people.'

'You had no intel come through on this?' McCorkell asked, noting the stack of daily papers that he didn't have the time to go through this morning.

'Nothing that's come up, just an anonymous tip-off about Greenland,' Dunn said. 'I've got a team on the intercepts now, going through everything in or out of France. We're scouring for any leads on this threatened coup too.'

'Well, it's a damn sight more credible now,' McCorkell said. 'We've got twelve dead French commandos on Danish soil, attempting to infiltrate a US base. The remainder surrendered to the Delta team, and the *La Fayette* is heading back to port with her tail between her legs. *Seawolf* is trailing her real close, F-15s buzzing overhead.'

'This wasn't just an act from their chief of navy working alone?' Dunn asked.

'That's yet to come through, but it's looking damn unlikely,' McCorkell said. 'Delta and the French soldiers are being picked up. Turns out there's a DGSE agent among them but he's staying zip. SSB agents are going to put him through the griller to see what his orders were.'

There was silence on the other end until he heard Dunn let out a defeated sigh.

'Look, Ira, with no Delta boys lost, this didn't turn out too bad,' McCorkell said. 'But we should all get together at the Pentagon later in the week and debrief on this one, otherwise the bad blood is going to settle in, from Larter and the DNI down.'

•

Dunn shut his office door and headed downstairs. He took the walkway into the COMINT supercomputer lab. He followed the passageway past the empty workstations, through the biometrically protected vault doors to the new quantum cryptography annex, where the shift workers were calibrating the new Crays with the quantum drives.

'How quickly can we switch over?' he asked of his head technician on the late shift.

'Sir – how quickly? We've never had to speed up before.'

'Well I'd like it sped up,' Dunn said. 'Can it be brought forward?'

'We may be able to shave a few hours off, but that's it. We need the quantum interface to be working in sync with the Crays in order to switch over. If we force it sooner and it doesn't interface, we can't guarantee the security of this network or any other system we're accountable for.'

'All right. Just get it happening as fast as you can,' Dunn said, turning to leave. 'And keep me posted on your progress.'

83

WIESBADEN, GERMANY

The room had one purpose: torture. It was small and dark, the walls and door made of steel and totally soundproofed. One neon light in the ceiling lit up the stainless-steel interior with an eerie blue-white incandescence. The only furniture was a metal chair bolted to the floor.

Strapped tight to the chair was the right-wing German national wanted for selling NATO arms to the Middle East. Except for his head, plastic bindings held every part of him immobile in the chair.

'You can't do this to me!' He spat blood from his split lip. 'You have laws! I have laws!'

The Strategic Services Branch agent was working the inter-rogation alone. He stood before the man, arms crossed. Watched as the German heaved breaths, the floor beneath his chair a pool of urine.

On the floor next to him was a large metal toolbox.

'I don't exist,' the agent said. 'So I really don't think your laws apply to me.'

The expression on the German's face was blank. Gritty. Real. Cold.

'What, you are going to keep me in this bright room for a week? Put a hood on me and take photos for your sick American friends?' The German laughed to reveal his bloodied teeth. 'Do your worst.'

The SSB agent was silent.

'Unfortunately I'm not what you would consider a patient man,' the agent said. He held up a picture of the German's wife and children, taken from the mantel in his house. Showing him had the desired effect, until a last wave of defiance came over him.

'Fuck you!'

Again the SSB agent was silent. He turned the photo to look at them, let himself linger over the image.

'Tell me what you know,' the SSB agent said, putting the photo in his top pocket. 'LeCercle. A coup in France. Sianne Cassel.'

The German's jaw tensed closed, a sure sign he was attempting to hold out for longer. *We'll see how long*, the agent thought, opening the toolbox.

'Every minute from –' he checked his watch '– now,' he said, bringing up a big set of bolt-cutters, 'I will remove one of your fingers.'

'Ha,' the guy answered, spitting out more blood. 'I could fuck you over. Do you know who I am? I have friends every-where. A quarter of the guns in the Middle East are supplied by me. Me! I could have you killed in a second! Your whole fucking family!'

The agent went on unperturbed. 'It stops when you tell me the location and people involved.'

'Fuck you.'

'Whatever. As I said, I'm impatient, so while we're waiting I'm going to cut a finger off.' The agent walked forward, put the open jaws of the heavy cutters on the German's immobile ring finger.

'This first one will be sent to your wife, so that she can see your wedding band forever,' the agent said, smiling. 'A memento.'

The German smiled too, still not giving in to it.

'Bullshit.'

The cold steel bolt-cutters snapped closed. A finger hit the metal floor.

'Arrrrgggggh!!!!!'

'Up to you,' the agent said, checking his watch. As the guy quietened a little, panting, the agent went on. 'This stops when you tell me what you know. A coup in France. Who's involved? What's their location?'

Fifteen minutes later the agent hoisted up the steel door behind the German and dumped his unconscious body out into the dark night. The summer wind blew through the beech forest, the leaves sounding like a million little sails at sea.

In the cabin of the truck he dialled a number on a satellite phone as another agent drove off into the night.

'It's real. Confirmed location is Fort Gaucher, and we have more names.'

84

WASHINGTON

Kate looked at her suitcase on the bed. She had packed and unpacked it four times, and the first tears finally rolled down her cheeks. She sat on the edge of the bed and held her face in her hands, biting her lip and sucking up the emotions.

She stood and wiped the tears from her eyes, taking in a deep breath. She pulled the suitcase onto the floor and pushed her folded clothes into it. There were far too many items, and she dragged the overflowing case into the bottom of her wardrobe and shut it away, the task far too final to do now.

Walking into the en suite, she put the plug in the bath and turned on the taps. Soon, steam filled the room and she climbed in, welcoming the feeling of warm water on her skin. She just couldn't do it. She'd get dressed, go to dinner, and tell him. Yes, she would definitely tell Secher that she needed time, that maybe they should try another way of selling his business rather than her stealing Cooper's NSA access key . . . she should never have told him about it.

She knew why Secher wanted it, and there was an irony in there that doing this would free them both. In that way, she understood why he needed to do it.

Laying back in the bath, she closed her eyes and thought back to when they'd met, trying to pinpoint the time he'd suggested using the key to find a suitable buyer for his business. Strangely, she couldn't remember when or where the conversation had taken place.

85

WASHINGTON

Dunn left Fort Meade and sat in the back of his town car heading home. He'd travelled fifteen minutes before his long-serving driver spoke up.

'Not feeling well, sir?'

'Why do you say that?' Dunn asked. *Did it show?*

'Just that it's mid-afternoon, and I've never known you to leave work before dark,' the driver said.

That was true enough, thought Dunn, as he looked out the window at the school traffic on his way to Annapolis.

'I'm fine,' he said. He stared down at the briefcase on the seat next to him, resting his hand on it. 'I have some things to do from home today. And I'll get you to pick me up late tomorrow. I have to be on the Hill at two o'clock.'

86

THE WHITE HOUSE

The Security Council had assembled in the Situation Room and had finished being debriefed by McCorkell on last night's events. They had been in an almost congratulatory mood, given the way events had unfolded, when the bombshell landed among them.

'The Force Océanique Stratégique . . .' Vanzet repeated as they listened to the French President's words in disbelief.

McCorkell shared a look with Vanzet and Larter that the President picked up on, and he pressed the mute button on the speaker telephone in front of him.

'Gentlemen?' he asked.

'The Strategic Ocean Force is France's fleet of boomers,' McCorkell said. 'Nuclear-powered ballistic-missile subs.'

'A force', said Vanzet, 'of four *Le Triomphant* class SSBNs, each armed with sixteen M51 missiles. That's ninety-six targetable warheads per boat, at over 110 kilotons a pop.'

McCorkell looked the President in the eye.

'Mr President, they have to find that sub, no ifs or buts,' McCorkell said. 'We asked the French President of the status of his navy assets last night, and he flat-out lied.'

The President flicked the mute switch to speak to the French President again.

'Mr President,' he said slowly. 'Do you mean to tell me that you have lost communication with and the location of a ballistic-missile submarine?'

'Correct,' the French President said, audibly shaken by the unfolding events.

'And the rest of the fleet is accounted for?' Vanzet asked.

'Yes. We have confirmation of the other three submarines. One is docked in the Maldives. Two are on the naval exercise in the South Pacific.'

'What was its last known location?' McCorkell asked. The Situation Room in the White House was a tomb of silence. Every pair of eyes at the table stared at the small speaker phones lined out before them.

'The last location was as of nine hours ago, when they received a message from Naval Command,' the French President's voice rang out over the speaker phone. 'Located in the Atlantic Ocean, three hundred kilometres from your coast. Heading west.'

87

ANNAPOLIS, MARYLAND

Dunn shut all the blinds in his study at home and sat behind his desk, flicking on his banker's lamp. He reached into his cupboard under the desk and pulled out a bottle of bourbon, pouring a tumbler full. He had a sip and savoured the taste, that first moment his senses said hello to the familiar liquid.

Leaning up against the wall opposite him sat the framed flag from the *Liberty*. He looked at it, his reflection staring back at him in the glass. He saw an old man with too little left to give. A drive that was diminishing with every day that his job sucked from his body. A life that he'd long ago given up to his country, putting every waking moment into his career. The photos along the picture rail stared down at him from the shadows. He knew the faces that were on them, those young men depicted in black and white posterity, capturing a moment and mood that was indifferent to the fears of the young men in uniform today of the world around them. They had been nation-builders back then, continuing to forge the greatness of the century that was theirs, building upon the generations that had gone before them through two almighty wars. They stood on the shoulders of giants in a time that lent itself to the possibilities of immortality. They'd landed on the moon, for Christ's sake. *Where have we gone since?*

Dunn put down his glass and poured another four fingers. He opened his drawer and considered a cigar. He pondered over the humidor, looking without noticing. He removed a parcel and put it on the leather-topped desk. He unwrapped the white handkerchief to reveal a Colt service automatic. The weight of it felt good in his hand, and he remembered his dad teaching him to shoot that summer so long ago in the White Mountains of Arizona.

He drained his glass and looked again at the flag, staring into the burned and tattered stars and stripes . . .

8 June 1967

Lieutenant Ira Dunn laid on the aft platform of the Liberty *soaking up the Mediterranean sun.*

'Pass me the half-inch,' Dunn said.

Boatswain's Mate Greg Clarke did so, staring up at the twelve-foot moonbounce dish.

'How's this thing work, sir?' Clarke asked in his own slow southern fashion.

'It's – what's that?' Dunn sat up, and looked out to sea on the portside. Three big torpedo boats were closing in fast on their unarmed American vessel. Instinctively, he looked up to

be sure the American ensign was flying at full mast. It was, and he knew they were well inside international waters.

'It's okay, looks like the Israelis,' Clarke said. He waved in their direction.

Dunn didn't hear anything, but felt the young sailor's blood splatter across his face as his head exploded. He didn't flinch as he watched the torpedoes streaking in at them. He couldn't hear or do anything.

88

WASHINGTON

Secher and Kate sat at a secluded table in the Citronelle restaurant in Georgetown. It was packed, the second sitting for the evening picking up the late working crowd of mainly political powerbrokers. Kate could not decide on what to order, so Secher ordered them a full degustation menu, and their second entrée arrived, a soft-shelled crab with accompanying champagne.

'I like your hair,' Kate said, taking a sip of Veuve Clicquot. 'Dark hair suits you.'

Secher touched his hair, a bit of feigned self-consciousness.

'How do you Americans say? A change is as good as a holiday?' Secher said with a smile, and he noticed she tensed her shoulders, traded looking at him to staring at her glass. He took a sip of his champagne as he watched her mind ticking over. He could see the conflict in her as clearly as he read all her emotions. Secher leaned across the table and took her hand in his, noting her palm was sweaty. She was vulnerable. Pliable. He felt her pulse quicken.

'I know you have been through a lot this week,' Secher said. He gave her his fawning look. 'I'm sorry I haven't been there for you. But that will change. From tomorrow night, I will always be there for you.'

She softened a little. Her hand relaxed. Pulse settled.

'We are going to have a beautiful life, you and I,' Secher said, topping up their glasses. 'We are going to sail the world, we're going to get away from everything that controls us and live our own lives. Isn't that what you want?'

She had tears in her eyes, which she wiped away with her other hand. She sniffled, nodded.

He wiped another tear off her cheek. Smiled warmly, held his hand on the side of her face and turned her gaze up to face his.

'What is it?' Secher asked.

Kate couldn't look him in the eyes. 'My parents . . .'

'You'll see them again soon enough, we don't have to be away forever,' he said as endearingly as possible. 'You are the one who said you wanted to get away for a while, remember?'

'My apartment . . .' she said, nodding her head in thought of all that she would be leaving behind. Secher could see that it was more than just real estate binding her here.

'Sell it. Rent it out, whatever,' he said. 'We'll organise it when we land in Malta, before we set sail. We will have the money to make these problems go away. If you ever want to visit home, just jump on a plane.'

Kate continued to stare at her glass, watching the bubbles as they rose and popped on the surface, escaping into the air.

'My work . . .' she said. 'I don't know if –'

'Kate. Twenty million Euros,' Secher said, the number putting a gleam in his eye. 'That is how much I can sell my business for, if only you can get access to that key you have spoken about.'

Kate had a sip of champagne, scratching her neck.

'You will pick up the key tomorrow as planned,' Secher said. 'We will use it, find a buyer who's willing to pay the right price, and hey presto – we put the business in their laps and take the money. Everyone wins.'

'I've been thinking –' Kate stopped mid-sentence. Looked down at the large envelope Secher put on the table in front of her.

'What's this?' she asked, a smile forming. Secher had surprised her with something the last time they'd met, a map with highlighted locations dotted around the Mediterranean where they would sail, brochures for diving in French Polynesia, a cabin over the water they'd rent in the Maldives.

'Take a look. Perhaps this is your hesitation?' Secher said, taking another sip as Kate opened the envelope and removed a stack of paper and photographs.

She stared wide-eyed, dropping the file on her side plate in shock. She looked up at Secher and caught a glimpse of iciness in his eyes before he turned on a calming presence. He reached an arm across the table and again took her hand in his.

'Kate, my dear. Those photos of you with that man, Lachlan Fox.'

'I – I can explain,' Kate said, her hand tense in his. Pulse almost too fast to count.

'There's no need, it is me who needs to explain,' Secher said, having a sip of champagne for dramatic effect. He watched as her eyes fell on the photos of her entering her parents' building with Fox on that first day back in New York.

'Kate, after that terrible attack on you in St Petersburg, I have worried about you, your safety,' Secher said as he stared into her eyes. 'As I cannot yet be by your side, I hired a security firm in New York to watch you, to protect you from a distance.'

Kate turned her head slightly to the side, as she did when she was considering new information.

'In the process of their job, they investigated this man.' Secher tapped the photo of Fox with his arm on Kate's back, leading her into her parents' building. 'He is investigating the Advocacy Center. He is investigating you.'

Kate looked at the photos. Flicked them aside, started skimming the biographical info. A look of puzzlement appeared on her face as she turned the pages.

'You must know he was in St Petersburg to investigate John Cooper,' Secher said, drawing her into conversation.

'Yes, yes, I know that,' she replied, frowning as she read the pages in front of her.

'You can see he has a military background. The thing is, he never left that job. Just changed countries, changed roles. He works for the US government, and it seems he may have had prior knowledge of the attack on Cooper,' Secher said. He held her hand a little tighter so that she looked up into his eyes.

'Kate, my darling, that man works for the CIA,' Secher said smoothly. 'They are in a power play to gain control of the Advocacy Center.'

Secher could see his lie was being taken in.

'Lachlan Fox is a spy. I'm sorry, but he is using you . . .'

89

NEW YORK CITY

It was late and Fox was still in his office at GSR, elbow-deep in research. Without looking up he noticed someone enter. He knew it was Faith, knew her gait, her sound, her smell. She quietly shut the door behind her. He was deep in research, files everywhere, background on everyone and everything involved with Cassel.

'Team's in the air from Greenland, it'll take them about twenty hours to get back, stopping over in Canada to cover their flight plans,' Faith said.

'Okay, thanks,' Fox answered. He read the open file in front of him but felt himself being distracted, right when he didn't want it.

Faith walked up to his desk.

'You missed your session with the psych today,' she said. He could feel her watching him read. Could smell her perfume, freshly sprayed.

'Huh?' Fox was deep in thought, pen in mouth.

'Dr Bender, she booked you an extra session at twelve o'clock today, she was quite worried . . .'

'Oh. Funny thing,' Fox said. 'I kinda feel better about things now. Been sleeping easier.'

'What, you're fixed all of a sudden?' Faith sat on the corner of his desk, her pencil skirt sliding up her long, crossed legs revealing through the split the pale skin above her stockings. 'I don't have a doctorate in psychology, but I don't think post-traumatic stress disorder ups and leaves overnight.'

Fox didn't answer but he knew he had lost in his battle of wills to ignore her.

'What is it – perhaps this woman you're seeing?' Faith asked.

Fox looked up at her, the long legs on his desk. It was late, near midnight, and her shirt buttons were undone low. She'd done that before entering his office. A new coat of lipstick flashed bright red, matching her locks of hair falling over her shoulders.

'She's sweetened your dreams?'

Fox looked away. Faith put a hand on his face, turned it towards her.

'You know I would have done that for you a long time ago,' she said. 'You know my door's always open.'

Again, Fox didn't respond. He turned back to the file.

'You're like the *Times* cryptic sometimes,' Faith said through a smile.

'You're like someone with an obsession with *Sex and the City*,' Fox replied. Again he looked at her. She cocked her eyebrow, as if asking, *Really?*

'The way you talk, dress, act,' Fox said, smiling. 'Admit it, you want to be Carrie Bradshaw.'

'I'd rather be Samantha,' Faith said. 'And I guess you think you're Aidan?'

'Probably more Berger,' Fox said.

'The novelist character? Broke up with a Post-it note? Ouch.' She gave him a mock-evil stare. 'Have you eaten? Why don't we go get some dinner?'

'At this hour?'

'This city never sleeps,' Faith said. 'Seems neither do we.'

'I really have to get moving with this,' Fox insisted. 'Things are coming to a head, there are too many events happening at quicker intervals.'

'Tell me about it over dinner,' she replied.

'I can't go out for dinner when Al and the security team are somewhere in the air,' Fox said. 'This investigation I'm working on is unfolding to become a radical power shift in Europe, I've got the Feds watching me . . .'

'Well then, tell me about it over breakfast,' Faith said, running her manicure up his long, tanned arm.

Fox looked at her. He was conflicted. She was attractive, smart, fun to be around, but the situation was just far too complicated. And too close to home. For both him and Faith it was too easy but didn't mean enough.

Faith saw the hesitation in her eyes. She got up, pushed his chair back and hitched her skirt up, opening her legs and sitting on his lap, then pulled him in by the collar and kissed his mouth. He sat there, compliant but not responding, letting her run her hands through his hair as she kissed his face and neck, licking at his day's stubble along his jaw line.

After a few minutes she sat back a little, undid her shirt and flung it over her head. Her lacy La Perla bra was full in Fox's face as she unzipped her skirt and stood, pushing it to the floor. She was naked but for her bra and suspenders and stockings. In the few times Fox and Faith had done this, it had always been the same: him working late in his office, her coming in. She sat on his desk, and leaned back on her elbows. She pulled Fox to her by her feet through the arms of his chair.

Fox rubbed his hands down her legs, and kissed her chest.

'You know this can't go anywhere,' he said.

'Yet we keep coming back for more,' Faith replied, pulling him up to her and unbuckling his belt.

90

THE WHITE HOUSE

McCorkell again pressed the mute button on the phone to the French President.

'There's no need for them to come anywhere near our coast to launch,' Vanzet said.

'That's right, Mr President,' McCorkell agreed, nodding along with Vanzet.

'What do you mean?' the President asked. He took off his reading glasses and pinched the tension away from the bridge of his nose.

'The missiles are intercontinental, Mr President, they could reach us from their homeports in France,' McCorkell said. 'Ballistic-missile subs do have another quality, though.'

'They're silent,' Vanzet said, adding to McCorkell's hypothesis.

'Wait, you think the French are quietly setting off some personnel on our eastern seaboard?' Larter asked. The Secretary of Defense was shaking his head in disapproval of this line of thought. 'Too far-fetched, too much work for something that could be done quicker via small aircraft or ocean vessel.'

'Ex parte Quirin,' McCorkell said, still looking at Vanzet. The highest-ranking officer of the DoD got it, he could tell.

'Gitmo?' Larter said.

McCorkell received a crooked smile from Vanzet.

'Wait, what the hell has Guantanamo Bay got to do with this sub – they headed down there?' the President cut in.

'Ex parte Quirin refers to the Supreme Court case back in 1942 that sentenced German combatants to death,' Vanzet said. 'It's the precedent used today for Gitmo detention and trial of suspected terrorists.'

'And a precedent in incurring our shores via submarine,' McCorkell said. 'German agents were deployed via two subs back in '42, coming ashore at Long Island and a beach in Florida. It's been done before and it looks like it will be happening again. Modern boomers – hell, particularly these nuclear-powered French subs – are practically undetectable. Quieter than the sea around them. It could be a drop-off, it could be a pick-up. Either way, Mr President, we have to take this to the next level.'

McCorkell and Vanzet shared a look.

'Mr President,' Vanzet said. 'I recommend that we go to DEFCON Three, sir.'

'And get you to a secure location ASAP,' McCorkell added. 'Bill –'

'Mr President, let's have this conversation in the air,' Fullop put in, standing up. The President was steadfast.

'Mr President, France is the world's third-biggest nuclear power,' McCorkell said. 'We know there's a renegade nuclear sub headed for our shores. We have had confirmation that all their naval assets are loaded with a full suite of arms at the moment, meaning nukes as well. Going to DEFCON Three will authorise naval and air combat, and we'll continue this conversation on Air Force One.'

'Mr President, I suggest we at least move the eastern seaboard to DEFCON Three,' Larter said.

'We've established there is no reason for the sub to come to our shores but to pick up or drop off agents,' McCorkell added.

'It could well be deploying a *biological agent*,' Larter suggested. 'Some kind of WMD, like a chemical attack in the water supply.'

'Okay then, we go to DEFCON Three in the European theatre, and here at home we step up the Homeland Security threat level from Orange to Red along the entire eastern seaboard,' McCorkell said. 'Every Coast Guard vessel is activated. This will give us flexibility in Europe without having to militarise things within the US. We go to DEFCON Three worldwide and everybody gets spooked, which may be enough for some crazy people to do crazy things. Things that aren't even on our threat board yet.'

'Or a mad Frenchman with jittery nerves taking that step too far. I agree with Bill, Mr President,' Vanzet said. 'It means we can get some strike power in the air to act if we need it. Lock and load some B2s out of Britain and have our European air force ready to play.'

An army major stood in the corner of the room, a slim case containing the nation's nuclear launch codes cabled to his wrist.

He stood more to attention than McCorkell had ever seen him. DEFCON Three in Europe would see dummy warheads replaced with live nuclear warheads.

'Bill – we have the French President on an instant com link here –'

'A president who has not had credible command authority over his armed services for twenty-four hours now – maybe even longer. Announcing DEFCON Three in Europe will wake up the world and show everyone in that theatre not to mess with us right now.' McCorkell looked to the Chief of Staff, who nodded, and then turned to the President's Secret Service detail chief, a man who had held his sleeve-mike to his mouth ever since he'd heard the content of the current conversation.

'Do it,' the President said.

Vanzet turned to the aides and barked orders to get things moving fast.

McCorkell motioned to the Chief of Staff, a man he genuinely loved to hate. He got the look.

'We're going to Air Force One and I want you to crash the White House once we're out,' Fullop said to the Secret Service detail chief.

'Code Black, Code Black. The Family and the Lakers are moving to Air Force One!' the detail chief said over his sleeve-mike. The coded talk meant that the President's full complement of serviceable helicopters from the HMX-1 Nighthawk Squadron would be heading in from the Marine One fleet at Quantico, landing in synchronised formation on the South Lawn for a full evacuation of senior staff – the 'Lakers' – and the first family from the Residence. Air Force One would be rolling from the hangar, fully stocked and fuelled, waiting with engines running for fast take-off from Andrews Air Force Base on their arrival.

'Now listen here,' the President said, standing. 'I'm happy for you to move my family, but –'

The detail chief and another Secret Service agent each took an arm and whisked the President from the room, his feet barely touching the ground. The senior staff and the joint chiefs followed, the aides at their heels.

91

WASHINGTON

Outside the restaurant, Secher passed the valet a tip and followed Kate into the back seat of a cab.

'Where to?' the driver said.

'Your place or mine?' Secher asked, squeezing Kate's hand.

92

NEW YORK CITY

'See you in the morning,' Fox said, closing the cab door and waving goodbye to Faith.

He walked off East 51st and headed back up Lexington Avenue, having had to walk a block to find a cab in the rank outside the subway station.

The streets were busy, despite it being after midnight, and he ran across the street between the intersection at East 52nd –

A car horn blared beside him.

'What?!' Fox yelled. He knew his path had been clear – and he turned to look as the honking cab went past him – but he wasn't honking at Fox, he was honking at a black Suburban SUV that had followed him through the red light and was ten metres away, engine roaring –

Fox sprinted past a news-stand, then turned to a building with big exposed columns the Suburban jumped the kerb, taking out a postbox and street sign with an explosion of the radiator. The news-stand was smashed backwards, its vendor screaming as he toppled into the street and magazines and papers went flying about.

Screams came from the sidewalk as Fox flew through the air, the remaining distance covered as he slid across the paved foyer. The three tonne Suburban came to a shattering halt as it wrapped its front end around the marble-encased column, the ground-level glass doors and windows of the building shattering from the force and showering down onto Fox.

He covered his face with his arms as the safety glass rained down, the noise pierced by the deafening sound of a nine-millimetre pistol firing four shots at close range.

PART THREE

93

AIR FORCE ONE

Vanzet hung up the phone to the Pentagon, turned around in the small Air Force One version of the Situation Room, and made a gesture to talk over the speaker phone. The President nodded.

'Mr President,' Vanzet said to the French President over the speaker phone. 'I have a report from my intelligence people. Sianne Cassel is confirmed as the leader of a planned right-wing coup d'état. Running the show out of your military base, Fort Gaucher.'

'I don't know of any military base there,' the French President said – a little too quickly to be convincing, McCorkell thought.

'Mr President, it's a military fallback command base in the Mont Blanc region,' McCorkell said. 'And operated year-round by your DGSE as a satellite relay station.'

'We have a list of names coming through of members of the coup,' Vanzet added.

He passed over a print-out of names. McCorkell scanned it and then passed it on to Boxcell and the President.

'Mr President, we are sending you this list now,' McCorkell said. 'You should note that while it lists some of your high-ranking officials and members of the defence community, such as your departed chief of navy, the list is not exhaustive.'

'We need to roll everything we have to safeguard our nationals,' Baker said, turning to Vanzet to organise their military assets in the area.

'You may not be in a position to know who to trust,' the President said over the speaker phone, reading through the list himself. 'While I offer my support to you, you must understand that I cannot send my military in to support you in what may be a bloodless internal political matter.'

'I understand,' the French President said.

The silence in the cabin was met by silence over the phone line to Paris.

'This list,' the French President said, reading through the names. 'My God, how can this be? I have known some of these people . . .'

'Mr President,' McCorkell said, leaning forward to speak on the speaker phone. 'Who is in your office with you right now?'

'The Prime Minister and Minister for Defence,' the French President replied absently.

'That's all?'

'Yes,' he affirmed. 'I will alert our national police force to arrest Sianne Cassel and these others,' he said. 'Outside of them, I do not think that I can call on the military to respond to Fort Gaucher. I wonder if I may be so bold as to ask for your help.'

'Wouldn't be the first time,' the President said quietly to those in Air Force One. 'What have we got in the region that we can use?'

'The Brits' 22nd SAS Regiment is tasked with a counter-terrorism and high-intensity support role with Europol,' McCorkell said. 'Legally, they can enter into this situation under the request of the French Government. Beyond that, unless we have a clear threat to our national security emanating from Fort Gaucher, we cannot make a pre-emptive strike.'

'Did you hear that, Mr President?' the President asked.

94

HEREFORD, ENGLAND

Major William Farrell, DCM, of the British 22nd Special Air Service Regiment, looked over his troopers as they strapped in. Satisfied, he gave the thumbs-up to the pilots in the cockpit.

On board the Hercules aircraft, thirty-two heavily armed SAS soldiers were buckling in as it taxied towards the runway. They were from A Sabre Squadron, grouped into two separate sixteen-man troops. Air Troop, and Mountain Troop.

He would have liked more shooters on this trip but the other half of A Sabre was in Afghanistan, while B Sabre was spread thin throughout Iraq. C Sabre was stuck in the UK, playing the counter-terrorism role.

They wore snow fatigues, many with their variants of M4 rifles fitted with white and grey coverings. Farrell himself was using an SR-47, something he'd fallen in love with in Afghanistan. Specifically developed for the allied special forces for use in

Afghanistan and Iraq, it looked like an M4, but was built for the bigger 7.62 mm round. The real kicker was that it could use AK-47 magazines, meaning you could use your enemy's ammunition.

None of the troops asked what they were about to head into, and only two men in the cargo area knew their destination and mission. He'd prep his troops soon enough, he wanted them to get locked, loaded and in the zone first. Not that a hot incursion into France would put a dampener on this lot.

Farrell turned to his trusted second-in-command.

'Jenkins, we're off to kick some Frenchy arse. Up to it?' Farrell said.

Warrant Officer Jenkins almost had tears in his eyes. His delivery was worthy of any Old Vic performance:

'It's what I was born to do, sir.'

95

NEW YORK CITY

Hutchinson looked around Fox's office before leaving, and put the empty coffee cup on a desk that was bathed in morning sunlight.

'Well, Capel's a damn good shot,' Fox said. 'I owe that man more than a few beers.'

'Should be in the Secret Service, but his heart's too far in the right place,' Hutchinson said. 'He'll be back on the streets tomorrow. The Bureau normally desks agents for a couple of weeks after successfully using their sidearm but I got some pull.'

Fox walked him to the GSR thirty-seventh-floor lift.

'I'll make sure I pop out front and thank him,' Fox said.

'He'd probably rather you stayed in the building,' Hutchinson replied, getting in the elevator and pressing the lobby button. 'I'll let you know what we find at the French Consulate. Heading over there this morning.'

•

'No way!' Goldsmith said.

In the security room, Pepper was updating Goldsmith on the events of the previous night.

'Way,' Fox said as he entered.

'Here's the man,' Pepper said on seeing Fox. He got up out of his chair with a sigh and slapped Goldsmith on the arm. 'Don't let him out of your sight, he's like a magnet for trouble.'

'Thanks Doug, you're all heart,' Fox said as the big guy tiredly walked off and gave the bird over his shoulder.

'Ready to try the team?' Goldsmith asked. Fox nodded and sat next to him at the radio controls. They got through on the third call.

'Copy that, Seagram. We'll be taking off from Canada as soon as the gale-force wind cuts back,' Gammaldi said. 'Should be in two hours if the satellite weather feed is good.'

'Come on, Al, you can fly in anything,' Fox said. 'Anyway, I'll meet you guys at the airport. I'm trying to track someone down, and hopefully by then I'll have a location so we can refuel and take off straightaway.'

'Oh, more travel into a dangerous area I hope,' Gammaldi said, his voice crackling over the satellite phone from the winds belting down on the small air station they were at.

'Shouldn't be too bad,' Fox said. 'I think you've missed the worst of it on this adventure.'

'Speak for yourself,' Gammaldi replied. 'I've been locked in a snow-covered spy base with a couple of pot-smoking nutters while two sets of commandos tried to kill everyone in sight.'

Fox smiled. 'Yeah, well you should try hailing a cab on East 51st.'

96

WASHINGTON

Secher watched from his sleeping position as Kate walked into the bathroom, her naked body silhouetted behind the frosted-glass shower screen. Once he heard the water running he rolled over on his side, the sun blazing through the bedroom window into his face.

He leaned over the side of the bed and got the cell phone out of his trouser pocket. He'd switched it to silent last night. One message.

Listening, he went out of the bedroom to the kitchen, and made a call to the intelligence attaché at the French Consulate in New York.

'Your man was killed, Major,' the consular official said. 'Apparently he was shot by the FBI last night while –'

'Do you have access to his office?' Secher asked.

'Yes, Major, I am in here now,' he said. 'The FBI said they would be back today with a warr –'

'I want you to find the file on Lachlan Fox and fax it through to me at my hotel right now,' he said, checking his watch. 'And then destroy that file straightaway.'

Secher hung up the call and turned back to the bedroom, Kate walking out with nothing but a towel wrapped around her wet hair.

'I was going to come back into bed,' she said.

'Sorry, my sweet, something has come up,' Secher replied. 'I have some business to take care of here. Can I meet you in New York this evening?'

'Okay,' she said.

Secher walked up to her and took her hands in his.

'You'll be okay with this today, won't you?' he asked.

She nodded.

'Just think. This business today will be the last thing I have to do before I sell out,' Secher said, smiling at the layered truth behind that line. 'I'll meet you in New York later today. Then, our lives start again. No worries, no pressures.'

Kate nodded, and he kissed her on the cheek.

'Do you have time for breakfast?' she asked.

'No,' he told her, buttoning up his creased shirt from the bedroom floor. 'I must get moving.'

'Okay, I'll leave with you,' Kate said, moving into her wardrobe and getting dressed.

'Listen, I have a private jet booked for a four o'clock departure, leaving out of Dulles,' Secher said, buckling his belt. 'You take it, as it's already paid for. I'll pick you up at your parents' around eight.'

'A private jet?' Kate said. 'Sounds like you're spending all the proceeds of your business sale before it's even sold. Leaving nothing for us . . .'

Secher recognised the humour in her tone and smiled along with her.

•

They walked out of the door ten minutes later. Kate looked around her apartment for one last time. She was not coming back in here, ever.

She closed the door behind her, rattling the knob as she always did to make sure it was locked, and the sound of the phone rang through the door. Kate looked to Secher and he checked his watch.

'Get it if you want, I'm leaving.' He kissed her on the lips.

'No, it's okay,' she said, and hand-in-hand they walked down the hallway.

97

NEW YORK CITY

In his office at GSR, Fox hung up the phone, deciding against leaving another message for Kate. It rang as soon as it was down in the cradle.

'Lachlan Fox.'

'Fox, Andrew Hutchinson,' he said. 'I'm over here at the French Consulate, just stopped a consular secretary from incinerating some files.'

'Yeah . . .'

'Sit down for a sec,' Hutchinson said. He spoke for five minutes, telling Fox of the contents of the file, the surveillance notes, Kate. And love interest, a Christian Secher.

'What does it say about Christian Secher?' Fox asked. He wrote down the name.

'Nothing other than a note of his name. Who is he?'

'Kate's boyfriend, I guess,' Fox said.

'Wait, there's more.' Hutchinson was silent on the phone for a while then came back. 'Seems your friend Secher is due to come to New York at some stage today.'

'Would you get copies of all this to me? A fresh pair of eyes might see something you don't,' Fox requested. 'My file say much about Kate?'

'Fair enough, I'll get them over. And nope, I just read you everything in yours,' Hutchinson said. 'Kate Matthews, on the other hand, has a file all of her own. Much thicker than yours.'

'What?'

•

Five minutes later, Fox leaned into the open doorway of Faith's office, and knocked hard on the frame.

'What the hell happened to you?' she asked.

'This?' Fox looked at his reflection in the glass case of a framed print. The left side of his face was grazed and gauzed. 'Rough night. Look, I need you to check some flight details for me.'

'For?'

'Kate Matthews.'

'The other woman,' Faith said. 'Okay, give me five.'

98

US ATLANTIC COAST

The US Coast Guard was on full alert, every vessel afloat that had a sonar tasked with trawling for submarine activity in an operation that eclipsed any Homeland Security exercise ever performed.

The cutter *Tampa* was sailing along the territorial water line, twenty-two kilometres east of New York City. For four hours she had been doing a search grid back and forth, her helicopter dipping active sonars into the water at random positions. For her part, *Tampa* launched passive sonar pods into the water along a grid. Usually tasked with picking up drug runners on fast boats, the sonobuoys formed a giant net. If it made noise, they'd find it.

Trouble was, the target they had been given the heads-up to look for wasn't going to be making any noise.

In the Combat Information Center, the officer on watch came over to check his chief sonarman's assessment. Again the noise came over the speakers. Between them, he and the chief had over forty years at sea. And having done many ASW training exercises with the navy, they knew what a nuclear-powered submarine sounded like. But not particularly one driven by pump-jet propulsion.

'That's a surface vessel,' he said. 'Cavitations are far too small.'

'Well damn if we're going to find an undetectable submarine using just passive sonar.'

'What, are you thinking to catch them with reverberation from active sonobuoys?'

'Close,' the chief said with a smile. 'We know these waters better than anyone. The helo's already set up the grid, how about we switch it all over to active and set it up as a net grid.'

'Picking up anomalies in the seafloor on the screen,' the officer said, going along with the idea.

'We'll get an echo sounding of the sub if it's down there,' the chief said. 'We know this seafloor.'

'Just like fishing.'

99

NEW YORK CITY

Fox entered his office to find copies of the files sent over by Hutchinson. He closed the door, switched on a pot of coffee in the small kitchenette cupboard, and flicked on some background music.

This file on Kate was far different to her personnel file from the Advocacy Center. It included a full report of her arrest, including a note that the federal prosecutor had pardoned her. No mention of the deal she cut, however. He flipped to the last pages, which were the up-to-date references.

The murder of Cooper was noted there, and he flipped to the last entry and worked backwards through the pages. His affair with Kate was there, complete with some photos of them on his houseboat. Their arrival in New York. St Petersburg. Another page, and Fox froze. It was the note on her lover,

Christian Secher, along with a photo of the pair together at a Washington café dated almost month ago.

The report was prefaced with the directive coming from a General Danton of the French intelligence service, the DGSE. Seems they had an interest in this man. But the caption was what made Fox freeze.

'Kate Matthews at café in Georgetown, Washington DC, with Major Christian Secher, DGSE case officer.'

For a moment Fox's world spun. He leaned up against a wall in his office, thinking hard.

Christian Secher. Kate's boyfriend. Works for French intelligence!

Kate Matthews. Works for the Advocacy Center . . .

'. . . he's Swiss . . .' she had said. She didn't know.

Or, did she?

'. . . about to sell his business . . . we're going to sail the world . . .'

She was in Washington now. About to leave, with him. She was using Advocacy Center information to help him.

'. . . that most powerful of weapons . . .' Lopin had said. 'Information.'

Information!

Kate might be about to use the Advocacy Center's information to start a new life, but she might not realise that she was playing a part in something so big.

The photo of Secher on Fox's desk triggered something. He flicked through some folders on his desk and stopped. What was it he was looking for? Seeing the photo of Secher upside-down generated a familiar image. A black and white photo that was seared in his mind. On a list of suspected and known

DGSE agents, he flipped through some pages and stopped. The third photo down was of a Swiss national, and although it was a passport-quality photo dated 1984, there was no mistaking the image. The three lines of information on the man stated:

'Alain Turenge, a known Swiss alias. This man is wanted in connection to the Rainbow Warrior *attack of 1985. Suspected as a French NOC agent working for DGSE.'*

There was no mistaking the face. Sure, twenty years younger, but it was him. Another shot showed the face of a known French agent exiting a car in Paris, dated January 1987, as hunted down by a New Zealand investigative journalist working on the case. Secher was standing by the man's side.

Alain Turenge *was* Christian Secher. A major in the DGSE.

Fox grabbed at the phone on his desk and dialled a number he'd written on a Post-it note by his computer. In five rings it was answered.

'Colonel, it's Lachlan Fox,' he said urgently.

'Lachlan,' Dunn said over his cell phone. 'I'm glad you called. Those transcripts you gave me were fakes. Good ones, looked like ours, but fakes.'

'What? Look, I've got something for you, and I'd like to be kept in the loop in return,' Fox said.

'Lachlan, you know I can't let you in on –'

'Your COMINT infrastructure may be under attack,' Fox said. 'I don't know how, but the attack at the Greenland base was part of it.'

'How do you know –?'

'There's a French agent working a person inside the Advocacy

Center,' Fox said. 'I'll give you a name and an alias, you'll need to check if he's come into the country.'

'French agent?'

'His cohort tried to kill me last night,' Fox said.

'Where's he now?'

'Dead.'

'Look, Lachlan, what is this weakness at the Advocacy Center? This part of your Cooper murder conspiracy thing? What do you think the target is, economic?'

'This is part of a planned coup d'état in France, and that's just the beginning,' Fox said. 'The target is information.'

'Yes, but what information?'

'Total. All of it,' Fox said, sitting on the edge of his desk. 'Is there a means for gaining access to the COMINT programs of NSA via the Advocacy Center?'

'No, we only provide them with the relevant economic info,' Dunn replied. 'And none of it is raw transcripts.'

'So Cooper's access was limited?' Fox asked.

'Yes, it was . . .' Dunn trailed off.

'There's no way for an Advocacy Center staffer to access inside the NSA?' Fox waited a while for Dunn to reply. 'Hello?'

•

Dunn hung up on Fox and looked at himself in the rear-view mirror of the car. He was as white as a ghost.

'Driver, the Advocacy Center, fast,' Dunn ordered.

'I might not be able to get you to the Hill on time,' the driver said as he did a U-turn in the street and powered off in the direction of the Center.

'You just let me worry about that,' Dunn said.

100

WASHINGTON

Kate walked onto the executive floor of the Advocacy Center, holding her handbag close and her head down with guilt. It was later in the morning than she had planned on coming in, the floor filled with staff that she didn't have the wherewithal to face. They all wanted to lend their support, to show how much they cared for her, that they were there if she needed them. She knew she should have shared in their conversations of condolences as they too were suffering from the loss of Cooper, but her mind had moved far too many paces beyond such action. She had an official purpose here this morning, signing her leave forms for the Deputy Director and clearing out her office. Her hands shook and the thought that she looked suspicious made her stomach spin.

In her office she went to her desk, rifled through the drawers and packed a few personal items into a file box. Some photos

372 • JAMES PHELAN

lined a picture rail along one wall and she packed them too, even the business ones. She had no intention of ever displaying them again, not even the one taken with her parents on her graduation day from Harvard. From her wall she took her degree certificates and awards, placing them on top of the box and putting the lid on. She was surprised that it was all packed so quickly.

She took a deep breath, looked about the room, and left – only this time through a side door.

Cooper's office immediately felt wrong. All the blinds were shut, a state she'd never seen it in, giving it a cave-like appearance. It was cold too, as if he'd left his zoned air-conditioning on its coldest setting. Her back, neck and face were wet with sweat. Her shoulders and hands tensed.

She took a breath and walked into the room, not exhaling until she had placed her box and handbag on the desk and partially opened the blinds. The horizontal light coming through the timber blinds hinted at life in this room that felt so dead.

Kate blew out her breath and was sure she saw it fog in the sunlight. She took in another deep one, waiting to let her nerves settle. She closed her eyes, and went over in her mind the location of Cooper's safe, his combination that he'd had her memorise due to his terrible memory with numbers. She exchanged breaths, her hands started to steady –

'Kate?'

The voice nearly made her jump out of her skin. She heard herself give a little squeal, the involuntary noise in turn surprising the speaker.

She turned around to see the Assistant Director at the main door to the office.

'Oh, hi, Fiona,' she said. She wiped the back of her hand across her sweaty brow in an attempt to regain some composure. Dried her sweaty palms down her dress as if smoothing out the crinkles.

'You okay?' the Assistant Director asked. She took a couple of steps inside the office and reached for the light switch.

'Fiona – do you mind if I just stay in here for a while, with the lights off?' Kate said.

Fiona stopped short of switching the lights on and stared at Kate for a few seconds before replying.

'Of course,' she answered, moving back out the door. 'I'll be in my office when you're ready, come and see me before you leave.'

'Thanks,' Kate replied. She watched Fiona close the door and felt her heart start to steady again. She moved to the desk, resting her hands on it to support herself. Her heart still pumped fast, her breaths shallow and short. She allowed herself a couple of minutes to settle, then walked around behind the big mahogany desk and opened a false panel under the side drawers.

She entered the combination in the electronic keypad and pressed her thumb on the biometric scanner. The thick door hissed open and she took out a small plastic box.

101

WASHINGTON

Dunn walked into the foyer of the Department of Commerce building that housed the Advocacy Center, straight through the metal detectors that alarmed as he went through. None of the guards would stop a full marine colonel in dress uniform. He waited for the elevator and stepped forward as it chimed, and a woman bumped into him as she rushed to exit, nearly spilling her file box in the process. He pressed the third floor button and rubbed the sweat from his hands as he rode alone in the lift.

Two minutes later he was at the Assistant Director's office.

'I'm sorry, Colonel, I don't have the combinations to John Cooper's safe,' she said, shocked at seeing the military leader of her department in the building.

'Get security to reset it, now,' Dunn said. He couldn't bring himself to wait the time out in Cooper's office, so he paced the hallway.

Twenty minutes later Dunn was back in his car, the driver flooring it up Constitution Avenue.

He sat there, slumped in the leather seat, stunned. While the key was not there in the safe, it could well be at Cooper's house. He'd organise a black-ops team to go in there tonight and sweep for it. How could he have overlooked that? After all, only he and John had one of these access keys.

He looked out of the window as the treasury building flashed by, not registering the sight . . .

8 June 1967

The General Quarters call blasted the air about the Liberty. *Still, Dunn felt himself stuck to the aft deck, unable to move.*

Three Dassault Mirage IIICs came from the direction of the sun, directly at him, in perfect attack formation.

Streams of bullets zapped into the sea broadside to the Liberty *and traced up and over the hull like lasers. Designed to penetrate tank armour, the cannon-fire from the Mirage fighters sank through the skin of the* Liberty *as though the old ship were made of cardboard.*

Dunn was blown high into the air as a line of tracers ripped up the middle of the dish behind him. The explosion was like a firecracker in a can, sending him clear over the railing to the main gangway below. Landing face-down, chest ablaze as several ribs cracked, his cheek came to rest on a red-hot bullet scar in the deck. The blistering pain jerked him to his senses. He could hear everything, smell the fires and burned flesh, see the gore.

376 · JAMES PHELAN

Instinctively jerking away from the pain, Dunn staggered to his feet and stepped over a dying crew member lying in a hatchway, the man looking wide-eyed at his own intestines strewn along the deck.

Inside the ship was chaos as Dunn charged toward the aft NSA spaces he was assigned to. There, intercept operators were shredding classified documents, smashing sensitive equipment and loading codebooks and intercepted voice tapes into 'Ditch Bags'. Made of heavy canvas and measuring five feet high, the bags were designed to take sensitive material to the bottom of the sea and out of other partys' hands. They had lead weights in the bottom and brass eyelets at points all around to allow water to pour in. They were designed to sink, and sink fast.

Grabbing the first of the loaded bags – there would be almost two dozen to be filled – Dunn dragged it from the room and up the stairs. It took every ounce of strength, and his chest protested with pain at every step.

Sparks flew throughout the ship as the tracers punctured the hull, burrowing through anything in their path until they hit structural steel, or passed out the other side of the vessel. The sound was like a hailstorm of rocks hitting a tin roof.

Dunn headed topside. He saw daylight through a hole in a man's arm. Saw another man cut in half. The decks outside were a tangled web of steel and wires, of explosions and shouted orders from the fire crews. As if knowing the use of every antenna, the fighter jets managed in three passes to put a hole in them all.

'The water's too shallow – we have to wait until the ship moves further out!' said another NSA man as he dumped his bag onto the deck next to Dunn and dashed off again, disap-

pearing in a cloud of smoke that billowed from the rocketed pilothouse.

His world a spinning daze, Dunn followed and paused at the door to the radio room. Through the ringing in his ears, he managed to pick up the staccato mayday calls from the only still-standing crewman – the room had taken a direct hit moments earlier.

'Flash, flash, flash!' the radioman shouted. Heavy jamming from the Israelis crackled over the speakers. 'Flash, flash, flash – I pass in the blind. All stations this is Rockstar, under heavy attack from fighter aircraft on position . . .' At that moment a fresh series of pinging noises announced the Mirages were doing yet another pass, augmented by a loud explosion and fireball that licked through the doorway behind Dunn, singeing his clothes.

The call, going out to any and all Sixth Fleet vessels in the Mediterranean, was picked up by the USS Saratoga *on the fourth try.*

'Rockstar, this is Schematic, please provide authentication code,' came the level reply from the aircraft carrier over four hundred kilometres away, sailing off Crete.

'Negative, Schematic, codes are down, repeat codes are down – we are under heavy attack!' the Liberty's *radioman called, squeezing the microphone as he yelled.*

'Rockstar, we require authentication –'

'Listen to the fucking bombs, you son of a bitch!' The radioman was red in the face and pounded his fists into the bench in front of him.

Dunn turned around and walked to the edge of the railing. Overboard, bodies floated, some survivors trying to swim to the safety of land they could barely see. He pushed the classified-intelligence ditch bags into the sea, hoping the water here was deep enough to hide them forever. He closed his eyes as the sound of another wave of aircraft washed over him, the unmistakable smell of napalm drowning the ship.

Crew attempting to abandon ship were targeted by the torpedo boats whenever they ventured above decks, and life rafts were strafed in the water and blown from their mounts with devastating accuracy.

Dunn fell over the side and felt warmth encase him as his senses went offline one by one.

102

NEW YORK CITY

Fox looked at his watch. Waiting in the arrival lounge at JFK, he walked up to the stewardess who was closing the door to the gate.

'Excuse me, there's no one else on this plane?'

'That's it I'm afraid, sir. Perhaps your passenger missed the flight. Want me to check?'

'Yeah, thanks,' Fox said as he gave her the details and waited for the response. A phone call later Fox was headed for the exit. He called Kate's cell again but it was still switched off. He looked up at the monitors on his way out; there were two more flights coming in from Washington in an hour's time.

He placed another call.

'Faith Williams.'

'Faith, it's Lachlan,' he said.

'Hey you, what's up?' she asked.

'Run another flight-ticketing check with your contact at the Feds for me?'

'She was a no-show?'

'Yeah, didn't board at Dulles. Check any of today's flights from Washington to New York, she may have rebooked a flight recently.'

'Okay, call you back in five.'

'Thanks.'

•

Ten minutes later, Fox was in a GSR SUV driving back to Manhattan. Not only was Kate a no-show for her flight, she was not booked on any others.

•

Two cars behind Fox, the French consular officer pulled into the traffic. He continually scanned his rear-view mirror, sure there were FBI agents out there somewhere. He changed lanes after the SUV, almost sideswiping an ambulance in the process. He dialled a cell number, sweat running down his temples.

'Yes?' Secher said.

'Major, he is driving back from the airport to Manhattan.'

'Keep on him,' Secher ordered. 'Let me know where he goes.'

'He is travelling with a driver, looks like a bodyguard,' the officer said. 'And I think the FBI may be following me, and I don't like that prospect, not since they shot your New York agent –'

'I will relieve you within two hours. Do not lose him, this mission is vital to France.' Secher hung up.

103

NEW YORK CITY

Fox walked quickly, spotted his target and took a right down the timber marina at the 79th Street Boat Basin. Most of the craft at this end were small sailboats and open-topped cruisers, with the odd larger catamaran thrown in.

'Your doorman told me I could find you down here,' Fox said.

Frank Matthews was polishing the timber decking of a vintage speedboat, much like the water taxis seen in Venice.

'Hey, Lachlan,' Frank said, wiping his hands on a rag before shaking Fox's hand.

'She's beautiful,' Fox said, running a hand over the pristine panelling. The interior had been re-upholstered in a sandy red leather, the chrome dials in the dash gleamed behind a white sports steering wheel.

'*Kate*,' Frank said.

'Ah, that explains it.'

'My father had her, kept the engine in perfect order but the body was worse for wear when I inherited her. Been doing it up for Kate, just not sure when to give it to her.'

'No time like the present,' Fox said.

Frank had a distant look in his eyes, then resumed polishing. Seemed letting go of the boat was as hard as letting go of his daughter.

'Yeah, I guess you're right.'

'I'm actually after Kate, I haven't been able to reach her,' Fox said, picking up a rag and helping buff the polish off.

'Still in Washington, had to push her flight back for some reason. Should be home early this evening I think, but best to check with Faye when she's back home in an hour or so, she has more of a mind for these things.'

'Okay. You'll be right with this?'

'Yeah, I wanna get it done today, what else are workdays for? Anyway, big storm headed in tonight, so I have to get her done before then and double up the moorings of the cruiser.' Frank pointed to the bigger modern boat next to *Kate*.

'They don't build them like *Kate* any more,' Fox said, shaking Frank's hand again.

'They sure don't.'

104

HIGH OVER FRANCE

The pair of B-2 Spirits flew at a height of 15,000 metres, and at over seven hundred kilometres per hour. The two pilots on board each aircraft switched through their laser-guiding systems.

Known more commonly as Stealth Bombers, the flying wing designs gave them an otherworldly appearance. The black paintwork was to camouflage them in the night sky, which is when they did most of their hunting. The stealth design and technology hid their massive bulk from almost all radars.

'Ghost, this is Fatal Beauty, running check on ground targeting, lighting up GATS.'

'Copy that, Fatal Beauty, lighting GATS,' the pilot of Ghost called, both aircraft switching over the laser-designated target below to be converted to Differential GPS coordinates.

105

NEW YORK CITY

Finally, Fox got through to Mrs Matthews.

'Hello?' she said over the phone.

'Mrs Matthews, it's Lachlan Fox,' he told her. He hoped his voice was coming across as measured and calm.

'Oh, hi, Lachlan,' she said. 'Kate's actually in Washington at the moment.'

'Yes, I know,' Fox said. He paced in his office, the cell phone held tight to his ear. 'I was expecting her on an early-morning flight back to JFK. Do you know what her movements are?'

'Yes, she rang moments ago,' Faye Matthews replied. 'She's arriving back on a flight this afternoon, still into JFK I think. Said she would make her own way home in a cab.'

'Thanks, I might pop by later today to see how she is,' Fox said. He ended the call, wondering how long he had to stop her.

106

FORT GAUCHER

'What is it?' Danton said. He didn't bother to look up at the agent who entered, instead he continued to type commands into the computer. Hitting 'enter', the twenty million Euros transferred into Secher's account.

The agent waited in silence until Danton looked up.

'Yes?' Danton asked, recognising the fresh-faced junior from the communications room.

'We have picked up unusual radio traffic, sir,' he said. 'Non-designated aircraft, intermittently coming up.'

Danton's eyes went wide for a second.

'Wake up the communications team,' he said, standing up from behind his desk and pulling his jacket on. 'No one leaves their stations until the aircraft are identified.'

107

MONT BLANC, FRANCE

The SAS split up into four fire teams in their assault on Fort Gaucher.

Three eight-man teams set off to climb the steep mountain slopes, two teams in a pincer manoeuvre above the cut-out tunnel that snaked into the mountain, and the third team entering from the opposite side, where the mountain was at its highest point.

The remaining team of eight soldiers split into two, one four-man team heading for the only road into the mountain, and the remaining team setting off for a small relief valve at a thin point in the mountain's wall.

At the road leading in, the four soldiers buried high explosives at a precipice, ready to blow out a twenty-metre stretch of blacktop. Digging themselves into snow-covered positions close to the entrance of the tunnel, they readied themselves for battle.

Farrell called in for each of his soldiers, and one by one they confirmed they had completed their initial objectives and were in position. Now it was a waiting game.

108

NEW YORK CITY

Fox walked back into his office after another update on Gammaldi and the security team, finally in the air from Canada and still a good six hours away.

'It's Fox,' he said, answering his cell.

'Hutchinson – you were trying to reach me earlier?'

'Yeah, thanks for calling back,' Fox said, and he rushed around his side of the desk, flicking to the info on Secher. 'Christian Secher, did you read his file?'

'Capel's going through that now,' Hutchinson replied. 'I've been working on a warrant to bring in the Consul General to see what he knows about all this.'

'You may not need to,' Fox said. He told him about Kate and Secher, about her job, the threatened French coup, the Advocacy Center . . .

'You told anyone else this?'

'Ira Dunn at NSA.'

'Okay, leave it with me,' Hutchinson said. 'I'll have an agent call past her apartment in Washington ASAP. You hear anything, give me a call.'

'Will do, thanks,' Fox said, about to end the call. 'Hutchinson!'

'Yeah?'

'Quick question. Kate said she was arrested at college and cut a deal not to have any charges left on her record. This was in DC, about ten years ago.'

'She certainly doesn't have a record, I know that much about her,' Hutchinson said.

'That's my point,' Fox replied. 'Who could totally wipe a record like that? Not even a mention, nothing, when the crime involved a congressman?'

'We could,' Hutchinson said. 'Need a damn good reason, though.'

'Like what kind of reason? If the charges were conspiracy to assault, blackmail, obstructing justice . . .'

'All depends. Most common is when we put people into witness protection,' Hutchinson said. 'Couple of other agencies clear records to protect undercovers, insiders, double agents . . . oh, you clever son of a bitch!'

109

ATLANTIC OCEAN

'Genius,' the officer said, slapping the chief on the back and picking up the line to the bridge.

As they watched, the profile of the seafloor had changed. Where there had been a flat area now showed an underwater ridge. They had the helo go back over the spot and dip its sonar – to find the area flat again. It took a few wrong turns until the next sector of the sonar net showed the same pattern. Something big, like a nuclear-powered submarine, was slowly heading east. And now they had a bearing.

The bulk of the big submarine was giving false echo readings from the seafloor.

'Captain, it's confirmed, we've got her,' the officer said. 'Contact bearing twelve hundred metres off our port bow, westbound at eight knots.'

'Roger that, Sonar.' The captain hung up the intercom and called to his XO. 'Have the helo keep on her and alert the navy.'

110

WASHINGTON

The hearing was in an annex meeting room in the Capitol Building.

Across the table from Ira Dunn sat the members of the Senate Select Committee on Intelligence.

Dunn was alone on his side of the table.

No press. No lawyers. No stenographer. This was as closed as a session could get on Capitol Hill.

'Mr Dunn –'

'Colonel Dunn, Senator,' Dunn said, accentuating the woman's title.

'Colonel Dunn,' the majority leader started again. 'You are here today to discuss the activities of your office in relation to illegal wiretapping. Of particular concern are recent findings by the UN security services in New York that the fibre-optic cables supplying the headquarters building were tapped into.'

There was a pause where it was expected Dunn would say something, but he remained silent.

'Also, we have evidence from the FBI that you intercepted telephone and email traffic between one of their agents and a suspected double-agent in the CIA.'

Again Dunn was silent. He tapped his pen on the closed folder in front of him, looking at the people before him.

'You have been conducting activities that are well beyond your mandated scope of responsibility,' the senior senator said, leaning forward with his elbows on the table. 'And you're going to be held to account for it, in a more public hearing than this one.'

'Senator, I'm mandated to protect this country,' Dunn said slowly. 'It's something I do a damn good job of.'

'Indeed, your record has been exemplary, Colonel.' The chairing senator looked down at her notes.

'Tell us about the activities of Echelon. As mentioned, of particular concern to us today is the illegal targeting of communications within the United States.'

Dunn looked at the six members in front of him. This had taken a turn from the 9/11 investigation he was expecting. Not that it mattered. He tried to look at them like he had all the Aces, even with a few spares up his sleeve.

'You ever served on the frontline? Any of you?'

'Colonel . . .'

'I'm happy to answer your questions, it's only fair you answer one or two of mine, only friendly,' Dunn said.

'We're not here to make friends with you, Colonel Dunn,' the senator said.

Silence. Dunn was waiting for an answer.

'Well, women weren't in frontline forces when I was of serving age,' the chairwoman said.

'Ever served in the military?' Dunn asked. 'I know none of you have.'

'Then why waste our time with the question?'

'We live in a big wide world, and as much as you like to think otherwise, no matter how big our military is, we are an open society. A nation without physical walls.'

'Thank you for that insight –'

'For the past thirty-three years, I've given everything to this country,' Dunn said. 'For the past thirty-three years I've seen and heard everything there is to do with defending this country. I was there when the sons of bitches in the Pentagon wanted to make phoney terrorist strikes within our own country to *start* a war with Cuba.'

'Admiral, I don't think this is the time or the place –'

'I was on the USS *Liberty* when the Israeli Defence Force shot us up all day –'

He was interrupted again. 'Let's not forget it was your department that intercepted the calls of the September eleventh terrorists prior to the attacks. Why don't we explore what you have done since to ensure that can never happen again.'

'It's people like you who think eighty thousand US soldiers in South Korea are the defence of this nation. It's people like you –' Dunn pointed at the entire panel. He'd reached the point of no return, and was going to go out with a bang, '– who believe that if we have a quarter of a million boots on the ground in the Middle East you will be able to drive your SUVs for another fifty years. You think *that's* where the walls should be. You want to make that the central front on terror, yet you don't have the capacity to realise the work that goes on by the quiet Americans like me.'

'Colonel Dunn!' This from the minority leader. 'I sympathise with what you are saying, and I know of that frontline of which you speak – my son's serving in Afghanistan right now. What we need to ascertain here today is the scope of operations your section has been conducting and whether that is outside the legal framework of the Patriot Act.'

'The Patriot Act?' Dunn leaned forward on the desk. 'That Godforsaken shit rag you passed overnight is a ream of bullshit. You think terrorist cells have oversight committees? You think al Qaeda has to waste time getting a court order to park a bomb in the car park at your kids' school? To send anthrax to your office?'

'There's provision to go to the FISA court after the –'

'There is no "after", this is fluid, this is constant,' Dunn said. 'We are engaged in asymmetrical warfare at its most simple, its most ruthless.'

'I think we've heard enough for today, Colonel, perhaps we'll pick this up tomorrow when you have thought about your answers,' the chairwoman said. 'I'm offering you that lifeline, Colonel, and I suggest you take it.'

'I'll answer the question,' Dunn said, not the least bit concerned about shooting his mouth off. 'The work we do saves more lives than you will ever know.'

'Does your office intercept local traffic?' the minority leader asked. 'Local calls, emails, faxes within the US?'

'There is no local, there is no boundary,' Dunn said. 'Communications and information travel and develop faster than you can ever pass laws. You send an email down the hall, it bounces to Canada and back first. Do we intercept? You bet your ass we do.'

'So you are confirming that the NSA currently intercepts domestic communications intelligence?'

'You could not fathom what we do on a daily basis,' Dunn said.

'We need to know.'

'You need to do your jobs and I need to do mine.' Dunn banged his fist down on the table in front of him and bit his lip to regain some composure. The silence in the room was palpable and Dunn grabbed it.

'There are more hostiles wanting to bring down this nation than you could possibly imagine. We at the NSA are *the* front-line. Forget intercepting illegal immigration, drug trafficking and terrorist attacks for a minute. We have more foreign ownership of our companies and land than any other country on this earth. We have more threats to our nationhood than the countries and entities that are pitted against us *combined*. We are knee-deep in the beginning of a century where we are destined to become a second-rate power in the world. The very ideas and ideals that make up this nation are eroding fast and being torn down from within as much as from outside.'

'So you are confirming, Colonel Dunn,' the grey-haired Senate minority leader said slowly, 'that your directorate of the NSA deliberately targets US citizens, within the country?'

'You have no idea of the enormity of what I do for this country.' Dunn's hands were fists, his knuckles white. 'When information is power, I hold that power. For America. You understand that concept: America? Or are you too busy worrying about bringing the troops home in time for your next election.

Too worried about which component of the Joint Strike Fighter will be built in your backyard.'

The panel shifted in their seats.

'I think it's un-American to suggest –'

'Un-American!' Dunn snorted. 'Abraham Lincoln used to say that the test of one's Americanism was not one's family tree; the test was how much they believed in America. Because we're like a religion, really. A secular religion. We believe in ideas and ideals. We're not one race, we're many; we're not one ethnic group, we're everyone; we don't speak only one language, we're all of these people. We're tied together in our belief of political democracy, in religious freedom, in capitalism, a free economy where people make their own choices about the spending of their money. We're tied together because we respect human life, and because we respect the rule of law. Those are the ideas that make us Americans.'

'It's the particular rule of law that we are questioning here today, Colonel. If you suspect a US target of terrorism, then your course of action is to apply to the FISA court to obtain the appropriate warrant.'

Dunn was silent.

'Colonel?'

'How do I ask a court for warrants to track the thousands of criminals tearing apart this country that I've helped build. Criminals who openly break laws that they so righteously defend in public? Criminals who make the laws?'

'What are you talking about, Mr Dunn?' the grey-haired senator asked, shifting in his seat.

'How do I tell the court I need a warrant to listen in to your phone calls to the VP at Raytheon regarding the fifty grand a month they deposit into your Cayman account?'

The senator went as pale as a ghost. He sat back in his chair, his colleagues looking at him. Sweat dotted his forehead.

'How do I tell the FISA court that White House staffers are raising political funds from government offices. That extortions and bribes are rife in this country. I don't go looking for these criminals, they pop up in the system. I don't commit the crimes in this country, my dear representatives. I protect this country, inside and out.'

•

CIA Director Boxcell listened to every word spoken.

He sat with a CIA technician in a cubby-hole office in the Capitol Building, listening to the discussion, picked up on by a tiny bug planted in the room.

'He's hung himself out to dry,' Boxcell said, over the small speakers on the technician's laptop computer. A smile crept over his face.

111

AIR FORCE ONE

Air Force One flew at cruising altitude, a pair of F-22 fighter aircraft flying ahead with another off each wingtip. The main level of the big Boeing 747–200B was full of the White House senior staff, most of the Security Council, their aides and twenty members of the US Secret Service. While through the use of aerial refuelling the aircraft was equipped to stay in the air for two weeks, they were headed for Barksdale Air Force Base in Louisiana.

'Are you certain?' Vanzet said into the phone. 'Okay, thanks.'

'Waiting on confirm from the Coast Guard,' Vanzet said. 'But they think they've found the sub, tracking westbound within twenty klicks of New York City.'

'That's it, it has to be a drop or a pick-up,' McCorkell said.

'What have we got on hand in NYC?' the President asked.

'ASW helos with SEAL support teams, and a Tico-class missile cruiser steaming south from Boston,' Vanzet said. 'If this is her, we'll rock the house good.'

112

NEW YORK CITY

Secher went to the car-hire desk at La Guardia airport using his Winston Smith ID, and retrieved the keys left for him the day before by his agent.

'Here are the keys, Mr Smith, your colleague left the vehicle in this parking bay.' The clerk handed over a printed diagram of the car park with a space highlighted in the far corner.

When he got to the car he popped the boot, and was glad to see that the last useful thing his New York agent had done had gone to plan. He took out the long duffle bag and threw it through the open driver's side door onto the passenger seat.

He waited until he was out of the airport lot and away from its CCTV cameras, settling into the afternoon traffic on the Grand Central Parkway, before opening the bag. A hardened steel case was on top of two wetsuits. He flicked the combination and revealed the Sig Pro 9 mm pistol with suppressor and two loaded magazines inside.

'I'm looking forward to meeting you, Lachlan Fox.'

113

WASHINGTON

Kate walked from the cab to the corporate jet terminal at Dulles and was met by a flight attendant bearing her name on a card.

'Welcome to NetJet Airways, ma'am,' the flight attendant greeted her and took her bags. They walked through the small terminal to the waiting Gulfstream 200 parked in close.

'Thank you,' Kate said, as she was shown up the steps into the plush nine-seater corporate jet. An ice bucket held a bottle of Veuve Clicquot and a bunch of yellow tulips were awaiting her, with a note from Secher. *'Relax and Enjoy.'* She took a seat and buckled in, and double-checked the NSA key was secure in her purse. To think that tiny little thing once connected to any computer via a firewire port would access information to facilitate the sale of Christian's business. She smiled and reached for the champagne.

114

NEW YORK CITY

'I'm on East 52nd, I can see your car ahead,' Secher said, pulling into a loading-zone park. 'I will take it from here. Thank you for your efforts, I will inform the Consul General of your dedication.'

'Thank you, Major,' the consular officer said, all too happy to be rid of the assignment. He put his Toyota into gear and drove into the evening traffic leaving Manhattan.

Secher called another number and hung up. While he waited for his cell to ring back, he screwed the long suppressor onto the end of the Sig Pro pistol, the action hidden from view under the steering column. His phone rang and he answered it one-handed.

'General,' Secher said with a big smile.

'Christian,' Danton replied.

'What, no more rank for me?' Secher asked. 'I checked my account, thank you for the payday.'

'Do you have the key?' Danton interrupted, audibly annoyed.

'Almost,' Secher said, feeling the weight of his unloaded pistol in his hand. 'Did you arrange for the pick-up to come in closer?'

'Yes. It will be there at nine-twenty your time, at the ferry slip.'

'Excellent. The key will be there. Goodbye, and good luck with your future.'

Secher ended the call before Danton could retort. Really, he could not care less about the mission from the time he handed over the key. Yes, he would be proud to see France become the jewel in the Super EU's crown. Yet jewels of his own were what he was looking forward to a lot more. Twenty million Euros bought a heck of a lot of luxury.

He leaned the seat back and settled in, looking up at the towering bronze monolith of the Seagram Building, glowing in the setting sun that broke through the overcast conditions. He was prepared to wait in the car with the air-conditioning running until he had confirmation that the NetJet flight had arrived in New York with Kate. Then, it would be time to move on Fox.

115

US WATERS

The Coast Guard had lost her.

'She won't be that way, I'm telling you,' the officer said. The sonarman continued to activate the net of buoys along their southernmost point.

'I reckon he's drifting, not making any noise.'

'Doesn't matter, we couldn't hear him anyway,' the sonarman said, looking over a chart of the seafloor.

'Where did you last see him?' the captain asked as he entered the room. He looked over the sonarman's shoulder.

'He was here; now he's gone,' came the reply, the sonarman pointing to an area around the southern tip of Long Island. The captain scanned the chart, following the depths of the water.

'Chart's wrong,' the captain announced. 'They dredged that section of the shipping channel last fall, it's much deeper now.'

The captain picked up the intercom to the bridge. They were back in the chase.

116

NEW YORK CITY

Fox walked out of the Seagram Building and strode across the open granite plaza, brushing past the commuters ending their day at work. The sun was a bright orange that cut through the big-city haze to give New York the sort of light seen usually in Bruckheimer's Miami. On the south-eastern horizon a dark bank of clouds was rolling in, beads of lightning crackling through the eerily still air. The humidity today had gone through the roof.

Goldsmith walked by Fox's side, scanning the crowd for threats. His Hawaiian shirt splayed out at his right hip where a Smith & Wesson .45 auto sat in a quick-release holster. A bumbag hanging at his front rode low with the weight of two spare mags and a police radio.

'Here's a cab,' Fox said, waving an arm.

•

Seated in the hire car, Secher could see Fox struggling to wave down a taxi. He pulled back the slide to chamber a round into his pistol, flicking off the safety.

Once the lights turned green, Secher stamped on the accelerator to get ahead of the traffic, and depressed the button to open his tinted window. Within ten metres of his target he brought the pistol up and sighted Fox, pulling the trigger repeatedly.

•

Fox had walked along the sidewalk, arm up, turning to look in the other direction –

He was pushed aside –

Saw a glimpse of a man with a pistol from inside a grey Ford –

A loud gunshot, close by –

He hit the ground hard.

•

Secher's side airbag exploded into the cabin from the one shot the bodyguard got off. Through the action, Secher knew some of the rounds from his full clip of 9 mm ammo had found their mark on both Fox and the bodyguard.

•

Fox did not hear the bullets firing from the silenced pistol.

Rather, he felt them, felt the rounds pound into his travel bag, felt the bullet that passed through his left shoulder.

Instinctively, he turned his head, and in the fraction of a second as he fell to the ground he saw the end of a silencer disappearing into the window of a speeding sedan.

Through the darkened rear window, he saw the profile of the driver as he looked over his shoulder.

He *knew* the driver.

And Fox knew where he was going.

•

Secher again floored the accelerator, taking off into the traffic, sideswiping a courier van in the process, when his windscreen was shot through from ahead. He looked up in time to see a suited man, unmistakably a federal agent, standing ahead in a two-handed firing position, and he ducked under the cover of the dash and turned the wheel, feeling the impact as the car hit the man and he was thrown over the roof and onto the road behind.

Secher sat back up, corrected the steering, and braked hard to avoid a head-on collision.

•

Fox's world was silent, devoid of all sensory stimuli for a few seconds. His vision returned, tunnelled at first, then back to full view. He looked up at the buildings that towered into the sky. A face came into view, mouthing words he couldn't hear, and he went to get up to find a weight pinning him. Goldsmith had thrown himself on him. Fox lifted his head, tried to push him off, only his left arm was useless. He looked down at his shoulder, saw a stain of crimson spreading from a gunshot wound. Strange, no pain, although his head rang with the force of having hit the ground.

Fox slid from under Goldsmith, who was fighting for breath as he'd taken at least two shots in his bullet-proof vest and one through the neck. The side of his face was splattered with blood that had erupted from the wound.

A security guy from the Seagram Building foyer arrived on the scene, calling emergency services over his radio. Pedestrians formed a ring around them.

Fox reached into his duffle bag, taking out his SOCOM pistol as he got up and scanned Park Avenue for the silver Ford – to see it disappearing as it turned onto East 57th Street.

Fox stepped onto the road, people screaming in the background as they realised what was playing out in front of them. He pulled the gun up level with a cab that came to a screech in front of him.

'Move over or get out!' Fox yelled at the stunned driver, who went from shock to utter bewilderment in under a second. He decided to move across to the passenger seat.

Fox got behind the wheel and took off with a squeal of tyres and smoke.

•

Roaring down East 54th Street, Fox raced through the red light of Madison Avenue without even blinking. Cars travelling through the intersection with the right of way skidded and swerved, smashing into one another as the cab hit forty-five miles per hour driving on the centre-line.

'Gringo – you're in some hurry,' said the driver.

Two Japanese tourists in the back seat went pale as Fox pulled on the handbrake and sloughed sideways onto Fifth Avenue, knocking the rear wheel off a horse-drawn carriage in the process.

'I have to save someone –' Fox said. He honked the horn and swerved between lanes. 'Outta the way!'

Fox stamped on the brakes as they came to Fifth Avenue, the cab screeching to a halt in a cloud of tyre and brake smoke. At best – breaking every road law on the journey – the Matthews' place was a good twenty minutes away.

'She is your . . . señorita?'

Fox looked at the driver while waiting for a break in the traffic and then turned right onto Fifth.

'Yeah, amigo, she's my señorita.'

Fox floored the accelerator and spun the wheel.

•

Secher settled into a comfortable drive along West 57th, heading for Riverside Drive. He loaded a full mag into the Sig Pro and unscrewed the silencer, placing it in his door's storage holder. He flicked the radio on – Edith Piaf of all singers.

'Ha!' Secher slapped the wheel with a grin. 'Fuck'n' America!'

•

'Where are you headed?' the cab driver asked. He hung on tight as Fox ducked between lanes and oncoming vehicles. He even took the time to return a few of the obscene gestures from cut-off motorists.

'West 79th and Riverside,' Fox said, taking advantage of an

opposing red light and driving down a relatively empty oncoming lane, overtaking the standstill they were in.

'This is your last turn before the park, amigo,' the cab driver yelled above the redlining engine and horns that blazed at them.

Fox wiped the sweat that ran into his eyes from his brow and cried out in pain from his shoulder. He yanked the wheel down as a result and grated his side of the cab along an oncoming bus, sparks everywhere.

The woman in the back screamed.

'Shit, you're bleeding,' the cab driver said, looking wide-eyed at Fox's shoulder. The tension in the cab stepped up a level.

'I can help,' the man said from the back seat. He leaned forward and inspected the wound.

'Clear exit,' he said, picking it for a bullet wound.

'That was 59th!' the cab driver said as Fox flew over the intersection. 'You'll have to take the Transverse through the park now!'

'Ahhh!' Fox yelled as the guy applied a folded handkerchief tied off with his wife's scarf.

'Thanks – buckle up back there!' Fox looked the passengers in the eyes via the rear-view mirror and they sat back and obeyed.

Fox braked and took a gap in the traffic to get across the lanes. He took the kerb gently, not blowing his tyres out, and entered Central Park as rain began to fall.

'This is gonna get slippery.'

•

Secher pulled up out the front of the Matthews' residence and looked up at the façade as he got out. The rain had picked up but he could just see her.

Kate was there. Looking down at him from the second-storey window. He waved, and she retreated behind the curtain. He didn't like the look on her face.

Secher bounded up the stairs and was greeted by the doorman.

'Evening, sir, do you have –' Secher cut him short with a three-punch judo move that left him out cold. He dragged the limp body inside and into a broom cupboard before bounding up the stairs.

•

'Left!' the cab driver said as Fox spun the wheel full turn, the back tyres flicking up rivers of mud as they barely missed a sunken walkway running through the Sheep Meadow.

The cab was snaking wildly from side to side as the grass became a quagmire under the spinning rear tyres.

Central Park West loomed ahead, as a group of tourists clamoured out of the way.

'That was the park,' Fox said over his shoulder to the Japanese couple holding on to each other, the woman throwing up in the back seat as the cab went airborne over a stone step that threw the car over the sidewalk and T-boned into a passing Fed-Ex van.

Fox backed up a few feet and tore off again.

•

Secher knocked on the door again, this time with a hurried staccato. He fingered his Sig Pro tucked into the back of his belt.

Mrs Matthews answered.

'Oh, hello Christian, lovely to see you again,' she said as she opened the door. 'Please, come in and I'll let Kate know you are here.'

'It's okay, Mom,' Kate said, coming into the hall.

'Are you okay, honey?' Faye Matthews asked. Kate's mascara was smudged under her eyes, her cheeks damp from tears.

'Fine, Mom, can you leave us for a sec?'

Kate watched as her mum walked into the lounge.

'You look –' Secher was cut off.

'I rang Lachlan about half an hour ago, confronted him,' Kate said, her stare absolute. 'He said you worked for the French government, or at least a faction of it.'

Kate looked into his eyes, searching for some kind of reaction.

'Of course he'd say that, he's a spy.'

'I'm not sure.'

'Baby, listen to yourself,' Secher said, taking another step so she was within reach. 'Do you think a government official dresses like this? You've seen my house in Bern – you think a public servant can afford that?'

Secher noticed her soften just a little.

'I – I don't know . . .' She wiped a tear on her sleeve.

'I'm sorry I'm late,' he said, and took the last step and hugged her. 'You know me. Come on, we're going to get away from all this, today.'

He could feel her relax some more.

'Did you get it?' he whispered into her ear.

•

Fox leaned on the horn as a couple of cars in a fender bender ahead were taking their sweet time exchanging numbers.

'Get off the fucking road!' he yelled out the window.

They waved back as if to say 'wait until we're done', and Fox took off beside them, the side of the cab grating along both cars, causing far more damage than their original incident.

•

Kate leaned her head against his shoulder, letting him hold her tight. She took in his smell as she stared off into the ether. She didn't say anything for almost a minute, and Secher allowed her this silence.

'Did you get the key so we can sail the world?' Secher asked again, clearly so he could be sure she heard him.

'It's here,' Kate said, letting go slowly, her hands coming from around his back and brushing against the butt of his pistol. Her mind was still registering what it was as she pulled the encryption key from her pocket.

'What's behind your back?' she asked as she raised the key for him to see.

117

NEW YORK HARBOR

'Captain, contact is rounding Long Island,' the sonar officer called.

'Chief, make it so and go to red,' the captain called.

'Aye, sir, going red.' The Chief of the Boat hit the klaxon and red lights all over the ship went ablaze. He picked up the PA handset. 'Crew, this is the Chief, we are weapons hot, weapons hot, weapons hot.'

'Son of a bitch is headed for Manhattan!' The captain pounded the table and surveyed his bridge team, all looking to him for direction, none of them believing the chase had come this far.

'Find out where our damn navy support is!' the captain yelled at his radio officer before turning to his air commander. 'Tell our helo if they lose her, it's their asses I'm gonna chew! No one fucks with Manhattan on my watch!'

118

NEW YORK CITY

Secher's eyes glinted at the sight in the palm of her hand. After a year of planning, months of groundwork, here it was. He had it!

'Sorry?' he asked as he reached for the key. His eyes shifted focus from the key to her eyes in the background.

'Tucked into the back of your trousers?' Kate's eyes had a sharpness that he'd never seen before. He cocked his head, trying to figure it out, interested.

'Shall I organise a spot at the dinner table for you, Christian?' Kate's mother entered the room. 'Frank will be home any moment.'

Kate held Secher's gaze.

His eyes shifted back onto the key.

'My phone,' Secher said.

'You're a bad liar,' Kate replied, closing her fist around the key as his hand reached hers. He closed his hand tight over hers and turned to face Mrs Matthews.

'Thank you, Madame, but I will be taking your charming daughter out for dinner.' He pulled Kate to him and her shoes slid across the marble floor.

'I think we'll stay,' Kate said, pulling back on her hand, still stuck in his fist, his grip tightening. 'You're hurting me!' she said.

Her mother registered confusion as there was a noise at the door behind Secher, then Frank Matthews entered the foyer.

'Hey there, Christian!' Frank said in good humour, dumping his bag and umbrella in the stand, and turning back before he could register the scene. 'It's really starting to come down out there –'

Secher chopped his pistol down on Frank's neck. He was down, out cold.

Secher pulled Kate into a headlock under his arm, his hand still clamped around hers. Mrs Matthews' eyes went from wide horror at the scene of her husband on the ground to staring at the pistol in Secher's outstretched arm. He was on her in a second, headbutting her in the face. Her nose erupted in blood, and he slammed the pistol grip against her forehead. Her head snapped back against the open lounge-room doorframe, and she slumped to the ground.

119

NEW YORK CITY

Fox did a handbrake turn at the front of the building, the rear end of the cab smashing up on the kerb as his door popped off its hinges and onto the ground.

'Thanks!' Fox yelled as he leapt from the still-rocking vehicle.

The cab driver and Japanese tourists were left there, shaking and sweaty.

•

Secher dragged Kate through Riverside Park, his hand still clamped over her fist that held the NSA key. His duffle bag from the hire car hung over his shoulder.

'What are you doing with me?' she asked, rain pelting down at such a force as to leave the park deserted.

'We're sailing the world, my love,' he replied, striding through the rain towards the boat basin up ahead.

•

Fox came to the open door of the Matthews' and bounded in, to find Frank on his knees holding a towel to his wife's face.

'Shit,' Fox said, nearly slipping on the blood-covered marble. 'Are you okay – where's Kate?'

'I've called an ambulance and the police,' Frank said.

'He took her!' Mrs Matthews broke down. 'Christian TOOK HER!'

'Where?' Fox said. He pulled the SOCOM pistol from his belt and chambered a round.

The Matthews looked up at him wide-eyed. Their second shock for the day.

'I need to help her.' Fox knelt down to their level, held a hand out to Mrs Matthews. 'I'll bring her back.'

Her shaking hand held his tight, and the parents read a familiar sense of protection in his eyes. It was a look they all shared.

'He took the keys to my boat,' Frank said. He went to the key bowl by the phone, slid open the small drawer in the hall table and pulled out a single brass key.

Fox stood and took it, knowing what it was for.

'Take *Kate*, she'll catch the yacht,' Frank said. 'Bring our daughter home.'

120

FORT GAUCHER

Major Farrell waited under the cover of a snow dugout, the seven men in his fire team doing the same.

'Sir, we've got company,' Jenkins said. 'Snowmobile coming up the ridge to our south-east.'

Farrell clambered up to the lip of the basin, peering down into the mist. Through his binoculars he could just make out the fast-moving shape of a snowmobile climbing the incline, fast.

'They on to you?'

'I think we tripped a sensor,' Jenkins said.

Farrell checked his watch. Two minutes to impact from the air strike.

'Wait till they're on you and take them. Cleanly,' Farrell ordered.

'Copy that.'

•

Jenkins moved to the well-worn patrol track he could see the snowmobile had traversed before, waiting at the top of the incline with another soldier on the other side.

The snowmobile came to a halt at the peak of the lip, and the three soldiers disembarked. Immediately, the three of them looked at each other, holding their radio earpieces tighter into their ears. Before they could turn around to defend themselves from a threat, Jenkins and his SAS corporal were upon them, slicing the three throats before they could take another breath.

Jenkins removed the earpiece from a French corpse and listened, while his corporal dragged the bodies out of sight. He stopped his subordinate from removing the last body.

'This is Jenkins,' he called to the rest of the SAS soldiers. 'They've triggered their alarm.'

'Copy that,' Farrell replied. 'Base team, blow the relief valve.'

•

Farrell could see from his vantage point that the French company of commandos never stood a chance. As they were emerging from their barracks, the five GBU39 Small Diameter Bombs came crashing home.

Designed to penetrate up to 1.8 metres of reinforced concrete, the state-of-the-art weapons streaked in to their targets via differential GPS locating. While specified to hit a target within five metres of the designated area, the 110 kg bombs hit their targets right on the money, thanks to the SAS's precision laser designators accompanying the GPS.

Within two seconds of the first guided bomb hitting home, the entrances to the compound were shattered, along with the two radomes and main defensive battery.

Before the shrapnel of the blasts even hit the ground, the SAS demo teams detonated their explosives.

The basin creaked with a muffled explosion that echoed off the cannon walls in the Mont Blanc range. The relief valve, set halfway up the mountain at a weak point in the base's wall, acted like a pressure seal that released a steady stream of water from the frozen lake inside. Now blown, a massive geyser of water erupted into the sky.

On the road that snaked into the mountain, a ten-metre section disappeared down the steepest slope, the SAS squad there moving forward and securing the tunnel.

Farrell called in reports before giving the go-ahead to move down into the base. For now, Fort Gaucher belonged to the British Special Air Service.

121

NEW YORK CITY

Secher cast off the Matthews' motor yacht and throttled up the engines, in the process knocking overboard the pilot of a smaller craft in the basin.

Kate struggled in the passenger seat that Secher had bound her to.

'My parents –'

'They will be fine,' he said, turning to her with a smile. The canvas canopy of the yacht rocked under the weight of the rain. 'Nothing more than a headache,' he added, as if their ordeal were a run-of-the-mill occurrence.

'Who are you?' Kate asked.

'I am Christian Secher.' He smiled at her again as he wound out of the basin and onto the Hudson. He pushed the throttle up to its stops and the craft slowly picked up speed.

'I'm offering you a new life, to sail the world,' Secher said. He grabbed at his duffle bag and pulled out a wetsuit, changing into it as he spoke. A spare suit was still in the bag.

'But it's up to you, of course,' he said. 'I have the key –' he dangled the chain around his neck that he'd hooked the key on '– that will afford us our wildest dreams.'

'What is it for?' Kate asked.

The orange setting sun gleamed through the rain for a moment and lit up the wet Manhattan glass like a billion jewels.

•

'Come on!'

Fox started *Kate* up on the third try. The inboard motor coughed to life and thrummed to a throaty reverb. He put her in gear and tore off, the keel rising into the air from the force.

The rain eased for a moment and the sun glinted off the river. His instinct told him to turn left, but he did a tight loop, unable to see the yacht in any direction. They could be going right, up the river, to a waiting car. Fox throttled off for a second, whipping his head around desperately.

The warning horns of a ferry caught his attention, far off to the left, and he turned just as the Matthews' yacht turned broadside to make way for the larger craft.

Fox pushed the throttle to its stops.

He looked like death warmed up, blood splattered across his shirt and wet to the bone from the torrential rain whipping down. Visibility was low, and a sea mist was blowing in as Fox hammered the boat, getting airborne every few seconds as he hit the wake of several larger craft.

•

Secher was nearing Liberty Island when his windshield disintegrated.

He turned around – and saw Fox, in a small timber speedboat, bearing down fast, some thirty metres back.

He pushed the throttle further but it was fully open.

'Shit!'

•

'Got your attention, arsehole,' Fox said, wedging his SOCOM in the dash while he double-handed the steering wheel.

He was on the yacht's tail now, and could see the back of Kate's head where she was tied facing forward in the chair. The rain became torrential, the wind picking up from the Atlantic and whipping the waves over the deck of Fox's boat, slowing him down.

Secher fired rapidly at Fox, but with both craft at full speed in the rough waters near Liberty Island, none of the bullets found their mark.

Fox closed fast on the yacht, and went portside as he watched Secher eject a mag and bend down to retrieve another.

'Kate!' Fox yelled.

She looked across and spotted him – he saw she couldn't believe her eyes.

Before Fox could do any more catching up, Secher was firing.

Fox ducked and leaned hard on the wheel. Secher wasn't ready, and he lost his footing as his craft was pushed across by the smaller timber boat.

Fox stood up on the chair of his craft, one foot braced on the framing of his windshield, SOCOM pistol in hand. He leapt onto the back of the yacht.

Secher got up and corrected course, away from the rocks that began at Liberty Island.

Fox was thrown across the slippery stern. He grabbed hold of the gang-rail – with his one good arm – as his pistol tumbled into the cabin by Secher's feet.

Secher turned and saw him. He smiled.

He raced the few steps to where Fox was hanging, as the yacht bumped past a craggy outcrop and rocked violently. Then Secher fell.

Fox used the motion to slide up and tumble into the cabin, right onto Secher.

The Frenchman had the wind knocked out of him, and Fox laid his elbow into his back, hammering away at his kidneys.

'Lachlan!' Kate screamed, trying to see what was happening over her shoulder.

The yacht rocked again, harder this time, and Fox looked forward to see the massive stones that cragged the shape of Liberty Island.

'Lachlan, we're going to –' and Fox was next to her, adjusting the wheel away from the coast. He pulled at the knot tying her closest hand and then reached for the throttle and was jerked forward, Secher kicking him square in the spine. He fell to the deck in agony.

Secher was on him now, with more kicks, as Fox used his good arm to catch a leg and pull, the slippery fibreglass deck working to his advantage for a second as Secher stumbled back.

Then Fox was up, SOCOM pistol in hand. He aimed, fired . . .

•

'Coast Guard cutter *Tampa*, this is USS *Gettysburg*, SEAL One and Two are inbound hot, two minutes out of your position, both helos armed with forty-eights.'

'Copy that, *Gettysburg*, what's your ETA?' the Coast Guard captain asked, looking over towards his sonarman's console at the French sub.

'On station within ten, *Tampa*, good hunting,' the captain of the *Gettysburg* called.

•

Fox felt wet and cold but for his shoulder, which burned hot with pain. He lifted his head and couldn't see for the rain, then found he was lying on coarse sand. He tried to push up but couldn't. His left arm was totally useless. He rolled onto his right and got up, his ears ringing.

The sun had dipped to just below the horizon, and the rain was pelting down. The yacht was beached next to him, its prow smashed against the granite wall that ringed Liberty Island.

Fox stumbled towards it, struggling to see in the water that whipped at his face.

A bolt of lightning flashed through the sky.

He saw Kate, in the yacht, still tied to the seat.

He ran the remaining paces, used his good arm to pull himself up the side of the boat.

The deck was covered in watered-down blood.

No sign of Secher.

Thunder rumbled as he bent down and felt Kate's pulse, there but faint. He untied her and laid her flat, looking her over.

'Lachlan . . .' Kate said, her eyes open.

'Kate, don't move,' he replied, stroking her face. A long gash in her hairline streamed blood across her eye and down her cheek.

'I feel okay,' she said. 'My parents . . .'

'They're fine, I saw them.'

'Lachlan, you have to stop him.'

'Just relax, I'll radio for some help.' Fox crawled over the angled deck to the radio.

'Stop him, please,' Kate said, as another lightning flash lit up the evening sky.

As Fox called out an SOS on the emergency channel, from the corner of his eye he saw movement.

Secher, limping; he must have taken the bullet in the leg when the yacht grounded.

Fox watched as Secher scrambled up the granite wall that led to the statue.

'I'm right here,' he said to Kate. He knelt next to her and put a hand to her head.

She looked at him through blood-soaked eyes.

'Lachlan, thank you,' she said. She squeezed his hand. 'I've done something terrible . . . please, don't let him get away.'

Fox passed her the radio. 'I'll be right back,' he said, running his hand down her face.

He climbed over the shattered windshield and canopy of the yacht, running up the prow and jumping the wall onto the grassed forecourt of the statue.

There, limping around the statue, along the pedestal covered with maintenance scaffolding, was Secher.

Fox took off, his left arm dangling by his side.

•

Two black US Navy MH-60R Seahawk helicopters came in low and fast, all lights out, even the tail navigation beacons.

'Coast Guard Twenty-One, this is SEAL One, on station at thirty by your five,' the helo pilot called, watching in night vision as the Coast Guard helo turned about on the spot to face them.

'Copy that, SEAL One. Contact bearing two-one-five at six knots, ninety metres out.'

'Copy that, Coast Guard, we have the ball.'

The Coast Guard's Sea King banked towards its mother ship, some eight hundred metres out on the Hudson, as the two black-painted navy birds moved in for the kill.

'Two, this is One, dropping active.' The pilot nodded to his quartermaster in the load bay, who hit the switch on the belly-mounted sonar buoy. 'Lighting up now.'

'Smoke 'em out, One,' came the reply over the encrypted radio.

As soon as the active sonar buoy hit the water, all hell broke loose.

•

Fox ran after Secher. The Frenchman limped in a half-run to get away.

A crack of lightning struck Liberty's torch and lit the wet twilight sky.

Secher took a glance over his shoulder before he turned the corner and Fox was on him.

Secher was knocked against the wall in a tackle that sent the wind out of him. Fox followed up with a punch to the face that Secher managed to move out from – just – and the Frenchman swung down with a double-fisted judo move into Fox's back.

Both men fell to the ground, and it was Secher who was up first, Fox soon after.

Secher stumbled to a stack of scaffolding, pulled out a metre-long steel pole and swung it at Fox.

Fox used his quicker leg speed to move away from the onslaught, and he was able to back around to the pile and get his own piece of scaffolding.

The pair swung and parried, slipping and sliding on the wet ground.

A well-placed blow beat Fox's defensive swing and he was hit in the ribs. He fell down on all fours. He rolled onto his back and raised his pipe, just in time to block a head-crushing blow. The force was enough to knock the pole out of Fox's hand, and Secher took a few steps around his quarry, wiping the water from his face, heaving breaths.

•

'Target just put down the pedal, we've got flank-speed cavitations,' the sonar chief said.

'Counter-measures in the water,' the sonar officer said, listening to his own headset.

'This better work,' the captain murmured. He picked up the external radio handset. 'SEAL One, drop your fish.'

•

'Copy that, *Tampa*,' the pilot of SEAL One said, his co-pilot releasing their Mark 48 torpedo. 'Torpedo in the water.'

The French submarine knew it had nowhere to go. In the shallow and narrow confines of New York Harbor, the chances of evasion were nil. With a blast of her klaxon, she blew her ballast tanks and prepared for an emergency surface.

•

'Target has surfaced!' SEAL Two called out, the prow of the massive ballistic-missile submarine rising out of the water at a thirty-degree angle. The water around her was a geyser of foam as she came crashing down.

'Killing the torpedo,' the co-pilot of SEAL One said. He flicked off the arming and propulsion systems, the weapon drifting to the seabed for later retrieval.

'SEAL Two disembarking aft the con tower.'

'Copy that, Two, covering with mini,' One called.

The pilot of SEAL Two hovered over the surfaced submarine, the aft section churning up spray as the pump jet worked in reverse to bring the vessel to a dead stop. The French sub knew they were beaten.

'Ropes, ropes, ropes,' the co-pilot of Two called, as the cabin gunners un-spooled four ropes, and the eight-man SEAL team was on the aft deck of *Le Vigilant* in seconds.

Six of the team advanced with their laser-targeted M4s trained on the conning tower, four immediately climbing the dripping ladder while the vessel fought to steady, the other two placing charges along the deck. The sub was going nowhere they didn't want it to go.

The *Tampa* closed the distance, its big spotlights lighting up the conning tower of the sub.

The captain squinted to make sure he was seeing right. 'Is that a French flag painted on that con tower?'

122

AIR FORCE ONE

'Mr President, confirmation that the Brits have taken the DGSE base at Fort Gaucher,' Larter said. The Secretary of Defense resumed his seat at the table, physically relieved.

The Security Council were in the briefing room, as the aircraft flew a circuit over the mid-western states. The F-22s were in the process of mid-air refuelling. Considering the firepower outside the windows, Air Force One was perhaps the most secure place in the world at that second.

'Admiral, how'd it play out?' McCorkell asked, the Chairman of the JCS just hanging up the phone to the op centre at the Pentagon.

'SAS with air support, two friendly casualties,' Vanzet said. 'General Danton, head of DGSE, was killed. No sign of Sianne Cassel.'

'The SAS will be doing an intel sweep of the location, they'll find her whereabouts,' McCorkell said to the room. 'They –'

'Bill,' Vanzet cut in. 'We have confirmation that a SEAL team has control of the French submarine in the Hudson.'

McCorkell considered the looks on the faces before him. The military aide with the nuclear launch codes seemed to shrink in stature out of relief. The senior political staff were relieved too, while the military chiefs looked more pensive.

'Have they confirmed that there are nuclear missiles aboard?' the President asked, and there was silence as everyone waited for the answer. 'I gotta know,' he said, to no one in particular.

Vanzet relayed the order over the secure radio link and waited a full minute for the reply.

McCorkell sat and watched his president tapping his pen on the table.

'Affirmative, Sir.' Vanzet paused, waiting to hear the list of the boat's inventory. The SEALs were trained to gather such information, fast. 'She's identified as *Le Vigilant*, *Triomphant* class ballistic-missile submarine. Fully loaded.'

123

NEW YORK CITY

Fox lay there on his back, heaving deep breaths. The rain eased to a drizzle, each drop falling as if in slow motion, lit from above by the powerful strobes that illuminated the great lady. Liberty Illuminating the World, Fox thought, his ears still ringing.

•

Secher knew Fox's vulnerabilities. He'd been in enough hand-to-hand combat to know what to do. He took two steps and fell onto Fox, forcing the pipe down onto his throat.

•

Fox caught the pipe, the force smashing the bones in his hand. His strength with just one working arm was not enough to keep off the weight of Secher. The downward pressure slowly closed off his air. The veins in his neck reached exploding point.

He gritted through the pain.

'Come on, then!' Fox tried to shout, the words a hoarse whisper. He kicked up, the move requiring all of his effort. The blow glanced off Secher's side, useless.

Fox knew he had seconds to live. He weighed up his options. If Secher was closer, he might have a chance to knock him off his feet.

'Drop it!' Kate called.

Fox and Secher looked across. She stood there, Fox's SOCOM pistol shaking in her outstretched arms.

'Drop it . . .' she repeated, more quietly this time. Fox couldn't tell if it was for threat's sake or if she were fading.

Fox could see her swaying on her feet.

Secher stared at her, keeping the pressure down on Fox, pinning him to the ground. Fox could see him smiling.

Fox slipped into a haze of unconsciousness as he saw Secher say something, just another hollow lie from a professional intelligence officer. But Fox couldn't make it out, it was so distant, it was gone before he could comprehend.

Two gunshots rang through the air.

The pressure was off his neck.

Fox gasped air, deep breaths into his lungs, coughing from the effort and sputtering out the rain he inhaled.

There was a dead weight on him. Secher. Two bloody holes were drilled through his chest. Fox pushed him off as he turned to see Kate falling.

'Kate!' He was hoarse, almost no sound came out. She hit the ground, lying in the grass. Motionless.

'Kate!' he called, scrambling to his feet, running, stumbling in the effort.

As Fox ran, a spotlight followed his progress, shining down from the Coast Guard's helo. For a moment it seemed as though everything was illuminated, blinding.

Fox fell to his knees, crawling the last few metres, and sat next to Kate, pulling her to him. He cradled her head on his lap, pushing her bloodied hair out of her eyes.

She was alive, but only just. She looked up into his eyes, and he saw her smile at recognising him, his body shielding her from the rain.

'Don't go. Look at me. Kate, look at me! Kate! Kate . . . !'

For that one sublime moment, they both realised what could have been.

Fox looked down at her, at times his tears dropping into her closing eyes.

EPILOGUE

ANNAPOLIS, MARYLAND

Dunn sipped his bourbon, the bottle empty on the desk, a fresh one on the floor yet to be opened.

He looked at the wall of his home office, this one with many more photos than he displayed at work. Leaning against the wall, under all those photos of too many good men lost too early, was the large framed ensign from the *Liberty*. Its battered and burned condition was an apt reminder of how Dunn viewed his country. His life.

Attached to his computer via a firewire connection was his NSA key. On his computer screen were a series of bank accounts, with cash totalling over three hundred and twenty million dollars. He typed in some details, got it all ready for one final transfer. This was what he'd been skimming off his Advocacy Center deals with John Cooper. Cutbacks from US companies. Money he knew how to use for the good of the nation.

A pistol sat on his desk, a shiny nickel-plated Colt automatic he'd been given by Reagan. He glanced at it, still unsure. A single bullet was there too, sitting on its base as if standing to attention.

Dunn drained his drink and reached for the fresh bottle but stopped short. He clutched at his chest, coughing violently. Burning, tight, no breath.

He went red in the face, the veins in his neck angry and enlarged. Before he could register another presence in the room, he was dead.

•

The SSB assassin moved in from the doorway, and checked for a pulse. No one would ever suspect it was anything other than a heart attack, that's how good these drugs were. His clean-up mission was almost over.

SOUTH OF FRANCE

In her secluded villa in the South of France, Cassel was in the process of quickly packing some belongings. She turned from her suitcases on the bed, one filled to the brim with used Euros, to eyeball the long silencer on a massive pistol.

Cassel recognised him immediately. Akiva Goldsman, the manservant of Pierre Lopin.

He pressed the IMI Jericho against her forehead, the hot silencer of the recently fired pistol searing her skin as he pushed her back onto the dresser.

'So this is where you have been hiding,' Akiva said. 'Lopin sends his regards in the afterlife.'

'He killed my father!' Cassel said in realisation. Her eyes darted to the small automatic she had in the open drawer of the dresser, almost within reach.

'No . . . I killed your father.'

Akiva pulled the trigger, and she rocked backwards, cracking the blood-splattered mirror and crumpling to the floor.

He stepped over her body and picked up the bag of cash. He unscrewed the silencer on his way down the staircase, pocketing it and the pistol as he stepped over the corpses of Cassel's bodyguards.

Outside the villa, he put on sunglasses, slung the bag over his shoulder and walked down the tree-lined gravel driveway.

WASHINGTON

McCorkell and Wallace walked along the Potomac Track at a steady pace, taking in the river and its early-morning traffic.

'Joint houses session starts in three weeks,' McCorkell said. 'A special task force in the Office of the Director of National Intelligence is trawling through Dunn's databanks now, collating information that is going to be vetted through the President and party leaders prior to any further eyes.'

'What will happen with the program?'

'NSA's COMINT programs? FBI has been granted control on the domestic front, so they now have access to intercept all communications travelling within the US. It has a sunset clause that comes up every six months, so it'll be kept on a tight leash, and everything goes through a new branch of the FISA court with additional oversight from a panel of three former FBI directors.'

'Sounds like the seeds to Orwell's Big Brother are sown,' Wallace said, pausing at a water fountain.

'They were sown long ago, old friend,' McCorkell replied. 'The Feds will keep it clean. There's too much heat on the program to do otherwise, plus although it's now going from the property of the Department of Defense to the Department of Homeland Security, it still falls under the Office of the DNI, which is more oversight than it would have received if it had fallen under CIA control – which it very nearly did.'

'How did you avert that?' Wallace asked.

'A good investigator in the FBI has put forward a case to the Senate Select Committee of Intel and the House Permanent Committee, on some dubious CIA action in relation to this. It's hitting the fan as we speak.'

'Meaning?'

'Meaning, you'll see a new director appointed in the next couple of days, someone in uniform this time. CIA has been the only departmental agency outside the scope of the DoD-run intelligence community. Having a general at the helm will get around that little issue, with the view to pulling them into the fold in the near future. That said, some agents and task forces are going to be taken through the ringer first,' McCorkell said.

'What happened with Cooper's NSA key?' Wallace asked.

'Wasn't even an access key into NSA data,' McCorkell said with a smile. 'Have to give Boxcell and his goons kudos on that one – they were never about giving foreign access to the storage banks, just the scandal that is Dunn and Cooper's little side project. They must have figured that if Fox got it out in the public, coupled with a major security failure on behalf of the NSA, it would be scandal enough for them to assume the reins.'

'The Advocacy Center kickbacks?' Wallace asked as they resumed jogging.

'Yep, the so-called NSA key accessed nothing but their black-ops bank accounts and related files. Over the years Dunn and Cooper accumulated over three hundred million dollars,' McCorkell said. 'It'll be interesting. Only the President and senior staff know of it, so they're looking at funding a few things that Congress doesn't let them get through at budget time.'

'I'm guessing that won't be a Kyoto measure,' Wallace said, a touch of sadness in his eyes.

'You never know, Tas.' McCorkell slapped a hand on his shoulder and smiled. 'You never know.'

NEW YORK CITY

The big charter boat cruised the slate-grey water of New York Harbor, rounding off the trip from Long Island and heading back to the 79th Street Boat Basin.

Faye and Frank Matthews sat in the covered cabin, surrounded by friends and family. All dressed in black, most with tears in their eyes and pain on their faces.

Fox walked up to the Matthews, whom he had not spoken to since Kate's death. He'd been there, at Bellevue Hospital, along with them. She'd died from a subdural haematoma, the doctor had informed them, Faye collapsing into her husband's arms, the old man dying inside before Fox's eyes. Another parent seeing their child go before them.

Faye looked up at him, her eyes red. Fox bent down to her, put a hand on hers, and squeezed. She squeezed back, and Frank watched and sat in silence. No one said a word, and Fox left the cabin and its silent tears and frustrations and went to the empty aft deck.

The cold wind whipped up off the water at him but he didn't care. He couldn't get a jacket on as his arm was in a hard sling to set his collarbone and cover his gunshot wound, but he felt nothing of that pain. Nothing. All he had were visions, like a slow-motion slideshow, a series of stills of the events that had happened and what could have happened.

He stood at the rail, gripped it hard with his right hand, watching the river water swell by. A hand pressed onto his good shoulder, strong, familiar. Without having to turn around he knew it was Gammaldi.

They stood there in silence, buffeted by the salt-laden spray. Fox watched the water slipping by, and looked up at the Statue of Liberty growing bigger as they rounded Manhattan.

Eventually, Gammaldi spoke.

'Wanna head off for a while . . . go fishing back home . . . do some diving?'

Fox gritted his teeth, his grip still tight on the rail, and closed his eyes.

'Thanks, mate. If it's all the same, I think I'll get straight back into it.' He looked across and could see that Gammaldi sensed his sadness was being replaced by anger. Burning white fury.

'You don't have to come,' Fox said. 'But as soon as I can move this arm, I'll be going to Africa.'

Fox felt Gammaldi watching him closely.

'You think you're okay to get straight back into it?' Gammaldi asked.

Fox let the anger subside a notch, released his grip on the rail and tapped his knuckles on the stainless steel.

'I think it's exactly what I need to do.'

•

On another boat on the Hudson River, Kate had watched her own funeral procession through binoculars. Her head was heavily bandaged; she was dressed in warm clothes with a blanket around her shoulders. She was protected but lonely.

Hutchinson sat next to her, on the deck of an unmarked police boat.

'What happened to my CIA case officer?' she asked, feeling she could do so now since she was about to enter the witness protection service.

'Dead before we could arrest him. Heart attack, apparently,' Hutchinson said. 'A shame, I would have loved to see that case go to court.'

'So that's it?' Kate asked.

'We need one last interview with you, regarding the deal you struck with the CIA to work for them in the Advocacy Center,' Hutchinson said.

'It was just to observe, they never asked me to do anything,' she replied, fighting back tears. 'A ten-year stint, they said, then I could do what I wanted with my life.'

'I know it's hard,' Hutchinson told her. 'This has sparked a big clean-out and reorganisation of a lot of things. After today, you no longer have to work for the US government. Your record is clear – hell, it's a brand-new record. Name, social security number, the works.'

Kate watched Fox's face again through the binoculars. She could see her death was killing him. She knew her parents were among friends, among family. If she could see them now she knew she'd really lose it. But all she had in front of her was Lachlan Fox, standing on the deck, his friend Al by his side.

'And if I contact my family? Let them know I'm alive?'

'Until we are sure we have this cleaned up, you may be in danger,' Hutchinson said. 'I'm sorry, it's not my rules. But, like that deal you accepted at college, this has its limitations of what you can reveal. You've got a new life now.'

'A new life with no one in it,' Kate said, looking at the tired face of Fox through the binoculars. She knew his life, like hers, was forever changed.

EUROPEAN COUP STOPPED, 84 ARRESTED

by Lachlan C. Fox

In one of the biggest simultaneous arrests ever staged in Europe, 84 suspects were taken into custody across 14 countries. In a joint operation between several police agencies, armed members of Europol raided homes and offices across continental Europe.

All of those arrested were attendees of this year's LeCercle meeting, where plots were made to stage coup d'états across Europe to place right-wing governments in almost every country. The isolationist principles of these parties, as well as a desire to create an EU superpower, were the motives behind the conspiracy.

LeCercle, also known as The Pinnay Cercle, is an extreme right-wing group of European military, business and government leaders. Its goal is to keep European identity strong and closed to outside interference and influence.

The European Parliament recently saw the offshoot of this group formed from its ranks. The Identity, Tradition and Sovereignty group is seen as a positive step, as it brings to light meetings that were previously staged in secrecy.

Sianne Cassel, the leader of France's National Front Party and the chair of LeCercle, was found dead in her coastal house in the South of France. Authorities have yet to release details.

Lachlan C. Fox is an investigative journalist with the Global Syndicate of Reporters.

GLOSSARY

ABS	Anti-lock braking system
ASAP	As soon as possible
ASW	Anti Submarine Warfare
AW	Arctic Warfare (Accuracy International Snipers Rifle)
CAVNET	1st Cavalry Division site on SIPRNet to share TTP (Tactic, Technique, Procedures)
CCTV	Closed-circuit television
CIA	Central Intelligence Agency
CNN	Cable News Network
COMINT	Communications intelligence
COFUSCO	Commandement des Fusiliers Marins et Commandos
CSI	Crime scene investigator
DARPA	Defense Advanced Research Projects Agency
DC	District of Columbia
DCM	Distinguished Cross Medal

DEFCON	Defense condition
DGSE	La Direction Générale de la Sécurité Extérieure, or General Directorate of External Security
DNI	Director National Intelligence
DoD	United States Department of Defense
DUMBO	Down Under Manhattan Bridge Overpass
ETA	Estimated time of arrival
EU	European Union
FAMAS	Fusil d'Assaut de la Manufacture d'Armes de St-Etienne
FBI	Federal Bureau of Investigation
FISA	The Foreign Intelligence Surveillance Act
FORFUSCO	Force Maritime des Fusiliers Marins et Commandos
FSB	Federalnaya Sluzhba Bezopasnosti, Federal Security Service of the Russian Federation
G8	Group of Eight
GATS	B2's GPS-aided targeting system
GBU39	Guided bomb unit
GCHQ	Government Communications Headquarters
GDP	Gross domestic product
GPS	Global positioning system
GSR	Global Syndicate of Reporters
HPCS	High productivity computing systems
HQ	Headquarters
HUMINT	Human intelligence
ID	Identification
IED	Improvised explosive device
IMI	Israel Weapon Industries

ITS	Identity, Tradition and Sovereignty group
JCS	Joint Chiefs of Staff
KIA	Killed in action
LCD	Liquid crystal display
MA	Master of arts
MCB	Marine Corps Base, Quantico
MO	Modus operandi
MRE	Meal ready to eat
MSC	CIA Moscow Station Chief
NASA	National Aeronautics and Space Administration
NATO	North Atlantic Treaty Organisation
NCIS	Naval Criminal Investigative Service
NCS	National Clandestine Services
NFL	National Football League
NFP	National Front Party
NGO	Non-government organisation
NIPRNet	Non-classified internet protocol router network
NOC	Non-Official Cover
NRO	National Reconnaissance Office
NSA	National Security Agency
NYC	New York City
PDB	President's Daily Brief
PI	Private investigator
POTUS	President of the United States
PSP	PlayStation portable
QANTAS	Queensland and Northern Territory Aerial Services
RPG	Rocket propelled grenade

SAS	Special Air Service
SEAL	United States Navy Sea, Air and Land
SF	Special Forces
SIPRNet	Secret internet protocol router network
SOCOM	Special operations command
SSB	Strategic Support Branch
SSBN	Nuclear-powered, ballistic nuclear missile-carrying submarine
SSCI	Senate Select Committee on Intelligence
SUV	Sport utility vehicle
UK	United Kingdom
UKUSA	Treaty between intelligence agencies of five English-speaking nations, United Kingdom, United States, Canada, Australia and New Zealand
US	United States
USB	Universal serial bus
VP	Vice-President
WMD	Weapons of mass destruction
XO	Executive officer

ACKNOWLEDGMENTS

Thanks to Nicole Wallace for being the first to hear about my crazy ideas before the words even land on the page. Living with a writer is probably about as hard as living with an opera singer, minus the high F's. Love ya babe.

Malcolm Beasley was, again, my wingman and this book is the better for it. My mum's critical eye and support was invaluable, as was the feedback and encouragement from: Emily McDonald, Tony Wallace, Martin and Cheryl Beasley, Tony Niemann, Seamus O'Keefe, Regan Baynes, Amy Hurrell, Steve Kynoch, Scott Hopkins, and Wendy Newton. Al Gammaldi, it's been great taking you on another adventure, and thanks to Cheryl for letting him do his bit to save the free world (see, I brought him back in one piece!). Andrew Hutchinson, thanks mate for telling me lame jokes when I needed to hear them. All my family are continually there for me and I thank them for their support and respite from the isolated world of being a novelist. Staff and students from Swinburne University have been a good distraction too, and continue to surprise me with their creativity.

To all involved at Hachette Livre Australia; bringing a novel to readers is a team effort and I'm among the All Stars being with you. Special thanks to Vanessa Radnidge, Judy Jamieson-Green, Louise Sherwin-Stark, Kate Taperell, Annabel Blay, Sara Foster, Pam Dunne, and all the sales reps out there on the front line. Pippa Masson, my beautifully talented agent, thanks for making sure that Lachlan Fox has a nice long future ahead. Unless he's killed, which I can't promise won't happen some day . . .

James Bamford, Nicky Hager, and Duncan Campbell have all written great material on UKUSA, the NSA, and Echelon, which proved a good launching point in researching for this book. I'm indebted to George Orwell for writing his masterpiece *1984*. Every day we take another step closer to his ideas in that book, and it's a frightening prospect.

Q&A WITH JAMES PHELAN

You hold a Master of Arts in Writing, are studying for your PhD, have published academic non-fiction . . . why write a 'commercial thriller'?

The freedom that the genre delivers to get across some interesting issues and themes in a thrilling framework. I love reading thrillers; I like that anticipation that I as a reader feel when the story is ripping along. The global political landscape is something that I am very interested in, hence setting my books predominantly in the US and locations that are often in the news. The themes that propel each story, such as WMD and the Star Wars Missile Shield in *Fox Hunt*, to the USA Patriot Act and the NSA's eavesdropping programs in *Patriot Act*, are areas that I have a great time researching and then figuring out how to get that information across to my readers in an entertaining way.

How do you create characters?

In many different ways. Lachlan Fox came about because I wanted a protagonist who worked as a journalist but had a military background so he knows how to handle himself. Al Gammaldi works well as a dual protagonist because in many ways he's the opposite of Fox, and I get to have a lot of fun with that. When it comes to naming characters, I quite often cheat by using the names of friends. Sometimes even their descriptions play a part but usually I let the reader make their own picture of each character rather than really spell out how each person looks.

When and where do you write?

When I used to work office hours and write on the side, I used to write at night and into the early hours of the morning. Since I've become published and do all my work from home, I find that the early morning to early afternoon is my most creative time. I use my afternoons and evenings to do all the other little writing things that come along, to go to the gym and to catch up with family and friends if I have any time left over. In what downtime I have left I read or watch DVDs. I live in a converted warehouse in Melbourne. I'm seconds away from heaps of great cafés, restaurants, bars and pubs which can be a bit of a distraction at times! Sometimes, if my study is boring me or I start to get cabin fever, I take my MacBook and walk to the State Library to work. There's a great café there too!

Where do you get your ideas from?

I try to carry a notebook around at all times, in case inspiration strikes or an idea comes to me. It's a great tool for a writer, as I can jot down overheard conversations or record something that I have seen. Every now and then I'll flick through my notebooks and find something really useful that I'd completely forgotten about. The central ideas of my books generally come from world news and current affairs. The so-called Star Wars Missile Shield appealed to me as a storyline when I heard that Australia was joining the US in the system. The ramifications of the USA Patriot Act are extraordinary, and some similar laws were passed here in Australia that, particularly for a writer, have worrying Big Brother-like hallmarks. Fox book three is about oil, and book four is on water, again both hot issues that I am wrapping up in a thrilling story.

What research do you do for your novels?

I love the research component that goes into writing thrillers, and each new book means another world that I get to inhabit for a while. I read heaps of non-fiction, which I generally buy (I am a bibliophile) but sometimes find at a library. I go over interviews with people who have been in the situations that I am depicting in the pages of my books, and I talk to them if I can. With the military pieces I am lucky enough to know some people who have served, and since publication I have some military fans and I've even visited some bases. I'm forever asking questions of people to fuel my stories.

The internet is an amazing tool if you can find your way around. There are heaps of honest and often very sad blogs of soldiers and civilians that are directly affected by the circumstances that I write about, and they are things that keep me grounded. I try harder and harder in each book to get an accurate portrayal of the lives that I am writing about.

Suspending the reader's disbelief, keeping the facts within the realm of entertaining fiction, is the fun part.

How much planning do you do for your novels?

Heaps. When I'm working with three book parts and up to seven storylines in each novel, I make sure I know who's who, where they'll be going, what they are after etc. I need to know the motivation of all my characters, the stakes involved, the hurdles ahead of them, and above all, I need to know where my story is going. I need to be sure before I type anything that I've written down what the end of the story is going to be. Once I know that destination, I may deviate from the hundred or so pages of notes I've made but I will eventually get there. And there's no feeling like writing that final scene and seeing everything come together.